KOSTAS KROMI

Dominion
of the Moon

Ouranoessa

With the kind support of

REALIZE

Via Donizetti 3, 22060 Figino Serenza (Como), Italy

Phone: +39 0315481104

Dominion of the Moon

More beautiful, the rays where you pass without stepping
Unbeaten like the goddess of Samothrace
atop the sea's hills
Like so I have seen you
And that will suffice
for all time to be exonerated

Odysseas Elytis, Monogram

Kostas Krommydas

The story you are about to read was inspired by real facts. However, all names, locations, and dates have deliberately been changed and any similarities are totally coincidental. The real heroes mentioned in the acknowledgments simply formed the inspiration for the writing of this book, and in no way is their real life depicted here.

Ouranoessa is dedicated to the archaeologists who have worked and still work in Greece, bringing to light all that has been hidden in the dark for centuries, sacrificing on occasion everything—even their own lives—to do so. It is especially dedicated to some who have inspired a great part of the story you are about to read:

Andreas Vavritsa, Elbeth B. Dusenbery, Karl Lehmann, and Phyllis Williams Lehmann, who worked for many years at the Sanctuary of the Great Gods in Samothrace.

And to Marina and Vaya, who fill my daily life with inspiration—and more.

*Ouranoessa

is another name for the island of Samothrace. The name refers to a woman filled with sky and is often likened to the famous statue of Victory of Samothrace, currently found in the Louvre Museum in Paris, France.

Contents

CONTENTS 5

1944, MACEDONIA, NORTHERN GREECE 7

THREE YEARS LATER, THESSALONIKI 19

OCTOBER 1948, KOMOTINI 27

1948, SAMOTHRACE 33

SUMMER 1949, SAMOTHRACE 47

PRESENT DAY 203

BUENOS AIRES. PRESENT DAY 205

ABOUT THE AUTHOR 437

MORE BOOKS... 438

Dominion of the Moon

1944, Macedonia, Northern Greece

As the remaining German troops haphazardly withdrew, an eerie silence descended over the ruins. A dense cloud of yellow dust raised by the speeding tires settled over the hamlet, blurring the outlines of the damaged buildings. By the church, a small truck waited for the few remaining soldiers to depart. When the last of the motorcycles had disappeared down an alley, a German soldier climbed on its back. He grabbed the mounted machine gun and turned it to face the rear, worried about a possible attack even at this final moment.

The vehicle sped away until it was a small puff of dust in the distance. The air began to clear, unveiling the full scale of the devastation. Bullet-riddled walls bulged dangerously under the weight of unsupported plaster, and smashed windows gaped open. Here and there, the embers of a fire still glowed red. Plumes of grey smoke wafted up to the sky in the stillness of the wind, whispered prayers carrying messages of destruction. Muffled explosions and bursts of gunfire rang out in the distance.

The figure of a woman timidly raising her head over a low garden wall broke the deathly stillness. She wore a long white dress that clashed with the dark hair spilling down her back. It gave her an otherworldly appearance as she glided over the fallen stones from the collapsed buildings, as if defying the laws of gravity. She planted her feet firmly on the ground and, fixed to the spot, shielded her eyes as she scanned the alley. Tense, she tilted her body in the direction of the departing troops, her heart quaking with fear that the Germans would return at any moment.

Once certain they would not be coming back, she ran to the church. The bell tower was the only building in the hamlet to have escaped unscathed. For some reason, bullets and shells had refused to injure the stones and the wooden beams that covered its weatherworn surface. She hurriedly grabbed the rough rope of the church bell and pulled back with all her strength, trying to coax the metal tongue against the bronze walls of the bell.

Her arms were not strong enough. The bell made a soft, hollow sound. With steely determination, she turned her back to the tower, brought the rope over her shoulder like a yoked horse, and pulled with all the strength left in her famished body. This time her efforts bore fruit and the first metallic peel rang out, as if the bell were clumsily trying to remember the long-forgotten tune of good news.

The heavy bell pulled her up in the air. Without resisting, she let the swaying rope guide her, the bell ringing louder with each swing. Her feet sprang up, and then touched the ground, back up, back down, up, down, her body dancing to the happiest tune to have sounded over the land in the three years since the war started. As if suddenly borne of the ruins and lifeless stones, villagers timorously crept out and approached the square where the woman swung in a frenzied dance.

Fear still etched on their faces, they looked toward the alley and all around them, checking that the Germans were gone. Some held small children in their arms; frightened, their young eyes followed the glances of their elders. It was the height of autumn, but their exposed limbs were milky white, as if they spent their days hiding from the sun.

The first whispers broke out, faint-hearted at first but slowly gathering strength, growing louder, turning into fragmented, confused sentences and laughter. The words became questions.

"Is the war over?" some asked.

"Are they gone?" shouted others.

Laughter mingled with tears of joy, and only then did the exhausted woman let go of the rope and run to them, ecstatically announcing the end of the war and the departure of the occupiers.

Skinny as scarecrows, they summoned up all the strength buried deep inside them and broke into a dance with no rhythm and no music, skipping to the sound of their own improvised singing. They rejoiced in the village square, flinging their clothes and belongings in the air as if exorcising the heavy burden that had been crushing their souls.

The breathless cries of a man running down the hill startled them. "Soldiers! Soldiers are heading our way!"

A chill descended over the square at the sound of his words, and icy fear gripped their hearts once again.

The ensuing silence was broken by bursts of gunfire near the road winding down the hill to the village square. The sound of spinning tires struggling to climb over the hilltop sent most of the villagers scurrying amongst the ruins and the crumbling houses. Only ten men, and the woman in white, stayed behind; she ignored their entreaties to go hide and stood stubbornly beside them, waiting for the unwelcome visitors.

Seconds later, a truck appeared at the top of the hill, its bed filled with men, their guns hanging like oars over the side. A hundred more walked behind the truck, taking cover against a potential attack behind the moving mass of steel. Their features became clearer as they neared. Most had not shaved in days, and beards obscured their faces. They wore army camouflage with bullet belts across their chests, and it was hard to tell whether they were the remnants of the defeated regular army or guerilla fighters, continuing the fight.

The first man to reach them appeared to be their leader. He stopped a couple of yards away and let his eyes wander over them, sizing them up. He then moved toward the woman, his hard features barely containing his rage. "How long since they left?" he asked, spitting insolently close to the frightened villagers' feet.

For a few seconds nobody replied. The memories of the last time they had provided this kind of information were still raw. They had paid a dear price for that act, the Nazis executing ten men and setting most of the village on fire.

The brave woman spoke up, and her voice rang clear among the silent men surrounding her. "They left about an hour ago."

The leader gave her a look of suspicion, slinging his gun from his shoulder. With soft, familiar movements, his fingers armed the rifle and the bullet slotted into the chamber. He raised it slowly and aimed it at the face of one of the villagers, who began shaking with fear. With menacing slowness, he moved toward the man and whispered in his ear, "How long ago?"

"Fifteen minutes at most," the villager replied, quaking under the guerilla's cold gaze.

The guerilla leader removed his side cap. His hair was drenched in sweat and coated with dust; his eyes were those of a snake ready to strike. He wiped his mouth with the back of his hand, deep in thought, while everyone around him held their breath. A large sword and a revolver in a leather case hung from his waist. The weight of the guns and the ammunition did not seem to bother him in the least.

"An hour ago, eh?" he screamed, the stench of his breath hot against the woman's face.

She did not even flinch, refusing to be intimidated by his strutting ferociousness. "I'm not afraid of you," she said calmly. "Whatever you're planning to do, do it quickly. Then you can catch up with them."

Stunned by her manner, he faltered for a moment. Then he threw his head back and laughed, mostly to disguise his unease before the woman's courage. Still cackling, he turned back to his men and shouted sarcastically, "Where is the rookie?"

As if they had turned to stone, no one moved. His scream tore through the air. "Where is the rookie, I said!"

Only then did one of the men, one of the few not to sport a long beard, timidly step up. With a look of rage, the leader gestured that he should approach. Having no choice, the young man went and stood beside him.

A couple of steps were all it took for me to reach him. My hands shook as I tried to hold onto my rifle. I sensed that the leader's intentions could not be anything other than evil. Barely two days had passed since I had been forced to join them. Ever since, all I could think about was how to escape. Wearing the clothes they had given me, unshaven, I looked like a typical guerilla. I could always feel someone's eyes on me, watching me. Having witnessed the savagery with which they treated both Nazis and Greeks, I was afraid to make a move.

In the two days I had spent in their company, I had witnessed unimaginable horrors, which instilled in me the unshakeable belief that the wildest, most bloodthirsty beasts on this planet were humans. The occupiers were finally running away, and instead of us coming together, a vicious circle of hatred and inexplicable vengeance was forming, a race to see who would grab power first after the end of the war.

I had waited as patiently as I could for the madness of the war to be over. Now, all signs pointed to the fighting continuing after the departure of the occupiers. Instead of peace, the hardest of all wars would begin: a Civil war. It would pit those who had spent the last few years fighting for a common cause—to free their country—against each other. This village had already suffered enough.

On the way here, someone had been saying the guerrillas would burn the village down as reprisal for collaborating with the Germans. However, there was nothing left to burn. Destruction lay everywhere. Over the years, I had become familiar with this smell. It clung to my skin like an invisible hand gripping my throat, suffocating me. I knew it well. It was the smell of death. Like fog, it had settled over the country and taken lives without paying heed to age, gender, or nationality.

One quick glance at the ragged band of villagers standing before me had been enough to make me wonder how any of them could be seen as friends of the Germans. Skeletal and filthy, they all stood stooped, their bodies ravaged by hardship ... except for the woman standing at the edge of the group of men in her white dress.

I could not take my eyes off her as I walked toward them, trying to decide whether she was of this world. She glowed with defiant bravery, in sharp contrast to the wide-eyed terror of the men around her. Her sunken cheeks highlighted her black eyes, and her pale face belonged on one of the ancient amphorae that had been discovered on my home island just before the war.

I froze when I felt the barrel of the leader's gun against my chest. For a moment that felt like an eternity, I waited for him to pull the trigger; I had no idea what he was planning to do. He held out his own, new rifle and barked, "Take her behind the church and send her to meet her traitor comrades."

He paused, and I thought I had misheard. A sinister bellow confirmed his nightmarish orders. "Take my gun; your piece of junk won't do the job properly. Here you are. This is your chance to show us whether or not you are a true patriot. Kill the traitor."

I cannot even recall how his rifle ended up in my hands. I stared at him, trying to find the right words to refuse. He sensed my reluctance and spoke before I had a chance to say anything. "Execute her, or I execute her, everyone else—you included. What would you rather? Choose!"

I thought I would collapse under the strain. I could not believe he had picked me to carry out his sick orders. Against all reason, I hoped he would burst out laughing and tell me it was all some macabre prank. His sadistic voice crushed my hopes. "If you don't make up your mind now, I'll just go ahead and execute you all anyway. Hurry up! Don't you want to go home and dig up all that ancient stuff? The sooner you do this, the sooner that will happen."

All eyes were on me except hers. Shoulders defiantly thrown back, she stared ahead, indifferent as to what my choice would be. It was impossible to decide. I could never raise a gun and shoot another human being, let alone a woman whose only crime had been a lie about when the Germans had left. On the other hand, if I disobeyed, he would kill us all. I had no doubt he would carry out his threats; the past two days had shown me he was capable of anything.

I summoned up all my strength but could not take a single step. As if they had a mind of their own, my feet refused to budge. The leader took a few steps back and the others, used to reading his signals, raised their guns against us. I felt the woman dash like the wind and stand beside me. As I turned to look at her, she clumsily struck my face. Without losing any time, she grabbed my shirt, signaling that I should obey and follow her behind the church to carry out his orders. Caught in a trance, the guerillas' laughter ringing in my ears like a nightmare, I blindly followed her.

Once outside their hearing range, she whispered, "Do as he said so the others can live. If you don't, he'll kill us all."

High up on her shoulder, a small spot of blood had tinted her dress red, as if something had scratched her delicate skin. I heard the guerilla leader order one of his men to follow us. If I disobeyed, he was to kill us both. I stumbled through the ruins. I walked as slowly as I could, hoping that something would happen to stop our march toward death. I would not be raising my gun against her. She pulled me by the hand and I struggled to think of a way out, but the clock was ticking against us. I could not come up with a plan that would save us, that would save her.

She did not look a day over twenty. What was she doing in this place, all alone? None of the men had tried to protect her. They had all kept quiet, heads bowed, trying to make themselves invisible.

Passing by the bell tower, I saw the bloodied bell rope and turned to look at her shoulder again. I now noticed the line the rope had left on the cloth and her skin. When we arrived behind the crumbling walls of the church, she turned to me and our eyes met, hers moist but not afraid. On a fallen piece of plaster behind us, remnants of an icon of the Virgin Mary bore witness to the sin about to be committed. I looked around, weighing up what I was about to do. The guerilla following us was still some distance away. I hurriedly whispered in her ear, "Stand in front of me so he can't see you, and I'll pretend to shoot you. Fall in the gap between the ruins over there and I'll keep firing beside you. Lie low until I walk away, and then run. Run, and hide wherever you can. Save yourself!"

I could tell she sensed my determination, but I did not detect the slightest fear in her eyes. On the contrary, she obeyed as if she were doing it for my sake. She lowered her eyes for a second, then cast me a look of gratitude. This was the only chance we would get; I could hear the guerilla's footsteps getting closer. Any minute now, he would be too close and see through our ruse.

I pulled her by the hair and pushed her to the spot that would give us the best chance to execute our escape plan. She did not turn to look at me once. She stood on the edge and I quickly raised my rifle. I aimed it toward her but not at her. I was unfamiliar with guns, so I pulled the trigger as carefully as I could. The blast and the force of the kickback knocked me back, and a cloud of smoke obscured her for a moment. She jerked, pretending to be injured. She then fell clumsily between two large rocks and rolled downhill, until she was out of sight.

My heart thumped as if it were trying to escape my chest and the agony that had descended upon me. Before the guerilla could reach me, I moved to where she had been standing and looked down. I froze. She had tumbled down a steep and rocky slope. I could not see what lay behind the ledge when I had picked the spot. Now, I stood aghast, staring at the sharp rocks that rose like deadly fingers waiting to shred whatever fell their way.

A sharp pang pierced my heart when I spotted the decomposing corpses that lay among the rocks, flung down the cliff and abandoned. Seized with terror, I looked for her body, but could not spot the white dress. All that remained were the wisps of settling dust where she had rolled downhill just moments before.

The guerilla came and stood beside me. He cast an indifferent glance at the rotting corpses. Having made sure I had carried out my orders, he smirked. "Well done. I didn't think you had the guts. I was getting ready to shoot you both, but now I see you've got it in you. Come on, let's go. Everyone is waiting for us."

He turned to go, but I stood there, staring at the cliff and the creek further ahead. No matter how hard I tried to pull my gaze away from the dismembered bodies, I could not. From the corner of my eye, I thought I caught a movement. My heart skipped a beat and I leaned forward to catch another glimpse. Was that a woman in a white dress, slipping into the small wood at the edge of the creek? It was an impression so brief, so fleeting, that I could not be sure if it was real or a figment of my imagination, an attempt to save myself from the guilt welling up inside me. A sharp whistle made me jump, and I turned as casually as I could. If what I had seen was real, I did not want anyone else to notice it.

Three years later, Thessaloniki

In the small library, I heard the elderly professor call out my name, and I jumped up. My legs shook imperceptibly, as if I were about to walk before a firing squad rather than receive an archaeology award. I had been lucky enough to unearth a dark suit in a second-hand clothes store. Slightly worn and frayed, it nonetheless added some formality to my appearance.

I had almost become accustomed to the stifling air of the sealed-off room. It must have been months since any sunlight had penetrated the windows. Fear and isolation kept even fresh air at bay. The joy of receiving the award, however, stopped me from dwelling on sad thoughts for too long.

A small number of people, mostly archaeologists and academics, surrounded me. I felt sad that my uncle had not lived long enough to be here tonight. My love of archaeology was all due to him. A historian, he kept a large library at his house that had formed the foundation of my education.

While I waited, I stared down at the old scars on my hands. The tragic day the guerillas had tried to turn me into an executioner came to my mind. I had managed to make my escape shortly afterwards, during a skirmish with a decimated group of Germans. Seeing them execute soldiers who wished to surrender, I had flung down my gun and run away as fast as my legs could carry me. Hours later, I found myself in Grevena, where at first I hid in a cave, then a village. There, at an impoverished farmhouse, I managed to dull my hunger. The family took pity on me and let me stay.

I lived with them, in hiding, for a long time, helping them toil the fields and tend to the few animals they still had left. When it became clear that things were calmer, I began the long journey to my uncle's house in Thessaloniki, where I could resume my studies, which had been interrupted by the war. My mother and older sister lived on Samothrace after the departure of the Bulgarian troops. My father passed away during that time and I did not even manage to attend his funeral, news of his death reaching me ten days too late.

We had all become accustomed to the idea of death, as if it were a common occurrence. We did not flinch, even when a life was lost unjustly. Survival instincts forced people to overcome any loss quickly.

I had not seen my father in years and was deeply pained that I could not be there for the funeral. However, even if I had received news of his death on time, I still would have been unable to return to the island—traveling was restricted at the time, making any journey difficult. Nonetheless, the goodbye I had not been able to whisper by his deathbed still haunted me.

A few days ago, I received the latest letter from my mother and sister. Thankfully, they wrote they were well. I could not wait to see them again, even in the present, impossible circumstances. Perhaps this award would prove to be my passport to my beloved island, even for a brief return.

In the few seconds it took to cross the room and receive the award, thoughts of the executions nearby came to complete my thoughts of the dead. Summary trials had led many people before a government firing squad. They were put to death like cattle taken to the slaughter.

I could not believe that the civil war still raged on, three years after the departure of the Germans. Vengeance was like a mother repeatedly giving birth to children, who gave birth to other children in turn, hungry for the absurd joy brought by the death of people who only held different ideals.

I caught a glimpse of the edge of the table, where my artwork proudly stood. It had earned me the award I would soon be holding in my hands.

The face I had sculpted on the plaster cast of the Winged Victory of Samothrace reminded me of the woman who had disappeared forever down the cliff, among the corpses of the executed. No matter how fervently I hoped she had survived, I was aware it was unlikely. All that remained were her features, forever etched in my memory. I had reproduced them on the missing part of the statue, which had been discovered in pieces, headless, long ago. Trying to reproduce the original image, I had completed it by adding the unforgettable face of the otherworldly creature that had crossed my path back then. It fit so well, as if she were the ancient woman whose likeness the sculptor had tried to capture thousands of years ago.

No one knew about that horrifying day in the ruins of the village. I had not spoken about the few days of my enforced recruitment. I kept it all buried deep inside me, haunted by it at night. I kept dreaming that I was carrying out the orders of that monster of a man and executing the woman, firing my rifle in front of everyone, while their manic laughter echoed in my head like the screeching of the Furies.

I had reached the lectern. A round of applause and the loud voice of the white-haired professor made me reach out and receive the award.

"Andreas Stais," he said, "on behalf of the committee judging the antiquities contest, I am pleased to award you first prize, and the gift that comes with it, for your reproduction of the statue of the Winged Victory. Congratulations!" He removed his glasses, shook my hand warmly, and handed me an envelope.

He then opened a small wooden box and took out a medal hanging from a silver chain. I caught a glimpse of my name on its surface as he placed it around my neck.

"A small, symbolic gift, so that you may always remember this moment," he said, and took a step back.

I was so nervous I felt my throat constrict. I could not utter the slightest sound. I bowed shyly a few times, thanking those present. When the applause died down, the professor urged me to open the envelope that had accompanied the certificate. Its worn corners betrayed that it had been used numerous times. The tightly folded piece of paper inside was white and shiny. I took it out and carefully unfolded it. Everyone's gaze was fixed on me as I read the short message and the president's signature at the bottom, my eyes welling up with emotion. From this day forth, I would be reporting to the regional branch of the Greek Archaeological Service. It was based on the island of Lesbos and supervised Greek archaeological expeditions in the Northern Aegean and Thrace.

When the war had forced me to abandon my studies, I never thought my dreams of excavating ancient treasure, artifacts which bore the marks of Greece and waited for the hand that would bring them to the surface, would materialize so soon. No words could adequately describe the magical feeling of knowing that the last time anyone touched what you were holding was thousands of years ago. The magical feeling of a discovery that could be shared with the whole of humanity. Unfortunately, I was fully aware not everyone thought this way. Too many finds had been destroyed, stolen, or even sold to the four corners of the world.

My uncle had mentioned in the past that countless artifacts had disappeared over the years. The main cause was war—one broke out every century or so, plaguing Greece and the rest of the world. It was common for many discoveries to be exploited for political purposes. The Turks had given away priceless Greek artifacts as if they owned them. One of those was my beloved statue of the Winged Victory, the Nike of Samothrace, which has resided in the Louvre since 1884. The piece of paper I held in my hands was my passport to the past, a world filled with symbolism, mystery religions and cults, ceremonies, and rituals. Rituals such as those that had taken place on my home island of Samothrace in ancient times and which I so wanted to research ...

A loud noise from the street directly below us interrupted my thoughts, and spurred some of the men in attendance to dash to a large window and timidly peek behind the heavy curtain. Their frightened faces made us all stop what we were doing and rush to the other windows.

A car slowly drove up the street dragging something behind it, the pedestrians impassively watching the gory spectacle. When the corpse came into view, a bundle of rope and flesh and torn clothes, my knees buckled. I turned away from the window, feeling all my reserves of strength were finally depleted. Although it was impossible for any smell to reach the room, the stench of death filled my nostrils once again. I was almost certain that if I kept seeing such things, I would go crazy. There was no end to the savagery of people, on both sides.

Still fresh in my memory was a story doing the rounds these days, of a young man who, returning from the front, had butchered the woman he was due to marry simply because her family was on the opposite side. I remembered Euripides's words, framed on a wall in this room, and sought them out. They fit the moment perfectly. The ink had faded with the passing years and the pale words now read:

"Stronger than lover's love is lover's hate. Incurable, in each, the wounds they make."

Euripides, Medea

Trying to lighten the mood, the professor urged us to step away from the windows. "Let's not allow anything to cast a shadow on this important day. And let us hope that people like dear Andreas will leave this madness behind them."

The president of the committee, who I had not managed to greet until that moment, crossed the room to join me. He congratulated me, then turned toward the window and spoke solemnly. "If I did not know how much you love Samothrace I would not be telling you this now, but I have been informed that American archaeologists will be resuming excavations on the island soon. We would like you to lead the Greek team, if you agree. Your tenure would officially begin there. You will be working under their supervision and I think you will do just fine."

The joy his words sparked briefly chased away bad memories and filled me with gratitude. Not only would I be doing what I loved, I would be commencing my career in a place I adored. As a young boy, I used to sneak inside the ruins every chance I got. There, I would watch the archaeologists and workers excavate the Sanctuary of the Great Gods. I would secretly wander among the ruins and try to imagine what it must have looked like back then. I would climb on the marble pedestals and pretend to be a statue. Whenever someone caught sight me, I would run away like a thief, fearing punishment. I was frightened by everything I had heard about the headless statue of the Winged Victory and always tried to guess where it might be. Local lore had it that someone had stolen it and kept it in their house, separating it from its body ...

We posed for a commemorative photo and, a few minutes later, we all realized it was time to leave. We slowly walked toward the narrow wooden staircase that led to the exit and onto the main road. I hoped that more savagery would not be waiting on the other side. Alas, the sounds coming from outside foretold more horrors.

Small frames depicting the busts of the Ancient Greek Sages and their words lined the small hallway leading to the exit. Just before following the others onto the street, I had enough time to read the words of Aeschylus, a sinister sign of what I was about to witness ...

"Act for act, wound for wound"

Agamemnon

October 1948, Komotini

No matter how hard I tried to scrape off the mud that clung to my boots and weighed my feet down like lead, I failed. The men accompanying me faced the same problem. We had spent the past two days struggling to determine whether statues had been hidden in Komotini in an attempt to save them from the Bulgarians' looting. The Archaeological Service had received information to this effect and sent me here first to salvage what I could.

The informant also asserted something else, something that had spurred me on to accept. He had heard that the missing head of the statue of the Winged Victory might also be buried here. Although highly unlikely, I still had to investigate the matter. No one knew what had happened to the missing head. Like a compass, my desire to find it determined my course. Inside me, the figure of the woman in the white dress had merged with the statue. Not a day passed by that I did not think of her. I hoped she had survived, even if I never saw her again.

We had set up a small, makeshift camp outside the town of Komotini and thrown ourselves into battle against the relentless rain and mountains of mud. The soil was very soft, a sign that it had recently been dug up, then shoveled back in. A bad sign; someone had beaten us to it.

With hands heavy as ploughs, I pulled the mud out of the large ditch. Sleep-deprived, we somehow found the strength to withstand the hostile conditions and long hours. We were committed to our cause, heart and soul. The drizzle seeped through our overcoats, piercing the cloth and condensing against our skin. The sun was setting and it was time to accept that our efforts had been fruitless. Whatever had been buried here was now gone.

Someone had probably shared the same information with the Bulgarians, who reached this spot long before us and collected what we were now looking for, exhausted and in vain. It had been a race against time and, sadly, we were too late. I fumed at the thought that the occupiers had violently snatched so many treasures—entire museums and priceless private collections—from their birthplace.

Even harder to bear was the fact that the information most often came from the Greeks themselves. I hoped that, even at this last moment, we might be able to salvage something. Information pouring in from all over the country told of the looting that had followed the German invasion. Every one of the stories filled me with rage. More than anything else in the world, I wanted to bring back everything that had been taken out of the country. Against all my principles, I would be very harsh toward anyone who had demonstrably participated in the crime that had taken place in the shadows of the Occupation. The Archaeological Service had already made official protestations after the end of the war and managed to secure the repatriation of some of the stolen artifacts, but it was a drop in the ocean compared to all the priceless treasures that had by now been dispersed all over the world.

One of the workers called out that he had found something and needed help. We all dropped what we were doing and, filled with excited anticipation, rushed to his side. A large piece of marble was visible beneath a thin layer of muddy soil. With our hands, we started to dig as fast as we could, scraping the mud away to see what lay beneath. My distress could not have been greater had I been trying to pull a man from the soil so he could catch one final breath.

The rain became our ally, the drizzle helping me wash away the mud, slowly revealing the white flesh of sculpted marble beneath. I could feel the small stones in the soil pierce the underside of my fingernails, but the desire to know what lay buried spurred me on. When I saw blood drops on the white stone, I looked at my fingers. The soil trapped under my nails had turned into a thick red mixture that slowly dripped over the cracks of my skin. As soon as I realized it was nothing serious, I resumed my task. It did not take long to perceive that the piece of marble was the base of a statue.

The others, sensing my despair to discover anything, had stepped aside. Smaller, broken pieces of marble slowly appeared around it. Absorbed as we were, we did not notice the man creep up and stand on the edge of the small ditch.

I saw him first, as I turned to throw away a handful of mud. I froze. Behind him, a group of men stood guard, stock-still in the rain, which was now getting stronger and soaking us from head to toe. His face frightened me, reminded me of my brief, coerced recruitment at the end of the war. I had heard of the deeds of a man they called Captain Lambros. The locals said that the guerilla leader was tough but fair. The nearby presence of the army had not discouraged this group of guerrillas from fighting the government. As for us, we ignored their conflict and worked hard, doing what we could to prevent even more antiquities falling prey to looters.

I stood up, mud covering my entire front. Rainwater dripped from my wet hair down my face to the edge of my nose, where it trickled like a faulty faucet. My feet slipped in the mud, and it was a struggle to keep my balance. I looked around, and shivered. The hole we had dug looked like a mass grave waiting to be filled.

The guerilla raised his rifle. "Why are you rooting around in the mud like pigs?" His voice sounded hollow through his thick beard.

"Archaeology!" I shouted. "We have a permit to excavate. From the Archaeological Service." I raised my arms, trying to prevent any unfortunate misunderstandings. My three companions, awkwardly and without being asked, followed suit. Wasting no time, I added, "We received information they buried antiquities here, to hide them from the Bulgarians. We are looking for them."

"Put your arms down," he barked, bringing his rifle to rest on his shoulder. He examined us for a while, pondering his next move. One of his men came near him and whispered something in his ear. He turned to look at me and said, "You are too late. They found it months ago. The Bulgarians smashed the bases, took the statues, and loaded them onto their trucks. Didn't the locals tell you? They only left what they couldn't carry. We found a broken statue head in the gully behind the mountain the other day. Someone had smashed it to bits."

I shuddered at his words. "Where is it? Can you show us the place?" I waited anxiously for his reply.

"The gully is filled chest high with water now, fast as a torrent. The pieces must already be in the sea," he said with a laugh. He gave us another appraising look, and then trudged back to his companions. Following his lead, they slowly walked to the woods. They had more pressing concerns than a group of lunatics struggling in the mud.

Night was beginning to settle over the clearing, and I decided it was time to stop our excavation. I tried to shake the mud from my hands along with my disappointment, and told the workers we were done for the day. We would have another look in the morning, if the ditch did not flood overnight.

Then I would set off for Samothrace and the others would return to Komotini. On the island, a couple of Americans and their team were already resuming the excavations they had abandoned before the war. The second American team that would be directing the excavation was due to arrive the following day. Perhaps it was best not to waste any more time. In any case, it seemed our efforts here would not bear fruit.

A terrifying thought seized me as we returned to our tent. To which statue did the smashed head in the gully belong?

Dominion of the Moon

1948, Samothrace

Any minute now the head of the second American archaeological mission would be arriving at the Sanctuary of the Great Gods, where we would be joining forces to continue excavations. Although German, French, and Czechoslovakian teams had excavated the island in the past, the only team on the dig now would be ours, in collaboration with the Americans.

Wanting to add a touch of ceremony to their welcome, I had elected to meet them for the first time by the *Hieron*, the Sacred Temple. The evidence we had pointed to it being the site of the ancient Cabirian Mysteries. I stood there silently, surrounded by once-majestic marble columns, which now lay broken and scattered around me like wounded guards. I mused, as I did whenever I found myself at the Sanctuary, on how little we knew about that strange religion. The Cabeiri were significant ancient deities, mysterious and even physically imposing, often depicted in the form of demons with stern faces and oversized genitals.

The occult rites to celebrate these deities were said to strike fear and awe. Rumors surrounding the merciless punishment unleashed by the Cabeiri's wrath abounded even back then. We still did not know the details of what the punishment entailed. On the other hand, the cult revolved around birth and fertility. Initiation was supposed to be a gentle, rather than violent, testing ritual. The cult's strict orders that the initiate abide by absolute secrecy regarding the ceremony sadly left little hope of uncovering enough information about the rites and rituals. However, that did not mean there weren't enough secrets, shrouded in darkness for thousands of years, waiting patiently to be revealed. That is what I yearned to bring to light.

Sometimes I would stand here and close my eyes, trying to imagine what it all must have looked like back then. Even now, when only a fragment of the site survived, the perfection with which the ruins framed the area and their artistry fascinated me. I wondered what had interceded to lead to the loss of such profound aesthetics, of what humanity was capable of creating.

Although the connection between the statue of the Winged Victory and the Cabirian Mysteries was still unknown and certainly not proven, the imposing nature of both made me strongly sense that perhaps there was a secret link to their mystifying existence.

A feeling of rage always rose inside me when I thought of the sale of the winged goddess's statue to the French. It was as if wars, as well as other human beings, were conspiring to prevent the elucidation of these unanswered questions. The Turkish occupiers had sold the statue a hundred years ago for a pittance. A French consul, Charles Champoiseau, had snatched the broken up Nike and transported her to France, unaware that the statue could not stand upright, having been mounted on a base shaped like a ship's prow, which they had neglected to take with them. They returned for the missing parts once they realized and the statue was eventually erected as the unknown ancient sculptor had intended. More than anything in the world, I wanted to bring it home when the local museum was finally complete. I would even give my life for it.

Vasilis arrived, wearing a black wool hat pulled low over his eyebrows and holding a gramophone as instructed. He carefully placed it on a flat, fallen slab and pulled a record from beneath his coat. He placed it on the turntable and slowly wound the tiny crank as I had shown him, so that it would be ready when our colleagues—our employers, for that matter—arrived.

I had told him to play this particular record, which I had selected from among the few pieces of Wagner I had been able to find. It was one of the few records left behind by the Germans, just before they handed over the island to the Bulgarian forces. When I gave him the signal, he would play Spring Waltz, which I liked very much. I didn't think the choice of a German composer would bother the American leader of the mission. I always believed music unites people. Besides, it was a beautiful melody, which would gently accompany our introduction.

In the brief time I had spent with Vasilis I had come to realize he could be rather clumsy, so I chose the tasks I assigned him carefully. I didn't have much choice as far as workers were concerned and had to make do with whoever was available. Despite his young age, Vasilis was kind and very eager. An orphan, he had managed to survive the harsh Occupation years on the island. He never spoke of those days, but I'd heard that the Bulgarians caught him stealing a couple of onions and sliced his ear off in punishment.

Dominion of the Moon

There were moments when he would stand still and stare at the sea, anticipation gleaming in his eyes as if he were waiting for something to suddenly surface. When I would ask him if he was all right, he'd jump in surprise. Even though most of the locals made fun of him, it was clear to me that he harbored many secrets. Whatever the reason behind his absentmindedness, I turned a blind eye, sensing that he was weighed down by great sorrow.

Winter was approaching and promising to be heavy; you could only stay outdoors if wrapped up in heavy clothes. I buttoned up my overcoat, feeling the northerly wind collude with the salty humidity and sneak through the opening like an invisible thief. The sea stretching in the distance was the same uniform grey color as the sky, dotted here and there with small golden sunbeams that crept through the cracks in the clouds and joined water and sky. Behind me, lost in mist, lay Mount Fengari, the island's highest peak, named after the moon. Countless sources sprang from its slopes, their water trickling down the mountain all the way to the sea.

I had not found time yet to walk through the woods and climb up as high as I could, ambling beside the streams as they made their course down to the island's shores. Whenever it rained, they would swell up and turn into treacherous torrents. Perhaps that was the reason the locals called one of the torrents *Fonias*: a treacherous murderer.

Longing and regret mingled inside me as I remembered the wonderful pre-war years on the island and the great void left by the war. The fact was that the preceding eight years had been lost, never to return, with only the memories of horror and war left to haunt us.

When I returned to Samothrace, I was saddened to discover that the Americans were in complete control of the excavations. Everything needed their consent, but there was nothing to be done about it. It was the Americans, under the supervision of the American School of Classical Studies, who had begun construction work on the museum and excavations in 1938. At the time, I was still filled with rage after the bombing of Japan and the thousands of deaths it had caused in a single day.

My first encounter with Karl and Phyllis, however—the couple who had returned to resume their work at the end of the war—made me change my mind. As I slowly recovered from the traumatic eight years I tried to leave behind me, I realized that, in essence, no one was responsible for the decisions made by their leaders. The people arriving here loved their work, sacrificed their private lives, and invested significant sums in the excavations, motivated by their love for archaeology at a time when Greece, injured by the war and its internal divisions, could barely feed its people. So now, I found myself looking forward to becoming better acquainted, working together toward a common goal.

In a short while, we would all gather at the museum's tiny hall. I intended to give the newcomers a brief tour first, before leading them to the museum. Even though works were still in progress, we had managed to transform that one small room into something suitable for the reception. Everyone who worked at the site and on the museum's construction had been invited. My mother, my sister, and other local women had prepared a small banquet to welcome them. Then I had to make sure they settled into the home allocated to them—an old mansion in the small village of Paleopolis, so they could be near the dig and move easily. Weather conditions permitting, we would be working throughout the winter, picking up where our predecessors had left off in 1938.

In the intervening years, the site had been abandoned. The Bulgarians showed no real inclination or sympathy for archaeology. On the contrary, they went on a looting spree of their own, selling everything they could get their hands on for a pittance, or removing much of the marble to use as building material in the construction of homes and stores. One of the greatest plagues to befall this island was the limekilns. Dotted around the land and on the actual excavation site, they were used to turn marble into quicklime. Malice was not the driving force behind these acts, just ignorance about the significance of antiquities.

From the moment I set foot on the island, I had been met with widespread suspicion. I had to belong somewhere politically, left or right, and my neutral stance displeased everyone. I could hear the locals whisper whenever I walked by.

I had been absent for nine years. Only the landscape and the buildings had remained unchanged. Many of my friends had disappeared, with no information available as to their fate. Some were certainly dead. Others abandoned the island when it passed to the hands of the Bulgarians. The civil war would end at some point, but it would take years for the hatred to be forgotten.

News of ferocious battles between the army and the guerillas had reached us from Epirus. I never took anyone's side; both sides were committing terrible crimes. As hard as I tried to enjoy every waking moment, relieved to have escaped the madness, my soul was filled with torment and blood; and the thought of her, and what had become of her.

No matter how busy I kept during the day, her image still burned in my mind, and I tried to exorcise my guilt by hanging onto the thought that she had survived, escaped, was living her life just as I was mine. Other times, I thought none of it had happened and that I had dreamt it all. When peace returned, I intended to travel back to that village and find out who she was and what had become of her. If I could find her … If she remembered who I was.

The archaeological mission soon appeared on the small path leading to the temple. Elizabeth, a young American archaeologist, walked ahead of the others, followed by members of her team and some locals. Her long blonde hair spilled out from a red scarf covering her head, and she held her thick woolen coat close to her chest.

I sensed another presence to my left; as they approached, I turned to look toward the small neighboring hill. A man stood at its peak, the wind whipping up his long overcoat and making him appear like a dark deity, an enormous shadow against the setting sun. A few steps behind him, a woman walked slowly. She reached the man and stood beside him, still as a marble sentinel. It did not take me long to figure out who they were: Nicholas Varvis and his wife, Marika. I had only seen them from afar since my return to the island. I had heard so many stories about them that I did not know what to believe.

Some said they had collaborated with all of the occupying forces, others that they had fought against them. Others yet claimed that they were not beings of this world. Whatever the truth may have been, I would soon meet them. Their land bordered the dig site and the excavations had to expand onto their property.

I found it hard to look away. It was as if my eyes were caught by the strange magnetic field exerted by the immovable, towering couple. With great effort, I looked at

Vasilis to signal it was time for music. He was already struggling to place the needle on the record. Disappointed, I accepted that there would be no musical accompaniment to this event.

The large smile that lit up Elizabeth's face chased away my sense of foreboding, and I spread my arms to greet her. Her freckles made her angular face appear sweeter. She gave me a tight hug with a strength that her fragile frame belied. The scent of freshly cut jasmine tickled my nostrils, and as I inhaled it deeply, I held her for a few seconds longer than was called for.

We pulled apart and looked at each other awkwardly. When I shook her hand, I realized a tough woman stood before me, not the delicate creature her appearance and perfume seemed to imply.

At first, I thought something had been caught between our palms, but a quick look at her hand showed a scar—a thick, knotted line. Some old injury, I hurriedly thought. She followed my gaze and pulled her hand away, closing her fingers in a fist. Her eyes were vivid, intense and I had never seen such a deep blue before.

"W-welcome," I stammered. "I'm looking forward to be working with you."

She opened her mouth to answer, and suddenly the air reverberated with the booming music from Vasilis's gramophone. Except that, instead of the sweet melody of the Spring Waltz, the majestic strains of the Ride of the Valkyries filled the air. A music piece most unbefitting the occasion. I bit my lip and gave her an apologetic look, trying to ignore my assistant's gaffe.

Elizabeth masked her startled look with another smile and pretended to ignore the loud music. "You may call me Elizabeth if you like," she said in Greek, in a slight American accent. Luckily, her Greek was good and we would be able to communicate easily; my English was still very poor.

"Thank you. I'm Andreas," I replied with a nod.

Vasilis, obviously unaware of his mistake, turned the horn toward us and Wagner's opera drowned out the rest of our sentences. Unable to pretend that this was all going as planned, I turned toward him and gestured that he should turn the horn the other way around.

Elizabeth could no longer stifle her laughter. "I've heard great things about you," she said, "and am looking forward to getting started. You have picked the right spot to welcome us; we will be spending most of our time here. And music, too!"

I couldn't tell whether she was joking or being sarcastic, so I kept silent. She looked around and added, "Who knows? We might already be standing over our future finds."

She was not joking. The area was crammed with artifacts and remnants of the temple. Some were already on the surface, but even more remained beneath.

After meeting the rest of the team, I showed them the area of the temple. Two other Americans accompanied Elizabeth, newly arrived from the US. They kept looking around ecstatically, filled with child-like enthusiasm. One of them—a tall, imposing young man—bent down and scooped up a handful of wet soil. He brought it up to his nostrils, wanting to smell the scent emanating from the humid ground. At such moments, I felt these foreigners loved the island more than we locals did.

The cold wind picked up and put an end to our wanderings. I dropped back to help Vasilis carry the gramophone. That's when I saw them again. Nicholas Varvis and his wife had not budged this whole time. Clouds now covered every naked piece of sky, and their silhouettes loomed darker.

Only when Vasilis suddenly lifted the needle and silence fell did they move, as if the music had been keeping them enchanted to the spot. I kept my eyes on them until they disappeared from view. A chill ran down my spine. I hurriedly attributed it to the cold. We picked up the gramophone and turned in the direction of the museum.

The smell of jasmine Elizabeth had left behind her enveloped me once again, and a smile crossed my lips. For the first time in years, a feeling of optimism and happy anticipation for the future timidly stirred inside me.

My mother and sister waited outside the partially constructed museum building. Although years had passed since my father's death, they still wore black all year round. Tradition held fast on this island, especially where death and mourning were concerned.

"My mother, Anna, and my sister, Calliope ... Elizabeth," I introduced them.

The Americans already on the island stepped outside to greet the newcomers. They all seemed to know each other well, and broke into warm, friendly chatter so fast that I could not follow a word. Their smiling faces were contagious and the atmosphere became festive as we stepped inside.

Sensing my admiration for Elizabeth, Calliope threw me a look of stern disapproval before entering the room. I knew how funny she could be about anyone who was not from the island, and I ignored it, hoping her prejudice would go unnoticed.

On the other hand, my mother had tried to impress all our guests with her culinary powers. This was probably the first festive gathering she was attending since the death of my father. She had been through her fair share of pain and trouble and, like the rest of us, only wanted to spend the rest of her days in peace. All that she wanted, she often said, was to see us married and have grandchildren to carry on her name.

The mouth-watering smell of food drifted outside and Elizabeth clapped her hands with glee. "I don't know what smells so good, but I can't wait to taste it," she cheerfully said, and any awkwardness between us disappeared. She had a warm, open nature, a beautiful woman inside and out.

I was the last one to walk in and, before closing the door, I cast one last look at the hill where our uninvited guests had appeared. All that glimmered in the darkness was the faint red glow of a fire burning where they had stood. Although not an unusual sight on the island, it struck me as curious. I stood there, watching the flames grow stronger, rise higher, until the bonfire lit the autumnal landscape all the way down the slope.

I heard my mother's voice sweetly instructing me to shut the door to keep the cold outside, and I reluctantly pulled the heavy wooden panel closed. Who would light such a big fire so close to the archaeological site, and why?

Dominion of the Moon

Summer 1949, Samothrace

The August full moon struggled to break through the thin clouds and spread its glowing light everywhere. It was the brightest full moon of the year, and it gave the evening a touch of majestic solemnity. I was waiting for Elizabeth to arrive so we could visit Nicholas Varvis, who had to give his formal permission for excavations on his land to go ahead. He had been avoiding us until a few days ago, when he sent a message through Vasilis requesting a meeting. His instructions were so precise, yet bizarre, that I feared Vasilis had given his imagination free rein rather than passed on the actual message. He was inviting us to dinner just before midnight, at the stone tower where he lived with his family. He requested us to be at his front door at 11 p.m. sharp.

It was a balmy evening and I had arrived on foot. Standing at the edge of the path leading to the Varvis tower, I waited for Elizabeth to arrive so we could be punctual, as per our host's instructions. A large torch burned brightly against a wall. The flickering flames licking the wall mingled with the moonlight, radiating an imposing aura of mystery.

The only worry to cast a shadow on my mood was the rumor that some of the locals were still secretly selling illegally procured artifacts to foreigners. Order had not yet returned to Samothrace, and certain high-ranking families were still running the island. One of them was the Varvis family. Pressed by time and more urgent affairs, we had thrown ourselves into work these past nine months and allowed the need to excavate the land of the man we were about to meet fall by the wayside.

The time to resolve this matter had finally arrived. I was dying to see how he would treat us. My mother had urged me to avoid the meeting and let the Americans bite the bullet. I, however, felt that facing him was my duty. It was our homeland, and it was time to take responsibility for it, rather than let the foreigners always do the talking on our behalf.

I would often see Varvis ride by us, watching us astride his black horse. Although he had not attended my sister's wedding the previous month, he had sent us all the meat for the wedding feast through Vasilis. I had been impressed, not only by the gesture but also by the way it had been done: he had sent the livestock and his steward, Simon, to slaughter and skin the animals, then collect all the blood in casks, as if he did not wish to soil our fields. We had invited the whole island to the wedding but, unfortunately, many had chosen not to come. The terrible suspicion that had hung over me ever since my arrival had not abated, and was now hurting everyone related to me.

The latest news to reach the island finally foretold the imminent end of the civil war. My intention was to take a short leave in mid-autumn, before the weather turned cold, and travel in search of the woman who had been haunting me ever since the day our paths had crossed. So many years had passed, yet her memory had not faded. Her face appeared before me every day, as vivid as that fateful moment.

I was nonetheless very happy; our excavations were progressing in the best possible way. Piece by piece, astounding finds were coming to light, changing much of what we knew about the temple and the initiation rites of the Cabirian mysteries. A feeling that we would soon be making a significant, life-changing discovery grew stronger with every passing day.

A white, ghostly figure appeared in the distance, reflecting the moonlight. I immediately recognized Elizabeth. Her blond hair, shimmering under the silver moonbeams, made it easy to spot her from afar. She was the only woman on the island with such fair hair. She quickly came beside me and greeted me with a wide smile. Then, slowly, she kissed me on the cheek, her lips brushing the edge of my mouth just enough to confuse me as to her intentions.

We had often come close during this summer, but neither one of us had crossed the bounds of propriety. She was a beautiful woman, and had aroused the interest of many men on the island. In her polite, cold way, she had discouraged every prospective suitor and, devoted to her work as she was, did not add water to the local rumor mill. We spent hours together, and many thought there was something more going on between us than there was.

Although very attractive, she kept her personal life very private. She tended to associate only with her fellow Americans and avoided contact with the locals. It was not surprising; she was not planning to settle on the island, after all. She seemed to enjoy all her time spent working with the other mission members. She would be returning to Athens before next summer. There, she would wait for her next archaeological post to arrive from the American School of Classical Studies.

I offered my arm, and we started climbing up the cobbled street leading to the large wooden door of the Varvis tower. Her hand slid down, and our palms met. Once again, I felt the hard, long scar that crossed her palm. Despite being curious as to its provenance, I had never managed to ask how she got it.

As we crossed the final yards to the front door, small ancient lanterns lit our steps on either side of the narrow path. We had unearthed similar lanterns at the site of the temple, and I wondered how they had come into Varvis's possession. I felt my temper flare when I saw them exposed to the elements outside like an everyday oil lamp. Elizabeth also seemed surprised to see them. She picked one up and examined it closely, before replacing it with a frown of displeasure. She gave me a look of annoyance, but we kept walking without exchanging a single word. As if an unseen eye had been watching our arrival, the door swung open with a long, low creak, revealing an inner courtyard lit by torches, candles, and tall lanterns.

A long, monastery dining table stood on a raised dais at the far end of the courtyard. We hovered by the entrance, waiting for someone to appear. The first person to greet us was Simon, Varvis's steward. He looked different than his usual self. Dressed in his Sunday best, he no longer looked like the coarse giant that made grown men on the island quake with fear.

Nicholas and Marika Varvis appeared on the landing, bestowing beatific smiles of welcome. I had never seen either of them smile. Both were dressed in white, as was Elizabeth, and the darkness of my clothes stuck out like a sore thumb. As soon as we reached them, they hugged us warmly as if we were old friends. I tried to hide my astonishment as they stood there, well to do and cheerful, so different to how I had become accustomed to seeing them.

I cast a quick, furtive look around me and spotted numerous artifacts that had no right to be there: amphorae, marble fragments of ancient buildings, and small statues. I felt my temples throb in anger at the sight of all these small treasures. I would not be leaving this evening without raising the matter. Lost in my thoughts as I took it all in, I missed their conversation with Elizabeth, who had succumbed to the enchanting atmosphere the hosts had created.

Nicholas was holding her hand, palm turned upwards, observing her scar. He did not shy away from asking the story behind the sharp, hard line. Years ago, on a mission in Italy, she had tried to hold onto a rope to prevent a statue dangling at its other end from falling over a cliff. She had stood there for quite a while before someone came along to help her. She did not think of letting go of the rope for a single moment, trying to save the statue from smashing against the rocks, all the while risking great damage to her hand.

As soon as Elizabeth finished telling the story, Marika offered her a drink. Then she turned toward me, proffering a cup of red wine. There was a strange glow in her eyes as she kept looking at me intently, having evidently divined my agitation and trying to fathom what I was desperately trying to hide. A thin woman, her hair was piled on her crown in an intricate knot. She seemed to enjoy my momentary awkwardness.

Behind us, Simon was lighting large torches along the walls and casting furtive glances in our direction, making sure nothing was amiss. I don't know why, but I had a strange sense of floating in a fog, not being truly present in the courtyard but watching what was happening from a distance high above.

I took a sip, felt the strong red wine warm my chest and wake me from my strange, slumberous state. At Marika's invitation, we all took our seats around the table. Varvis smoothed down his thick mustache and raised his cup. "Welcome. We are honored by the presence of such distinguished guests in our home. May tonight be the beginning of a warm friendship."

We all raised our glasses and took a sip, and I wondered what had caused this sudden show of affection and conviviality. A child appeared at the other end of the courtyard. He solemnly walked up to the table and stood beside Varvis. I guessed he was their son, Alexandros. I had heard about him but had never seen him before. With the exception of his blond hair that reached his shoulders, he was the spitting image of his mother.

He looked at us indifferently as his father made the introductions. He did not look older than nine. As soon as his father finished introducing us, he bowed and kissed his hand goodnight, without uttering a single word. He then approached his mother and repeated the gesture, before disappearing up the stairs that led to the first floor.

I followed him with my eyes as he walked along the balcony and stood before one of the doors. As if sensing my gaze, he turned toward me and stared at me with such hatred that I gave an involuntary gasp, wondering what could have caused such animosity.

The first dishes were being served as we resumed our conversation. "How good to finally have the war over," I said. "I hear the guerilla war will end soon."

"Every war happens for a reason," Varvis slowly replied, and looked at Elizabeth. "Your government has invested a lot in our land."

"Yes, and they intend to continue," she replied. "We love Ancient Greece, the civilization that was born here and shone its light on the rest of the world." My American colleague gave me a knowing look. "For our part, we thank you for welcoming us on your beautiful island."

"It will become your island too, soon," Varvis said, raising his glass. "Our island carries ancient stories, unique stories ... So many people have passed through the island since those times. Some looted whatever they could find; others lived peacefully with the locals for a long time. Our ancestors made sure to safeguard our heritage. Their legacy passes from generation to generation, a legacy no occupier or war has ever managed to spoil."

Hearing his last words, I was about to seize the moment to raise the issue of all the antiquities he kept, which could fill a museum on their own. As if reading my thoughts, he looked at us and raised his voice. "My wife and I have decided to donate everything in our possession to your museum. When it is completed, they should take their place where they belong. For many generations we have kept these treasures and traditions safe. Now, it is time for all Greeks to enjoy them. Well, at least the treasures."

He paused and savored the surprise on our faces. It was completely unexpected. It all sounded so perfect, even I believed him. Elizabeth was the first to let out a cry of joy. She had been drinking steadily throughout the evening and seemed a little tipsy.

Varvis turned to his steward with a small nod. Simon immediately approached the table. He held a small chest, which he placed with near religious solemnity beside Marika. She opened it carefully and removed two small cases. She gave one to Elizabeth and handed me the other. Inside were pieces of bronze eyelashes, evidently removed from statues.

My colleague placed her wine on the table and examined the eyelashes attentively, suddenly alert. Her eyes glimmered with the familiar thirst for discovery as she looked at them. The other case contained coins and small objects.

"A Bulgarian had collected all these and was about to sell them years ago for a pittance," Marika said. "Luckily, Simon, our steward, found out and bought them for a slightly higher price. They will be among our donations."

She offered Elizabeth her hand. "Come, let us leave the men to talk and I will show you what else you will be receiving shortly."

As if in a trance, my friend put the case down and took Marika's hand to stand up. The drink made her unsteady on her feet, and she lost her balance, falling into her arms. Aware of my companion's state, Marika held her up and smiled as if nothing was amiss. Putting an arm around her waist to support her, she gave me a reassuring look. She then led Elizabeth away through an arched passageway that led inside.

As they passed under the vaulted arch, I noticed a piece of marble bearing an inscription mounted above it. The light was too dim, and I sat too far away to make out what it said. On either side of the arch, the heads of two rams with oversized horns stood guard. As the two women moved further inside, their laughter echoed under the stone roof and bounced back into the courtyard, so altered that it sounded like it came from the depths of the earth.

Once alone, Varvis and I resorted to polite conversation that had nothing to do with excavations, before succumbing to an awkward prolonged silence. He stood up and asked me to accompany him to the other side of the courtyard, where the moonbeams on the sea stretched out as far as the eye could see. I got up and followed him without thinking about it. He must have been two years older than I was, but his lean physique made him look younger. The wine dulled my thoughts, but I still felt in full command of myself.

"Some people arrived today by boat just to enjoy the full moon. They'll spend the night in the forest, apparently, and return to Alexandroupolis on the mainland tomorrow."

I had heard of that group, but had not seen them arrive. We had been told that they might visit the archaeological site, and were asked to be prepared to give a small guided tour. "Many people will start visiting our beautiful island from now on," I said.

Varvis's next words had nothing to do with the topic he had just introduced. "Tonight is a very special evening for my family. Every full moon in August, we celebrate the circle of life and fertility. We will hold a wake until dawn. Tonight, and tomorrow night when the moon starts waning, we confess all our sins so that we may find catharsis," he said, looking up at the moon.

I had no idea which festival he was talking about, but I waited for him to continue. "I picked tonight so that the grace of the gods could be with us," he said. "They come closer to us on evenings such as this. The ceremony will take place tomorrow, and you are welcome to join us."

I knew some people on the island believed in the *dodecatheon,* the twelve Olympian gods, but I didn't think that was what Varvis was referring to. I could sense Simon behind us, discreetly following our every word.

"I'll get straight to the point, Andreas Stais, because I know you are an intelligent man so you will understand. I don't know what business all these foreigners have to be on our land; what gives them the right to decide what will happen to the legacy of our ancestors."

Even though the same thoughts had sometimes crossed my mind, I had never placed the Americans in the same category as the others who had occupied our land. I decided to keep my mouth shut and see where he was going with this.

"As I already mentioned, we will donate much of what we have safeguarded for years, what we protected from thieves and looters. My family has been keeping tradition alive for centuries. Some of my ancestors gave their lives for what is here today."

Trying to nudge the conversation in my favor, I said, "I appreciate your gesture, and I promise that, as soon as we have catalogued all the artifacts, I will propose that part of the new museum be named after you. We could even construct a new wing to house everything discovered on your land, now that excavations will be underway ..."

Varvis tensed and stood very still at these words. He slowly turned toward me, his face hard and unfathomable. The familiar glassy film descended over his eyes. "There will never be excavations on my land. You will make do with what I give you, and you can forget all your schemes, you and your Americans. You will make sure they never take place. In return, I will make sure you and your family lack for nothing. Anything to be found on my land has already been found. If you start digging, you will just end up seizing the largest part of my property for who knows how many years, all for nothing. I cannot allow that. Most of the land you are already digging on was taken from my ancestors anyway."

I tried hard not to let my unease show. I turned toward the passageway, looking for Elizabeth. The two women had been gone for quite a while, and I was beginning to worry.

My composure regained, I turned back to Varvis and spoke determinedly. "Everything you say you will gift us is not yours to gift. I understand you kept it safe all this time, but the antiquities belong to the island. They are not your family heirlooms; they are the heirlooms of humankind. If the Archaeological Service approves excavations, they will go ahead. It is beyond anyone's influence ..."

"You have no idea who you are talking to!" he shouted, and I felt Simon creep up behind me.

I did not know how to react. At a loss, I tried to diffuse the situation. "I think we should leave now and arrange for a meeting with everyone another day."

"The matter is closed," he said flatly.

I realized that the best thing to do would be to take Elizabeth and leave. I turned to go look for her, but in the blink of an eye Simon stood before me, barring my way. Varvis's menacing voice rang out behind me. "I will only say this once. If you don't want an archaeologist to dig up your carcass in the future, call off the excavations now."

I had anticipated many things, but I never dreamed he would have the gall to threaten me directly. A woman's voice cried out in pain from the depths of the passageway. Elizabeth! I shoved Simon aside and ran in that direction. Just before I reached the first arch, I felt him grab my arm and pin me to the spot. I saw Elizabeth appear. She stopped before me, out of breath, holding her wrist. A tight red belt circled her waist. Walking slowly, Marika appeared behind her, looking as inscrutable as ever. Elizabeth's hand was bleeding

"W-what happened?" I stammered.

"Nothing," Elizabeth whispered, and came nearer, looking puzzled at Simon, who was still gripping my arm. Only then did I feel him slowly release his grasp. She flung herself in my arms as if looking for a place to shelter.

With shaky hands, she nervously fumbled with the red belt, trying to undo it. I helped her and, as soon as it came loose, she grabbed it and flung it in a nearby flowerbed. Nicholas and the steward walked around us and stood beside Marika under the arched entrance. Marika bent down and picked up the belt, straightening it ceremoniously and giving Elizabeth a look of annoyance. It was time to leave.

"Thank you for your visit. We hope you will come again. If you change your mind, you are welcome tomorrow at the same time," Varvis said coldly.

I took Elizabeth's hand and turned toward the exit, casting a quick look at the Latin inscription on the marble slab above the arch.

Dominion of the Moon

«Deorum sacra qui non acceperunt non intrant»

Still shaky, we descended the cobbled path away from the tower, hand in hand. I did not look behind me until we reached the dirt path that led to the village. On the tower ramparts, a large fire burned brightly, the tongues of the flames appearing to lick the moon from this distance. On either side of the bonfire, Varvis and his wife stood still as statues, looking in our direction. Not wanting to alarm Elizabeth further, I picked up the pace and pulled her away as fast as I could.

I never managed to find out what had actually happened to Elizabeth that evening. All she said was that she had a bit too much to drink, stumbled, and cut herself on a sharp wall stone. I did not believe her, but I could tell she did not want to talk about it. Her injury was superficial, anyway, and she decided to resume work as normal.

She seemed embarrassed by her tipsiness and momentary loss of self-control. Despite burning with curiosity, I waited for her to reveal what had happened when she had been alone with Marika, if she wished to do so. I could not fault her reluctance; I had kept Varvis's threats to myself as well. I intended to send a report to our headquarters in Thessaloniki, explaining the situation so that we could decide how to handle the matter.

I did not manage to sleep for more than a couple of hours that night. My anger had abated, but I kept tossing and turning, trying to make sense of the evening's events. What did the red belt Elizabeth had been wearing mean? Why had she flung it away like that?

The inscription above the arch still played in my mind. In 1938, the Millers had discovered a column at the entrance of the *Anaktoron*, the House of the Lords. It bore the exact same inscription. *The uninitiate may not enter.* Was the marble slab at the Varvis home an archaeological artifact, or had someone just etched that phrase, a prohibition linked to the initiation rites that took place at the Sanctuary in ancient times? I thought it unlikely that a second such inscription existed. Its discovery before the outbreak of the war had caused a stir and changed much of what we knew about the Sanctuary of the Great Gods.

Although systematic excavations at the site of the Sanctuary had begun as early as 1873 by an Austrian group of archaeologists, the most significant finds were made after Karl and Phyllis began excavating in 1938. The American couple had already discovered many buildings, statues, and part of the Temple Complex. Piece by piece, they reconstructed the history and rituals of this ancient religion and tried to solve the mystery shrouding the Sanctuary of the Great Gods. It was now clear it was the site of a complex *myesis*, an initiation of many stages. We were still unable to determine the order or nature of those rituals.

Sleep deprived and exhausted by the din of thoughts churning in my mind, I decided to take a rare day off. I planned to walk to *Gria Vathra*, one of the most beautiful fresh water pools on the island. Then, I would hike as far as my legs could carry me.

I left the two teams excavating close to the temple behind and, after a long walk, reached the mouth of a small stream. I bent down like a thirsty animal and plunged my face in the water, taking large gulps. I resurfaced to catch my breath and slowly started walking upstream toward the mountain. I had not been here since the beginning of summer, when the water current was twice as strong. I walked on, through the arbutus shrubs and beneath the tall plane trees, whose roots played hide and seek, spreading on the ground and burrowing under the soil and beneath the large stones.

It was a land sculpted of wood and rock. A cormorant suddenly sprung from the foliage and I felt the flap of its wings ruffle my hair as it headed out to sea. So many memories linked to this spot, moments shared with old friends, long departed.

I reached *Gria Vathra* a few minutes later. A large bowl, as if scooped out of the mountain by a mystical hand, it loomed in the middle of the forest. The flowing, crystal waters of the stream pooled there before continuing their course down a small waterfall. Legend had it that it was named after an old woman, a *gria*, who had drowned as she bent down to drink. Her flock of goats dispersed the moment they saw her fall in the water. Days later, people discovered her body on the shore, where the torrent joined the sea. That was how the locals realized that the river continued its course underground and underwater all the way to the sea. The island's waterways were treacherous beasts, flowing with strong currents and littered with rocks like sharpened knives. Some said that the woods were haunted with lost souls seeking redemption; others said they were full of nymphs and sprites.

The trees were already shedding their leaves, dropping them in the water like missives to the sea. Although I wanted to dive into the cool lagoon, I decided to keep walking. The route upstream was dotted with other water pools. I walked on, trying to put the previous evening's events out of my mind. The landscape helped, soaking up all my negative thoughts and soothing my senses: the sound of

Dominion of the Moon

flowing water and the scent of the old trees. Their rotting trunks resisted the passage of time and made me long for my childhood, for the times we spent hiding in tree trunks and jumping out to scare each other.

Steaming embers in a circle of stones caught my eye, remnants of a fire that had been lit there recently. The trampled ground beneath the large rocks showed that a group of people had spent the night here, possibly the visitors Varvis had mentioned the other evening.

As I stood observing their tracks, I thought I heard the sound of splashing water further up, carried by the soft breeze stirring the branches as it blew down the mountain slope. I sprang up the rocks and held my breath, ears pricked to every sound. Silence.

It must have been a trick of the wind, creating otherworldly, indefinable sounds as it whistled though the rocks. Many of the locals believed it was the sound of sprites and nymphs, lurking in the woods and trying to chase intruders away. I shrugged and carefully walked further up. Winter and the torrents reshaped the way of the land, so that every new trek felt like a foray onto virgin ground. Nature on this island was an incomparable artist whose creations overflowed with generosity. I had decided to spend the rest of my life here. Whatever travels came up, my base would be Samothrace, and I intended to request that my post here be made permanent.

An elderly plane tree, uprooted by the torrential waters, lay across the ground, barring my way. I could either slither like a snake through the small opening, or walk along the trunk to reach the other side. I opted for the latter, and slowly edged along the tree trunk, like a novice tightrope walker. It had fallen in such a way as to create a natural shortcut. If I managed to walk to the other end, I would save myself a circuitous climb and reach a small clearing offering a magnificent view.

I was almost halfway along the trunk, walking among the tree's foliage, when I spotted another, smaller water pool beneath me. I had forgotten all about it. Its surface rippled, a sign that someone or something was swimming in it. It must be the visitors, I thought, and hesitated for a moment, trying to decide whether I should walk on or make my presence known in some way. I could not see anyone from where I stood, so I took a hesitant step forward. Suddenly, I had a clear view of the entire pool.

At the center of the pool, as if she had been patiently waiting under the water's surface all this time, a woman with long black hair rose like a dolphin cresting the water's surface. Before I could see her face, she turned around and started swimming toward a large flat rock that stood on the edge of the pool like a diving board. I looked around but could not see anybody else. Her white arms split the water in ever-wider circles as she reached the pool's edge. She reached the ledge and tilted her face toward the small flowing stream that poured fresh water into the small lagoon. She then gripped the rock and pulled herself out. The cool water had been her only garment. It dripped away, revealing her naked form.

I felt myself blush with embarrassment, but I could not pull my eyes away from the milky figure thrown into sharp relief against the craggy grey rocks. She looked more like an elf than a creature born of man. My eyes were drawn to her only flaw, the scar of an old wound that started at her shoulder and faded between her shoulder blades. The spark of an old memory stirred inside me.

As if sensing my stealthy presence, she suddenly turned and looked at me, standing still. She did nothing to hide her statuesque perfection; she simply raised her hand to shield her eyes from the sun, to see me more clearly. I could not believe what the voice in my head was now screaming at me. Even when she slowly pulled away the wet strand of hair that partially hid her features, I refused to believe that standing before me was the same woman for whom I had gone from executioner to savior a few years ago.

Varvis nervously paced up and down beneath the vines in the tower's garden. On a nearby chaise longue, Marika lay holding their son in her arms. Lulled by the tranquil garden and his mother's voice, the boy lay on her bosom, eyes heavy with sleep. She half-whispered, half-sang a melody that sounded like a lullaby, and stroked his blond hair, gently playing with his curls and trying to untangle them with her caresses.

It was nearly noon, and the sun snuck through openings in the vine's thick foliage to warm the cobblestones. Simon pulled up a bucket of water from the stone well and emptied it into a clay jug, the overflow cooling down the stone slabs. He then brought it to the table and filled their glasses.

Varvis interrupted his nervous pacing and thirstily emptied his glass. He put it back on the table with a sharp thud and turned to his steward, who had remained by the table, silently watching him. His voice was tense but low, so as not to wake his precious son. "Stais does not seem to heed any warnings. I want you to teach him a lesson tonight."

His wife raised her voice and sang more loudly, to cover the sound of his voice. Unperturbed, he spoke on, swept up by the vision his words were painting. "The flames will reach the sky. He must understand that if he fails to dissuade the Americans from digging on our land, he is doomed. Do what you must. Just make sure you are not seen."

The silent nod from Simon was enough to show his acquiescence, and his master dismissed him with a wave of his hand. Varvis slowly walked to the edge of the chaise longue, where his wife sang on, seemingly indifferent to everything around her. Her chant rose like a low murmur from her chest, like an Orphic hymn. Soothed by her voice, Nicholas stretched out his hand and touched his son's head, gently running his fingers through the child's soft hair.

"No one will set foot on our land. Our child's child will be the one to pull from the bowels of this land that which awaits its master to reveal it. It will all come to pass when and how it should. Tonight is significant," he said, tenderly looking at Alexandros.

Marika fell silent and looked at him intently. She untangled her fingers from the boy's hair and tenderly placed them around her husband's temples, like a wreath. Murmuring something under her breath, she drew him near and kissed his forehead. Steely determination etched on his face, Varvis stood and picked his son up carefully as not to wake him. He slowly moved inside the tower, Marika by his side, the sleeping boy in his arms.

Like a startled hare, Elizabeth sprinted through the archaeological site, hastily skirting around the marble column fragments that dotted her path, risking a bad fall in her excitement. As she ran, she looked around, anxiously searching for someone. As soon as she spotted Vasilis in the distance, she loudly called out his name. Startled, Vasilis lost his footing and dropped a wooden beam he had been hoisting on his shoulder.

"Where is Andreas?" she asked. "Have you seen him? I've been looking for him everywhere; do you know where he's gone?" She peered at Vasilis from under her wide brimmed hat, hands on her knees, her breath coming short and fast.

Puzzled at her unusual deportment, he pointed in the direction Andreas had taken. "I think he's gone to Gria Vathra ... He'll be back in the afternoon, though."

Pulling herself upright, she gripped his arm and spoke intently. "Run and fetch him. Find him and tell him to get here as fast as he can. Please, hurry!"

"Miss Elizabeth, what's wrong? What shall I tell him?" Vasilis asked, as he prepared to go in search of Andreas.

Mixing English and Greek in her agitated state, Elizabeth settled for a few scattered phrases. "Tell him we found a woman ... the goddess ... marble ... buried ... pieces. He must come now. Run!"

Vasilis somehow managed to make sense of what she said, his eyes widening in surprise. Then he ran, skipping over the scattered marble pieces and stones and clearing the makeshift enclosure in a single, easy leap. He could still hear her voice shouting, and he picked up speed, like an experienced athlete.

He climbed up the slope with the ease of a mountain goat, lightly crossing even the most arduous parts. It did not take him more than an hour to reach *Gria Vathra*. He stopped, needed to catch his breath for a moment. He leaned against a tree trunk and, as soon as his heart stopped beating like a wild drum, he pushed himself off and started walking upstream, convinced that Andreas must have done the same.

Walking carefully, he moved between the trees, agilely stepping on the stones that were firm enough to allow him to move fast. A short while later, he arrived at the first large pool and looked carefully around him, without spotting Andreas. He rested for another moment and then resumed his search, still walking against the flow.

A triumphant smile crossed his lips when he spotted the man he was looking for standing on a fallen plane tree. Without wasting a moment, he called out at the top of his lungs. Like a sudden clap of thunder, his cry pierced the forest and did more than catch just Andreas's attention.

We both stood transfixed, unable to make the slightest move, like statues facing each other across a wooded garden. A few moments later, I hesitantly decided to approach her, spurred on by the need to make sure that the woman before me was real, not a figment of my imagination.

A scream pierced the air behind me, startling me. Turning sharply to see who it was, my foot slipped on the mossy trunk of the old tree.

I flung my arms wildly, trying to grab onto a branch and keep my balance. I caught a fleeting glimpse of Vasilis's frightened face before plunging backward into the cold stream. Thankfully, it was not a long drop, and I fell in with a quick, clumsy splash. I felt the icy water soak my clothes and, at the sight of the large stones menacingly protruding on the stream's banks, realized I'd had a lucky break. A few inches to the left or right and it would have been a much more painful drop.

In the blink of an eye, Vasilis was wading through the water and helping me stand up. He started talking, but I ignored him and hurriedly started to clamber up the rocks, trying to return to my previous vantage point. As if in a trance, driven by some mystical impulse, I ignored his cries to turn back and quickly reached the top of the rocks, from where I could see the water pool and the area surrounding it.

All was calm and still, as if no one had been swimming there minutes ago. Deathly silence, interrupted only by the trickling of the water and the splattering sounds it made as it wove through the rocks. The shouting must have startled her, but she should still be around. Maybe she had hidden somewhere to get dressed. But I had a panoramic view from where I was standing—she should still be visible.

I climbed back down and took the small path circling the lagoon all the way to the other side. Countless thoughts crossed my mind as I tried to understand how she could have disappeared during the brief moments it took me to climb up the rocks. I was at a loss as to what to do. I wanted to call her, but what could I possibly tell a woman I had just seen naked, who had most likely been frightened by my presence? Call her by what name? I could not rationalize what had just happened.

I felt Vasilis tug my sleeve, shouting out my name, and I snapped out of my trance. He was the reason I had lost her. With rising anger, I abruptly asked him what he meant by screaming in the forest like that.

"Miss Elizabeth sent me. She wants you to get back immediately ..." he said, eyes bulging and out of breath.

His words worried me. I gave a last, fleeting look around me, should that strange creature reappear, and then grabbed Vasilis by the shoulders. Water still dripped from my hands. "What happened? Why should I go back? What's the matter?"

In the jumble of sentences that tumbled out of his mouth, I seized on the words he kept repeating. "They found a woman ... buried ... Marble, pieces ..."

I felt the water become one with my sweat and freeze down my back. Buried? Pieces? What did he mean?

"Speak clearly, man. What woman? Murdered how? Where did they find her? Who is it? Calm down and tell me, slowly."

"I told you, Andreas. She told me to run and find you. You need to go there right now. She also said 'goddess'. I think."

He was making no sense. They had clearly just unearthed something, but what? A person, or a statue? Whatever had happened, it must be serious or Elizabeth would not have sent Vasilis to find me.

At the same time, what had become of the woman I had just seen with my own two eyes? I wondered whether the creature I had just encountered had never really existed, whether it was just my imagination playing tricks. All the island lore that had colored my childhood came flooding back, stories of people seeing or hearing things in the woods that were not really there. Was that what had happened to me?

I took a couple of steps forward, hoping that even at this last moment she would reveal herself. But nothing happened. Whoever or whatever she was, she had disappeared as if a magic hand had lifted her from the water to the sky, from one expanse of blue to another.

"What are you looking for, Andreas? Is anyone else around?" Vasilis whispered, sensing my agitation.

I looked down at my dripping clothes and tried to shake the mud off. "Just give me a moment," I replied, and walked around the small clearing in desperation, scanning the foliage.

A loud howl of frustration escaped my lips, a last, hopeless call beseeching a reply, but it was met by silence. My body sagged, worn out. Sensing the urgency of Elizabeth waiting back at the site, I reluctantly decided to abandon my search. The climb down would take whatever reserves of strength I had left, so I turned to Vasilis and said with a sigh, "Nothing. It must have been some forest critter; it's gone now. Let's go!"

Without waiting for Vasilis to catch up, I hastily started climbing down, hoping to at least solve the second mystery of the day: that of the buried woman.

Even when we reached the archaeological site, exhausted by the hurried trek back, I could not get her naked form as she stood by the water pool out of my mind. I snapped back to reality only when I saw all those gathered at a corner of the *Hieron* Temple, where one of the American teams had been excavating. As soon as they noticed me, they parted to make way for me to approach. My heart was about to burst, thumping with worry and the exertion of the fast walk. I took deep breaths, trying to compose myself.

Only when I caught a glimpse of Elizabeth's face did I begin to calm down, the excitement lighting up her eyes reassuring me that nothing was wrong. In the trench, Phyllis Miller, Karl's wife, kneeled down covered in dust. She wore a stripy dress and a large white hat. All around her lay marble fragments tied with thick ropes, evidently belonging to the same find.

Like a mother nursing a baby, she cradled a part of the broken statue in her arms. Its edge touched the ground, and I could just make out the statue's tunic and a part of her hand. With her free hand, Phyllis was carefully wiping away the earth stuck on the statue's surface. Sensing my presence, she stopped and looked up at me.

Everyone was silent, as the sun set to the west and the southerly wind gently stirred up dust over the mound of soil recently dug out. Only our ragged breathing as we tried to catch our breath broke the silence of anticipation.

Elizabeth came and stood beside me. Her hand was roughly bandaged where she had injured it the previous night, but she did not seem concerned. I felt everyone's eyes on me. They were all waiting to see my reaction. I still felt disoriented, unable to think clearly. With great difficulty, I asked what was going on.

She did not wait for me to finish my sentence. She knew my love for excavations and my impatience for a significant discovery. Taking my hand, Elizabeth led me to the edge of the trench and pointed to the opening.

I jumped in, landing near Phyllis. She stretched out her hand and pulled me toward her, the soil on her hands rubbing into my skin. As soon as I could get a closer look, the realization of whom the headless statue was began to sink in. My eyes filled with tears I fiercely fought to hold back. The fragments lying before me revealed that the third statue of the goddess that haunted my dreams had just been found.

The setting sun was but a distant orange slice on the horizon as we all cheerfully went about covering the statue to shelter it as best we could. I was bursting with joy. There had been no time to move the statue to a safer place, and I was ready to spend the night beside it, guarding it on its first night out in the open air after so many years.

We would resume the search for the missing head of this Nike in the morning. The heads of the previous two statues had disappeared many years ago, if they had ever been found. Three similar statues without a face; it seemed like the goddess had been cursed. I secretly hoped that this statue would finally yield the missing puzzle piece ...

Vasilis had gone to my house to fetch me a change of clothes. This new discovery superseded everything else that had taken place that day, until I heard Vasilis say he had to stop at the boat that had arrived the previous night to ship something to the mainland. Fast as lightning, a thought crossed my mind. If the woman at the water pool had arrived with the other full-moon visitors, she would surely be returning with them. Provided she was real, and not a vision I had conjured up.

I vacillated between my reluctance to leave the statue and my desire to go with Vasilis and solve that other riddle. I made up my mind quickly; such was my desire to meet her. I asked Vasilis to wait up for me and, as soon as I found someone to stand guard in my absence, I hopped inside the old Jeep and we drove to Kamariotissa, the island's small port.

It was getting darker by the minute as we watched the boat arrive at the dock, where a small crowd was waiting to board. Sitting on pieces of luggage, they seemed to have arrived much earlier, trying to beat nightfall. I was still surprised they had not arranged to depart earlier. Maybe they wanted to enjoy the moonlight on the boat. The sea was calm, still as a mirror, ideally suited for a night aboard. Most of them held small lanterns, as if they were outside a church waiting for Midnight Mass. Other than the waiting passengers, the port was nearly empty. A small group of children sat on a derelict old wall at the edge of the port, curiously watching the unusual gathering.

We parked nearby and I left Vasilis to unload the car, making my way toward the waiting group. I could hear them speak French as I came nearer, and I wondered if any Greeks were among them. Her back turned to the sea, a woman was explaining something, pointing to the sky, then the ground by her feet. I could not understand a word of what she was saying, but felt drawn by how expressively she spoke. In the dim light of the lanterns and the shadows they cast, I could not make out anyone's features. I circled them discreetly and then stopped to face them, a few feet away from the woman who addressing them. Some curiously examined me with a frown, as I stood peering at them in the hope of spotting her. Their guide seemed annoyed at my presence and abruptly turned toward me. "Can I help you?"

I shook my head and apologized, feeling bad at having invaded their space so indiscreetly. I pulled further away, without having managed to spot her. Now they were nothing but grey shadows in the dark. Suddenly, one of the shadows stirred and turned toward me, pushing her way through the crowd. She walked slowly, the glimmer of her lantern lighting the ground by her feet and keeping the rest of her shrouded in darkness. When she reached me, she stopped and slowly raised it between us, like a barrier we would soon be crossing.

Transfixed, we stood staring at each other, ignoring the calls of her companions who had started to board the boat. Rooted to the spot, we tried to grasp how once again fate had brought us together in the strangest way. The woman I had seen in the forest that morning was no longer a fleeting vision, but a reality that stood before me. A tear glimmered at the corner of her eye, ready to course down her cheek. I could sense she was helplessly trying to find the right words, as was I. All I could do was take a step toward her.

"I-it can't be you," she stammered, breaking the silence. She raised her hand and hesitatingly touched my cheek, as if to ensure I was real. I opened my mouth to speak, but words were beyond me. I had so much to say, but my thoughts were spinning, giving me no chance to voice them. She looked the same as that cursed day, though more tranquil, without the vacant expression she had worn as she waited for death at my hands.

"I'm Andreas," I said awkwardly, trying to set our strange encounter in motion.

"I'm Zoe," she immediately replied.

A man walked up behind her and gave us a curious look. He said something in French, and she gave him a brief reply. I felt the ground sink beneath my feet when she turned back toward me and pointed to the others. "I must go … I came with them. Thank you for saving my life. It feels strange to see you again. I always wanted to find you and thank you, and now here we are. I don't know what to say …This is all so strange. I don't know what to do …"

I did not want to let her go. If I lost her now, I knew it would be forever. She spoke to me so openly that I concluded she did not realize I was the man who had watched her swim naked in the forest. I decided not to mention that part.

Without asking anything further, not even how I came to be here, she moved the lantern aside and brushed her lips against my cheek. My body quavered at her touch. She slowly pulled back, her gaze still locked on mine. She made an imperceptible move to turn to the boat, and I realized time was up.

"Don't go …" The words burst out of my mouth, imbued with all my sincerity. She seemed taken aback, and paused in her tracks. The spark of joy in her eyes gave me the strength to persevere. "Please stay …It can't be random, our paths crossing for a third time." I bit my lip as soon as I realized I had just revealed our previous encounter. Her reaction confirmed that she had no idea what I was talking about.

She looked at me questioningly, trying to understand what I had just said. Feeling the sands of time flowing ever faster, I spoke hurriedly. "I saw you swimming at Gria Vathra ..." Her eyes widened in surprise, as if she could not believe what she was hearing. "It can't just be a coincidence," I insisted.

Without a nod or a word, she looked at me for a moment, then turned and walked straight to the boat. I realized confessing my little sin had been a mistake. The men at the port were untying the ropes as I watched her walk swiftly up the gangplank. The acrid smoke of the oil lamps filled my nostrils. I saw Vasilis waving at me that it was time to go; he had been waiting at the other side of the port all this time, unaware of what was happening.

On the horizon, behind the craggy mountain peaks, silver light shimmered majestically, announcing the arrival of a bright, round moon. I felt caught up in a rapidly flowing tide of events, unable to react, unable to pull my eyes or thoughts away from her.

Unable to bear the tension any longer, I slowly dragged my feet down the dock. The visitors' lanterns now dotted the deck, making the boat look like a dark rock festooned with tiny stars. At the captain's urging, they began to put them out, so he could see his way out of the port. As the flames vanished one by one, so did my hopes that she might return. The boat was now nothing but a dark mass bobbing in the water.

This cannot be the end to such a fated meeting, I desperately thought.

Just before the boat pushed away from the dock, I saw her climb the prow and take a reckless leap onto the dock, holding a small cloth bundle that landed clumsily beside her. Behind her, some of her companions leaned over, calling out her name, but it was too late.

The boat was sailing away, and she stood there, silhouetted against the rising moonlight. As still as a statue, she waited for me. Trying to control my excitement and ensure that her presence was not a trick of my fevered mind, I walked toward her.

In a cave filled with candles and small lanterns placed on the indentations of the scraggy rocks, a group dressed in white held hands in a circle. Their faces were hidden behind black, expressionless, genderless masks. Their eyes were turned to the mouth of the cave, as if expecting someone to arrive at any moment.

Like an altar, a block of white, shiny marble stood at the center of the cave that nature had hollowed out of the mountain. Smoke rose from a bowl carved into the marble block's surface. It seeped through the cave like fog, filling it with an intense scent.

A woman appeared at the mouth of the cave. She wore a deep crimson dress that swept the stones as she walked, holding a clay vessel in her hands, like a compass leading her steps to those waiting. Another figure, dressed in white like the others but wearing a tight black belt, walked closely behind her.

The woman entered the circle and stopped at the altar. Her companion stood at a gap in the circle, and the bodies closed once again, sealing the woman in the center.

The deep beat of a drum sounded outside the cave, giving the proceedings a note of solemnity. She slowly raised the clay vessel above her head and, following the rhythm of the drum, started chanting an ancient hymn. The red cloth, tied roughly around her body, slipped as she swayed to the beat of the drum until it fell to the ground, spreading like a pool of blood around her and exposing her naked body. Only her face remained hidden behind the securely fastened mask.

Still undulating, she gently tilted the vessel, and shiny drops of blood dripped onto the white marble. When its contents had fully covered the surface of the altar, it looked like an animal had just been sacrificed in this otherworldly ritual. When the last drop of blood had been emptied, she flung the clay vessel against the wall of the cave, where it shattered.

It was the signal for the drum to pick up its pace, beating faster and faster as she turned to face the mouth of the cave and lay on the red cloth on the ground. Going against the rhythm of the drum, she slowly spread her bare legs. Her companion stepped forward from the circle and stood before her. He untied his belt and flung off his white cloak with a sudden movement, revealing his chiseled, muscular body. He snapped the thin thread that hung around his neck, a ring dangling from it, and knelt beside her, placing the ring on her finger.

The drum reached a frenzied beat and the woman slowly raised her pelvis, inviting the man inside her. He shifted before her, getting nearer and nearer. The white clad figures of the circle stepped closer, as if trying to shield what would follow from any wandering eyes. The name of a woman, an indistinct murmur, rose to their lips. *Axieros* ...

The man crouched on top of the woman, placing his palms on either side of her head. She tilted her body like a bow, welcoming him inside her. At the moment of their union, the drum beat wildly, like a rumble threatening to bring the cave crashing down. The figures in white turned and ceremoniously began to blow out the candles, until the cave sank into complete darkness.

The drum stopped abruptly when the last flickering flame died out. Only the wild moans of the couple caught in the primitive throes of the union ritual echoed around the cave.

We had just arrived at the archaeological site. I had spent most of the drive trying to explain to Vasilis who Zoe was and why she was joining us. He seemed unable to grasp what I was saying, so I asked him, rather abruptly, to go home and rest. He gave me a hurt look, but did not protest, and left, still casting impressed looks in her direction and trying to fathom what was happening in his own way.

I had been struck by Zoe's strange silence during this time. Only when she saw the flames and torches lighting up the Varvis tower did she ask what was happening, but I avoided giving an answer. The fact was that I did not fully understand what was happening there that evening myself. Although Varvis had extended an invitation, I did not think he would have been happy to see me on his doorstep.

Nightfall had shrouded everything in darkness, and only the moon high in the sky shone its silver light over the site. Holding the bundle with her belongings, Zoe looked around the temple. She wore a long, dark dress and a thin jacket of a similar color. Her long hair cascaded down her back, reaching her waist. Elizabeth and the others had placed a couple of oil lamps around the trench where the headless statue lay, and were seated around it, their satisfaction evidenced by the peals of laughter that echoed in the night.

During our short walk from the port to the car, I'd had just enough time to tell Zoe who I was and what I was doing on the island, and fill her in on this latest discovery. She had been impressed, and asked that we go there first, before trying to find a place for her to spend the night. My eyes flitted from Zoe toward the resting place of the statue of the winged goddess, unable to grasp fully that in the space of a few hours my two greatest wishes had come true.

I shyly touched her shoulder, urging her to join the others. She looked at me and took my hand, letting me lead her there. As soon as they became aware of our presence, they all stood up to greet us, curiously looking at Zoe. I realized we had not thought of an explanation to give the others for her presence on the island, by my side, but she spoke without hesitation. "I'm Zoe. I'm an old friend of Andreas, and we ran into each other at the port. I missed my boat, so I have to spend the night here."

I faltered upon hearing her fiction, and all I could do was nod with an awkward smile. Elizabeth walked up to us carrying a blanket, which she spread out on the ground beside her, beckoning us to sit down. She gave me a look filled with surprise at Zoe's presence. The smashed statue lay at the center of our impromptu circle. The trench and the light of the flickering stubby candles burning beside the marble fragments created a scene reminiscent of a funeral wake; it was as if we had gathered to bury the statue, sink it into eternal darkness rather than bring it to light.

I thought of the long hours of work that awaited us the following day, when we would join forces with the American couple and their team, focusing on this particular spot. Phyllis brought over two cups of wine for us. I felt compelled, as head of the Greek team, to say a few words. I raised my cup, toasting Zoe first, and then the others.

"Today is a great day for us. The discovery of the Winged Victory by our colleagues raises our hopes for further significant discoveries. May this goddess someday be rejoined by her two sisters who were forced abroad. May this meeting take place at the museum being constructed by the American School of Classical Studies."

We all raised our cups and took a generous sip of warm wine. My chest was already aflame, warmed by the presence of the woman sitting silently beside me. The image of her naked beauty emerging from the water had been burned onto my retinas, try as I might to chase it away.

Elizabeth's soft voice caught my attention. "We still do not know how the statue ended up here. By this, I mean whether it has been transported to this spot. At this early stage, we surmise that it is a statue from the *Hieron* Temple pediment and fell following an earthquake, which is why it is in pieces. Whatever the case may be, this is one of the most significant finds to date, and we owe a debt of gratitude to Phyllis and Karl, whose perseverance and love have bestowed this great gift upon us ..."

Trying to keep the spark of my connection to Zoe alight, I shifted closer to her and whispered, "Would you like something to eat?" She stifled a laugh and raised her eyebrows, showing that she was so absorbed in everything she was seeing and hearing that the thought of food had not even crossed her mind.

Across from us, Karl slowly stood up and ceremoniously emptied the last dregs of wine into the trench in libation. A respectful silence descended; Karl rarely spoke, preferring to let his work do the talking. His natural reserve meant that relations between us were rather formal and strictly professional. He spoke in clear, concise Greek, tinted with a rounded accent. "All the latest discoveries lead me to one conclusion. When we complete excavations at this site, everything we have believed so far may radically change. At this very moment, we may be standing on one of the most mysterious and important temples of the ancient world. It is very likely that Samothrace will be recognized as one of the chief religious sites of Ancient Greece. It is too early to say, of course, but I share my thoughts with you based on these finds. I could be jumping to conclusions, but I think we are on the brink of unearthing one of the most ancient religions in the history of mankind."

Zoe was drinking in every word. I was moved— impressed, but impatient for the two of us to be alone together, to talk freely. Karl gave a brief outline of how work would proceed in the coming days, and then it was finally time to leave for some well-earned rest, after what had been, at least for me, one of the most intense days since my arrival on Samothrace.

I still had to find a place for Zoe to spend the night, and I wondered how my mother would react if I returned home with a woman who was a complete stranger. I immediately rejected that plan, certain of her displeasure, and tried to think of an alternative. When everyone started to leave, Zoe leaned close to my ear and whispered, "Can we stay here a little longer?"

"Yes, of course," I replied, and motioned to Elizabeth to go ahead without us. She gave me look of stunned surprise, but left without a word.

I suggested that the worker who would be standing guard go rest for as long as we were there, and he gladly agreed. I was savoring every moment of our meeting, without giving any thought to what was right or wrong, what propriety dictated or what would follow. Ten minutes later, we were all alone. She sat back down on the blanket, looking at the trench. I put out most of the candles and torches. A couple of lanterns gave enough light, aided by the bright moon that bathed us in its silvery light.

The sea breeze blowing inland chilled the air, and she gladly accepted the blanket I placed around her shoulders. She touched my hand in silent thanks and our eyes locked in an intense gaze once again. I sat beside her, enjoying the evening's stillness. Dozens of crickets provided a musical accompaniment to this peaceful, enchanted evening. In the distance, a startled owl pierced the darkness with an eerie screech like an old witch.

Zoe took my hand and tugged at me to sit down beside her. She then stretched out on the blanket, gently pulling me along. As soon as her head touched the ground, she turned to face the sky. I followed her gaze, watching the faint twinkle of the stars glimmer around the moon. My heart beat loudly in my chest and I desperately tried to think of a way to break into conversation.

She stretched her arms, playing a game of cat and mouse with the moon, chasing it between her fingers. As if sensing my sudden shyness, she spoke first. "Andreas, do you mind if we say nothing about the past tonight? I promise you we will talk about everything tomorrow, but I want to leave the past buried tonight."

I was so happy to just have her beside me on this most beautiful of nights that all I could do was give her hand a firm squeeze to show my acquiescence. We let our eyes wander across the heavenly expanse above, as if searching for the star that governed our fates. The sea breeze, stroking us with its briny chill, carried the voices of the others who had already drifted some distance away.

Emboldened by the touch of her fingers stroking my palm, I spoke up, careful not to allude to anything in the past. "I want to apologize about what happened at lunchtime. I was just taking a stroll when I ran into you, but instead of hiding, I just stood there, staring ..."

"The sun was behind you so I could not see your face; you were just a shadow. You don't need to apologize for something that wasn't your fault. Anyway, you almost killed yourself up there." I heard her stifle a laugh at the memory of my clumsy fall, before steadying her voice. "I heard all the shouting and I got such a fright that I ran off to find my friends. I had no idea who you were or what you were doing there. I've been through a lot ..." She stopped talking abruptly, and her mood became somber.

I felt her squeeze my hand during the silence that followed. I did not know how to handle any of this. I had so many questions, so much I wanted to know, that I did not know where to start. Taking no time to think before speaking, I blurted out, "From the moment I first met you, I've been hoping we'd meet again someday. Not a day has gone by that I did not think of you, wishing our paths would cross. Deep inside me I felt—I believed—that you had managed to survive that nightmare. But tell me, what brought you here?"

She turned to look at me. I did the same, and we found ourselves facing each other in the dim candlelight. The lanterns casting their feeble light behind me flickered like two hopeful sparks in her eyes.

"My father is from Maronia, and I have spent the past few months living in my family's home, trying to repair it. I am all alone; my parents have passed away, and I only have a couple of relatives who are helping me out. We lived in Naousa before the war, then Thessaloniki. I speak French, so I was asked to accompany some foreigners, first to Alexandroupolis and then here. I overheard them talking about a Frenchman, who left Samothrace with a statue he took to France, but I did not fully understand, not until I heard the full story. They seemed to feel ashamed about it, and maybe that's why they chose not to visit the archaeological site. They were on their way to Istanbul and stopped over to see the full moon. We spent last night in the forest, and it was a very special experience for everyone. They weren't exactly pleased when I abandoned them. But I could not help it."

I felt tongue-tied all over again. She spoke as if we were old friends, picking up a conversation where we had left off. She was exquisite. I remembered well how beautiful she was, but it had been a beauty tempered by the terror of that day.

"I can't describe how happy I am that you decided to stay, Zoe. Even if you had left, I would have come to find you. I don't believe fate brought us together on a whim ..."

"On a night like this ..." She pointed to the moon.

"On a night like this ..." I repeated, following the motion, mesmerized.

I felt as if I were caught in a dream, lying between the injured Winged Victory and the woman who had left a searing mark on my heart. I so wanted to lean against her and kiss those red lips, but my skin froze at the thought she might get angry with me for daring to get closer than she would allow.

I had never been with a woman. I had never felt the warm flesh of a woman's body. The few, snatched kisses of my past seemed like insignificant pebbles flung in the vast ocean of my desire to feel what I had heard other men brag about. I never considered paying for a night of passion, although it was a prospect that had presented itself often. I would rather take a vow of celibacy rather than pay for love.

Our intertwined fingers did not part for a second. Hot desire swept through my body like an iron bar held to the flames, which only grows hotter and hotter if you do not pull away your hand. That was the flame I felt burning inside me, that I tried to tame to no avail.

A flurry of feet stamping the ground startled me. I dropped her hand clumsily as I jumped up. Vasilis arrived, panting, and called out my name in a voice filled with terror. His wild-eyed look filled me with foreboding.

"Come quickly ... fire ... your house is on fire ... Run!" he shouted, gesticulating wildly. I turned and looked in the direction of our house. An icy fear gripped my heart at the sight of the faint reddish glow glimmering over the ridge.

My throat constricted at the thought of my mother. Vasilis tugged at my sleeve, begging me to hurry. Alarmed, Zoe was now standing beside me.

"Stay here. I'll be back ..." I said, and walked off.

I heard her footsteps behind us. "I'll come with you," she declared, and fell in step with us.

The moonlight was our ally, lighting our steps as we hurried along the path to my house. As we came nearer, cries of despair mingled with the smell of burning wood, foretelling a disaster I did not want to imagine. It was not long before the house came into full view. It had surrendered to the large, flaming tongues that hungrily consumed it, and belched out dark clouds of smoke. Shadow figures moved in the grey haze, carrying water buckets that only seemed to cool down the flames for a moment.

I looked for my mother among those gathered, crying out her name. Calliope, my sister, fell into my arms, screaming that our mother was trapped inside.

The front door appeared through the flames, a tiny opening just wide enough for me to dash inside and save the woman who had given me life. I ran toward it without thinking, with no sense of the terrible danger. With a piercing cry, my sister flung herself at me, knotting her arms around my waist. Vasilis snatched the back of my shirt, pulling me back, and Zoe, in tandem with the other two, stood before me, spreading her arms to block my path.

I struggled to escape their grasp, to launch myself into the flames. Like a chained beast, I tried to break my human bonds, but more and more people gathered around me, forming a tight circle that trapped me at its center while the nightmare that held my mother in its burning bosom relentlessly consumed her.

A roar of despair surged into the night air from the depths of my being, and I felt the hot flames melt my vocal cords as I sank to my knees, any strength left inside me a pile of ashes. The tears dried in my eyes before they could even roll down my cheeks. The flames kept getting higher. I desperately looked to the heavens, and through the curtain of tears that filled my eyes, saw a blurry moon ...

Dominion of the Moon

Only a few mourners remained at the cemetery. Zoe was one of them, dressed in dark clothes she had borrowed from one of the women in the village. I, too, had borrowed a black suit from the woman's husband. The wind had risen, whipping up the surface of the sea to match the storm raging inside me.

It was late afternoon by now, and most had returned to their chores after the service. Almost everyone had stared at Zoe in puzzlement, trying to understand who she was and what business she had to be there with me. My nostrils were still filled with the acrid smoke the fire had released all through the night. Everyone had advised me to keep away once it died out, but I made it clear that I wanted to be with them when they entered the charred ruins to look for my mother. I did not want her found by a stranger. I had wept and mourned all through the night, so that when we found her remains, all I could feel was horror, but also an inexplicable sense of release.

The entire archaeological mission had attended the service. They all stood numb, the women comforting my sister, who softly lamented the woman who had brought her into the world. Vasilis took care of all the arrangements that I should have been making. He did not leave my side for a moment, always keeping a watchful eye over me. When the last of the mourners turned down the path leading to the cemetery gates, Zoe wordlessly moved close beside me, patiently waiting for me to turn and follow them.

We had buried her beside my father, so they could keep each other company in the land they had now reached. My mother had taken good care of his grave, keeping it neat and tidy, and would visit him every day, telling him how much she missed him. I found comfort in the thought that they were together again.

I looked at the freshly dug earth that now covered her, and wondered how it was possible for my mother to be there one moment and gone the next, taking everything we could no longer share with her. I was filled with guilt about everything I had not found time to do for her, everything I had not managed to tell her or show her.

Most of all, I felt guilty about the time I had not spent with her since my return to the island. I had dedicated myself to the excavations, and she had dedicated herself to me, always there, always patient, never complaining, compassionate, making sure I wanted for nothing.

My heart had been smashed into a thousand pieces. I had learned in the most brutal way that death can catch you unawares, snatching your loved ones in the blink of an eye, so you never know when you are seeing someone for the last time. You might not even have time to say goodbye. The future is so uncertain; it turns suddenly into the past, and everything you never found the time to say will haunt your nights forever. A gaping "Why?" was now etched inside me.

Vasilis approached me silently, waiting for my instructions. He was sleep deprived like the rest of us, his eyes red with tears and smoke. A small wound beside his missing ear testified to his losing battle against the flames. I asked him to go get some rest, and as soon as he had moved some distance away, I turned to Zoe. In an hour, a boat would be leaving for Alexandroupolis, and she had told me that she would be making the crossing at the end of the funeral.

She stepped closer and looked at me. A black shawl was tied around her long hair, and she stood as still as a statue, as if waiting for me to determine what she should do.

"Don't go yet," I beseeched her in a shaky voice.

I remembered her eyes so well. Their image had been so firmly imprinted in my mind from the moment I first saw her. I knew that, no matter what happened next, it would be a memory to last a lifetime. One last tear ran down my cheek, and she wiped it away with her handkerchief. She then moved it to her face and dried her eyes.

"When tears unite, souls become one," she said, wrapping her arms around me like a mother shielding a child. Her body snuggled against mine and calmed me down, soaking up the pain and sorrow.

The hope that she might stay a while gave me strength. "Will you stay?" I asked her, wanting to make sure that was what she meant.

"For as long as you want." She gently stroked my cheek.

Hope surged inside me. "You'll stay with Calliope. I'll ask her; I'm sure she won't mind."

"And you?" she asked, seeming more concerned for me than for herself.

"I'll find a place to stay, don't worry about that," I replied, and wondered whether I had optimistically miscalculated how welcoming my sister would actually be toward Zoe. I turned one last time to look at the grave, and then followed her to the exit with a heavy heart.

I had been trying to figure out how our house could have burned down so quickly that my mother did not have a chance to get out. Some supposed that she must have had a heart attack while she was cooking. Everything had turned to ash, and only a couple of the walls remained, tarry, smoke-smudged reminders of the house that had once stood there. There was no way of finding out how the fire had begun.

We silently walked up the narrow path until we caught up with Calliope and her husband. They gave us a questioning look as we approached. Calliope asked to speak to me alone, so her husband and Zoe kept walking, giving us some space. I had a sense I would not like what I was about to hear. Sadly, I was right.

Night was rapidly descending when we found shelter at Elizabeth's house. My sister had refused to accommodate us, saying that she would not let a woman who slept in the forest, whose reputation no one could vouch for, cross her threshold. She even went so far as to inform me that her husband had threatened to kick her out of the house if she dared bring that woman into their home.

I did not say a word. Such was the turmoil raging inside me that a bitter argument was sure to follow if I opened my mouth. I thought it better to leave without saying a word and seek shelter at Elizabeth's house.

Without asking any questions, Elizabeth readily agreed to accommodate me in the basement, and gave Zoe a bedroom across from hers on the first floor. I chose not to tell Zoe about my sister's decision; instead, I lied and said that it would be better if we stayed with Elizabeth, whose house was roomier, and that we would be more comfortable there.

Although I am sure Zoe understood what had really happened, she did not comment, and followed me, saying she did not care where she stayed. I was displeased at my sister's behavior; angry. Under the weight of our shared grief for our mother, however, I opted to let things cool down. My colleagues had wanted to suspend excavations at the Sanctuary the following day in a gesture of compassion, but I asked them to carry on as normal. I firmly believed that life must go on no matter what, and I did not want my sorrow affecting anyone else.

Suddenly, we heard a soft knock on the wooden front door. I nodded that I would get it while Elizabeth and Zoe made the spare beds. I opened the door without asking who it was, and came face to face with Vasilis, who stood frozen on the spot. For a few, brief seconds I had forgotten what had happened; seeing Vasilis at the door, I broke down in tears once again. I realized that from now on, for the rest of my life, I would think back to the moment he told me the house was on fire every time I saw him.

He gave me a bundled up sheet, stuffed with clothes. For me, he said, now that my belongings were gone. I did not know how to thank him, and I hugged him in gratitude. He was not used to people being demonstrative; with a hasty goodnight, he left as silently as he had arrived. The two women came to join me, and we all stepped out into the courtyard.

Elizabeth was the first to break the prolonged silence. "It's time for you to rest. You have had a shock, Andreas. You need to rest." She turned to leave, perhaps wanting to give us some time alone.

"Is someone guarding the statue at the Sanctuary?" I asked.

Elizabeth nodded, and gave my shoulder a squeeze. "Everything is taken care of, don't worry. Goodnight." She walked inside and closed the door behind her. Silence descended on the courtyard once again.

"Elizabeth is right," Zoe said. "We all need to rest. Try not to think anymore. Try to sleep. It will help you. Tomorrow, a different life begins for you. I've lost both my parents; I understand what you are going through." She tiptoed close to me and reached up to brush her lips against my cheek. I turned my head and kissed her lips.

The need to feel something strong, the need to erase the horrifying images playing in my mind, melted my shyness away. She did not seem surprised as our lips met in a soft, gentle kiss, which did not last long. She brought her fingers between our lips and pulled away, tenderly whispering goodnight. Light-footed as ever, she glided up the few steps leading to the front door and disappeared inside the house, leaving me alone, her taste lingering on my lips.

Happiness flared in my heart, struggling to overcome the sorrow. In the end, sorrow won out. Just before disappearing inside the house, she turned back toward me. In the darkness, I felt her eyes pierce my soul. It was as if we could see each other's depths through the black shroud of the night. Elizabeth's soft voice forced Zoe to step inside, her gaze still fixed on me.

I looked up at the top floor of the house. Only when I was certain they had retired to their rooms did I go in search of some rest, my legs shaking with fatigue. I walked into the basement urgently, needing to feel the coolness of water against my face. I splashed hesitantly from a pitcher on the dresser, not wanting to wash away the taste of Zoe's lips, which still lingered on my mouth.

I took off my clothes and stretched out on the bed, the image of my mother twirling through the shadows and the darkness. The pain of the realization that the person who gave you life and raised you is gone forever is indescribable. Especially when it is coupled with the knowledge that she passed away so tragically, so painfully.

I wondered what fate had determined that a woman who had never hurt anyone should meet with such an end. I thought I had no more tears to shed. But when I closed my eyes, the moistness on my cheeks proved me wrong.

Nicholas Varvis sat at the long wooden table in the tower's enclosed courtyard. Simon stood across the table from him. Not a candle or torch was lit; only their soft whispers betrayed their presence.

"You should have been more careful. I did not want the mother dead. It was a step too far," Nicholas scolded the steward sternly.

"Forgive me, master. I made a lot of noise before I set the oil on fire, and no one called out. Stais was at the Sanctuary with the newcomer, and his sister was at her house. I thought their mother was out, too, so I lit ..."

"It's better this way," Marika's voice interrupted them, approaching like the shadow of a ghost. She spoke again once she came to a stop behind Varvis's chair. "This is no time to play games. We had to send a strong message. Nothing is possible without sacrifice ...No one will miss his mother. It was the perfect night for it. She was probably destined to leave this world then ..."

No one spoke for a while, only the northerly wind whistled eerily as it glided over the stone walls.

"So be it." Varvis's voice rang out stronger in the dark. He paused and conspiratorially whispered, "However, it means we must be extra careful now as we proceed with our plan. Tomorrow you go to the policeman and tell him what we agreed. Everything else will fall into place on its own. Go now, go get some rest."

Simon turned and carefully edged toward the staircase. Alexandros appeared from inside the tower, holding a lantern. He walked up to his parents, raising the lantern high to shed its light on their faces. "What are you doing out here? I heard the sound of your voices."

"Nothing, my love, we are only talking business," Marika replied, and pulled him closer. She kissed his lips tenderly and stood up. "Light all the lanterns to brighten up the courtyard, and I will prepare our dinner."

As she walked away, her son lit a candle. Carefully, he lit the wicks one by one, stealing glances at his father, who watched him, deep in thought. The wind impeded his task, shortening their flame and putting out some of them. The boy, familiar with the sheltered corners of the courtyard, moved them there so they could stand bright against the wind. Nicholas looked on, admiring the way his son tamed the night.

When all the lanterns had been lit, Alexandros sat next to his father. Varvis stroked the boy's long blond hair and spoke tenderly. "Alexandros, time goes by as fast as a swallow. One day, all of this will be yours, and when you have a son, he will not just inherit the land, but something far greater. My grandchild, your child, will be the Varvis descendant who will fulfill the prophecy of the old scriptures: he will be the spark that will revive our old religion!"

Alexandros nodded obediently, showing he was fully aware of his destiny. His parents spent many hours instructing him so he would not stray from his path as he grew up.

Marika arrived carrying a clay platter, which she placed at the center of the table. From a drawer on the table's side, she removed cups and glasses and laid them out. Varvis stood up, took a jug of wine, and started filling the cups. When he reached his son's cup, he stopped and looked at him. "Tonight is the night you taste our wine, Alexandros. You are a young man now, and will have your first drink with us.

The boy jumped up from his chair in excitement. He had been waiting for this moment for so long. Varvis raised his cup first, proudly looking at his son. Before taking a sip, he tilted it ever so slightly so that a few drops of wine dribbled onto the stone floor, muttering something under his breath. He then raised it high, a sign for everyone to take their first sip.

Alexandros's cheeks flushed as the crimson liquid burned down his throat and warmed his chest. He tried hard not to show it, and tried to mimic his parents, who sat, pleased, at the table. His mother reached for the platter to serve them, and Nicholas raised his cup to the height of his eyes, and then toward his son, urging him to take another gulp. His lips broke into a taunting smirk until Alexandros followed suit, and emptied his cup in a single gulp.

Nicholas and Marika broke into delighted laughter, showing their pride that their son had managed to drink all of his wine so nonchalantly, as if it wasn't his first time. The boy's proud grin turned to loud laughter. A few drops of wine spilled out from the side of his mouth and dribbled down his chin like blood drops.

Like a dog waiting for its master to rise, I sat on the sill of the basement's sole window, waiting for a sound indicating that the two women had woken up. I had surrendered to a brief sleep, just long enough to rest somewhat and forget the woes that had befallen us. There were times during the night when I would open my eyes and think that it had all been a terrible dream. Sensing the truth around me, I would squeeze my eyelids shut, imploring sleep to come mask the pain for a moment.

Zoe's presence gave me hope and courage to face the difficult hours that lay ahead. I was certain by now that I was not searching for some temporary comfort, but hoping that she would stay by my side for as long as possible. Without my mother, and following my sister's stance, Zoe seemed to have come into my life not simply to replace them but to fill the void in my heart. It was as if I had saved her life that day so she could be here today, lighting the path I should follow.

The sound of creaking floorboards upstairs alerted me that they had risen. I stood up, splashed some water from the pitcher on my face, and stepped out into the courtyard to make my presence known. A large pomegranate tree struggled to hang on to the red fruit that bowed its branches to the ground. I walked up to it and tried to cut a pomegranate for Zoe. Cutting a pomegranate is not always easy—like a mother clasping a child to its bosom, the spiny branch refuses to be parted from its fruit.

Hearing their footsteps getting nearer, I pulled with all my strength. As the fruit came free, I felt a sharp pang as the tree sank its thorns into my flesh. My father had always warned me to be careful about pomegranate thorns; they are painful and hard to remove, burrowing under the skin. I looked at my finger and saw the small brown edge of the thorn trapped inside. I brought it to my lips and sucked the drops of blood, then turned toward the women, one of whom was walking to a stone table carrying a tray.

The sun had just risen and beamed down on the courtyard. Elizabeth and Zoe greeted me with a smile, put the tray down, and beckoned me to join them. Zoe was wearing one of Elizabeth's dresses, reminding me of the first time I laid eyes on her. I needed to forget the nightmarish events of the previous day, and the sight of Zoe whisked me away from sadness, even for a brief moment.

I walked up to Zoe and gave her the freshly cut pomegranate, giving Elizabeth a small look of apology. She smiled and said, "I don't like pomegranates anyway."

The smile washed my worries away, and Zoe gently squeezed my hand in thanks. She brought the pomegranate to her lips, as if wishing to give me a small sign of what she felt. We breakfasted, making small talk and avoiding any allusion to the terrible fire.

Sensing my confused state about all the arrangements that needed to be made, Elizabeth had solved the most imperative issue—the matter of Zoe.

"Zoe can help out the conservation team for a few days while they handle small artifacts," Elizabeth said. "I spoke to Karl yesterday, and he said it's fine. You can both stay here for as long as you like. It's a big house and Zoe is excellent company." She gave Zoe a friendly wink.

Even though this new set of circumstances muddled my thoughts and feelings, I felt better that Zoe could stay a little longer. The thought of my mother struck me once again, and I was overwhelmed with the need to go light a candle by her final resting place. It would be hard for me to move on with my day before I went near her. I felt that she would appear at any moment, with the wide smile she always kept for me every time I came home.

I jumped up, startling them, and said, "I'm going to the cemetery to light a candle. I'll meet you at the Sanctuary."

Neither of them seemed surprised, and Zoe stood up to escort me to the garden gate. "You know I owe you my life," she said. "That is not the reason I am staying, however. I wanted you to know that. Would you like me to come with you?"

"I want you to stay here, to rest. I think it's better if I go on my own this time."

She acquiesced without a word, and raised herself to her toes to kiss my cheek. The desire to keep her close coursed through my body once again. Unaware of my innermost thoughts, she turned back to my colleague.

I picked an armful of yellow roses from a rose bush in the garden, recalling that they were my mother's favorite flower. The pain in my finger where the pomegranate tree had extracted its revenge was far too great for such a small thorn, and I wondered whether the pain welled up inside me had found a way to pour out through that small crack in my skin.

I started the uphill climb that led to the cemetery path, stopping at the church to pick up two candles. Then I walked to my mother's grave. I saw my sister on her knees beside it, tending to the soil, affection and sorrow etched on her face. Despite the argument of the previous day, the sight brought tears to my eyes. The years we had spent apart may have put some distance between us, but we still shared the same blood.

I walked up beside her and placed the roses on the mound of soil. Calliope, sensing who it was, did not turn to look at me. She placed my roses beside another bouquet and stood up slowly. She turned to my father's grave, bent down, and pulled up a couple of weeds. Giving both graves one last look, she crossed herself and walked off without saying a word. Understanding that she felt ashamed, I did not speak either.

The morning breeze gently stroking my face was my only company among the graves and the dead. I had been near death so many times that the atmosphere of the place felt oddly familiar. Many of those resting here were people I had known. The thought that one day my turn would come seamlessly led to the thought that I should try to enjoy every day as the generous gift it was.

I still held onto the candles. The wind howled. They would barely stay alight for a couple of seconds before the wind snuffed them out. I planted them between the two graves to be lit another day. I sat there for quite some time, my gaze flitting between the grave and the sky. I could not remember another day when I had spent so long beside my mother since my return to the island, and the irony that I was doing so now was too bitter to bear.

Feeling my tears dry up, I stood up and looked out at the stormy sea. A boat was struggling in the waves, trying to reach the port. I was surprised anyone had risked sailing in this weather; the waves were so high they could easily sweep it off its course.

I was making my way down the hill when I noticed some of the locals approaching. I discreetly avoided any contact with them. The last thing I wanted was conversation. We all confined ourselves to a polite nod from afar.

I decided to go to the Sanctuary. I wanted to see how work was progressing on the spot where the statue had been found, and to see Zoe. The matter of my accommodation kept swirling in my mind. Elizabeth's house was but a temporary solution and, despite her kind hospitality, I had to find a place of my own. I wished Zoe would join me then.

Lost in my own thoughts, I did not even realize how I ended up before the fence enclosing the Sanctuary. Vasilis was impatiently waiting for me by the entrance. I prayed he was not going to give me more sad news. I could tell by the look on his face that being the bearer of bad tidings seemed to be his new role in my life from now on.

"The policeman passed by half an hour ago and told me to ask you to go down to the station," he said, before I even had a chance to ask what the matter was.

"Did he say what about?"

"No, just what I told you. But he seemed nervous and worried."

I thought it probably had something to do with the fire, and turned to leave, but Vasilis tugged at my sleeve and lowered his voice. "Andreas, there is something else I want to tell you ..." He paused, casting a frightened look around himself, like he wanted to make sure there was no one to overhear what he had to confide. "I heard people in the village say that when they arrived at the fire, they could smell burning oil. I wondered whether someone had soaked the wood."

Despite my fatigue, my mind worked fast. "Maybe they smelled the oil we kept in a vat when it caught fire. It doesn't mean anything."

"Yes, but there is also what Constantis said. He passed through here with his goat herd earlier."

I kept quiet, waiting for him to finish.

"Someone threw a big clay jug down the gully behind your house. It's smashed to pieces against the rocks."

"So what?" I asked nervously.

"It happened recently. The broken pieces are still dripping with oil."

The information I was being bombarded with matched the questions I already had, and confused me even more. Why would someone want to kill my mother and burn down our house? I did not want to show my agitation, so I interrupted him abruptly. "Fine, we'll talk when I'm back. Do not say anything about this to anyone! Agreed?"

Vasilis nodded. Troubled by his words, I took the path to Paleopolis and, walking across a small wooden bridge, reached the police station. On such a small island, we had only three officers, and one of them—a man who had only arrived on Samothrace a few months ago—sat behind the front desk. He was all alone, and when he saw me he pointed to a worn, wooden chair, indicating that I should sit.

I sat carefully, and the old wood gave a treacherous creak. I was too thin to be blamed for the sound, and I tried to keep most of my weight on my legs, worried that the chair would collapse beneath me.

"Hello." My greeting hung in mid-air without any response from him. A military march fought to be heard through the crackling sound of radio static.

The officer's hair was stuck to his scalp, combed over in a failed attempt to cover the bald patch stretching from his forehead all the way to his nape. Ever since he set foot on the island, the only thing he had done was collect information on suspected left-wingers. He was convinced that law and order rested on everyone's ideology.

He scribbled something on a piece of paper and placed it on a pile of similar-looking yellowing sheets, then peered at me suspiciously. He came straight to the point. "My condolences. One of my men had a look at your house, and told me the fire started after some accident. Poor woman."

I realized that his words were but a prologue of fake compassion leading to what he really wanted to say. I replied with a dry "Thank you" and let him carry on.

"These are hard times, but I am forced to inform you of a serious accusation against you. You visited the Varvis tower two days ago with the American woman—is that so?"

I was surprised to hear Varvis's name. I could not imagine how our visit to the tower had anything to do with what the officer had to say. "That's right. We were invited to dinner, and we went."

"I have been informed that Varvis showed you a chest containing pieces from his personal collection. Is that so?"

That phrase he stuck to the end of every sentence was starting to irritate me.

"That is so," I snapped back, trying to understand where he was going with this.

"That collection disappeared the following morning. It has been stolen!"

I immediately recollected the bronze eyelash fragments that had once decorated the eyes of statues, and the coins. "What does this have to do with me? What are you trying to say? I don't understand."

"How long have you known the woman who is your guest? Why did she stay behind when all the other visitors left?" His voice became harsher, and his eyes took on the beadiness of an interrogator.

"I have known her for years, and we happened to meet again here. She stayed on to visit the island. I don't see how this has anything to do with the theft you claim took place."

"We have reason to suspect the visitors did not leave empty-handed. I have asked the mainland police force to search for them, but it will be difficult as they are headed to Turkey. Varvis's steward has stated that he saw someone acting suspiciously near the tower two days ago, just before nightfall. Then the foreigners sailed away, possibly taking the collection with them. You were the last to see the collection. Is that so?"

I tried to keep my cool, but failed. "My mother has just been laid into the ground, and you dare call me here to accuse me of a theft Varvis claims took place! Don't you dare drag the Americans into this," I shouted, outraged at the unacceptable insult.

The officer seemed startled to hear me raise my voice. He recovered quickly enough, and went on the attack. "A theft took place, and I must follow the appropriate procedure. We have lost much of our heritage, and still the thefts continue. Some will not stop at anything to enrich themselves."

I did not disagree with what he was saying. My outrage was at the insinuation that Zoe and I were criminals. "Let me make myself clear. It is a grave insult to suggest we may be connected to this matter in any way. You obviously know nothing about yesterday's discovery and what it means for this island."

"I know everything, sir," he said, resuming his interrogatory manner.

"Very well then. As you are so well informed, you must be aware of who you are talking to. For my part, I will immediately inform my department in Thessaloniki as well as Lesbos …"

He stroked his mustache and took a sip of water. "Do you know how many of your colleagues are responsible for the smuggling that happened during the war?"

I stood up, unable to stand his presence for another minute. "I refuse to listen to these unfounded accusations. If you have any proof, you know where to find me. Until then, leave us alone to do our job in peace, and you do yours. You should also know that these collections do not belong to individuals but to the Greek nation. Refusing to relinquish possession is a mistake. The war is finished, and they must be handed over. Moreover, don't you dare drag my friend into this; she has nothing to do with your ridiculous, baseless claims. Now, if I may, I would like to leave. I have more important things to attend to."

He smiled awkwardly and stood up. "Listen to me, Andreas Stais. A lot is said about what you did after the war, and whose side you were on. If you don't want the gossip to spread, you'd better cooperate. It's hard to clear your name once it's been tainted …"

Dominion of the Moon

He took out a packet of cigarettes and lit a match. He offered me one, but I shook my head. Blowing the smoke toward the ceiling, he said conciliatorily, "I advise you to ask your friend what the foreigners were doing here. You do it in your manner, or I will do it in mine. I want the chest found and returned to its owners."

It took all my resolve not to curse him as I turned and stormed out. If the sea had been nearer, I would have dived right in to cool down the rage that was thumping against my chest, protesting the series of blows life was handing me.

I almost ran back to the Sanctuary. As soon as I passed the enclosure, I felt all my negative thoughts and feelings drift away, as if they surrendered to the breeze blowing down over the temple toward the sea. All the talk about Samothrace's energy fields, and the Sanctuary in particular, seemed very real just then.

Zoe was crouched on the ground at the dig site, hand buried in the soil, looking in my direction. I caught her eye. She drew me toward her like a magnet, and shortly I was standing beside her. I cast a quick look around and saw that everyone was busy at work. Through the open door of one of the museum rooms, I saw Elizabeth turn toward me and greet me with a smile before resuming her work.

"Is everything all right?" Zoe asked. "You were gone for a while. We were worried."

Zoe's bright face made me determined not to spoil the mood, and I resolved to stick to my original plan and not mention any of the things that were said at the police station. "Everything is fine. The police officer only wanted to discuss some details concerning the fire, but all is well ... How are you getting on?"

"I'm trying to help, but I'm not sure I'm managing to ..."

"She is managing just fine," said Elizabeth, exiting the museum. She placed a tender hand on Zoe's shoulder. "She is a natural ... Come, let's make our way to the trench and see what our goddess is up to."

Zoe took me by the hand, heedless of the soil encrusted in her palms. Giddy as young children, we made our way to the spot where the other team was already at work on the spectacular find. The soil rubbing against my palm as she gently stroked my hand was one of the most tender sensations I had ever felt.

In the brilliant sunshine, the team was working feverishly, clearing away soil and carefully separating the pieces of the broken statue. I pulled Zoe toward a broken column and we sat on what had once been a part of the temple that had stood here. Its restoration was another great wish of mine, even with the limited means at our disposal.

Zoe, still looking in the direction of the statue, asked, "What did it look like back then? Is there a painting of it somewhere, something that depicts it as a whole?"

I jumped up as if I had just been stung, freed my hand, and ran to the building which we hoped would one day become the Samothrace museum. I remembered a photo of the statue I had presented at the competition in Thessaloniki was lying in a desk drawer somewhere. For a moment, everyone was startled by the sound of my thumping feet as I sped away. They paused what they were doing, watching me run down the hill.

I was back in a couple of minutes. On the day of the award ceremony, a photographer had taken a few photos of the plaster copy that had won me an award and a place at the Archaeological Service. I had forgotten that my model for the head of the Winged Victory had been Zoe's face, as I remembered it from that first meeting. For a few minutes, work stalled as everyone watched me run, out of breath, toward her.

I sat down beside her and showed her one of the photos. Despite being taken from afar, it still gave a clear impression of what the statue would have looked like, with the addition of the head as I had imagined it.

She looked at the photo in admiration and then asked, her voice filled with innocent wonder, "Will you be able to piece her together again, just like this?" It was evident she had no idea that she had been the muse behind the sculpture she was looking at.

"I hope we can find all the missing pieces, although it's unlikely. Both of the other statues found on the site were missing many parts, including their heads. Based on what I can see, this one will be missing parts too. They could be anywhere on the site. I wish we could find the head. Three winged goddesses ... all without a face. It's as if they were cursed. Finding it would make one of my greatest dreams come true. When we cease excavations for a while this winter, I intend to go to Paris and visit her sister statue. If you like ..."

I caught myself and stopped, suddenly realizing that I was being inappropriately familiar given the length of our brief acquaintance.

"That would be lovely ..."

Like a torrent, her unexpected response washed away any embarrassment caused by my haste.

"I've been meaning to tell you ..." she continued. "You saved my life that day, Andreas. Those monsters would have killed me. I arrived at that village looking for my two brothers. I found them lying dead, executed along with countless others, at the village square. That was their punishment for the death of a German soldier, killed by the resistance."

I caught the catch in her voice and turned toward her. She swallowed hard and carried on, undaunted. "Forty Greek men for one German soldier ... I stayed behind after their burial to help the locals, now that most of their men were gone. Fighting intensified and I became trapped there. I could do nothing except wait for the war to be over. By then, I was all alone in the world ... When they asked about the Germans, I lied because I knew they were leaving. I wanted the torment of war to be over, right there and then. Catching up with the departing troops would only lead to more bloodshed, on soil already soaked with the blood of so many. And then you appeared ..." She squeezed my hand tightly. "I'm sorry to be telling you all this when you are grieving for your mother, but I wanted you to know. I feel so at peace here, it helps me open up."

"I don't mind hearing any of this," I told her. "I've always wanted to know how you ended up in that village, and what became of you afterward. I think that during the war we became used to death; it does not surprise us anymore. Most of the people I knew on Samothrace are either dead, or we have no idea what has happened to them. I want to stop feeling this strange familiarity with death. I want to expel the apathy that has taken root inside me. I'm ashamed to confess this, but I just lost my mother and I feel like I am not mourning her as I should."

"There is no right and wrong in grief, Andreas. Everyone grieves in their own way. No one can say how or when one should mourn; no one can impose their will on grief itself. Showing grief when you don't feel it because that is what others expect to see is meaningless."

She was right. What others thought of me preoccupied me more than it should.

Seeing the American team struggle with the ropes, I interrupted our conversation and stood up to help. Even Vasilis abandoned a wheelbarrow piled high with weeds and came to help lift the statue's torso. We heaved with all our strength, and when it stood on the ground, we stepped back to admire it. One of the team, who always carried a camera with him, stepped across and stood there, waiting for us to assemble for the photo.

In her wide-brimmed hat, Elizabeth smiled in the sunshine, her arms wrapped around the largest intact piece of the statue that stood beside her. Arms and head missing, wounded by time, the statue of the Winged Victory shone in all its splendor, like a star that glows brighter than the light of day.

We all gathered under the shade of a large oak tree at the edge of the *Hieron* Temple, where Vasilis had spread the food he had brought from the village. We lunched and rested, accompanied by the loud chirping of the last cicadas. The weather was gradually turning, and soon the bright clear skies would give way to the first rains. When the heavens opened above Samothrace, they forgot to close up again.

Zoe sat beside me, crunching an apple. With every passing minute spent by her side, I worried about how much time I still had left with her. I dreaded the moment she would tell me it was time for her to return home, to Maronia. At the same time, I wondered whether it would not be best if she left, given the threats made by the policeman. At least until the matter was settled. I didn't intend to share what had happened with my American colleagues; neither the policeman's threats, nor Varvis's. However, I could not stop thinking about them for long, especially Varvis's words. Although I found it hard to believe, I still caught myself wondering whether he was linked to the fire.

My first task would be to send a formal request for permission to excavate the Varvis grounds. The Americans were in charge of the site up to where it bordered the land, but their influence remained within the archaeological site. Instead of deterring me, his threats had strengthened my resolve. I was determined not to give way. I was certain that, following the discovery of the statue of Nike, the Archaeological Service would rubber stamp any request to extend excavations anywhere we deemed fit.

Elizabeth cleared her throat. "I will be taking the boat to Alexandroupolis this afternoon. Tomorrow morning, I will pick up the tools needed for the dig in Thessaloniki. I will return in two or three days, and then we can make the formal announcement of the find. I expect many visitors in the following days ..."

This trip would normally have fallen to me. I caught her eye, and realized she was taking on my responsibilities to allow me to stay here. Her trip to Thessaloniki meant that she could deliver my letter as well.

We all agreed, and began to disperse. Soon, everyone was back at work, and only Vasilis, Elizabeth, Zoe, and I remained. I tried to signal to Vasilis that he should leave us, but my pointed look went unnoticed, forcing me to ask him to go. Once he had shuffled out of earshot, I turned to Elizabeth. "Thank you. Would you not prefer me to go?"

"No, Andreas. It's best if you stay here. You have so much going on right now; you don't need the extra hassle. You can stay at my house with Zoe for as long as you like."

Hearing this, Zoe turned toward me without a word, waiting to hear my response. "We thank you. I appreciate your support during this difficult time. I need to send a letter to my department in Thessaloniki. I'll give it to you before you set off."

"It's about the excavations on Varvis's estate, right?" I nodded, and Elizabeth carried on. "I want you to be careful while I'm away. I will report to my department on the matter, too. Don't you think it would be better to drop it for a while? Focus on the discovery of the Winged Victory and then decide how to approach the matter? There are buried antiquities all over the island. Let's focus on those that we can excavate freely."

I understood she was trying to ease tensions, but I was determined not to back down now, especially with so many other suspicions swirling in my mind. "No, I think it's very important to begin excavations there. I have a hunch that our find is connected to the part of the temple that extends beyond this point. Besides, nothing will happen to the family if we dig up their land a little. If we find nothing, it's still their land. However, I am convinced we will. It's what the location of our find indicates, at least the way I see it."

"I disagree. As you already know, even if we find something, it will not be of any significance. I will not stand in your way, so long as you promise to be careful until we receive formal permission to expand excavations. You need to rest and let yourself grieve, Andreas. I am not asking you not to come to work—I understand that it is not something you would consider—but please be careful. I am going to the museum. Prepare your letter; I have to set off in three hours."

She stood up and kissed both of us goodbye, then left. The silence that always descended between Zoe and I every time we found ourselves alone was becoming familiar, and strangely calming. It was as if we had no need for words to communicate, as if the ground between us was acting as the conduit of all our thoughts and feelings.

Zoe gripped my hand and pulled me away from the tree. "I haven't seen the rest of the site. Is there time, or must you go?"

Despite the pressing need to go draft my letter, I could not refuse this, or any other, request coming from her. "Of course ...There is enough time for a quick tour. I'll tell you everything our own searches and analysis have brought to light. Most of it hasn't even been announced yet ..."

She smiled, and her eyes shone with happiness. We walked away briskly and soon found ourselves among the marble pieces that dotted the ground all over the site. The small village of Paleopolis came into view, nestled between the wooded hills and flowing creeks.

Succumbing to the peaceful calm exuded by the site and the view, I began my tour with a whisper. "The ancient Greeks called Samothrace the Sacred Island, as well as *Ouranoessa* …"

She froze and looked at me, stunned, as if she could not believe what I'd just said. Her eyes welled with tears.

"What's wrong?" I asked, worried at the sudden change that had come over her.

Zoe dried her eyes and fixed her gaze on a fragment of marble by her feet. "My father used to call me that, when I was a girl. Our house in Maronia has a stone path that leads to the shore. He'd take me there and point at Samothrace, across the bay. He would tell me how a fairy in the sky pulls the mountain up, so the peak can touch the blue heavens … *Ouranoessa* was the fairy's name. He'd lift me up to reach the sky, my arms stretched out, and he'd call me by her name."

Her face came alive with the memory. A sigh, like an apology tinged with guilt, escaped her. Sensing her turmoil, I tried to lighten the mood. "Please, don't apologize. I loved that story and, believe me, it's not a random folk tale."

Zoe gave me a puzzled look as we walked toward the *Hieron*.

"Legend has it," I explained, "that the mountain peak of this island is so high it reaches the sky, almost blocking out the moon. According to Homer, the throne of Poseidon, the god of the sea, was perched there, so he could watch the Trojan War from that high vantage point. The war not only divided the Greek gods into two factions, it symbolized the standoff between the divine and the human worlds."

I fell quiet, waiting for her response.

"Please continue," she said, still looking ahead.

I obeyed gladly. "I believe, and it is a view shared by many others, that the Sanctuary of the Great Gods was one of the most important sacred sites of ancient times. Every day we uncover small details that support this theory."

We were walking more briskly now, and reached the remains of the theatre. We paused at the highest point, beside the ruins of the long gallery. The view before us was spectacular. Everywhere we turned, the deep blue of the surrounding waters greeted us, seeping into our every pore. I walked a little further along and stood, awed, before the sad remains of the niche where the statue of the Winged Victory of Samothrace had once stood.

Wanting to impress Zoe, I assumed my most professional tone. "This where the other statue of Nike once stood; it is now housed in the Louvre. It was fragmented, and it took a while to collect all its pieces, which were spread all over the site."

"How did they join them together?" she asked curiously.

"It was reassembled in France, piece by piece. I understand they removed it from the Louvre during the war. I guess now they will display it once again. The irony is that it was hidden in a safe place alongside the Venus de Milo, accidentally setting up a unique meeting of goddesses ..."

She seemed so absorbed in what she was hearing, I forgot all about my letter and kept talking. "The Sanctuary was a complex of many magnificent buildings. I wish there was some way we could see an exact reconstitution of the site. It may happen someday in the future, although we may not live to see it."

She gave me a puzzled look, then turned back to gaze at the site as it stretched out on the terrace below. From the faraway look in her eyes, I guessed she was trying to imagine everything I was describing.

"Our winged goddess, perched on a marble ship's prow, seemed to float above the site, symbolizing absolute freedom," I said. "Her widespread wings and her flowing *chiton* made her visible to approaching ships from horizon to horizon. I hope we will soon have more information about the statue, as well as the ceremonies that took place here, and if there is any link between the two."

"I heard the French I accompanied to Samothrace talk about this," Zoe said. "I have a feeling they may have tried to reenact one of those ceremonies during the night we slept in the woods. They did not want me to go with them. If their mood when they returned is anything to go by, there must have been some terrible argument, so I guess the ceremony did not go according to plan."

"It is said that many have tried to revive this ancient cult," I said, "but given the scarcity of any information about its rites and rituals, it's unlikely we'll ever know much about its true nature. Maybe, as I already said, we'll know some day whether the statue of the Winged Victory has anything to do with it, as I believe it does ..."

Zoe looked at me admiringly as I described everything I knew about the site. She then walked ahead and climbed onto the marble slab that may have been the base of the statue. Carefully, she turned to face the sun, closing her eyes. Pushing herself up on her toes, she spread her arms wide and stood still.

Mesmerized, I took a few steps back to gaze at her form as a whole. The breeze ruffled the folds of her long white dress, as if gently trying to strip it away and expose her naked beauty to the elements. Her long hair fluttered down her back, obeying the Aeolian choreography as it spun in an unruly dance.

Slowly, she raised her arms high above her head, as if she wanted to reach the sky. For as long as she stood there, I felt as if the Winged Victory had materialized before me in flesh and blood ...

Vasilis drove the Jeep that would take us to the port. During the drive, I was tormented by a multitude of conflicting thoughts over the events that had happened these past few days. I suspected that our walk through the site had been more beneficial for me than for Zoe, a respite from my unpleasant thoughts.

We had returned to Elizabeth's house, and Zoe had gone to lie down while I drafted my letter. Still curious about everything Vasilis had told me, I had dashed to the gully behind the burned shell of my house as soon as I heard Zoe close her bedroom door. I wanted to see for myself what the goatherd had found.

Indeed, after a brief descent, I found myself standing before a shattered clay jar, its insides still dripping with oil. I glanced around and saw an assortment of discarded items, everything from rusty old shotguns to torn military clothing. I had never realized the gully was being used as a dumping ground.

Another broken jar lay further ahead, but it was half-buried under a small mound of trash, showing it had been there for a while. On the contrary, the jar by my feet had been recently smashed. I could not see it as evidence of anything. Anyone could have gotten rid of it. It might not be connected to the fire at my house in any way.

I spent some time sifting through the grass and stones, unclear as to what exactly I was looking for. Then I abandoned my cursory search and returned to Elizabeth's house to write the letter.

Nothing betrayed Zoe's presence on the upper floor, and I assumed she must have fallen asleep already. I wrote the letter as quickly as possible, wanting to get it to Elizabeth at the port before sunset so I could return to the cemetery while it was still light out.

I'd left a note at Zoe's door that I would be back before nightfall, and had then walked outside, where Vasilis was waiting for me in the Jeep. I'd climbed in, telling him we needed to hurry.

On the one hand, I felt guilty for busying myself with so many other things when my mother had only just passed away. On the other hand, I thought about how right Zoe was. No one had the right to determine how I should grieve my mother except me.

Lost in my thoughts as we drove to the port, I did not hear Vasilis ask a question until he became so exasperated he almost screamed it in my ear, giving me a sudden fright. "What are you going to do about the fire, Andreas?"

"Nothing. I went to gully and saw all the rubbish that has been dumped down there. I don't think it's linked to the fire; there's a whole pile of broken jars."

I must have replied rather abruptly, because he hunched down over the wheel and kept silent the rest of the way. We arrived at the port, and Vasilis stepped on the brakes so abruptly I almost hit the dashboard. I gave him an angry look but held my tongue.

I jumped out of the Jeep and almost ran to the building behind the port. Elizabeth and her colleagues were sitting patiently around a table under a rickety canopy. She smiled at me and pointed to the chair beside her. I sat down and removed the letter from my breast pocket.

"I didn't have time to put down a lot of detail, but I reported the main facts," I said, placing it on the table before her. She picked it up and put it in her handbag.

"Don't you worry," she said. "I will fill in any missing details. I know exactly what you want …" Although her American accent remained strong, her Greek was better than many of the locals.

"The sea is calm; you'll have an easy crossing," I said. The voice of a crier calling all passengers to board forced us to get up. I had never seen that particular ship before. It wasn't new, but at least it was big, and the waves would treat it with greater respect than the fishing boats that usually made the crossing.

Everything was changing on the island, even if it was at a snail's pace, and I hoped it would not be long before, rid of occupiers, we would finally be able to live free.

I hugged Elizabeth, holding onto her longer than was usual. "Thank you for everything," I whispered in her ear, and then let her go.

She tenderly stroked my cheek. "Look after Zoe. She has been through a lot. You have impressed her, but she still harbors an open wound that needs to heal."

I felt the familiar, hard scar on her palm against my cheek. She smiled and moved to the edge of the small dock. The sun was hovering above the water's surface, ready to dip down. I wanted to make it to the cemetery before nightfall. As soon as they lifted the gangway, I waved goodbye. Then I rushed toward the Jeep, jumped in, and asked Vasilis to go.

He drove quickly but carefully. Despite the gaffes of his early days, he was impressive in his desire to learn and adapt. I had even caught him reading history books in his free time. His clumsiness aside, Vasilis was proving steadfast and reliable, and I felt he was one of the few allies I had on the island.

As soon as we pulled up outside the church, he quickly got out of the car and came around to my side before I had time to walk away. He put his hand in his trouser pocket and pulled out something wrapped in a crumpled piece of paper. "I went down the gulley too, Andreas, before you did. I found this."

Filled with curiosity, I tore away the paper. It was a broken piece of pottery, about the size of my palm. I looked at him, confused. "What is this? Why are you giving it to me?"

He kept silent. Frustrated, I raised my voice. "I don't have much time, Vasilis. Speak up!"

Angrily, he grabbed the piece of pottery and turned it over. "Look," he said, and pointed to the word etched in tiny letters.

"*Axieros ...*" I whispered.

"The jars and barrels that belong to the Varvis family all have this word engraved on them," he whispered conspiratorially. "So does everything that belongs to them; knives, swords ... everything. It's like their coat of arms."

I did not want to believe that the Varvis family had anything to do with the fire, but the evidence in my palm strongly raised that possibility. Feeling pressed for time, I placed the jar fragment into my pocket and walked toward the cemetery, calling to Vasilis, "You head back; don't wait for me. Not a word to anyone about all this."

I did not even turn back to look at him. I heard the sound of the engine and the tires crush the gravelly road as he drove away. The breeze had died out as the sun began to set, and I could now light the two candles I had left there that morning.

I was surprised to see three small flames flickering between my parents' tombs. The figure of a woman hovering above them made me think it might be my sister. *Maybe it's Zoe*, I thought for a fleeting, joyful moment.

As I approached, I realized it was neither Zoe nor Calliope, but someone else. She stood slightly stooped over my mother's grave, her head covered with a long, dark shawl that kept her features hidden. At the sound of my footsteps, she turned and looked me straight in the eyes. It was the last person I expected to see there.

The voice of Marika Varvis rang out in the empty cemetery. "I am sorry, Andreas Stais, for the misfortune that has befallen you. May you live long to honor her memory."

I spat out a dry "thank you" through clenched jaws. "Did you come to threaten me by my mother's grave?" I asked, unable to contain the anger surging inside me.

Marika pulled the shawl away from her face, letting it drop to her shoulders, and fixed me with her gaze. "Do I look like I am here to make threats? All I wanted was to light a candle in the memory of Anna. I didn't expect you to turn up, and I certainly do not intend to stay now that you are here." She pointed to the grave. "Your mother knew how to be respectful, but did not have enough time to teach you, as you were absent."

Under any other circumstance I would have shouted at her to go away, but I tried to keep my cool. We were at my parents's grave and I didn't want to disturb them. The Varvis family had not evolved with the times; they still thought they were better than the rest of us. We both stood our ground, locked in a staring contest. After a few seconds, she covered her head with the shawl and turned to walk away.

Unable to contain myself any longer, I took out the broken jar piece and shouted after her, "I think this belongs to you."

Marika paused, and turned to look at me. I strode toward her, proffering the piece in my outstretched hand. Impassive, she slowly picked it up and brought it close to her face. It was getting dark; it was possible she could not make out the writing. She examined it for a little longer, and then smirked. "By gods, I don't understand why you are walking around with this."

"Because it belongs to you," I said firmly. "I found it today, in the gully behind my house. It is soaked in oil. I don't know if that says something to you."

As far as I could tell, her expression remained as impassive as ever, masking anything she might have been feeling. "What it says, Andreas, is that you are losing your mind," she said in a voice dripping with sarcasm. "I will leave you to mourn your mother, and we will meet again when the time is right. I hope we will only have good things to say then."

She turned and walked uphill, away from the cemetery exit.

A torch came to life at the top of the hill, straight up the path she seemed to be following. Simon held it high above his head, to light her way. My heart was thumping. Her cool demeanor had confused me even further. If she were pretending, then she was a consummate actress.

When they were both out of sight, obscured by the leafy trees, I found myself alone among the graves, my only company the flickering candlelight. I knelt down and felt the freshly dug earth. No matter how hard I tried, I could not chase away thoughts of what had just happened.

I stood up, crossed myself, and turned to go. I had only taken a couple of steps when a sudden thought nailed me to the spot. She had not returned the broken fragment of the oil jar. If she did not know what it was, why did she take it with her?

Marika hurriedly followed Simon up the footpath leading to the tower, the steward holding the torch high to light the way. Through gritted teeth, she hissed in a barely audible voice, "I heard you say you were careful to cover your traces. How could you throw away the jar just behind their house? Didn't you think someone would find it there?"

The steward froze. Turning slowly toward her, he asked, "What do you mean?"

Outraged, Marika flung the jar fragment at him. With lightning reflexes, he caught it before it hit his chest.

"The archaeologist found it in the gulley," she snapped. "Our coat of arms is engraved on that piece there. Now he will accuse us of arson. Luckily, I managed to hold onto the evidence. You should have been more careful. I know you told Alexandros, too! Big mistake! He might let slip ..."

Simon did not seem to share her concern. Nonchalantly, he raised his arm and flung the piece of pottery as far away as he could. The sound of the fragment shattering against the stones echoed down the hill.

"Now it's gone," he said. "I didn't think anyone would go looking in the trash, and I didn't want anyone to see me carrying a jar in the dark, with a fire burning behind me. I made my way back through the gulley; I couldn't climb out and carry the jar at the same time. As for your son, he is used to keeping secrets."

He stepped toward her and, grabbing her elbow, pulled her closer. "There are dozens of those jars all over the island, gifts of wine and olive oil to people. Anyone could have one. Do you think anyone would dare accuse us of being responsible for the fire? Let them try and you'll see."

His words seemed to calm her down. She placed a hand on his chest and spoke with greater composure. "In any case, Stais now suspects us, so we have to be careful. Agreed?"

The piercing screech of a nearby nighthawk tore through the still night. Startled, they stepped away from each other. The steward raised the torch high and, without another word, they went on their way, walking in conspiratorial silence until they disappeared around a rocky outcrop.

I found Zoe standing beside the garden gate, holding a lantern. As soon as she saw me approach, she dashed toward me.

"I was worried," she said, and hugged me tightly. Once again, I was overcome with the sense of completeness her physical proximity exuded.

I was glad she had been waiting for me so impatiently. Awkwardly, I said, "I'm sorry I'm late; something came up that needed to be dealt with. Now I'm back for good."

Our eyes met hungrily. We stood facing each other, neither of us making a move, until she took the initiative and pulled me toward a table in the garden. It had been laid out for dinner, candles flickering in the darkness.

"Come, I made dinner," she said. "Elizabeth told me I could use everything, and I decided to take advantage of all the goodies in her pantry."

The beautifully laid out table in the secluded garden chased all my worries away. This part of town still had no electricity, and I wondered whether it was better if it stayed that way. I knew that once progress reached us, it would chase some of the magic away.

Elizabeth had set up the gramophone on one of the stone benches, but it sat there silently, needle poised over a record. "I didn't know whether it would be appropriate," she said.

"Better leave it," I replied, thinking that anyone passing outside would think we were celebrating rather than mourning. She nodded, understanding, and pointed to the seat across the table. I sat.

She filled our glasses with wine, and waited for me to raise my glass. Before I could reach for it, the sound of my sister's voice calling out from behind the garden gates interrupted us. Puzzled, I signaled to Zoe that she should stay, and I walked back to the gate.

A black shawl tightly wrapped over her hair, Calliope stood at the entrance, looking like she had followed me to the house. Her husband stood further behind her, holding a lantern and looking ill at ease.

"I see you are mourning our mother with the respect she deserves," she said sarcastically, pointedly looking at the table. I did not get a chance to reply, for she hurriedly added, "I came to tell you that after the forty-day memorial service, we'll cross to the mainland. We'll make our way to Komotini—forever. My husband found work there, and I think it is best that we leave the island. With all the rumors circulating, we cannot stay here any longer."

I was speechless. Although I had been hurt by her stance, I could understand why she had not welcomed me into her house when accompanied by a woman I was not married to. Her announcement that she was leaving, however, caught me off guard. The furtive glances she was now casting around the empty street showed there was more she wanted to say.

"What happened?" I asked. "Why are you leaving in such a hurry, and why are you telling me this in the dark?"

She pursed her lips and turned to go. I caught her hand, forcing her to stop. "Calliope, what is going on? Don't forget I'm your brother."

Tears ran down her cheeks. Looking away, she said in a shaky voice, "Maybe we should forget each other for a while. Yes, we may be siblings, but I have heard all the things they are saying about you. That's why ..."

She did not complete her sentence. She pulled her hand away abruptly and disappeared down the street.

Her husband gave me a dark look, then turned to follow her. I did not understand what she meant. I could not believe that Zoe's presence had upset her to this extent. Perhaps I was forgetting how little society on the island had changed during my absence. Still, I did not want anyone else determining how I lived my life, or how I mourned my mother. Unless something else had happened, of which I was unaware.

I feared that Varvis might have played his part. I turned to the table and found Zoe standing up, staring in the direction of the sea. I was sure she had heard it all. I walked up to her and gently placed my hand on her shoulder.

Without turning to look at me, she spoke calmly. "Maybe it would be better if I left the day after tomorrow. There is a boat at dawn. I seem to have brought you nothing but trouble since we met again."

Just the sound of those words was enough to open up a great void inside me. I gently pulled her around to face me. "Zoe, I will never stop you from leaving. I just want you to know that ever since we met, not a day has gone by that I did not think of you. I understand how you may think this is your fault, hearing all the nonsense people are saying, but there is something you should know ..."

I took a deep breath, and decided to lay all my cards on the table. "I don't care what people say. I want to show how I feel about you. I want to experience everything I have been dreaming of. Think of all we have gone through just to be standing here together. We did not meet by chance, and I will not let anything else get in the way. I do not care about anyone else, only the one I truly desire. I feel like I've known you for years. I understand this is happening very fast, but I don't want you to go. Not now."

She gripped my hand and held it tightly. "Andreas, many things have happened to me, things we haven't had a chance to talk about. Even though I too feel like fate has brought us together, I cannot face any more pain, any more humiliation. It is best that I leave now until things calm down. Everything happened so suddenly; I really don't understand what I'm doing here. I do want to get to know you. I owe you my life."

"You owe me nothing! I don't want you to stay out of a sense of obligation." I must have spoken louder than I intended, for I saw her cower.

I tried to calm down, realizing that I was taking my pent-up anger and frustration out on her. A few silent seconds later, I continued. "You are right. So much has happened in two days that even I feel dazed. Of this one thing I am certain, though: now that I've found you again, I don't want to lose you."

"I don't want to lose you either," she cried out, cupping my face in her hands.

The silence that followed this time was sweet, as her words echoed in my ears.

She spoke next, softly yet urgently. "However, at this point, it's best if I leave for a while. You have so much to deal with, and I feel like I'm a burden. Your colleagues are welcoming, but they don't know me. In these circumstances, I really cannot stay. I do want to see you again. Please believe me."

Her words shattered any lingering hopes I had that she might change her mind. I realized it was no use insisting, at least not at that moment. It was probably best that we both calm down and talk it over again the following morning. I gently pulled her toward the table. "Let's not talk about it anymore. This looks lovely. Let's enjoy our evening, I really need a respite from all this."

"Come sit, then. I'll bring dinner," she said, softening, and turned to go inside the house.

A small spark of hope that I might persuade her to stay flickered inside me. While she was inside, I tried to order my thoughts, to re-examine what was happening. Elizabeth would be returning in a few days, and I would have to find my own place. As Zoe said, we could not impose on her much longer. Despite the thought of her absence filling me with dread, I wondered whether her leaving might not be the best solution for the moment, a chance to deal with all those pending matters. Even unwittingly, her presence was a distraction in that she became the center of my universe whenever she was around.

Zoe always came first for me—more important than the discovery of the Winged Victory, more important even than my mother's death. Besides, I wanted to shelter her from the accusations about the alleged theft at the tower. I was sure Varvis was behind it all, a scheme to pressure me to abandon my plans to excavate their land.

Maybe I should follow Elizabeth's advice: back down for a while and deal with other matters until a more opportune time. My analysis was indicating that many important finds lay buried on Varvis's land, but maybe they would have to wait.

Zoe stepped outside carrying a large platter of food, and I decided that it was best to postpone all decision-making for the moment. She served us both, and then sat across the table. The shadows cast by the flickering candles on her face reminded me of the first day I saw her. Light fought darkness across her features, altering her expression with every flicker. At least, that is what I thought as I watched her through the bouquet of yellow roses in the middle of the table. She seemed much calmer, and I stood up and picked up the gramophone.

Fork frozen in midair, Zoe frowned as she tried to understand what I was doing. I pushed the basement door open with my foot and placed the gramophone on a table at its far end. I wound it up and, fumbling in the dark, placed the needle on the spinning record. The sound of violin strings belting out a tango spilled out from the great horn. I hurried outside, closing the door behind me. The muffled music just about reached the table. I raised my glass and made a toast to an uninterrupted, quiet evening.

We did not say much while we ate. I told stories of my student days before the war, and Zoe shared some family memories. It was evident we were both preoccupied by what was to come the following day. I helped her clear the table, and then stepped back into the garden. I hovered by the exterior stone staircase until she appeared. She came down the stairs and stopped a couple of steps above me, leaning leisurely against the railing.

With a gentle motion, she gathered her loose hair at the nape of her neck. The grace of her movements captivated me every time. I yearned to lie down beside her, to hold her in my arms. I would be unable to sleep a wink tonight, lying all alone in my basement bed, knowing she was a couple of floors above me. I knew that if she allowed me into her room I would be unable to contain my desire.

She cut my thoughts short by bending down and brushing her lips against mine. "Goodnight," she whispered, and disappeared back inside the house before I could reply.

I returned to the table and finished my wine, secretly hoping she would reappear and beckon me to her. It did not happen. I only caught a fleeting glimpse of her for a moment, when she lifted the curtain of her bedroom window to see what I was doing. Stillness and silence fell over the courtyard.

Realizing that insomnia was going to be my sole companion that evening, I decided to go for a walk up the hill behind the house. Luckily, I knew it well so I could find my way in the thick darkness. A few minutes later, I was standing at the top of the hill beneath the vast dome of night that sparkled with a thousand pinprick stars, as if a flock of fireflies were crossing the heavens above.

Turning toward the Varvis tower, I saw the red glow of a massive bonfire that had been lit at the highest rampart. I looked at the waning moon and wondered whether the bonfire had anything to do with the full moon of a few nights ago.

Back in my bed, I tried to chase Zoe from my thoughts. Had I not feared her reaction, I would have knocked on her door and taken her into my arms without a word. At this thought, my eyelids closed heavily, and I could do nothing but surrender to the dreamy vision of Zoe, standing on the marble base, arms stretched out to the sky, her long dark hair flowing down her back.

A soft knock on the door woke me up, and it took me a moment to remember where I was. The events of the last couple of days came rushing back, and I jumped out of bed, hastily throwing on my clothes. The birdsong of blackbirds and robins filled the air outside and hastened my impatience to see Zoe. I hurriedly ran my fingers through my hair, then flung open the basement door.

My smile vanished at the sight of Vasilis, hand raised in mid-knock. Though I liked the man, he had become the unfortunate bearer of bad news in my mind. Curious to hear what he had to say, I ushered him in.

"Good morning, Andreas," he whispered, looking around the room.

"Good morning," I replied. "Are you looking for something?" I added, trying to figure out what all the secrecy was about.

"Is she not here?" he asked, obviously referring to Zoe.

"No," I dryly replied.

"I passed outside the police station at dawn. I overheard that they will come take you to the station when the sun is up."

I was impressed by Vasilis's uncanny ability to be everywhere and hear everything on the island. "Who knows what they are scheming this time," I muttered. I did not intend to give them one minute of my last day with Zoe.

"They'll be here any second," Vasilis said, giving me a look full of meaning.

Despite the abrupt wake-up, I felt unusually alert. I stared at him for a few seconds as I worked out what to do next. "If you run into them as you are leaving, stall them," I determinedly said. "Tell them we are not home, that we've gone to the Sanctuary. Do not tell them that we met."

"Where are you going? They'll start looking for you both, especially you."

"Would you believe me if I said I had no idea? We are certainly not staying here."

I heard the floorboards creak upstairs. Zoe was up. I pulled him outside and grabbed him by the arm. "Go now, Vasilis, and please do as I asked, nothing more."

He shook my hand, gripping it tightly. "Be careful."

His grip was so firm that I struggled to free my hand. He would not let go, and I had to pull hard. Dumbfounded, he gave me another look, and left without saying a word. Zoe had watched the scene from the top of the stairs.

"I don't have time to explain," I told her, "but if you want us to spend the day together, you have to follow me. I know it sounds strange, but this could be our last day if you decide to leave tomorrow. Please, let us spend it together. I ask nothing else of you. If you want to thank me for saving your life, come with me, and I will take you to the boat at dawn."

She gaped at my torrent of words, but quickly regained her composure. "Tell me what I should do."

I nearly skipped with joy at her response. "Take some warm clothes with you; we might need to spend the night outdoors. And some bread."

She ran back inside, casting quick looks at me over her shoulder as she went. I walked inside the basement and picked up my overcoat and a jumper Elizabeth had left. Back in the courtyard, I snatched two pomegranates. This time I pulled so hard that the tree offered no resistance. I fleetingly thought that the thorn was still in my finger, and almost laughed aloud; it was the least of my concerns at that moment.

Zoe ran down the stairs holding a small cloth bundle. I hastily shoved my things inside it and took her hand. We ran up the path leading to the back of Paleopolis and into the woods. I thought I heard someone call out my name behind us, but paid no heed. A few minutes later, we had disappeared under the leafy plane trees.

The two men rushed out of the police station. As soon as they were out of earshot of the other officers, the policeman sternly turned to Simon. "I can't arrest him just because you showed him a collection. It will cause trouble with the Americans; don't you understand?"

"My boss is very annoyed the bronze eyelashes have not been found yet," Simon said. "He will have to go to your superiors if you don't do something. I don't think you'd like that."

The policeman halted at the sound of the steward's veiled threat. "Look, I'll send my officers after him and have him brought to the station. But I need evidence to lock him up. There is no evidence."

"Find it," Simon coldly said, letting a small bundle fall from his hands. He gave the policeman a pointed look and turned away.

The policeman stood staring at the fallen bundle. As soon as the steward was some distance away, he bent down to pick it up. He looked around to make sure no one was watching, then untied the handkerchief carefully. He slowly removed a coin and brought it close to examine it, then all the other contents one by one. He rubbed his mustache, troubled.

He slowly placed the bundle in his coat pocket and went back inside the station. The other two officers rose to attention, awaiting their orders. He paced the room, trying to decide what to do. He took his cap from a hook on the wall and paused at the doorway. "You two—go to the archaeological site and find Stais. If you find the woman, bring her, too. I have some business to attend to; I'll be back in an hour."

The three men stepped outside and separated, moving in different directions. Arriving at Elizabeth's house, the policeman entered the courtyard and called out Andreas's name. Receiving no reply, he walked further inside and paused outside the basement. He peered through the window, and then went upstairs. All the doors were open.

Calling out once again and receiving no reply, he stepped inside the house. In the cool shade, he pondered his next actions, and then returned to the balcony. Making sure no one was watching, he stepped up on a chair. He pulled out the bundle and emptied its contents on the stone ledge between the wooden roof and the wall of the house. He crumpled up the handkerchief in his fist and nonchalantly climbed down. Whistling indifferently, he exited through the garden gates and walked away from the house.

Vasilis stepped out from behind the hedge where he had been hiding. He had followed the policeman to the house and seen him plant the evidence. Once the policeman disappeared around the bend, he ran inside the courtyard. He stood, fists bunched in anger, looking up at the balcony and then in the direction Andreas and Zoe had vanished.

We had been walking for a while, and it was time to have a rest. We had made our way silently into the forest, like predators stalking prey, until we put some distance between the last houses and us. Zoe did not ask a single question; she simply followed my instructions obediently throughout the journey. I had already picked out a spot for our break: a large stone next to a gurgling fresh water spring further up the hill. I wanted to get to the shore as soon as possible.

A few hours of trekking, and we would be arriving at one of the island's most beautiful beaches. Luckily, Zoe was a strong walker and did not seem to tire. The perfection of the landscape at this spot was unparalleled, as if the invisible hand of a great artist had daubed perfect brushstrokes on a vast painting.

The red fruit of a pomegranate tree caught my eye. I jumped up and started to climb, gathering the fruit. Zoe smiled as she watched me hang from the branches. I filled my pockets and climbed back down, looking to quench my thirst at the spring where Zoe was already wetting her lips. I drank, placing my lips beside hers at the source of the spring.

We sat across from each other, the small creek trickling between us. I broke open a pomegranate, scooped out some seeds, and offered them to her. She did not reach out to take them; she just looked at me intently. Captivated by her intense gaze, I slowly lowered my hand. Time seemed to stand still as she leaned over and gently kissed me. Mesmerized, I did not respond. I closed my eyes and kept them shut, even when she pulled away. The coolness of her lips lingered on my mouth.

I felt her fingers trying to steal the small, juicy seeds from my palm. Teasingly, I pulled my hand away. One tiny, disappointed grimace, and I was putty in her hands. I picked a pomegranate seed and gently placed it in her mouth. Her lips parted just wide enough to receive the fruit. For a while, as patiently as a mother bird feeding her young, I fed her fruit, occasionally keeping a delicious seed for myself. When my hands were empty, she stared down the gully before us and spoke calmly. "I hope I am not the cause of our sudden flight."

Honestly, I had not decided whether to tell her about Varvis's imaginary theft and his accusations, but I worried that if she heard it from someone else she might give it some credit. I calmly recounted the events at the police station and the reason behind our sudden departure. I also explained why Varvis had an axe to grind.

She did not seem surprised. She seemed so at ease with fear, I guessed events in her past had made her tragically familiar with danger. More than anything, I wanted to hear the rest of her story, an explanation for the dark shadows that would cloud her eyes and then vanish as quickly as they'd appeared. The thought that this might be our last day together made me realize that when she left I would be all alone, dividing my time between mourning and work.

Sensing the clock was ticking against me, I pulled her up to continue our journey. It was still some way to the shore. I picked up the bundle and flung it over my shoulder, then started to climb down. The blackbirds hopped before us like small black shadows accompanying us on our journey.

The policeman and his two officers, one of the local men, and Varvis himself, accompanied by his son, stood outside Elizabeth's house impatiently waiting for someone. Indeed, a few seconds later, the American couple who had discovered the statue of the Winged Victory appeared. They greeted the waiting group politely, and the policeman informed them that he desired to search Elizabeth's house for the artifacts stolen from the Varvis tower.

Phyllis spoke up first. "You have no right to search for anything while Elizabeth is away. On her behalf, I forbid you to enter her house. If you do so, I will notify our embassy."

Varvis, acting as mediator, stepped up and, with feigned outrage, turned to the police officers. "I told you we should wait. It's not right to enter the house while its permanent resident is absent."

Turning to the archaeologists, he said somberly, "I apologize for the inconvenience. I am not in any way accusing your colleague."

Karl, who had been watching the exchange without a word, interrupted him. "You are accusing Andreas of stealing a collection that included coins, bronze eyelashes, statuettes, and rings."

"Yes. It disappeared the night he and Elizabeth visited our home."

With a look of surprise, the archaeologist said, "Why would he do that? Andreas has one single purpose in life: to discover as many antiquities as possible and ensure they remain or return where they belong. He is one of the most honest men I have met in my life. Why would he steal your collection?"

Varvis did not seem taken aback. Haughtily, he rested his arm on his son's shoulder and said, "For a long while, many antiquities have been stolen from this island. They are sold for small or large amounts. When the group of Frenchmen arrived, we paid no heed, but the theft of our collection coincided with their departure. I was about to donate it to the museum, as I informed your American colleague that evening. We believe that one of them handed it over, and they vanished with the stolen goods. They have been impossible to locate since then. We suspect they left the Greek woman behind to steal what she could and smuggle it to the mainland."

"This is impossible," Karl exclaimed. "The woman you are referring to is an old friend of Andreas's. They ran into each other at the port entirely by chance! How could they have colluded in such a complex scheme? We are asking you to leave. Please remember that any accusations you make against Andreas also tar Elizabeth with the same brush. She was with him that evening. When she returns, you can ask for her permission to search the house."

The policeman stepped closer to Varvis and Karl, and cleared his throat. "This man here," he said, pointing to the villager, "saw Stais hiding something in the house, and alerted us."

"How could he? How did he get inside the house?" Phyllis asked with genuine puzzlement.

"He wasn't hiding it inside the house, but outside."

A stunned silence fell over the group. Seizing his chance, the policeman went on. "Panagiotis here will point us to the spot, outside the house. We will not search the inside of the house. With your permission, of course. It won't take more than a couple of minutes."

The couple exchanged a look, trying to decide what to do. "Even if you find something," Karl said, "it does not prove what you say; especially anything you find outside the house. However, as the man is here, let us see where all this leads. Go ahead." He pointed to the garden.

Hesitatingly, the villager moved toward the stairs. Once on the balcony, he glanced at the policeman, then pulled a chair below the spot where the artifacts had been hidden. The chair swayed and buckled under the villager's weight; one of the officers rushed up to hold it steady.

Panagiotis placed his hands on the ledge and started to feel his way along the length. He was too short, and he ended up suspended in midair, one foot gingerly perched on the chair, the other kicking wildly as he desperately searched the gap between the roof and the wall. Eyes bulging, he turned to the others, saying there was nothing there.

Evidently annoyed, the policeman asked him to step aside, and climbed on the chair himself. Five minutes of desperate searching later, he climbed down, failing to mask his agitation. Raising his voice, he scolded the villager, accusing him of playing tricks. When he returned to the others, he gave a helpless, theatrical shrug, as if taking a bow at the end of his act.

Varvis pulled Alexandros closer, trying to understand how their careful set up had become a spectacular fiasco. The American couple stared at them, trying to understand what was happening. Trying to save face, Varvis said, "Maybe the man did not have a clear view, and the stolen artifacts are hidden elsewhere in the house. As you said, we will wait for Elizabeth—or Andreas, if he returns first. I understand he is also a resident of this house now."

"Yes, his own house burned down, causing the death of his mother," Phyllis pointedly said. "This is all well and good, but I am now asking you to leave. We will be informing our own authorities, of course."

Varvis, trying to salvage what was left of his dignity, turned to the policemen. "I guess there must have been some misunderstanding. I suggest that we forget the matter and apologize to our esteemed visitors for all the inconvenience caused. I would also like to take this opportunity to inform you that, as soon as Elizabeth returns, we will go ahead with the plan to construct a large wing of the museum, a donation from our family. It will house everything we have been safekeeping during the war."

"That is a different matter and not something to be discussed at present," Phyllis coldly replied, and turned away, followed by her husband.

The remaining men turned to go with their tails between their legs. Only Varvis and his son remained in the garden. Alexandros turned to his father and asked in a low voice, "Have they beaten us, father?"

Varvis smiled and cast a dark look toward the house. "For the time being, my son. We've lost a battle, not the war ..."

He put his arm around the boy's shoulders and led him toward the garden gate, the followed the others down the path that led away from the house.

Vasilis crept to a distant corner of the Sanctuary, not far from the trench where the statue had been unearthed. He dug a small hole, looking around all the while to make sure no one was watching. When he was satisfied with its depth, he flung the hoe aside and placed a flat piece of marble at the bottom of the shallow well.

He put his hands in his pockets and scooped out a few gold coins, some rings, and the bronze eyelashes. He carefully placed them on the stone, then hurriedly swept the freshly dug soil over them. Once the hole was filled up, he positioned another stone on top, marking the spot. He stood up, picked up the hoe, and moved a couple of feet away, hacking at the weeds clustered around the base of the fallen column.

We both stood still before the tranquil splendor of the clear blue waters stretching far into the distance to greet the sky. We had just stepped out of the thick foliage of the path, and suddenly found ourselves on a sharp ledge overhanging a rocky outcrop that dropped all the way down to the sandy beach.

We had been walking for hours, and I wondered how tired Zoe must be. My own two feet felt leaden as I paused in the brilliant sunshine, and sweat trickled down my forehead.

Zoe had tied her overcoat around her waist long ago, and her long, white dress clung to her back, drenched. The hemline of her dress was brown with mud, but she didn't seem to care.

I was about to suggest we sit on the ledge and rest before making the steep descent but, drawn by the sparkling sand and water, she pulled me by the hand, indicating that our next stop would be on the salty shoreline.

I watched her skip over the sharp rocks, and it suddenly became clear how she had managed to escape that day, when she had thrown herself down a very similar cliff after the pretend execution. As if she were weightless, she gingerly stepped from pointy rock to pointy rock like an experienced mountaineer, leaving me far behind. I struggled to catch up to her, and in the blink of an eye, she would vanish once again.

The only way to reach the water was through a small passage between the rocks. Honed by the salty spray and the sun, nature enchanted us at every turn. Many years had passed since my last visit to this beach, and I had almost forgotten the way of the land. The sun, blazing in the azure sky, made our descent even harder.

Whenever she needed to climb up, Zoe would raise her dress, revealing her naked legs as if she were all alone in the world. I almost tumbled off a rock, mesmerized by the sight of her alabaster flesh. She asked if I was okay. I hastily nodded, not trusting myself to speak. I kept my eyes on the path the rest of the way, until I felt the soft sand give way beneath my feet. We were finally there.

The white sand and pebble beach stretched before us, broken up only by two large tamarisk trees. The bubbling sound of running water joined the gentle gurgle of the waves, as a small creek became a miniature waterfall that tumbled over the rocks onto the shore. Large rocks encircled the beach, creating a natural fortress that made it impossible to access the secluded cove from any other direction.

Zoe stood at the mouth of a cave formed by the rocks. Other than the sound of our gasping breaths, a peaceful silence reigned. The water, still as a painting, stretched as far as the eye could see.

I caught Zoe scanning the horizon. "The island of Imbros," I said, pointing to the hazy blue mass of land in the distance.

"Have you ever been?"

"No, but I would love to. Many artifacts are waiting to be discovered there, too." I smiled. "My grandmother came from Imbros, a daughter of one of the oldest families on the island. It was an arranged marriage. They met for the first time on the day they got engaged."

"And the second time they met was their wedding day," Zoe added with a grin.

"Precisely! That's what it was like back then." I turned back to face the sea. "Imbros and Samothrace, two sisters separated by the sea, so near and yet so far. That's what they used to say in the old days."

"People are separated by borders, or by bits of paper, not by the sea," Zoe replied, crouching to unbuckle her shoes.

I flung the long-forgotten bundle I had been carrying to the ground and removed my drenched shirt. Turning my back to Zoe, I removed my vest, then draped both over a bush to dry. I felt the heat of the sun warm my shoulders and back, slowly evaporating the sweat that clung to my skin after our long trek.

I turned back to Zoe, and my heart stopped. Naked, like that morning by the pool, she stood by the waterline, ready to surrender to the sea's cool embrace. Her clothes lay in a bundle behind her, carelessly flung on the sand. I tried to look away, but it was impossible. She was glowing in the sunlight, her white skin reflecting the warm rays. Without any false modesty, she pulled her hair over one shoulder and stretched out her hand. "Are you coming in?"

Feeling my cheeks burn, I looked down and replied in a shaky voice, "You go in. I'll join you. I ... I'll spread the clothes out to dry first."

Zoe smiled, and started to wade through the crystal waters, which rose to hide her naked form with agonizing slowness. A scar on her shoulder looked like someone had painted a thin, dark line that faded as it reached the small of her back. She kept walking until she was neck-deep, and then let herself sink down. I don't know how long she took before resurfacing, but it felt like an eon to me. She swam with strong, confident strokes.

I picked up her clothes and spread them out next to mine. When I looked up, she was already some distance away. That would be the right moment for me to go in.

I removed the rest of my clothes and hurriedly dived in. The water was cold, a welcome release. As soon as she saw me in the water, she started swimming back toward the shore. I stood up, the water coming up to my shoulders, and wiped the salty water drops from my face.

"I have never seen such clear waters before. It's beautiful," she said, finding her footing beside me. A flock of seagulls landed on the rocks behind us, their loud screeching disturbing the peace.

"This is the kind of place where I'd like to live," she said, looking up at the sky.

"Why won't you stay, then?" I blurted out before I could stop myself.

She pushed away the wet strands of hair that clung to her forehead, and then turned to look at me. "I would have loved to, Andreas, believe me."

I looked away again. The clarity of the water meant that I could see her naked form when she stood so close. Oblivious to the thoughts tormenting me, she said, "Why do you think Varvis doesn't want you to excavate their land?".

I welcomed the change of subject, and replied at once. "There could be many reasons. They are one of the oldest families on the island, landowners, who own vast estates and great wealth. Their tower seems to be filled with archaeological artifacts. I feel something important is buried on their land bordering the *Hieron*. Somehow, they know that. They also know that if it is discovered, they will lose their land."

"What about the ceremony you mentioned on the way here?" she asked, intrigued.

"Elizabeth never shared the details of what happened to her at the tower that night. We had all had a little too much to drink. She seemed embarrassed, and I didn't press her. I believe they think they are the heirs, the guardians, of the ancient mystery cult of the Cabeiri. There seemed to be some ... protocol they were following the night we were there. Then there are the mysterious bonfires, the inscriptions inside the tower ... It all points to something like that."

She let out a small, startled cry, as if suddenly remembering something. "One of the Frenchmen in the group said that the island would once again become what it had been in ancient times."

"Well. Many things are said about what used to happen here, but we reconstruct history based on evidence, not embellished fantasies. It was indeed one of the most sacred sites in antiquity. Some say that Philip II of Macedon and Olympias were initiated to the mysteries here, and that Alexander the Great was conceived during their sacred union. But, as I said before, this is still unfounded lore."

"It's all fascinating." She gave a little shiver. "I'm getting cold. Shall we get out?"

Zoe was standing right in front of me, and I made sure to keep my gaze averted as she stepped out of the sea. I turned to follow, and saw that she was standing under the small waterfall, rinsing the salt water off. I rushed to where I had left my clothes and tried to dry myself with my overcoat. Hastily, I pulled on my trousers. Wet patches appeared on the fabric immediately, as I had neglected to dry myself properly in my haste.

Zoe stepped back and twisted her hair in a knot to squeeze out the water. My torment returned when she asked me to hand her the bundle to get some dry clothes. I handed it over, keeping my gaze firmly fixed to the ground. Out of the corner of my eye, I could see her getting dressed, leisurely, as if she were all alone on the beach. She pulled a crumpled black dress over her head, and tried to untangle her hair, running her fingers through the long tresses.

She picked up the bundle and walked to the largest of the tamarisk trees. Dropping down, she sat cross-legged in its shade, resting her back against the twisted trunk. I remembered we had brought some food, and crouched down beside her, untying the cloth knot. The scent of corn bread filled the air, and I had a vision of my mother removing a freshly baked loaf from the oven and handing me a wedge of the warm bread. I tried to hide the tear that rolled down my cheek and stifle the guilt that surged inside me.

I cut a large piece for her. She tore off half, and as if sensing my turmoil, held onto my hand, looking me in the eyes. She spoke softly. "I don't care about myself, but I don't want to cause you problems at work. You love your work. I was wondering whether it would be best for both of us to go to the police station before I leave, see what their accusations really are. I don't think they have any evidence against us. Based on everything you've said, I think they are trying to frighten you."

I didn't want anything unpleasant to come between us that day, so I instantly changed the subject. "Let's not talk about this now. I wish we had more food. If you are hungry, have mine. I'm full after all those pomegranates."

"I'm fine, too," she replied, waving the piece of bread she was still holding.

We turned to watch the sea, munching on the delicious corn bread. When she swallowed her last bite, she rose and came near me. To my great surprise, she buried herself in my arms and gently pushed me down on the sand. She rested her head on my chest, over my heart, her wet hair soaking my shirt. Our chests rose in tandem as our breaths synchronized, and we both looked up at the sky, enjoying the blessed calm that fell over the beach.

She stretched her hands, trying to reach the clouds that were beginning to gather in the north, a reminder that autumn was coming. I felt her breath deepen, and her hands dropped by her side as she drifted off to sleep. I smiled contentedly and closed my eyes, hoping to meet her again, as I desired, at least in my dreams ...

A sudden clap of thunder woke me with a start. Zoe was nowhere to be seen. Dark clouds covered half the sky, racing like warhorses to conquer the remaining patches of blue. A bolt of lightning forked through the heavens down to the surface of the water.

I jumped up and looked around for her. I saw her standing on the rock, fearless, as if preparing to confront the coming storm. Once again I was reminded of the statue of the Winged Victory, as I had imagined it standing on the ship's prow, face turned to the open sea.

I wondered how she had managed to clamber up there. I smelled the rain before I felt the first heavy drops. Another bright fork split the sky in half, and the earth shuddered with the menacing rumble of thunder that closely followed. Zoe, defiant, stood against the wind that tore through her clothes and hair. I called out her name, worried, and she jumped down from the rock, landing as light as a feather.

She beckoned me to her and, hastily scooping up our belongings, I obeyed. Everything would be soaked in minutes. By the time I reached her, the light had turned a hazy grey, and the leaden clouds had blocked out the sun. She grabbed me by the hand and stooped low to enter the cave. It was a small space, but enough to shelter us from nature's wrath. I pulled her close.

"I couldn't see you. I was worried," I whispered.

"Standing on that rock, I felt as if I had become one with the sea and the sky," she replied, looking into my eyes.

Lightning lit up the small cavity, blinding me. Before my eyes could readjust, I felt Zoe's body nestle against me. Our lips met, blindly, thirstily. I dropped the bundle of clothes to the floor. She wrapped her arms around me, tugging at my clothes wildly. Two shirt buttons bounced off the rocks. Hastily, clumsily, I pulled her dress down until it lay crumpled at her feet. We were both naked, gasping with unbridled desire.

She stepped back, startling me. Like a magnet, my body tried to meet hers once again, but she gently put her hands on my chest, keeping me at arm's length. Her gaze slowly took on a softer expression as she stroked my chest, exploring the rest of my body with delicious torment. My every pore ached with the desire to make her mine.

Unable to stand it any longer, I pulled her roughly toward me. The moment our naked bodies touched, I felt an overwhelming feeling of warmth, a shivering completeness wash over me. Slowly, she leaned back until she came to rest on our discarded clothes. I followed her lead and knelt before her, then lay down between her legs, waiting for her to guide me. The wind and the rain hammered the rocks with a nightmarish whistle as my body moved toward Zoe, who seemed to be burning with anticipation.

I was a novice; this was the first time I had ever been so intimate with a woman. None of the descriptions I had heard could compare with what I was experiencing inside this small cave. She stretched out her arms and gripped my back, pulling me closer to her. Flashes of lightning lit our shaking bodies as they came nearer and nearer. Slowly, I felt the warmth of her flesh inundate me, piercing my body. She dug her nails into my arms, pulling me further and further inside her until our bodies became one.

The more the weather raged outside and lightning split the sea and sky in two, the more we became a single being. Unable to control the waves of ecstasy coursing through me, I abandoned myself to the pleasures of her body. I did not stop even when she pushed herself up and sat astride me, hungrily seeking more pleasure. Her moans, merging with the thunderclaps and the roar of the wind, excited my desire, urged me to pull her down, again and again, feverishly craving to feel every inch of her body.

She had me pinned there, her thighs keeping me a prisoner to the ground. Her nails scratched my chest as her moans became louder, accompanying the frenzied dance of our bodies. It was impossible to control myself any longer. I made to pull away, to protect her. She roughly pushed me back against the stones, showing me we would be finishing together what had begun when we first met so many years ago.

The cave, the beach, the island all melted away as wave after rapturous wave of unbridled pleasure rippled through our bodies, the world swaying with us in this primal dance. Our bodies alight, we moved in tandem like puppets no longer in control of their bodies. This river of drunken delight that coursed through my veins seemed to know no end. Her spasms became stronger, became mine, as if we were one body. She trembled and quivered as her body burned up, consumed by the fire that spread through our loins as we scaled the mountain of pleasure and reached its peak.

Gently, she lay against me, our bodies still one, and we lay still as she stroked the scratches on my chest. The weather seemed to calm as our ragged breaths slowed. It was as if nature's startling outburst had coincided with our sudden union.

A few minutes later, all was tranquil, our bodies and the sky above. I kept silent, unfamiliar with the kind of words usually spoken at such moments. I stroked her arms gently as her fingers gingerly touched my neck and my lips. I picked up the dress and covered her back, pulling her closer to keep her warm. I have no idea how long we lay there, sheltering in each other's arms. Zoe was playing with the medal hanging from the chain around my neck. She was trying to make out the engraving in the dim light.

"It's my name," I said, anticipating her question. "Our winged goddess is engraved on the other side. Were it not for this award, I would not be here today ..."

She examined it for another moment, twirling it between her fingers, then ceremoniously placed it on my naked chest. "Andreas Stais," she whispered, and thus the hard journey of parting began.

It felt like my heart was torn from my chest when she rose and pulled on her dress. Following her lead, I grabbed my trousers. She knelt on the cave floor, folding the clothes she had brought. Ill at ease once again, I knelt beside her and took her hand in mine. "Please don't leave."

A dark shadow crossed her face, and for the first time I became convinced she would not be changing her mind. She rose carefully to avoid hitting the roof of the cave, and gave me a small tug, urging me to get up. "It's time to head back, Andreas. It will be dark soon."

My spirits sank when I heard that. We gathered everything we had brought and stepped outside the cave. The dark clouds were galloping away, to spread their wrath over other seas and lands. The sun hung low on the horizon, and it was true we had to hurry if we wanted to return safely. The humidity left behind by the rain rose from the thick white pebbles in misty tufts.

Without a word, we walked to the small waterfall. Zoe drank thirstily. She then stepped aside for me to join her. Despondently, I shook my head. Sensing my despair, she turned to face me. "When we are back at the house, I will decide if I stay. For all we know, you might not have a job tomorrow and I might end up in jail."

I followed her as she climbed back up the rocks, thinking about how the realization of our union had surpassed anything I had ever imagined. With a violent jolt, I returned to the present. The gaping chasms opening up inside me at the thought of parting weighed down my feet as I dragged them behind her ...

In the tower's courtyard, Simon filled a large burlap sack with the tools they would need. The paving stones were slippery after the storm. Soon, it would be nightfall. The torches and candles offered all the light that they needed. He quickly tied a rope around the mouth of the sack, through which two thick wooden poles protruded.

Varvis stomped toward him, followed by Alexandros. "I'm going to see the policeman, see if they found Stais," he barked. "Then I'll go meet our man at the port. I will find you on the estate once I am done. Start digging now that the ground is soft. Just be careful not to break anything. It was all buried in haste back then. Wait a while and then go; make sure no one sees you. We need to unearth everything by dawn. That's when the boat leaves."

"Don't worry, boss, it will all be done in time. Make sure you keep the archaeologist away, and leave the rest up to me."

Varvis turned to go, but Alexandros hovered beside Simon. "What's in the sack?" he asked with childish innocence. He received no reply.

His father pulled him away gently, urging him to hurry. "Let's go, we'll be late. It's work tools. Come, follow me."

Without another word, the child followed his father, keeping his eyes on the steward as he departed. Simon hastily followed them, and bolted the large wooden door behind them. He then took an old dagger attached to his belt and examined it.

Marika, who had been watching everything from the shadows, made her presence known. "I see you keep my gift on you at all times."

Although startled, Simon turned an expressionless face toward her. "I have never parted with it since that day ..."

They exchanged a hungry look, ready to pounce on each other. Marika took the dagger and sat on the stone bench, testing the blade against her palm. "Once he gets the money from the foreigner, we have to decide what we'll do."

Simon placed a rough palm over her mouth. "Everything will happen in good time. Tonight we must dig everything up. If the Americans find them, they will go to the museum and it will all be over. Nicholas has arranged to be paid tonight. Then, we'll see how we go about it."

She looked at him with a frown. "What happened with the archaeologist? Have they found him?"

"Not yet. He will have to reappear eventually. The policeman doesn't want to lock him up, not without any evidence, especially after today's fiasco. I still wonder what happened to all the things he hid at the house. Anyway, the important thing is that everything goes well tonight. Then, it won't matter what they do ..."

Still fondling the knife, Marika raised a leg onto the bench, letting the fabric of her dress fall down her thigh. Simon's breathing became heavier, and he wiped his forehead. Having achieved the desired effect, Marika pushed the folds of her dress back down, covering her legs.

"What about that woman who is always with him? Know anything about her?" she asked, changing the subject.

He took a deep breath and fumbled with the sack. "I heard they'd met during the war and somehow he saved her life. They met again by chance ... I didn't ask for more details." He hauled the sack onto his shoulder. "It's time for me to go. We'll all be back by sunrise."

He turned to go, but Marika grabbed his hand and pulled herself up. Their breaths met as she brought her face against his. She raised the dagger and pressed its blade against his chest. Their lips came closer as their fingers entwined around the dagger's handle.

"You forgot this ..." she breathed heavily, then pushed him away, vanishing under the passageway. Simon, disappointment chasing away the glow that had briefly lit his eyes, clipped the blade to his belt and stormed out of the courtyard.

We would shortly be arriving at Paleopolis. It was already after midnight, the trek back proving slow and arduous in the dark. I confess I did not expect the walk back to be this pleasant. All the while Zoe had been in a cheerful mood, sharing stories of her life before the war. She had wanted to be a singer back then, and was studying at a conservatory in Thessaloniki. She even sang a couple of verses of a French song in a beautiful, clear voice.

Despite the pleasant reminiscences, however, I felt tormented by the thought of her impending departure at dawn. I did not broach the subject. After what had happened at the cave, I sensed she felt the same.

I did not know if all women were like her, but I could have stopped anywhere just to feel her body against mine once again. My passion had not been spent and, while she spoke, her moans against the sounds of the storm swirled dreamily in my mind.

When we spotted the lights of the village in the distance, she stopped and turned toward me in the dark. "Let's go to the Sanctuary, the Winged Victory, please. We can talk there, and I'll answer the question you asked at the beach."

A small spark of hope suddenly burned brightly inside me. "Let's go," I cried out enthusiastically, leading her by the hand.

I avoided all the busy alleys and, following an overgrown footpath, we arrived at the top terrace. The guard was sure to be at the lower terrace, next to the building that would house the museum one day. I didn't think anyone would be out looking for us at this late hour. Luckily, I knew the area well and could avoid all the fallen pieces of marble.

We shortly arrived at the trench. The torso rested against a makeshift wooden support; it would be transferred to the museum in the coming days. The other pieces we had unearthed would soon follow, and then it could be reassembled. I felt a tinge of guilt at the thought that I should have been here, helping everyone. Once the matter of the police was settled, I would throw myself into work. I also determined to stop at the cemetery on the way back to the house. My guilt might not have prevented me from spending the entire day with Zoe, but now I felt I needed to stand beside my mother even for a few moments, having neglected her entirely that day.

I dropped our things on the ground, and we sat at the edge of the trench, feet dangling inside. A chorus of crickets filled the night air with their relentless chirps, bidding goodbye to the fading summer. Gazing at the statue, Zoe resumed her story.

"As I said, I wanted to be a singer before the war. When the Germans entered Thessaloniki, it all came to a stop. I watched as people I knew disappeared or lost their lives, and everyone pressed me to join the guerillas. I did not. I always believed that if you try to win a war with another war, you enter a battle that will never end. Only love can chase away hatred. It makes death seem small and insignificant. If people acted with love, there never would be war. At the same time, I did things very few people knew about, things that were more helpful than picking up a gun and killing anyone who crossed my path, be they German or Greek."

I did not know what to say. It sounded more like a confession than a story, so I kept silent, letting her take her time.

"One day, someone mentioned to the Germans that I was a singer. Drunk as they were, they asked me to sing a French song for them in the middle of the square. I refused at first, but then they threatened to kill a child. I sang. Yes, I committed that crime … I sang for the occupiers. That same night, a group of men were waiting outside my house. They accused me of being a traitor, of betraying my country with that song …"

Her voice broke, and she swallowed hard. I reached for her hand in compassion, but she pulled it away, determined to go on.

"They took me to a house and tortured me, violated me, telling me that that was the punishment for my crime. When they let me go, I was at death's door. A midwife nursed my wounds, saved me. She told me that I would never be able to have children … That is something you should know … I can't take any more pain …"

Shocked, I listened to her, unable to utter a word. She took a deep breath. "Time healed my body, but not my soul. Today, for the first time, I felt the ice that has gripped my soul begin to thaw …"

I could not see her, but sensed the hot tears running down her cheeks. I did not know what to say, how to comfort her. With a sigh, she talked on.

"When I found out my brothers were dead, I no longer cared about my life. I stayed on in the village, to help others and try to forget. Then, like an angel, you appeared. You saved me, and then we lost one another. When you reappeared, I felt as if a higher force had sent you into my life again."

She turned toward me. "Andreas, I have never felt like this before. All these years I kept away from people, afraid. A while ago I decided to trust someone, but even he ..." She brushed away her tears, her voice breaking. "I saw the next person to hurt me in the face of every man I met ..."

I couldn't bear to see her tormented like this. I took her hand. "Don't think of all this, Zoe. It's the past, it's gone ..."

She raised a finger to my lips, shushing me. "Let me finish my story. I want you to know who I am, and then you can decide if you want me to stay. If you still want to, we ...."

However, I was more determined than ever that the past be left behind. "I don't care about the past," I said firmly. "You look at anyone's past and all you'll find is misery and pain. All I ever wanted was to find you again. Fate brought us back together. What happened at the cave ... my body is still trembling ..."

"Mine too ..." she whispered, pulling nearer.

I pulled her even closer. She straddled my lap. Kissing me tenderly all the while, she unbuttoned my trousers and raised the skirt of her dress, bringing her hips closer. She cast a furtive look around to make sure no one was watching, and then took me inside her gently.

Catching me off guard once again, all I could do was hold her in my arms as she swayed against me, silently surrendering to the waves of pleasure that washed over me. Our union beneath the statue of the Winged Victory had none of the ferocity of our lovemaking at the cave, but was more intense as I slowly moved inside her. Whenever I opened my eyes, dizzy, quavering with ecstasy, I would catch a glimpse of the white marble of the statue that had played its part in our reunion, and now silently bore witness to its divine completion.

Her breathing got heavier, and a small moan escaped her lips. I placed my hand over her mouth to stifle her cries. She rocked her body gently, with increasing tempo. I could not control what was coming, and I surrendered to the deepest, most intense sensation I had ever felt.

Biting my lip to stifle the urge to cry out as I approached climax, I pulled her face against my shoulder and felt her tears soak the nape of my neck. I could sense they were not tears of sadness. It had taken me years to make a woman mine, and now I felt as if my thirst would never be satiated. I had always been afraid I would not know what to do when that moment came, but now everything was happening so naturally. Her trembling lips met mine and I tasted her salty tears as we both found release.

An otherworldly silence fell over the Sanctuary. Even the crickets were silent. All that moved was the soft breeze bringing the scent of the sea over the island, a hint of jasmine, a hint of thyme as it ruffled the bushes around us and we, calmly, tenderly, rested in each other's arms.

I felt the chain slip down my torso and grabbed it, pulling it out carefully.

"I'm sorry, is it broken?" she asked with a worried frown.

I placed it in my pocket. "I'm amazed it lasted that long, after everything it's been through today," I joked. "Don't worry. I'll have it fixed tomorrow."

The sharp crack of a snapping twig made her jump up, hastily brushing her dress down. I looked around in the dark, but all I could make out were the lanterns that lit the entrance to the lower terrace. "Must be an animal," I soothed her.

Indeed, a pair of bright eyes sparkled among the tall weeds before the fox revealed itself. It stared at us for a moment, then at the statue, unable to make sense of the beings that had invaded her territory. She then turned around and disappeared into the bushes.

Zoe smiled and helped me up. "Now that you know everything about me, you can ask me again. Just know that you are under no obligation to repeat the quest—"

"Will you stay?" I interrupted, without hesitation.

"I don't think I can do otherwise, Andreas. Events seem to be conspiring to bring us closer to one another."

Kostas Krommydas

I did not know how to express the joy I felt. I let out a happy cry, pulled her close, and covered her face with kisses.

"This is how we'll do it," she said, firmly placing her hands on my shoulders to emphasize her words. "We'll make a deal."

"Anything you want," I said with unbridled enthusiasm.

"I'll return to Maronia at dawn. I have to take care of some business there. I also have no clothes with me here. I will return in a week when things have settled down here. Besides, you have your winged goddess to attend to right now." She pointed to the statue. "Provided I'm not arrested at the port."

I didn't know what to say. I did not want her to go. On the other hand, everything she had just said made sense. "No one will arrest you. I want you to do what you feel is best," I mumbled.

"And when I'm back, we'll live one day at a time, whether good or bad. Agreed?"

"Agreed!" I nodded enthusiastically. Besides, the more I thought about it, the more her plan made sense. I had to focus on work, on finding a new place to live.

"I will have found a place for us by the time you get back," I said. "Then, possibly during winter, I could start building a house on a small plot of land we own ..."

"One day at a time," she repeated, temporarily halting my dreams.

.

"Yes. One day at a time."

The creak of a wooden door opening rang out from the side of the museum, and Vasilis appeared at the porch, holding a lantern. He couldn't see us in the dark, but I pointed at a bush and signaled that Zoe should hide there, just in case. Then I carefully moved toward Vasilis. He worked as a night guard some nights and slept here, but I didn't know he had a shift that night. I approached, giving a low whistle as a signal, and he jumped high in the air like a startled cat. He raised his lantern and came nearer when he realized it was me.

"Are you on your own?" I whispered.

"Andreas," he hollered. "Where have you been all day? We were worried!"

"Shush! Be quiet. They'll hear you."

Vasilis slapped his forehead. "That's right! You weren't here, so you don't know they're not looking for you anymore ..."

I thought I had misheard, but laughed with relief as he recounted what had happened that morning. I felt a tinge of satisfaction at their humiliation in front of my American colleagues. This was the perfect moment to begin excavating their land. I would wait for the authorization to arrive, and then I would dig from dawn until dusk, on my own if need be.

I asked Vasilis not to mention seeing me, took his car keys, and left without giving any explanation, ignoring his perplexed expression. I walked back to Zoe and asked her to walk down with me. Varvis was standing next to the museum as we walked past; he stared at us as if he had just seen a ghost. Zoe bid him goodnight, and giggled as he opened and closed his mouth, unable to utter a reply.

We drove back to the house, and I brought her up to date on the latest developments. I planned to stay up that night, and drive her to the port at dawn. When we entered the garden, my first thought was to light the lantern that stood on the table. As I struck the match, I grimaced.

"What's wrong?" Zoe asked.

I had forgotten to stop at the cemetery. I had spent all day outdoors, and had not found a moment to light a candle. "I haven't been back to her grave," I replied, wracked with guilt.

"If you don't want to wait until the morning, why don't you go now? I'll wait here for you; unless you want some company?"

The truth was that I felt torn. I did not want to miss a single moment with Zoe, now that I knew she was leaving, but I also thought it would be faster if I went on my own.

"Stay here and rest," I said, giving her a hug. "It will be dawn in a few hours. Sleep. I'll wake you up when I'm back. I need to go. I will feel bad if I don't."

"Of course, you should go. I'll borrow some of your friend's clothes and return them when I'm back, if that's all right. She said I could."

"Yes, of course," I replied absent-mindedly.

I looked at Zoe's face, trying to commit her features to memory. "I shouldn't be saying this," I said, "in light of what happened two days ago, but I want you to know today has been the happiest day of my life."

"Mine too, Andreas." She gave me a tender kiss.

"It's up to us to make sure many more such days follow," I declared, carried away.

She put her fingers on my lips and shook her head playfully. "One day at a time, remember?"

"One day at a time," I echoed. I wanted to return as quickly as possible, to savor the hours we had left until her departure. I sprinted to the garden gates, calling out over my shoulder, "I'll come wake you up, you know. Goodnight, Ouranoessa!"

Her face lit up. "I'll be waiting," she cried out, running after me.

I turned, and our lips locked in a passionate embrace. She then pushed me away, urging me to go. Walking backward, she raised her hand and waved.

I skipped the two steps that led to the street and ran to the Jeep. As I put the keys in the engine, I thought that maybe I should stay, and go to the cemetery in the morning. For a few seconds, I could not make up my mind. Then I turned the key and sped off, intending to return as quickly as possible. The round-trip would not take more than half an hour by car.

Further down the road, a fox stood frozen, caught in the car's headlights. I slowed down, but she would not budge.

Like a sentinel refusing to let anyone pass, she sat on her hind legs and stared at the car. I had no time to lose. I inched closer. When the car was but a hairsbreadth away, she reluctantly stepped aside.

I saw her eyes in the rearview mirror, following the car as I drove away. *Could it be the fox from the Sanctuary?* I wondered as I stepped on the gas.

Dominion of the Moon

I swiftly arrived at the cemetery. Anyone seeing me walk inside at this hour would take me for a grave robber. I found a single candle in the box outside the small church, and picked it up. Someone, possibly my sister, had placed a vigil lamp in a wooden box, its wick flickering in the oil that remained. I lit the candle and placed it on the ground beside my mother's grave.

The scent of the candle set off a chain of painful memories—the flaming house, the smell of burning timber, the terrible feeling of helplessness as we stood outside watching everything turn to ash. Without any concrete answers as to origins of the fire, I did not know how to react. I found it hard to believe it was arson, that someone had deliberately tried to harm us, and yet ...

My mind was overwhelmed by my whirling thoughts, by the flood of memories. I had expected to be plagued with guilt for spending the day with Zoe instead of mourning. Once again, reality and expectation were worlds apart. I had separated the two events. Horrifying as it may sound to a stranger, it seemed natural to both grieve my mother and delight in Zoe. I did not think it a coincidence that she appeared in my life when I was all alone in the world. I did not feel any great pain at the thought of my sister leaving, as she had announced. After everything that had come to pass, it was probably for the best—for everyone involved.

I stayed beside the grave for a little longer. Bending down, I gently stroked the mound of soil that covered the grave; a silent goodbye. As I turned to leave, I saw the glow of fire burning behind the hill. I wondered who could have lit a bonfire at this hour. It looked like it came from the Varvis estate, specifically the fields that bordered the site of the Sanctuary.

I felt torn between the need to return to Zoe, and the need to satisfy my curiosity. Maybe they had lit a fire to burn tree trimmings earlier in the evening, and neglected to put it out properly. At the same time, who would think of going out to do field work after a raging storm? The top of the hill was only a short distance away. Despite my weariness, despite my desire to return home, I decided to climb up and see.

A few minutes later, I reached the small peak of the hill. By the light of the burning branches, I could see the shadowy outlines of two men digging. I was too far away to make out their faces. The die was cast. I could not turn back, not without finding out what they were up to.

Cautiously, I crept forward, grateful for the muddy soil muffling my footsteps. If they were thieves, I would have to alert the police.

The sight of Varvis made me stop in my tracks. He stood beside Simon, who was shoveling earth knee-deep in a shallow pit. The neighing of their horse, grazing a short distance away, jolted me back to my senses. I hid behind a bush, trying to understand what was going on.

Standing on a large stone behind them, Alexandros gripped a small sword. He was obviously meant to be keeping a lookout, but the boy seemed to have forgotten all about it. He was lost in his game, fighting off an imaginary enemy.

I turned my attention back to Simon. As my eyes adjusted to the darkness, I noticed a wooden trunk next to the pile of soil at the edge of the pit. No more was needed to divine what they were up to.

I did not know what to do. If I went away to alert the village, they might be gone by the time I came back. Besides, whom could I alert? The policeman was in cahoots with Varvis. If I told him Varvis was digging something in the middle of the night, he would reply that the man could do as he pleased on his property. I was convinced that what they were doing was illegal, otherwise why would they be doing it now, under the cover of darkness?

Something snapped inside me. I stood up and revealed myself.

Alexandros was the first to notice me, turning the blade of his sword toward me. He called out to his father, who signaled to Simon to stop. Agile as a cat, Simon jumped out of the pit and moved toward me, raising the shovel threateningly. He stopped a couple of steps away, swearing, spraying me with spittle as his raged. He swung back the shovel to hit me, but Varvis barked at him to stop. Like an obedient dog, he froze.

I instantly realized the gravity of my error, but it was too late. I would not run away like a coward. Varvis came to stand beside his steward, as did his son. The flickering flames cast their faces in shadow, but I could feel their hatred pierce me like a poisoned dart.

"Well, well, if it isn't our esteemed archaeologist," Varvis spat out in his hoarse voice.

I decided to go on the offensive. "So I was right, Varvis."

"About what?" he asked sarcastically, looking at the others.

Alexandros shifted a little, and the red glow of the flames lit up his face. I gasped when I saw the loathing in his eyes, wondering how it was possible for a small child to harbor such hatred.

"I know what you are up to," I said. "If you hand everything over to the Greek Archaeological Service, I may not report what took place here tonight. But you will have to return everything that doesn't belong to you."

Varvis walked up to me and shoved his face in mine. "*Everything* here belongs to my family. I told you time and again, but you don't seem to understand. It's mine."

"Are you telling me that this chest is filled with your personal belongings?" I asked, wincing at his wine-laced breath.

"See for yourself, if you wish. Family heirlooms we hid from the Bulgarians." He stepped aside to let me pass.

I was taken aback by his gesture, but I was running out of options. Hesitantly, I walked around the fire to the chest. Simon lowered his shovel and followed me. I felt the flames burn my face, which had frozen with fear. I could hear them walking behind me. The horse stomped on the ground and let out a fierce snort.

The two men stepped around me and stood by the chest. Varvis nodded at Simon. My heart stopped at the thought that he would hit me with the shovel. I breathed more easily when I saw him place its cutting edge against the rusty lock. With a sharp twist, he broke it open and flung back the lid.

"Here, take a look." Nicholas pointed to the interior. I approached and leaned over. A rotting piece of cloth, covered in mud, hid the chest's contents.

"Unwrap it," he ordered. "We have nothing to hide."

As I bent down to pull away the cloth, I caught the nod he gave to his steward, but it was too late. There was a sharp pain at the back of my skull, and I fell forward, hitting my nose and teeth on the chest's edge. The taste of warm blood filled my mouth, and everything became a blur.

A strange sense of calm came over me. My body was numb from the waist down. I felt no pain. My eyes were tightly shut. I could feel Varvis and Simon beside me, removing something from the pit. I could hear their voices as if they were coming from afar, and I wondered if I was alive or whether I was experiencing the final flashes of reality as I left this world.

My eyelids felt so heavy; steel trapdoors keeping me locked in the dark. I lost all sense of time, could not tell if seconds, or minutes, or hours were passing, whether I was drifting in and out of consciousness.

The shock that ripped through my body as I landed on hard ground was a sign that I was still alive. My mouth filled with soil and blood. With great difficulty, I moved my tongue around my mouth, pushing out the thick paste, trying to breathe. I tried to open my mouth, to say something. No sound came. My voice refused to obey; it no longer belonged to me.

Suddenly, everything went quiet. A tiny spark of hope rekindled in my heart. Maybe they had just abandoned me here. Blindly, I began to feel the ground around me. My fingers brushed against a soil wall, and I realized I was lying at the bottom of the ditch they had dug. I sank my nails into the walls, trying to shuffle further up, to see if there was a way out of this shallow grave. Unable to see, unable to move my legs, I dragged my unwilling body behind me.

After what felt like a lifetime, the crown of my head brushed against the back end of the ditch. I raised my hand and began to scrape the soil, trying to carve some kind of hold that would help me haul myself up. The effort proved too much for my injured body. Once again, I sank into oblivion.

I was woken by the sound of a strange, otherworldly voice. I could not tell whether it was coming from outside or whether it was in my head, but it gave me the strength to sink my hand into the soil once again.

Somehow, I had managed to dig a small hole in the wall of the ditch. Desperately feeling around the hole, my fingers touched something cold ... a nose, a mouth, the shape of eyes ... I spread out my palm and felt the shape of a face. The otherworldly voice became louder, filling me with new strength.

Suddenly, I was shaken by the thud of feet landing beside me. I felt a hot breath against my ear, whispering about a house fire. Something cold pierced my chest.

Nothing made sense. I could not see. I could not feel.

I smiled and opened my eyes. In the dim light of the fire, I saw her alabaster face surge through the soil, a look of tenderness, giving me courage. The features shifted, and for a second I saw my mother; then Zoe, smiling and calling me to her. She was at the house, waiting for me. She would leave in the morning, and I wanted to see her again, before we vanished from each other's lives for who knows how long. Then the face reverted to its original form and, before the darkness engulfed me, I saw her rise in a flash of white light and call me to her. She looked exactly like I had envisioned her in all my dreams ...

Varvis grabbed Andreas by the armpits. Simon gripped the injured man's legs, and they clumsily flung him into the ditch.

"We need to carry the chest up the hill," Varvis told his son. "You stay here and keep guard. We'll be right back. If he tries to get up, call us." The two men grabbed the wooden chest and walked away.

Alexandros coldly looked at the motionless body at the bottom of the ditch, and began to sing a tune his mother had taught him. Suddenly, he noticed that the man had moved. The boy inched closer to the hole in the ground. He could tell the man was trying to get out, and wondered what he should do.

He looked at the distant figures of the two men, then leapt into the ditch. He kicked the man to see if he was alive. Andreas gave a jolt. Alexandros leaned into his ear. "We burned down your house," he whispered, bringing the blade of his sword over Andreas's heart. Without flinching, he plunged the sword into his chest. "Now, we win."

The smile on Andreas's lips startled him. When he saw the man's eyes open, he jumped out of the ditch, stifling a yelp. A few seconds later, he cautiously crept back to the edge. He dispassionately observed Andreas's final struggle to pull himself out of the ditch. He could see the man's hand, scraping away at the soil, but could not understand why he would do that. Soon he lost interest and sat back, singing loudly as he watched his father and Simon return.

Nicholas saw the handle of the sword sticking out of Andreas's chest, and grabbed the boy by the hand. "We'll take this chest, it's lighter," he told Simon. "You stay behind and clean up. When we load the horse, we will set off. There is no time to wait for you. Cover the ditch with leaves and branches; make sure the fresh soil doesn't show. Another storm is on its way." He pointed to the forked lightning tearing up the sky in the distance.

Alexandros picked up one of the chest handles and walked away without saying a word. When father and son had moved away, Simon looked inside the freshly dug ditch. He was surprised to see Andreas's outstretched hand, but felt no inclination to find out why. He kicked the glowing embers into the ditch and started to fill the hole with soil, without even checking if the man he was burying was dead.

The first heavy raindrops began to fall on the moist ground. There was a bright flash of light, and then the ground shook with the rumble of nearby thunder.

The storm had just died out, leaving devastation in its wake. Wet mist covered the port as the sun rose, and the handful of passengers gathered at the dock were informed by the loud voice of the crier that the boat would soon be departing for Alexandroupolis. Few had managed to reach the port in the aftermath of the storm.

Even though the land had been ravaged, the sea remained calm, as if obeying a different god. Slowly, the passengers walked up the gangway and boarded the wooden boat. Last in line, her back turned to the sea, Zoe scanned the dock in the hope that Andreas might still appear. Her heart raced faster when she saw a man running down the street, then sank when she recognized the familiar figure of Vasilis.

He ran up to her, gesticulating wildly, pointing to the boat. Zoe looked lost. She hesitated, until a voice asked her if she would be boarding. She fumbled in her bag and pulled out a scrap of paper and an old pencil stub. She scribbled something down hastily, and gave it to Vasilis. Then she ran up the gangway, following the two men carrying a muddy wooden chest. She stepped aside as the sailor pulled it up, then stood there, face always turned to the port, hand gripping the railing so tightly her knuckles turned white.

Even when the boat had sailed into open water, she kept looking toward Samothrace, hoping to catch the face of her beloved one last time. Even though they would be reunited in a week, it seemed like an eternity away. But the port remained deserted. Even Vasilis was nowhere to be seen.

Clouds were circling the mountain peak like a ring of steel, cutting it off from the rest of the island. It looked as if it was rising to the sky, lifted by the hands of an invisible god of wrath. It was hard to tell where sea ended and land began until the early morning rays burst out from the east.

To the west, a pale half-moon slowly descended. Still as a statue, Zoe's eyes had become one with the island shores, hopelessly searching for a sign from Andreas. She was bursting with the urge to ask the captain to turn back, to dive into the deep waters and swim to Samothrace.

She shook her head, trying to chase away a mounting sense of dread. Beside her, an old woman dressed in black, hair covered by the traditional dark headscarf, held a small girl by the hand, and pointed to the mountain. Like a folk tale from days long gone, her words reached Zoe ...

"Where sea and sky merge,

Like sugar and water,

Where the moon paves a road of silk,

That is where the fairies weep ..."

It was nearly dark when Zoe finally arrived home in Maronia. As she wearily dragged her feet up the stone steps leading to the front door, she bitterly regretted her departure. She resolved to return to Samothrace and look for Andreas the following morning. She had listened to her fellow passengers' reports of the havoc wreaked by the storm with escalating distress, despite Vasilis's attempts at the port to calm her fears.

She flung her few belongings down by the front door and ran around the house to the balcony, as her father called the long cobbled corridor that led from the back of the house to the sea. She did not stop until she reached the end of the corridor, which was suspended over the gaping cliff.

In the distance, Samothrace glowed in the afternoon sun. The clouds had dispersed, leaving behind a crisp clarity that made the island appear closer than ever. Yet to her, it seemed so very far. She stood there, looking at the homeland of the man she had loved in the space of a few days. She could not wait to go back, to find him.

A tear, sharp as a diamond, stung her cheek. She swallowed hard, but the crushing waves of grief that overwhelmed her refused to be suppressed. Great sobs raked her body as she wept for Andreas.

Present Day

Leaning on her cane, Zoe stood at the edge of the balcony, eyes turned to the island across the sea. With great difficulty, she had just managed to stand up. Her long white hair fluttered in the light breeze. The wrinkles around her moist eyes had not dimmed the keenness of her gaze, despite the passage of so many years. A wooden gazebo and an armchair stood behind her. She would spend many hours in its shade every day, gazing at the familiar view.

Sophia, the girl who had been looking after Zoe in her old age, watched her every move carefully. Zoe took another shuffling step, reaching the small marble columns that acted as a railing.

Her trembling hands leaned against them. The sun dipped low on the horizon as daylight gently gave way to dusk. She never took her eyes off the island, even when Sophia approached her.

"You'd better sit. I brought a jacket for you; there's a chill in the air."

Zoe obeyed, showing no sign of recognizing the girl. She turned her eyes back to the island and raised a frail hand, beckoning Sophia toward her. "Do you know what they call that place?"

Sophia did not reply. She knew how this exchange would go: the old woman would ask the same question every afternoon these past few days and, without waiting for a reply, would add, "It's Ouranoessa, and one day he will be back.

But this time was different. The old woman sighed, and then added, "The winged goddess will bring him, on a night with a bright full moon ..."

Sophia was puzzled. Zoe had never mentioned a winged goddess before, and she could not understand what the old woman meant. She paid no more heed and smiled, admiring the island shores as they blended into the water. She enjoyed spending the afternoons here with her, taking in the sprawling view.

A few minutes later, Sophia stood up. "Come, Zoe. It's time to go back inside. It's getting dark, and your grandson will call you."

She gripped Zoe's arm to help her get up. Eyes fixed on her Ouranoessa, Zoe did not move. Sophia shook her gently. She placed her fingers on the old woman's neck and kept them there, hoping for a small sign of life. She pulled them back sharply, stifling a sob. Covering her mouth with her hand, Sophia tried to keep her composure as she ran back inside the house to call for help.

The wind blew Zoe's hair in the direction of Samothrace. Her lifeless body sat turned toward the island she had loved more than any other place in the world. She had never stopped believing her beloved was somewhere on it, and had waited for him to return until her final breath ...

Buenos Aires. Present Day

The lights in the Teatro Colón dimmed, and the curtain slowly parted to reveal the orchestra, unblinking under the strong spotlights. Although the auditorium was packed from the stalls to the very last seat in the gallery, absolute silence reigned. The conductor, seated before the piano and wearing a red tux that made him stand out from the other musicians, clapped his hands to the rhythm, encouraging everyone attending to join in. Hesitatingly at first, they followed suit, tapping the opening beats of the composition to follow.

The exquisite sounds of Astor Piazzolla's *Libertango* flowed from the piano keys and, on cue, a woman in a long red dress appeared stage right. Her dance partner waited across the stage. To the first sound of the violin, accompanying the piano in its increasing tempo, the couple met at the center of the stage in a passionate tango. Audience and orchestra clapped to the frantic pace of the music and the swaying couple, who met and parted in a dance of seductive domination.

It was not the first time I was watching a show based on Piazzolla's music. However, Argentinean rhythms never failed to enchant me. Maybe because they reminded me of our life together before she was lost to me forever.

In those few minutes of swirling red dress and violin strings, I kept my eyes fixed on the stage, recalling her face.

At the spectacular finale, with a musician playing the accordion upright and a passionate kiss sealing the dance, everyone rose to their feet in a standing ovation. I knew then it was time to return to reality.

A crackle in my ear, and the orders came through on my headpiece. I turned to the front row of the dress circle, where the man we had been tracking was sitting.

I made eye contact with my colleagues, who had positioned themselves around the stalls. Before the acclamations died down, I swiftly exited to the bottom of the stairs that led to the upper level. There, I met the others. I clipped my pin onto my lapel and opened the door. I paused, signaling to the others to wait. The show continued on stage. A guitarist and an accordionist had just begun to replay the Libertango, slowly, gently, flooding the house with sweet melancholy.

The dancers drifted off to the wings, entwined in each other's arms, swaying to the soft melody. I did not want anything to disturb this wonderful spectacle before it was completed. Arresting the man a few minutes later would not change anything. Caught up in the atmosphere of the opera house, I longed to hold her in my arms once again, to feel her touch.

Another wave of loud applause swept through the audience at the conclusion of the final piece. It was time to act.

I spoke into the microphone hidden under my shirtsleeve, and we all walked up the dress circle and down to the front row. Startled by our sudden intrusion, people stopped as they left and turned to stare. The other agents held back, letting me reach him first.

I looked down at the fragile relic of the monster who had been responsible for the deaths of thousands during the Second World War. All our evidence indicated that he must be well over ninety years old. For a second, I wondered what the point of arresting him now was, in front of all these people, beside the evident symbolic value of the act.

He had spent many years hiding behind an assumed identity. Up close, it was clear he did not have long to live. We knew he was ill, and that he moved with difficulty. Living under an assumed name, enjoying the protection of high ranking members of various governments, he had managed to go undetected for so long. It had taken DNA identification through a close relative of his to uncover his identity at last.

A much younger woman sat beside him, accompanied by a man we knew was his security detail. I addressed him by his real name, in German. He did not seem to hear me. He only turned toward me, following the startled gaze of his companions. His smile evaporated as he took in my pin and the handcuffs in my hands.

His eyes were sunken in a face crisscrossed with deep wrinkles. Wisps of white hair did not manage to cover his baldness. An old scar split his forehead horizontally in half. I took a deep breath, and spoke.

"Lazlo Werner, you are under arrest for crimes against humanity committed between 1942 and 1945 and leading to the death of thousands."

Everyone around us fell silent as the former SS officer stood up, aided by his bodyguard. "You speak very good German," he commented in heavily-accented Spanish.

Before I could reply, he proffered his wrists, nodding to my handcuffs. "I am ready ..."

I was taken aback by his words. They were the last thing I had expected to hear. For a moment, I faltered. *How could he be so well prepared, so calm?* I wondered, and the answer came to me in a flash.

He knew we were coming for him today. Someone had alerted him. I knew many war criminals made secret agreements with various agencies, but I had not expected to come across such a case. Anger swelled up inside me, and I grabbed his wrists and snapped on the handcuffs.

"Where are you originally from? You don't look American," he said, trying to hide a small grimace of pain.

I was unmoved. "Greece," I replied, tightening his bonds. This time he could not hide his discomfort.

"Not a bad race ... Among the most resistant to our methods," he cackled. I pulled him hard, wanting to fling him down to the ground. He stumbled, and I propped him up, realizing I was letting my feelings rule my head.

My colleagues were already escorting his two companions outside, so I pulled him by the sleeve, trying to control my temper. I struggled to find the delicate balance between duty and emotions.

Seeing me waver, Jill walked up to me. "I'll take over," she said, giving me a look that mixed concern and compassion.

The Nazi turned back toward me. "See you soon," he said sarcastically, and turned to go.

"Not in the circle of hell waiting for you," I replied coldly.

He stopped and gave me a look filled with hatred. "*Der Weg zur Hölle ist mit guten Vorsätzen gepflastert,*" he spat out, and followed Jill, who had been following our exchange with a frown.

I became aware that everyone around me had been watching the whole scene. Some had taken their phones out and were busily recording everything.

Shortly afterward, Jill approached me in the theatre lobby. She announced that the German was on his way to the airport, where a plane would take him to New York. Then, with a sigh, my supervisor took out her cell phone and pulled up a video.

"It's gone viral," she said, turning her phone sideways so I could better watch myself manhandle the Nazi in an opera house.

"I'm sorry," I said, "I thought I had everything under control." I shrugged apologetically.

"Come on, Andreas. You know how it is. They blow everything out of proportion, just to get more clicks. You have been through so much lately. Maybe it's time to take a break. You shouldn't have returned to work so soon after …"

"It's not that!" I said, wishing I had kept the anger out of my voice.

"What did he say that upset you so?"

"He said a lot. At the end, when I told him he'll burn in hell, he said 'the road to hell is paved with good intentions'. It was his expression, not just the words. I could tell he doesn't regret a single thing he did."

Before Jill could reply, I felt my cell phone vibrate. I apologized and picked it up, noticing just then ten missed calls from my grandmother's summerhouse in Maronia. I remembered I had promised to call her that day. I would return the call from my hotel, if she was still awake. I was in no state to make a call at this moment. I knew that if she had seen the video I would get a telling-off for the way I had behaved.

We walked to the exit and the waiting car. In the end, I gave in to temptation. I strapped on my seatbelt and dialed the number. Sophia's voice presaged that something was wrong. As she explained what had happened, I recalled the few times I had been with Zoe at that house. She had passed away peacefully, sitting at her favorite spot under the gazebo, where she spent every afternoon of her retirement. *Her balcony to the sky*, she used to call it.

I had not seen her since her visit to the US two years ago. I had not realized so much time had passed. Time waits for no one. You think you are controlling your own time, and then one day you suddenly realize it has slowly eaten away moments that you could have experienced but never found time for. It had been Zoe's choice to return to Maronia and spend her twilight years, as she used to say, there. I made sure we spoke on the phone and Skyped. Jill could tell something was amiss while I spoke, and squeezed my hand in heartfelt condolences when I told her the news.

An hour later, I was at the hotel busily packing my bags, preparing for the long journey to Greece. I would have to return to New York and catch a flight from there. I thought about calling my mother, who had been living in Canada for many years now, but I did not think she would genuinely care about Zoe's death. We spoke rarely these days, and only when necessary. I had last seen her at my father's funeral, many years ago. I still remembered how reluctant she had been to attend. The reunion between her and Zoe had not been pleasant. Since I was a boy, my grandmother had taken the role of my mother. I owed her so much, and I hoped she realized how grateful I was for the sacrifices she had made for me.

The knock on the door interrupted my reminiscing. Jill stood in the hallway, and I invited her in. She cut straight to the chase. "Andreas, we are all sorry for your loss. I know you loved your grandmother. I spoke to the director, and he would like you to go on compassionate leave. He mentioned a month."

I frowned. I did not want to be away for that long. I had lost the two people I loved the most in the space of six months. I could not stand to be alone. Work kept me busy, provided respite from the pain. "It's the video, isn't it?" I asked, stuffing toiletries in my bag.

"Look at it as an opportunity. I speak as a friend. You haven't been the same since Eva passed away. I know you well. I understand. It all happened so fast that you haven't had time to grieve properly. It might be a good opportunity to rest. To find closure and then return, make a new start."

I had no wish to get into that conversation. I was still too angry, too sore, and I didn't want to risk taking it all out on Jill, who was only trying to help. Just then, I realized that someone was waiting for me in New York. Destine the German Shepherd, bequeathed to me by Eva. What would happen to her while I was away? She had been staying at a kennel during my absence, but I would have to make other arrangements for a longer absence. On the other hand, it would be nice to have her with me in Greece. She was so well trained, it wouldn't be a problem. In any case, I had plenty of time to make up my mind on the flight out of Buenos Aires.

"I think I'll head back home on the same flight as Werner; otherwise, I risk missing the funeral. I'll arrive in New York in the morning, and catch an afternoon flight to Athens. I'll literally be up in the air for the next couple of days."

"That's why it's a good idea to stay there, to rest. I'll let them know you are traveling with them, but please keep away from our prisoner. You promise?" Jill asked as she stepped outside the room.

Instead of answering, I looked away.

As soon as the door closed behind her, a terrible sense of loneliness came over me. I threw the rest of my stuff in my bag and dashed off to catch my flight. The funeral would be taking place in four days. As if sensing the end was near, Zoe had made a point of constantly reminding me where she wanted to be laid to rest: Samothrace. I would be setting foot on the island that had cast a long shadow over my family for the first time. All my life, I had only ever seen it from afar.

In the airy auditorium of the recently renovated building in the Chora, the crowd filled the seats and lined up against the wall, spilling out into the corridor. Above the main entrance, an inscription greeted the latecomers: *Welcome to the Axieros Foundation. Renovated by the Varvis family, in loving memory of Marika and Nicholas Varvis.*

A large banner beside the entrance depicted the statue of the Winged Victory and announced: *The Mystical Nature of Greek Mythology: Earth, Wind, Fire, and Water.*

An elegant woman walked to the podium. Her tight, white suit highlighted her shapely body and contrasted with the long black hair that flowed to the small of her back. Admiring glances followed her as she walked.

Someone turned on the microphone, and everyone fell silent. They all turned to the large screen mounted behind the podium. An aerial view of Samothrace came into sharp relief, rising from the sea like an island just spewed by a volcano. The woman tapped the microphone to test the sound, then turned on the tablet she had placed on the podium. Her eyes were the same dark shade as her hair, and she scanned the crowd to make sure she had everyone's attention.

With an assured voice, she welcomed them. "On behalf of the Axieros Foundation, I welcome you to the Sixth International Philosophical Symposium *The Mystical Nature of Greek Mythology: Earth, Wind, Fire, and Water.* Let us begin with a brief introduction."

The lights lowered, and a movie started to play on the big screen behind her. The woman noiselessly walked to the front row and took a seat beside an elderly man. To her left, a much younger man leaned and whispered something in her ear, receiving a look of disapproval.

On the screen, a black horse ambled carefree through the archaeological site of Samothrace. The camera followed it in slow motion as it galloped through the woods until it reached a large pool of water. The shot faded to black as the horse lowered his head to drink. Imposing music accompanied footage from the Sanctuary of the Great Gods and from all over Samothrace, as the sites visited alternated while a voiceover in English shared information on all the latest discoveries. The movie then moved on to the excavations that had taken place at the Sanctuary since the Second World War. Black and white pictures of mostly American archaeologists flickered across the screen, accompanying a timeline of all the significant discoveries.

The entire last part of the screening was dedicated to the ancient religion of the Cabeiri and their initiation rites. It ended with a night shot of a great bonfire, around which a large group of men and women stood, all dressed in white. The credits rolled as the camera zoomed in on the full moon hanging above the flames, zooming closer and closer until its bright yellow light filled the screen and invaded the auditorium.

At the end of the screening, enthusiastic applause filled the room until the lights came back on. The same woman rose, and beckoned the young man sitting beside her to rise as well. He stood up and thanked the audience with a brief bow. She returned to the podium and, once the applause died out, pointed to the same man. "We would like to thank Miltos Ramiotis for his excellent film, shot on Samothrace last summer with his crew, all the way from Australia."

Looking straight ahead, she continued. "I forgot to introduce myself. My name is Iro Varvis, and I have been the president of the Axieros Foundation for the past five years. Before officially declaring the symposium open, I would like to thank my father, Alexandros Varvis, for his tireless work in actualizing my grandparents' greatest wish. The Axieros Foundation's mission is to make Samothrace the Great Mother of all ancient religions once again, and one of the most important tourist destinations. An idea conceived by my grandparents, who sadly did not live long enough to see it become a reality."

She glanced at her father, who was watching her with a look of encouragement, then continued. "Soon, the construction of a large hotel will begin, built according to the architectural principles of Ancient Greece, always based on the evidence we have to date."

The strong murmur that rippled through the audience made her pause, but Iro's stern and irritated expression imposed silence once again. Trying to hide her disquiet, she pressed something on her tablet, and the lights became brighter. "It is my great pleasure to invite Mr. Christos Kanellopoulos, the symposium coordinator, to the podium."

She returned to the front row. Her father shook her hand as she resumed her seat. Miltos, the film director, gazed at her intently even though she did not turn to look at him once.

The first day of the symposium had just ended, and everyone was gathering in the foyer. A large table set up in the center served as a bar, and a woman dressed in black dominated the space, sitting on a small stage set against the wall. She held a cello between her legs, and provided the musical accompaniment to the hushed conversations of the attendees. Her thin fingers slipped on the musical instrument, weaving a gentle melody.

Iro stood beside the stage, gazing at the cellist in admiration. Her father and Miltos were engaged in conversation beside her. The waiter, failing to entice them with his tray of drinks, made to leave, nearly running into the woman who had suddenly materialized beside them. She grabbed one of the glasses, thanked him, and then extended a hand toward Alexandros Varvis. "Good evening, my name in Alkistis Cosma. I'm an archaeologist. I've been working at the Sanctuary of the Great Gods these past few months."

Alexandros ignored her hand and nodded indifferently, watching a blush spread from her neck to the roots of her closely-cropped hair as she awkwardly stood there. Trying to make up for her father's rudeness, Iro took her hand and shook it warmly. "Pleased to meet you. Iro Varvis. This is my father, Alexandros Varvis, and my fiancé, Miltos Ramiotis. Welcome to Samothrace. We hope you enjoy your stay here, and please don't hesitate to contact us for anything you may need."

Despite Iro's obvious disinclination to engage in anything other than polite formalities, the young archaeologist smiled, undeterred. "Thank you for your welcome, but I've been here for a while now. I am leaving for Athens tomorrow to visit the exhibition at the Acropolis Museum. It's on the mysteries of the Great Gods. When I return, I would like to meet to discuss a matter concerning old excavations that took place on your land. Any information you have on that subject would be useful. I tried to contact you before."

Alexandros gave the young archaeologist a look of disdain. "Excavations have never taken place on our land. There has never been a need for excavations on our land."

Iro, acting as peacemaker once again, spoke up, handing over a business card. "Please call me at the foundation offices one of these mornings to make an appointment, and we'll discuss whatever you want. Now, if you will excuse us ..."

"Yes, certainly, I did not mean to interrupt. We'll talk soon. It's been a pleasure." Alkistis moved to the other side of the room.

"Father, you don't always have to show what you feel," Iro whispered to Alexandros. "Everything is under control. Why don't you go to the evening reception with Miltos? I'll make sure everyone gets on the buses, and join you later."

"I wish your mother could have seen you like this," Alexandros said. "You were wonderful today. The nine days of the symposium will pass quickly, and as the big day approaches, you seem more and more ready for it ..."

She picked up his wrinkled hand and kissed it respectfully, then turned to go.

Miltos touched her elbow. "Don't you want me to stay with you?"

"No, you'll be bored. I still have many things left to organize. You'd better go with my father. I don't want him driving at night."

Alexandros had anticipated her reply, and smirked. Looking displeased but saying nothing, Miltos leaned over and pecked her cheek before accompanying the elderly man to the exit.

Iro turned to the woman playing the cello, and they exchanged a complicit look before she began to mingle with the other guests, urging them to move toward the buses. The music rose to a feverish crescendo, then abruptly stopped, as the musician gathered up her cello and left the room.

Miltos drove along the coastal road to the reception area. Alexandros sat comfortably in the seat beside him, looking out to the sea.

"My daughter has too much on her plate. Perhaps you should hasten your marriage," Alexandros said, without turning to look at him.

Miltos cast him a furtive look, then turned his attention the winding road. "Iro doesn't seem to be ready, if you ask me. I feel like she's been avoiding me lately."

Alexandros turned around sharply. "She is not avoiding you, son. She is a perfectionist, and all her attention is focused on work. However, it's time she took a break and gave me a grandson. It would be nice to set the wedding date tomorrow. Why don't you get married a month after the big day? Give your family some time to come over from Australia." He paused, giving his words some time to sink in, and then changed the subject. "What do you know about that archaeologist girl?"

"She arrived a few months ago, worked with the Americans during the summer. I don't think her contract will be renewed, so she'll be gone soon." With these words, Miltos gave Alexandros a conspiratorial wink.

The old man gave a satisfied chuckle. "So, I needn't worry about it, then? You've taken care of it? Excellent. Miltos … I don't know how many years I've got left. I want to make sure that the hard work of our ancestors does not go to waste. You are the son I never had, and I want you and Iro to further our vision. You are the guardians of their legacy. What I have will be yours. Everything we own has been paid for in blood and toil."

Listening carefully, Miltos pursed his lips and gave no reply. He was well aware of the importance of his fiancée's family. Their meeting had been no accident. Like Iro, he was born on Samothrace, and came from a rich island family. His parents now lived in Australia, having accumulated great wealth. He'd chosen to return to the island after completing his studies, and now spent most of him time travelling all over Europe. He was trying to establish an annual thematic film festival on Samothrace. Space had been allocated to this purpose in the hotel complex the Foundation was planning to build.

Iro's father had engineered their meeting, discretely arranging their introduction while Iro studied in Melbourne for two years. Now, with less discretion, he was pushing them to get married. Miltos, madly in love with Iro, was not convinced she felt the same. He tried to keep his possessive jealousy in check, realizing she was an unpredictable woman who would not tolerate being confined. He took a deep breath, trying to decide whether he should confide in Iro's father.

"What's the matter, son? If you have something to say, speak up!"

Alexandros's perceptiveness caught Miltos off guard. "I do not know how to say this without upsetting you. Iro mentioned something a few days ago. She asked me how I would feel if we were to leave the island at some point."

Alexandros's mouth twisted in an ugly grimace. They were near the reception venue when he spoke again, sharply. "What did you tell her?"

"That it's something we'll need to discuss, and ..."

"There is nothing to discuss! She will do as you tell her. You are her husband. She must obey you," screamed the old man, bringing down his fist on the dashboard.

Stunned, Miltos could only nod his acquiescence before his future father-in-law's imposing wrath. The old man's hair may have turned white, but the passage of time had left no mark on his eyes, which still sparkled with the fervor of youth.

Miltos pulled up by the front steps of the venue and handed his car keys to the valet. Another attendant helped Alexandros Varvis step out of the car, and Miltos caught up with them at the front door. The two men exchanged a glance, but did not say another word.

Standing some distance away from the milling guests, an elderly man leaned heavily on his walking stick, his keen eyes scanning every guest to cross the threshold. His ascetic stooped form, his whole demeanor, made him an incongruous presence. One of his ears was missing. The other ear protruded through tufts of white hair, making him appear almost comical.

Noticing him, Alexandros raised a hand in greeting. "Hello, Vasilis! Welcome!" he shouted heartily. The other man reciprocated with an awkward nod.

Miltos looked at the man with the missing ear curiously, and in a low voice asked who that was.

"He's a ghost from the past. I'll tell you some other time," Alexandros replied through gritted teeth. He looked at Vasilis, who was shuffling toward them, flattening his long white hair against his cheek with his free hand, trying to cover the missing ear.

"Good evening," Vasilis cried out to both of them when he came within hearing distance.

Alexandros seemed in a hurry to move away from the strange guest. "How come you are here, Vasilis? Will you be joining us?"

"No. I only came to tell you the news," he said, and looked pointedly at Miltos.

"Speak freely; Miltos is my son. I have no secrets..."

Vasilis hesitated, and then uttered a few words with great difficulty. "She ... Zoe ... passed away."

Alexandros froze, but quickly recovered. He pulled Vasilis further inside the room and said, "It was about time..."

Miltos watched them, curious as to whom this strange little old man could be. Vasilis bowed his head as if he regretted having spoken, turned around, and slowly moved toward the exit.

Kostas Krommydas

With the assistance of the manager of the kennel, I had just completed all the necessary paperwork for Destine to accompany me to Athens. We planned a trip that included a stopover in Zurich, and then a connecting flight to my final destination.

A beautiful German shepherd, Destine was a trained police dog who had been Eva's faithful partner. Destine had refused to leave her side, staying with Eva until the very end. I still remember how Destine kept looking for her, whimpered and whined until she could meet her, even for a few minutes, in the hospital's specially allocated area. Eva, weak, a shadow of her former self, smiled at her beloved dog; her eyes shone whenever she saw her. The cancer had spread rapidly from her breast to the rest of her body, and Eva fought hard. When the end was inevitable, she asked me to look out for Destine.

We had met two years previously, investigating the disappearance of a couple in one of the northern States. Eva, special investigator with the FBI, and Destine, trained police dog. The two of them were inseparable, the bonds between them as strong as those of a lifelong friendship.

Following Eva's death, the bureau had tried to pair up Destine with someone else. The dog refused. She had sunk into a deep grief, mourning the death of her beloved master. They asked me if I wanted to take her in. I did not have to think twice about it. She was my closest link to Eva.

Although it took us a while to get to know one another, we had been getting along fine these last couple of months. Destine only sulked or became angry if I was away for a long while. Like now, when she did not even deign to look at me.

She mostly responded to French commands, although I had managed to teach her a few English commands. She had been born in France, and her trainer had been French.

I decided to take her for a long walk before returning home to pack. The poor animal would be spending most of the next two days cooped up in the belly of a plane.

I felt rested, having spent most of the flight from Buenos Aires asleep in a large, comfortable seat. I had ignored the Nazi, leaving him to my colleagues. He was one foot in the grave as it was; they would not even have time to punish him. News of his arrest made headlines everywhere. For about seventy years, he had lived his life as any other law-abiding citizen. Nevertheless, I had read all about the horrific crimes he had committed in the concentration camps. Although a young man at the time, he had been one of the most ruthless torturers at Dachau.

The paperwork regarding Destine's travel completed, I stepped outside. She followed. I kneeled on the pavement and spoke to her in Greek. "We will be going on a long journey, to a beautiful country. We'll be spending lots of time together, just the two of us."

She pricked her ears as if she had understood what I had just said, and licked my cheek. As soon as she spotted the tennis ball cupped in my palm, she wagged her tail enthusiastically. Around her collar, the silver tag with her name, a gift from Eva, sparkled in the sun. We made our way to Central Park, man and dog strolling in the melancholy autumn breeze, in silent companionship.

At the old family tower, a young woman was serving breakfast to Alexandros and Miltos. Iro appeared in the courtyard, holding a tray she had preferred to prepare herself. They exchanged good mornings and, after kissing her father's hand first and then Miltos's cheek, Iro sat down with them. They ate in silence.

Alexandros was the first to speak, complimenting Iro on the success of the symposium. "Everything was wonderful yesterday, and I imagine our guests will enjoy today as well. I think I'll stay here, though, and rest. I need to prepare for the coming full moon."

Iro waved her glass of orange juice in agreement. "Yes, father, I was going to say the same. You don't have to attend. Everything is going as planned. "

"Yes, I know. Now, it is time to focus on other plans. "

His daughter looked at him, perplexed, trying to fathom what he meant. Alexandros nodded at Miltos, urging him to speak up.

Miltos's coffee cup clattered against the saucer as he put it down determinedly. "Your father and I had a long talk yesterday, and then I spoke with my parents. Iro, I believe it's time we set a date for the wedding. "

She turned to Miltos in surprise. "That is something you and I need to discuss," she said, nervously fondling her knife.

Her father was following their conversation with a keen, evaluating eye. He wanted his son-in-law to impose his will.

"It is not just our wedding, as you know. It involves everyone around us. Our families, I mean. I wouldn't think you'd want your father excluded ..."

"No, Miltos, I wouldn't, but some things are best arranged between us. Besides, now is not the right time to be making wedding plans."

"You're wrong, daughter," Varvis interrupted. "Now is the perfect time. It would be good to hold your wedding after the full moon ceremonies. There is no reason to delay it any longer. You know how important this year is to us. In a few days, you will be anointed. There is an opportune time and place for everything, and your union to Miltos should not be delayed any longer. Do you forget the promise you made to your mother on her deathbed?"

Iro was clearly uncomfortable, cornered like a rat in a trap. She didn't feel ready to make a lifelong commitment to Miltos. All her instincts cried out that she should wait a little longer, until she felt certain.

In the early stages of their relationship, everything had been great. Miltos gave her everything she had yearned for, as if he understood her better than anyone ever had. But in time, that feeling had begun to fade, as routine replaced the novelty of the early days. She was sure that she was not ready to marry him. She did not want Miltos to perceive her refusal to set a date as a rejection. She just needed more time.

"Perhaps it is better to wait until the end of the symposium," she said. "Once the full moon festivities are over, we can think about making wedding plans. I don't think we should be confusing the two. The night of the full moon and the wedding are two very separate things. As far as the wedding goes, I was thinking of next summer. You men think everything is easily planned, but these things take time to organize, time which at present I don't have."

Paying no heed to what his daughter was saying, Varvis mused loudly, "Mid-October would be perfect. It would leave more than a month for preparations. "

Realizing she was getting nowhere, Iro stood up. "Please excuse me, but I have a lot on my mind and it's time to go. They must be waiting for me."

She picked up her tray and, apologizing once more, walked to the arched passageway that led inside. Above the first arch, the old inscription forbidding entry to the uninitiated still stood intact after all these years.

Miltos stood up to follow her, but Varvis grasped his hand and pulled him back down. "Don't run after her. Show her you have the upper hand. She'll nag a little, but eventually she'll acquiesce. I give you my word that after the full moon ceremony, she won't be able to refuse. Then, everything will be as it should be. "

He spoke to Miltos with the tenderness of a father talking to a son, and of his daughter with all the indifference of someone referring to a perfect stranger.

"Sir, I think it's best that we wait for the symposium to be over before raising the subject again," Miltos said. "I'll talk to her the day after tomorrow, I promise. I'm sure I'll manage to persuade her to change her mind."

"I'm sure you will, son. And I think it's time you started calling me 'father.'"

"That would be a great honor. If you will excuse me, I must get ready."

Varvis nodded, and stood up himself. He walked to the ledge facing the sea and let his eyes wander over the blue expanse.

Several hours had passed since take off, and we would be soon landing in Zurich. Luckily, we wouldn't have to wait long for our connecting flight. Although I generally kept up to date with what was happening in Greece, I had spent most of the flight reading all the latest news about the state of the country.

Greece's economic crisis was still deeply felt by its people, who were struggling to land on their feet. At the same time, large waves of refugees were creating huge problems in the wider Mediterranean region. Last year, I had found myself in a closed meeting with security officers from around the world. One of the issues discussed was the refugee and general crisis in the Middle East. I will never forget the words of a Turkish colleague. He stressed that what we were witnessing was only the beginning; that the world would be experiencing the greatest humanitarian crisis since the Second World War in the years to come. It would be caused by the outbreak and protraction of civil wars, which would not stop but only intensify, as well as climate change, which would cause mass migrations of people in search of better living conditions.

In the distance below, the lights of a big city sparkled, probably somewhere in Germany. Memories of my grandmother flooded my mind. She had been one of the bravest people I had ever met. Pregnant with my father, she had sailed for the US. There, with the help of some

American archaeologists who had worked with my grandfather, she managed to make a life for herself. She worked at the American School of Classical Studies, close to the people who had known the man she had loved.

A veil of mystery covered the disappearance of my grandfather. He had been accused of antiquities smuggling, but no evidence had ever materialized. Not only did my grandmother refuse to believe these accusations, she refused to believe my grandfather was dead. She'd spent her whole life waiting for his return. She had searched for him for a long while without finding a single trace. It was as if the man had suddenly vanished from the face of the earth. She had asked me to continue looking for him, to investigate his disappearance, but I confess I had not. Now, I was plagued with remorse. My conclusion, however was that he must have died. Many crimes at that time went unsolved, committed in the shadow of war and civil strife.

I chose to keep the good memories of that story, their love that was so brief yet lasted a lifetime. I could tell that the few days they had spent together had given birth to a great love affair, feelings so strong they could not be dimmed by the passage of time.

He had been an archaeologist on the island. Zoe had recounted how he had saved her life as the war neared its end, how they had met again by chance, years later, on Samothrace. What a pity they never managed to live together ... When my grandmother returned to visit Maronia, she repaired her family home and returned to Greece regularly. The last time I had visited was years ago, with my father. I still remembered how beautiful it was, and I could not wait to find myself seated on her *balcony to the sky*. Zoe used to spend so many hours there, and on a night with a full moon, she would not come back inside until dawn had chased the moon away.

My father had grown up in New York. There, he met my mother, and I was the result of that brief, ill-fated relationship. They never married, and I was still a young boy when my mother returned home to Canada. I felt no bitterness about her leaving. My grandmother immediately filled the void created by her absence. Mother had chosen to leave, and I made my peace with that early on. Having formed no strong emotional bonds with her, to me she was just my biological mother. I did not miss her, because the great love I got from my grandmother immediately covered any gap. Nor did I ever feel the absence of an extended family. I always felt sheltered by the band of archaeologists who had worked with my grandfather and become surrogate uncles and aunts. They guided me, spoiled me, and helped me, as if they owed it to his memory.

Elizabeth was the other custodian of my grandfather's memory. She gave me other insights into the man; she claimed he was a passionate archaeologist, obsessed with the statue of the Winged Victory. Compassionate, yet rational. Elizabeth always maintained that my grandfather had probably drowned in a flash flood caused by the storm that hit the island on the night of his disappearance, and that there was no substance to the allegations that he was involved in anything illegal.

It is hard to find the words to describe Destine's unbridled joy when she saw me again in Athens. I had never seen her like this, wildly clambering all over me, trying to reach my face and lick it. Everyone at the airport laughed heartily at her antics. A Greek officer stepped out at passport control to greet me. Destine gave a low growl, but I reassured her with a caress.

"Mr. Stais, welcome to Athens. Headquarters briefed us about your arrival. I wanted to let you know that we are here for anything you may need during your stay. I think you do not have a weapon with you, but if you need to ..."

I simultaneously shook his hand and my head. "Thank you. I don't think I'm going to need anything, especially a gun. But I appreciate the offer." I was surprised at how quickly my Greek was coming back to me.

"And if I may," he continued, "I would like to congratulate you on the arrest in Argentina. You people have done great work in this field. We are proud a Greek was involved in such a large operation. I watched the video. I confess I enjoyed it very much. The bastards need to pay, even after so many years."

"It's probably too late for this guy to pay, " I said and, without wasting any more time, I thanked him and pulled Destine toward the car rental kiosk.

Minutes later, we were driving toward the center of Athens. I decided to spend the evening in a hotel near the Acropolis that accepted dogs, rest, and begin my long journey the following morning.

After about half an hour, having crossed the entire center of Athens, I parked the car at the hotel. The Acropolis was very close. I took what I needed for a walk, and headed out with Destine. The weather was warm, but the light breeze made it a pleasant walk. We ambled up the pedestrian street beneath the Acropolis, intending to walk to the Temple of the Olympian Zeus.

The Parthenon dominated Athens atop the sacred rock. We passed people from all over the world, their faces blending into a cultural mosaic of humanity. It did not take long to reach the main entrance to the impressive museum, where visitors patiently stood in a long queue waiting for a ticket.

I would have continued walking had it not been for Destine, who stubbornly refused to budge, stretching the leash. Surprised, I tugged lightly and encouraged her to follow. But she stood her ground, her gaze fixed on the museum's entrance. I turned to see what had caught her attention, and that is when I noticed the banner. It showed the headless statue of the Winged Victory and the title of the exhibition: *Samothrace. The Mysteries of the Great Gods.*

I'd had no idea this exhibition was on, but I could not believe it was mere coincidence. Sitting comfortably beneath the banner, a cat enjoyed the shade it cast. That must have been what caught Destine's attention, but ultimately led to me finding out about the exhibition. I approached one of the guards, who informed me animals were not allowed inside. Without wasting any time, I returned to the hotel and left my disappointed canine companion in our room.

Minutes later, I was standing in line for a ticket. I entered the exhibition area full of curiosity. Numerous exhibits filled the room, some in display cases and others behind a thick cord. Music that sounded like a mechanical roar mixed with the sounds of countryside animals rose and fell in the room. A film of the Sanctuary of the Great Gods was being projected on a wide screen. It was more than halfway through as I entered, so I continued my tour, hoping to catch the next showing.

I joined the small crowd gathered before the statue of the Winged Victory. Softly lit, it rose in the middle of the exhibition space as if it had just emerged from the ground. Though wounded by time, the sculpted marble seemed alive, ready to spring toward me.

I inched closer to a woman who seemed to be acting as a guide, explaining to the visitors the history of the statue's discovery.

I immediately remembered the words of my grandmother, who, along with my archaeologist grandfather, was there on the day the statue was discovered. As far as I could tell, I was now looking at the exact same statue. A strange and nostalgic feeling forged a bond between the past and the present.

Distracted by these thoughts, I thought I heard someone call me. I looked around me, and realized the guide had just mentioned my name. She was not referring to me, of course, but to the work of my grandfather. I felt deeply moved. As soon as her talk was over and the visitors began to disperse, I walked up to her.

"Good afternoon. May I ask you something?"

She nodded with a bright smile.

"Please excuse my Greek. I have only just arrived, and I haven't spoken it in many years. I heard you mention someone called Andreas Stais, if I'm not mistaken."

"Yes, he was part of the team that discovered most of what you see around you."

I fumbled for the words that would explain who I was, but she beat me to it. "I should probably introduce myself," she said, smiling warmly. "My name is Alkistis Cosmas. I'm an archaeologist at the Sanctuary site and the museum of Samothrace."

I shook her hand. "Pleased to meet you. Andreas Stais."

She looked at me, and tried to stifle a giggle. "Yes, as I told you, he was one of the archaeologists who..."

I took a deep breath and tried to explain. "No, what I'm saying is, *my name* is Andreas Stais. I'm the grandson of the archaeologist you mentioned."

Her face lit up and she gaped at me, trying to determine whether I was joking. We stood there a while, me explaining who I was and how I came to be here. Impressed by our meeting, she offered to show me around. It was becoming very clear that she admired my grandfather and knew much about his life. More than I did.

"Andreas Stais is one of my heroes. I've been on the island since early summer. Although I tried hard to find some information about what happened back then, I couldn't. People shut down the moment they hear his name. I am writing a paper on the Mysteries of Samothrace, the rites that still take place on the island, and how they may be the remnants of ancient rituals. I go as far back as the end of the second world war, which is when your grandfather returned to Samothrace."

I hung on to her every word with mounting interest. Unfortunately, one of the museum guards interrupted us before she could tell me more, saying she was needed elsewhere. She hastily pulled out a card and, propping it on her knee, scribbled something on the back. "I have to go. Would you like to meet up again when you are in Samothrace? You and I have a lot to talk about, believe me. Why are you visiting now, at this time of year? "

"I'm going for my grandmother's funeral, the day after tomorrow. She wanted to be buried on the island."

"Your grandmother? You mean..."

"Yes," I said, as a light of understanding dawned in her eyes. I understood she was pressed for time, so I added quickly, "I know it's not customary, but if you wish to attend the service..."

"I will be there," she replied with great fervor. "Call me tomorrow with the details, although I imagine I'll hear about it anyway. It's been a pleasure meeting you."

I stayed on for a while, looking at the exhibits she had not had time to show me, and left after watching the film on Samothrace. I was bursting with curiosity. I had been won over by the images on the screen, and was now looking forward to immersing myself in the beauty of the island.

The sun was setting, crowning the Parthenon with purples and pinks for a final few minutes, the white marble a mirror for its setting glory.

A long nap would sort out my jetlag and prepare me for the long road trip ahead. I took out my phone and called Sophia to find out how the funeral arrangements were going. Some distant cousins on my grandfather's side had suddenly appeared and intended to attend the funeral. My father had never liked them much, and my grandmother had called them vultures. All I wanted was to say goodbye to Zoe in the way she deserved. She always used to tell me, "Do not fear death. Love beats death. I beat death, twice!" Those were the words I turned to whenever I felt my courage might fail me.

An old man's voice answered the phone, a voice I had never heard before, yet it sounded strangely comforting. Familiar.

"Hello Andreas," he said, as if he had been expecting to hear from me.

Night had settled around Samothrace, with clear, starlit skies. Nightingales perched on the branches of the plane trees by the stream, filling the air with sweet song. Small lanterns lit the atrium of the house that nestled under the tall oak.

Iro and Erato, the cello player at the symposium, relaxed on chaise lounges sipping wine and enjoying the tranquil evening.

"I expect everyone will be drinking through the night now that the symposium is over," Iro said. Taking a long sip, she added in a serious tone, "Erato, I don't feel ready for the ceremony."

As if struck by lightning, her friend bolted upright and leaned toward her. "You will never *feel* ready, Iro. You are the Chosen One! *That* will give you immense strength when you need it."

"I don't think I'm the Chosen One," Iro said, hiding her face in her hands.

"Why would you think such a thing? Your family is the guardian of the legacy of the ancestors, and it all leads right down to you. In a few days, you will be the Great Mother," Erato said affectionately.

Iro lifted her face up and looked around, worried. "Did you hear something?" she whispered.

Kostas Krommydas

Both women kept very still, ears pricked for any unusual sound camouflaged by the birdsong.

Erato earnestly grabbed her friend's hand. "You are fretting over nothing. After the initiation ceremony, not even death will frighten you."

"I'm not fretting. I just don't want to become something I do not think I was destined for."

"I've never seen you like this; what's wrong with you?" Erato said, frowning.

"My mother might have died when I was very young, but she still had time to tell me something I've never told anyone... She tried to rebel against my father. But there wasn't much she could do. She told me that they all expected a boy, an heir to carry the mantle. I ruined their plans. When she fell ill and died without having any more children, I was chosen as a last resort. Not as the Chosen One!"

Erato raised her voice, almost scolding her. "Listen to yourself! You are your father's flesh and blood, and that is all that matters! Everyone might have wanted a boy, but fate chose you! Your father adores you and is very happy to have you as ..."

"My father wanted to have a son. He found that son in Miltos. That is why he wants us to marry so quickly."

"I don't know what's gotten into you, what's making you so morose, but you're exaggerating! You love Miltos, don't you? "

Iro pondered the question before replying. "Yes, I think so. I don't understand what's happening to me. My head is a mess. It's as if the moon is growing inside me, haunting my thoughts." She turned to look at the moon rising from the east.

The muffled rumble of thunder issued the clarion call for moon and clouds to engage in a battle for the sky. Erato put her glass down on the floor and came to stand behind her. She tenderly pulled her up and began to knead the nape of her neck. Iro let out a contented sigh.

"I've never seen you this tense," Erato said.

"I always thought something would happen, and we would not get this far. Yet, here we are."

Erato's hands pressed harder, and Iro slowly started to unwind. She leaned back and listened to the murmur of her friend's voice, grunting softly in reply. For the first time in days, she felt herself relax, the pent-up tension inside her finding some relief. "Thank you, I feel better already," she said hoarsely.

Erato picked up her glass and returned to her seat. She grabbed the wine bottle from the ice bucket and refilled their glasses. "To the gods who always show us the way," she toasted, giving Iro a look full of meaning.

Dark shadows fell over the island as the clouds sped toward the mountain, swallowing up the stars in their path. The moon disappeared, and only flashes of lightning lit the windows as Iro dozed on the chaise longue.

"Rain's coming. I hope the weather holds for the full moon," Alexandros told Miltos, as the two men sat at the long wooden table in the courtyard.

"Forecast says no rain, but Samothrace has its own weather god. You never know," Miltos replied, watching the storm come in.

"Whatever the weather, the ceremony will take place. The moon will still be there, watching. Nine days pass quickly! I need you to look after our people. Make sure no one tries to gatecrash. Only the initiated. No one else," Alexandros said briskly.

"Everything has been taken care of ... father."

Alexandros gave Miltos a look of satisfied approval. "These days the island is filled with hippies who think they are gods. They go to the water pools and leave their filth behind them like scavenging hyenas. This time last year they trampled over our vines, but this year, they will not dare. I have taken precautions. Although, what I'd really like to do is grab them all and fling them down the gorge, see if the gods they worship can save them from the vultures feasting on their bones."

Miltos smiled at watching him get so riled up. "We have nothing in common with them. Like you said, nothing but a handful of quacks braying at the full moon, high on drugs and cheap wine."

Varvis smiled and leaned back in his wooden armchair. He knew the man sitting across him was the best choice he could have made for his daughter. For years, his father, Nicholas, had heaped scorn upon him for failing to sire a male heir. On his deathbed, with no grandson in sight, he made Alexandros promise that Iro would mate with someone from Miltos's family.

"The old man at the reception yesterday, the one who told you that someone had passed away. Who was he talking about?" Miltos asked.

"I told you yesterday, son. A ghost, now dead. It's a very old story, faded with time." He changed the subject. "Where's Iro, by the way?"

"She went to see Erato after the symposium. I'm going to pick her up in five minutes. If I may ... there is something I would like to tell you."

Varvis nodded, curious as to what it might be.

"That woman, Erato. I know she is one of the chosen, but something does not sit right with me. I only know her a little, as a friend of Iro's ..."

Varvis shook with laughter, his loud guffaws echoing around the cobbled courtyard until a choking cough forced him to stop. Miltos stared at him, unsure how to respond. Finally managing to catch his breath, the old man cleared his throat and looked at his future son-in-law admonishingly. "Do you think me so foolish as to trust my daughter to choose her own friends? If Erato did not meet with my approval, she would not even be allowed to see Iro from afar."

Miltos was taken aback. He had no illusions that Varvis was capable of many things, but he did not expect him to be spying on his own daughter, to be checking on her friends. "So you are telling me that..."

"Yes, Miltos, I know everything. Once you pick up Iro, Erato will call me. She reports to me every time she sees her. If I left our lives to chance, my dear boy, we would be just like everyone else: sheep, the blind followers of stupid leaders. Iro was born to fulfill a mission. "

He stood up slowly and walked around the table. He stood behind Miltos and pulled at the young man's shirt, exposing his right shoulder blade and revealing a small tattoo. "Here's your real name, son, beside my daughter's. You will unite under these names and become what they symbolize..." He pulled the shirt back up to cover the tattoo, and patted Miltos's shoulder. "Go bring your wife home now."

Miltos obediently stood up and headed to the large wooden door. The smell of rain coming filled the air. A woman appeared as soon as Miltos left, and walked to the table. She placed a small clay dish filled with milk before Alexandros. "Would you like anything else, sir?" she asked in a low voice.

She was barely older than his daughter, and spoke in a foreign accent. He put his arm around her waist and slid it down to her thighs. "No. You can go to bed now. I might join you later. Leave the door unlocked."

The woman nodded submissively and only left when he pulled his hand away. Alexandros picked up the small plate and placed it by a crevice on a nearby wall, before turning to go back inside.

In the darkened courtyard, a small black snake crept out of the crevice and slithered to the milk ...

I was already nearing Thermopylae. No matter how hard I tried to keep Destine in the back seat, she would come to the front and sit in the passenger seat, looking straight ahead. It was pretty dangerous; a sudden brake, and she would be flung against the windshield. But try as I might to impose my will on her, she was her own dog. I could only hope I would not regret giving in and letting her sit there.

The man who had picked up the phone yesterday was Vasilis. I had heard my grandmother talk of him, but I had never met him or spoken to him before. He was one of the last people to have seen my grandfather alive the day he disappeared. My grandmother had asked that he be informed of her death as well.

He seemed happy that he was going to meet me. He lived on Samothrace, had taken care of all the funeral arrangements. His voice had sounded so familiar. For a split second, before he introduced himself, I thought that was what my grandfather's voice would have sounded like if he were still alive.

I tried to remember the last time I had spoken to my grandmother, and what we had talked about. It was as if my mind remained stuck on other, much older conversations. Even under these circumstances, I longed to be near her. We had become accustomed to living apart, and I would not be surprised to find her waiting for me at the front door. I always kept thinking that about the people I had loved and lost. That something would happen, that I would suddenly discover that they were not really gone, that they were still near me. There were times when I woke up in my flat and went looking for Eva, as if she had just gotten out bed.

The weather was good, and I enjoyed the ride as I drove past the place where Leonidas and his three hundred men had made history resisting the Persian army. Knowing that the fight was lost, that they were outnumbered, they still fought on. Despite growing up in America, I never lost touch with my Greek side. My father made sure of that, and then my grandmother.

I was surprised when I saw Jill's number flash on my screen; it was still dawn in New York. I replied happily, and we chatted about my journey. When she asked if I was stopping at Thermopylae, I realized she was tracking me through my cell phone, and could locate me with scary precision. It didn't bother me. We had had to track each other often, quietly, during operations.

She informed me that after the first wave of reactions to the arrest video, a second wave of sympathy toward me had surfaced, people applauding the way I had handled the arrest. Scrolling through the news the previous evening, I had noticed something to that effect, but had not paid much attention. She also told me that the Jewish community intended to give us an award at some special event. Trying to get out of it, I told her we would see when I got back, and that I wasn't interrupting my trip in any case.

When we hung up, I thought about disabling tracking and vanishing from the world for the next couple of months. My finger hovered over the screen for a second. But I decided to leave it for another day. Anyway, only she had access to my phone.

Between talking to Jill, and all the memories that came gushing like a river as I passed familiar places, we reached the place where we would make a long stop to stretch our legs. The imposing castle of Platamonas appeared around a steep bend, and Destine wagged her tail wildly when she heard the magic word—walk!

I had rarely heard Destine bark since she had moved in with me, and then only if we came across a cat on one of our walks, bearing testament to the eternal vendetta between the two species. As soon as I pulled up under a shady tree, she growled impatiently, wanting to get out.

I gazed at the archaeological edifice before me in awe. I had only ever encountered such a well-preserved castle once before, in Scotland. We left the road behind us and began to climb toward the castle walls. I removed Destine's leash, and she started to run all over the gentle slope of the hill, delighted.

It was not an arduous climb, and we reached the walls refreshed. The view that stretched before us was spectacular. On the one side, the sea, its unique shade of bright blue stretching as far as the eye could see. To the north, the tall peaks of Mt. Olympus, home of the gods in ancient times.

Absorbed by the view, I did not notice Destine sprint off toward a small dog she had spotted among the trees. I called out her name just in time. She froze to the spot and then obediently returned. A middle-aged woman rose from the bench where she had been gazing at the mountain and called the small dog to her. We exchanged a smile as I attached Destine's leash to her collar and urged her to return to the car.

Ignoring me, Destine pulled at the leash until we reached the small dog. They sniffed one another hungrily and wagged tails as I greeted the woman on the bench, apologizing for giving her a fright. She had beautiful, clear eyes, framed by a web of laughter lines. The breeze ruffled her white hair as she explained, in a quietly charming voice, that she lived nearby and often came to sit on this bench and enjoy the views toward the *Holy Mountain*, as she called it.

We chatted for a while, but time was pressing; we had to resume our journey. As I said goodbye, she quickly informed me that if I was in the area on the night of the full moon, I should come up to the castle and join in the festivities. I quickly counted the days in my head and told her that I would most likely be in Maronia at that time. Her face lit up, and she said in a low voice, "If you are so close to Ouranoessa, you should go watch the moon from there. Especially *this* full moon ..."

Before I could reply, Destine suddenly pulled on the leash, and I trotted down the hill behind her, trying to keep my balance and shouting a hasty goodbye over my shoulder.

Back in the car, Destine spent five minutes at the back and then came to sit beside me. She gave me a look of complete indifference, and settled down for the rest of the drive. We drove to Mt. Olympus, and I looked back up at the peak, covered in clouds. I wondered how the weather could change so fast, and sped on, in a straight line toward Thessaloniki. My distant cousins lived there, as had my grandparents before the war. Zoe had told me she had lived through horrors in that city, but had never gone into any detail.

Cities followed one another on this long journey, which resembled some rite of catharsis for me. All the hours spent on the road, hands gripping the wheel, helped me sort through my feelings, examine my own thoughts, settle my scores with the past in some way. People are afraid to spend time with themselves, but sometimes that is exactly what is needed. My grandmother had made her peace with death. Even when my father passed away, she did not grieve, not in the usual manner. She always said that living was the outcome of chance, and that only by accepting Death will find you whenever he wants could you exorcise your fear of dying.

A large road sign informed me that we were approaching the town of Komotini. Its wide roads and spacious layout initially impressed me. However, everything became narrower and more compact as we approached the center. The smell of fleshly ground coffee wafted through the windows, a smell I associated with summertime in Maronia when my grandmother made my father a Greek coffee in the morning.

Looking at the tall, beautiful buildings and the minarets of the mosques, I missed a turn. I hastily turned to my GPS, which was now pointing to the opposite direction of where I'd been headed.

Without realizing, I found myself in a shantytown and, to my great surprise, saw that people lived there; people who now stepped out and gave me strange looks. A group of stray dogs on the street made Destine rise up on the seat and give an angry growl. I patted her neck, trying to calm her down. I had seen similar neighborhoods in Mexico, but had no idea that a shantytown lay this close to Komotini.

The houses looked like old, roughly patched rags. Mounds of rubbish filled the narrow gaps between the slum houses. Small children ran naked and barefoot around a burning tire as thick black plumes of smoke wafted up to the sky. Every narrow alley I turned into led to a dead end. I spent some time hopelessly trying to find my way out of this maze, and then accepted that I would have to ask for directions.

On the outskirts of the gipsy settlement, I spotted a Muslim woman walking in my direction. She wore modern clothing and a headscarf, which highlighted the whiteness of her face. I smiled as I rolled down the window and asked for the way to the town center. She waved her hand and spoke a few words in Turkish. I was surprised she spoke no Greek. The only words I knew in her language were 'good morning,' and it was too late in the day to say even that.

I helplessly shrugged, and looked around to see if I could spot anybody else who could help. The street was deserted. I waved goodbye and made to turn around, when I suddenly heard her ask me if I spoke English. I grinned with relief and asked for directions once again. Her English was perfect, as she pointed to an alley behind her and explained the way out of this tangled web. I thanked her and, before she left, she came nearer and put her hand through the car window. She tenderly stroked Destine, whispering a few words in Turkish, like a blessing. My German Shepherd lay down on the seat as if obeying an order.

The woman smiled and mumbled a few words in English I could not make out clearly. I thanked her and replayed her words in my mind, trying to understand what they could mean. It was something about Destine and, possibly, how she was a dog with a human soul...

Finally, I arrived at the summerhouse in Maronia. A narrow dirt road led to the entrance of the small property. Two large plane trees guarded the passage to the house on either side. I remembered how, when I was a child, I would try to climb up their branches without great success, how Zoe would shout at me to be careful. Ivy covered nearly half the stone house. Olives and other trees hugged the old building, and the palm tree in the front garden was much taller than I remembered. The sun hid behind the clouds as it set, tinting the wet ground with a purple haze. It must have rained.

I spotted a number of parked cars in the yard. Someone saw me and ran to open the wide metal gates. I did not recognize the man who greeted me. He said he was the gardener who had been looking after the property for many years.

Once I parked, I ran to the passenger seat to let Destine out. I was surprised to see her hesitate. We had been driving non-stop for at least two hours, and I thought she would be jumping out in joy. I had to coax and pull her before she took a leap onto the grass. She walked around gingerly, tail hugged between her hind legs as if she was afraid. I paid her no more heed as I turned to Sophia, who came up and hugged me, her eyes brimming with tears.

Behind her, an elderly man ambled toward us, leaning heavily on a walking stick. Sophia introduced me to Vasilis, and returned to the house. I instantly noticed his missing ear, despite his attempts to hide it behind longish white hair. More people appeared on the steps behind him, raising a hand in greeting. The sudden, mournful sound of church bells reminded me that here the whole village would mourn the departed, young or old.

"You look so much like him..." Vasilis said, peering at me closely. I wasn't sure if he meant my father or my grandfather. "You look just like he did when I first saw him, seventy years ago. Same spark in his eyes ..." His own eyes welled up as he spoke.

I put my hand on his shoulder. "I am very happy to meet you, Vasilis. Sophia told me you took care of everything, and I want to thank you. I know my grandmother thought very highly of you, and I imagine my grandfather did, too."

My words seemed to touch a chord, and tears spilled down his wrinkled cheeks. Embarrassed, he brushed them away roughly. His voice shook when he spoke next. "I wish I had gone with him that night. At least that way I would know what became of him. There is no worse curse, my boy, than to not be able to mourn a man like you should. That sadness never left your grandmother ... never left me ..."

I pulled him in and gave him a hug. A few seconds later, he gently pulled back and pointed toward the house. "She lived a full life, and left when her time came. That is what Zoe wanted ...Today, we do not mourn. We celebrate her life, her legacy. That's the only way to look death straight in the eye." He took a deep breath and changed tack abruptly.

"Come inside, come see her. We'll hold a wake tonight and leave for the island in the morning."

He pointed his chin toward Samothrace, across the bay. Just like on Mt. Olympus, clouds had settled on Mt. Saos's peak. It was as if the gods hunched down behind the thick clouds, plotting the paths of mortals away from prying eyes.

We walked toward the house and reached one end of the corridor that led to Zoe's *balcony to the sky*. Beneath the gazebo, her chair stood turned toward the island. I could not pull my eyes away as I stepped inside the house.

Several people I did not know greeted me, giving me their condolences and the customary platitudes that go with such circumstances. I found these formalities insufferable, but I was patient. The church bells did not stop ringing. As soon as we crossed into the living room, I heard a low lament, a woman's soft voice.

A woman came up to me holding a tray of small glasses and offered me drink. The taste of cognac burned on my tongue as I slowly drank. Zoe's coffin stood in the middle of the large living room, filled with white and yellow roses. For the first time since news of her death reached me, I felt my chest burn as I tried to swallow my tears. The alcohol had nothing to do with it.

A group of local women standing around the coffin parted to let me through. Even the woman singing the lament lowered her voice, sounding barely louder than the rustling of the wind. I approached and stood beside Zoe silently. I leaned over and kissed her hand. Whatever had been Zoe, the essence of Zoe, was no longer in the body lying there, but somewhere around us, watching us.

I held her hand in mine for a few moments, then turned and walked outside. I was intrigued by the custom of holding a wake for the dead. It was an intermediary stage, when the worlds of the living and the dead met through the open souls of those mourning, refusing to be separated from their loved ones.

As soon as we were outside, Vasilis stopped at the top of the staircase, leaving me alone. The gardener was already by the car unloading my luggage. Destine walked ahead, down the paved corridor toward my grandmother's chair. She walked past the gazebo and stopped at the end, looking at the sea.

Dusk was falling, and I did not dare approach the spot where my grandmother had spent so much of her life at sunset. I could vividly sense her presence there. I preferred to sort out our sleeping arrangements, and returned to the car to pick up the rest of our things.

The small guesthouse, tucked away from the main house, would do perfectly. I used to spend many hours hiding there as a child, showing myself only when I felt they were really getting worried. Outside the bedroom, Destine curled up on a large carpet, showing that she had settled on her spot for the evening.

I unpacked a few things and pulled on a jumper, ready to take Destine for a walk. I was going to stay awake all night, too. It was the least I could do for the woman who had raised me.

Dominion of the Moon

Destine's low growl directed at the door coincided with the sound of knocking. Opening the door, I greeted a couple accompanied by two young children, who were looking at me curiously. I shouted at Destine to settle down, and then shook their hands. It did not take me long to figure out that they must be my second cousins, the grandchildren of Calliope, my grandfather's sister. The woman proudly announced that she was called Calliope too, named after her grandmother. I struggled to understand why they were here. My grandmother had had nothing to do with them during her lifetime. She had once mentioned that my grandfather's sister had not behaved well toward him, again keeping the details to herself.

I was in no mood to talk to them here and now, so I tried to worm my way out of a conversation, saying I had to walk the dog. They replied that there would be plenty of time to talk, as they would be joining us on the trip to Samothrace. The only silver lining was that they would be spending the evening at a hotel. I bid them goodnight and walked off, leaving the property and making my way to the sea.

It was getting dark, but the few street lamps along the way were enough to see by. The rocks on either side of the house were steep, but a small dirt path wound its way along the shore. A stone staircase at the side of the path led down to the beach, but I preferred to make my way along the coastline.

The waves below crashed on the shore. The land, with its sharp vertical drops toward the water, reminded me of parts of Scotland, where the only access to the shore was by the sea. I remembered my grandmother climbing down the rocks with such ease; whenever I asked how she did that, she would reply that that was how she had survived. During the day, the face of the small cliffs would be reflected in the waters below, mixing their earthy colors with the blue expanse.

I freed Destine and felt like she looked: as if I had just been released from the bonds that had been holding me captive. The cool breeze was a breath of freedom against my face. I turned toward the island, where the bright pinpricks of lit windows and streetlights flickered, a sign of life.

How wonderful it would have been to have Eva here with me. We had often talked of the island, but had never made it here. Her illness cruelly put a stop to all our dreams.

I paused and dreamily watched the island that had marked my family's existence. So many years had passed since then. It all seemed like a fairytale. I walked to a streetlight and sat on a large, flat rock beneath it. Destine, panting, ran up to stand beside me, enjoying the wonderful evening view of Samothrace. At times like this, I was convinced she and I felt exactly the same way.

Iro stood on the highest stone rampart, gazing across the sea toward the mainland. The wind tore at her long white dress, the fabric fluttering behind her like a pair of wings ready to carry her away. Her hair streamed behind her in all directions, dark slashes against the white fabric.

Erato stepped onto the rampart and walked toward her. Sensing her friend's presence, Iro pointed to the lights of Maronia and spoke without turning to face her. "In ancient times, the prospective initiate would sail over from there. If they were not worthy, the gods would prevent their arrival, raising large waves that swallowed up their vessels."

Erato did not reply at first, giving her friend a few more minutes of quiet solitude. Then she gently touched her hand and said, "It is time. They are waiting for you. Remember, today is the first stage of my preparation. All will go well. You know what you must do."

Iron nodded and turned to follow her down the stairs that led to the courtyard. A crowd was gathered there. All along the wall, torches cast their red and orange glow on the expectant faces and black tunics. As soon as the two women appeared, the crowd parted. A drum could be heard from the depths of the passageway, drumming out the pace of their footsteps.

A large chair stood on a wooden dais at the center of the courtyard, covered in purple cloth. Erato, keeping her gaze fixed firmly ahead, slowly lowered herself onto the chair. Alexandros and Miltos stood in front of her, looking at her aloofly. Iro walked behind her and began to weave Erato's hair into an intricate knot. She then raised a clay amphora and poured its contents around the chair, forming a red circle. The smell of strong wine wafted up from the flagstones. She handed the amphora to Erato, who raised it to her lips and hungrily gulped down the remaining drops.

Two men appeared from under the arches, one of them holding a torch high above his head to light the way. The other man tightly gripped a black lamb. Ceremoniously, he approached the chair and laid the frightened animal in Erato's lap. As soon as the helpless lamb felt the strong hands release their grip, it kicked and jerked in a desperate bid for freedom. Startled, Iro helped Erato take the animal into her arms. Holding the lamb tightly against her bosom, Erato rose and stood before the two men.

The man who had been carrying the lamb now held an iron rod against the flames until it glowed a deep red. Alexandros stepped forward and received the rod. His daughter's frightened glance met his, and he glowered at her to come to her senses. Iro, fully understanding the stern message in that look, gripped the animal's hind legs to hold it steady. Varvis raised the branding iron and seared the animal's flesh.

The lamb let out a bleat of agony as the hot metal made contact with its skin, and desperately struggled to escape. Iro, standing beside Erato, turned her head away, unable to stand the sight of its agony. Varvis handed the iron back to the man, then raised his hands to the sky. Accompanied by the bleating of the lamb, his voice rang out across the courtyard.

All is born of fire.

His phrase echoed three times, repeated by the gathered faithful. One of them took the lamb and exited through the passageway. Erato returned to her chair as one by one they knelt before her, each leaving a small pouch wrapped in black fabric beside her feet.

Once the last gift had been left beside her, Erato stood up. Her clear voice broke out in a hymn as she picked up the pouches and emptied their contents onto the circle of wine that surrounded her. Soil fell on the red liquid and became thick, blood-colored mud.

She then gripped Iro and led her to the chair. Iro sat and lowered her head, closing her eyes as if she did not want to see what would follow. Each of the men took a torch and approached her. Alexandros stepped forward and lifted her chin. She opened her eyes, expressionless, and stood up. She bent down and kissed his hand.

Alexandros slowly removed one of his rings and pulled a leather cord through it. Under the sound of a whispered chant that grew louder and louder, he placed the leather cord around her neck and tied the two ends together. The chant died down abruptly when he stepped back.

"In three days, with the coming of the full moon, we will be celebrating the beginning of a new era," he solemnly announced. "You will be the witnesses, the partakers of that great moment, set by our ancestors in their scriptures. The ring will anoint the Chosen One's finger during the ceremony. The earth you have brought from all the sacred lands will house this new dawn. In three days, all shall die, and all shall be reborn, through the body of the Great Mother."

He beckoned Miltos to join him. Taking the young man by the shoulders, he gently guided him so he stood beside Iro, who looked on, stunned. She froze at her father's next words.

"With the union of the next generation, the first great cycle ends. Tomorrow, we await the remaining chosen ones for the second phase. With the blessings of the Moon, we will come even closer to the gods and their commands."

Holding a large tray laden with clay cups, a woman made her way through the gathering, handing out drinks. When the last cup had been handed to Iro, Alexandros raised his cup in a toast. "The initiation rites have been passed down from generation to generation, to reach us today, unsoiled by the scum who would taint it. Those who dared betray the vows of silence were punished as they deserved, without mercy."

He brought the cup to his lips and downed the drink in a single gulp. The others did the same. The sound of the drum grew louder and louder. Like a swarm of bees, everyone gathered around Iro. The beat and the rhythm became stronger, faster, mingling with their voices in a chaotic song that came to an abrupt end as soon as it reached its peak.

For a few seconds, only the whistle of the wind through the cracks in the tall walls broke the silence. Alexandros, annoyed at his daughter's awkward stance, discreetly nudged her to move toward the passageway. As if in a trance, Iro walked away. Everyone parted to make way, breaking their cups on the flagstones as she moved past them, Erato accompanying her exit with a soft melody.

As they made their way into the dark shadows, a man raised his arms to the sky and began to chant loudly in ancient Greek:

Awful mysteries which no one may in any way transgress or pry into or utter, for deep awe of the gods checks the voice.

Happy is he among men upon earth who has seen these mysteries; but he who is uninitiate and who has no part in them, never has lot of like good things once he is dead, down in the darkness and gloom.[1]

---

[1] To Demeter/The Homeric Hymns and Homerica with an English Translation by Hugh G. Evelyn-White. Homeric Hymns. Cambridge, MA.,Harvard University Press; London, William Heinemann Ltd. 1914

I took a long shower as soon as we returned to the guesthouse. After that, I felt ready to enter the house, to be close to my grandmother. I left Destine behind, lying on her chosen spot, worn out by the long walk.

It was past midnight, and all was quiet. The soft sea breeze greeted me as I stepped outside, and it accompanied me to the front porch of the house, where Vasilis sat on a deck chair waiting for me. The door was open, and I could see a handful of women inside, settled on couches and armchairs, ready to spend the night. I pulled up a chair and sat beside Vasilis.

"How was the walk?" he asked.

"Good. I don't remember the last time I walked around in these parts. It's still as beautiful as it was back then." I turned to look at the sea. "Have my cousins left?"

He smirked. "Yes, they only stayed a short while, and then went to have dinner. We'll meet them on the boat tomorrow, in Alexandroupolis."

I was dying to find out why they were suddenly showing such concern for a woman they had spent most of their life ignoring. "Why are they here now?" I asked, and he smirked again.

"You'll find out tomorrow, son." Seeing my worried frown, he hurriedly added, "It's nothing to worry about. They are here for a very specific reason, and you will find out tomorrow. It's up to you what you decide. Now is not the time to concern yourself with them ..."

He bent down and picked up something wrapped in paper. "Your grandmother had given this to Sophia, with strict instructions that I should give it to you if I were still alive. You understand ... She knew the end was near, and she wanted you to have it. She drew the story of her life, from the moment she met your grandfather. It's all here, like a picture diary, as she remembered it and put it down on paper."

I carefully unwrapped it. A full moon and Samothrace's dark outline were drawn on the sketchbook cover. I struggled to read the word written above it, but as soon as I made out the syllables, I remembered having heard that word before. The voice of the woman at the castle came to my mind as I whispered, "Ouranoessa," trying to understand what it meant.

Vasilis picked up the question in my voice and tried to explain. "It's what some people call Samothrace," he said, pointing in the direction of the island. "You'll see the rest inside the sketch book."

I turned over some of the pages, glancing at the beautiful drawings. I wanted to be alone when I looked at it more carefully. I stood up. "I think I'll head inside."

"You do that, son. You do as your heart desires."

I walked inside, leaving Vasilis on his deck chair. The house was lit by dozens of candles. A woman pointed to a chair where I should sit. I sat there silently for a long while, surrounded by the quiet women, the sketchbook resting on my lap. Hushed conversations would break out briefly, and then silence would return.

What a shame I had not spent more time with Zoe. I knew she was having health troubles, but I did not do everything I could to visit her. I had thrown myself into work, told myself there would be plenty of time later. I so wanted to share the news of the Nazi we had arrested; I think she would have been glad to hear it. She had been so interested in that case. She kept saying that, eventually, we all pay the price for our actions. Even though she had become forgetful in her old age, she retained the things that interested her.

From the corner of my eye, I caught Vasilis beckoning me. I tiptoed in his direction. He whispered that he was going to bed, and that there was no reason for me to spend the night sitting there. He urged me to get as much rest as I could. We had a difficult day ahead of us tomorrow. I wished him goodnight, and went to the garden for a walk.

There was no way I could manage to get some sleep. I walked down the paved corridor and reached the gazebo and her empty chair, the last remnant of all her memories. Strangely, I felt her presence more strongly here than when I had been staring at her dead body. Maybe her soul was still sitting here, at her beloved spot.

I walked to the edge, feeling uneasy as to what I should do. After a lot of thought, I decided to sit in her chair. I thought something might happen when I did, but everything remained the same.

Dominion of the Moon

I gazed up at the carved roof of the gazebo. A sudden thought made me sit up straight. In the chaos of last-minute travel arrangements, I had forgotten to notify Zoe's old friends and colleagues in New York about her passing. None of the archaeologists she had met on Samothrace were still alive, but my grandmother had kept in touch with other people she had met at work, even after her retirement. It was obviously too late for anyone to come to the funeral, even if they had wanted to, but I felt she would have wanted me to let them know.

I typed a short message and sent it to the person in charge of human resources, feeling bad about having neglected to inform them. I did not think anyone would come all this way, but in any case, they ought to know. My phone buzzed and, to my great surprise, I saw a reply. "We are sorry for the loss of your grandmother. The head of archaeological research is in Alexandroupolis already, and will be attending the funeral tomorrow, representing us all. Please accept our deepest condolences."

Someone had obviously informed them, and I was stunned anyone would attend. I was glad, in any case, that those who had known and loved her would be present for tomorrow's last goodbye. It confirmed what I already knew, that she had been admired and respected.

I opened the sketchbook, but it was too dark to see. I leaned back against the chair, taking in the view she had enjoyed all these years. Tears filled my eyes, and a flood of memories broke through the dam of my defenses.

I sobbed, alone under the gazebo, feeling the grief for my grandmother and everything that had hurt me ...

Most of the guests had left the tower. Only a handful remained in the courtyard, sweeping up the clay shards that lay scattered on the flagstones. Varvis asked Miltos to send them away, and then tell Iro to come see him. Miltos did as asked, and a few minutes later stepped back out, closely followed by Iro. Her eyes were red and puffy.

Alexandros motioned for them to join him at the table, and immediately turned to his daughter. "I understand you are under a lot of pressure, my child," he said calmly. "Luckily, everyone thought your awkwardness was just nerves. I know you will be ready by the full moon and we will not have a repeat of tonight."

He paused, waiting for an answer, and when Iro bowed her head in acquiescence, he continued. "You understand that you carry the history of countless generations on your shoulders, and that you must rise to the task. Until you bear a son, you will be everyone's Great Mother." Suddenly, as if he could no longer contain the rage boiling inside him, he brought his fist down hard on the table, sending a glass flying to the floor. "Don't you ever dare question what we stand for, not for as long as I live!" he shouted.

Iro and Miltos froze. Even the wind seemed to pause and stand still before this angry outburst. "Do you understand? Or are you going to humiliate us again before our guests?"

Iro was shocked. She had never seen her father like this before. Shaking, she nodded, showing she understood. She stood up to leave, but her father grabbed her arm, forcing her to sit back down. "Do you understand?" he screamed in her face.

Unable to do anything else, Iro looked him in the eye and drily said, "Yes." She then pulled her hand away and went back inside.

Miltos stood up to follow her, but Varvis motioned for him to stay. "Bring us a drink," he shouted insolently, sweeping the remaining glasses off the table. His face had turned red, the veins at his temple visibly throbbing. He turned to Miltos, who stood rooted to the spot. "It is time you know which part you play in the initiation ceremony. My daughter needs to understand once and for all what it means to submit to our beliefs."

Confused, Miltos sat back down and waited. As soon as the servant brought a tray with drinks, Alexandros shooed her away and lowered his voice. In great detail, he began to explain what would happen in a few days ...

We had just reached the port of Alexandroupolis, the ferry already waiting at the dock, "Saos" written in large letters on its side. I had decided to take Destine with me and spend a few days on the island. Vasilis occupied the passenger seat beside me, so for the first time on this journey, Destine had to content herself with the back seat of the car.

Ahead, the hearse that carried my grandmother was pulling up by the ferry. All I had asked of Sophia was that things be kept simple, without any extravagant floral displays or wreaths. All of us formed a small funeral procession; only a few neighbors had joined us from Maronia.

I had fallen asleep on Zoe's chair the previous night, to be woken a couple of hours later when one of the women at the wake covered me with a blanket. I got up then and stayed beside my grandmother until the morning, when the hearse arrived.

The ship would be departing in a few minutes, and I was impressed by the number of travelers waiting to board. "How come there are so many people today, in September?" I asked Vasilis.

"It's the full moon in a few days. Most are here for this full moon," he solemnly replied.

"What's so special about this full moon?" I asked.

Vasilis shifted uncomfortably in his seat and did not reply, pointing instead to the port guard checking everyone's tickets. He picked up his ticket from the dashboard and stepped outside the car, saying he would meet me inside. I was puzzled by his odd behavior, but did not press him. Instead, I drove on and parked in the ferry's garage, right behind the hearse.

I walked up to the car carrying my grandmother's lifeless body and placed my palm against the tinted window. Unlike Eva, Zoe had lived a full life, despite the difficult war years. A couple of other passengers gave me strange looks as they walked toward the stairs leading to the decks, but made no comment.

I turned to my car and saw Destine anxiously looking at me. It was a brief crossing, so I preferred to leave her in the car with the windows rolled down. She would initially go with Vasilis once we arrived, until I checked the hotels to see if any of them accepted pets. Vasilis's house had a large, enclosed garden, and he had offered to host us for the duration of our stay. I had politely declined, saying it would not be easy with Destine. Vasilis had no children. His wife had passed away a few years ago, and he lived alone. However, I needed to spend time alone. I wanted a quiet, peaceful break.

I walked to the lounge and found my travelling companions gathered around a coffee table. As soon as I had taken a seat beside Vasilis, my cousin came near me, asking if I wanted a drink. I politely declined, but Vasilis replied that he would like a coffee, despite not being asked.

She gave him a look of displeasure, but got up and went to the bar.

"That buys us five minutes of quiet," he said in a low voice, suppressing a chuckle.

"I think I'll step outside," I said. "It's stifling in here."

"You do that." He winked.

I stepped onto the deck, and suddenly felt as if I had been transported to another decade. A large group that sat on the floor reminded me of people in the sixties, with their hair and clothes and guitars, which they strummed in an indeterminate melody.

I heard someone clear his throat behind me, and saw a middle-aged man with a thick moustache. He asked me, in English, if I was Zoe's grandson. I nodded. He introduced himself, and I shook his hand warmly; he was the head of the American team of archaeologists on Samothrace. He mentioned Alkistis, and said that Vasilis, whom he knew, had pointed out who I was.

He spoke fondly not only of Zoe, but of my grandfather, too. He had been in France, at the Louvre, when he had heard about Zoe's death. They were attempting to make a digital map of the Winged Victory statue, so that two exact replicas could be made. If they succeeded, one of the replicas would be placed at the Sanctuary, and the other at the port we had just left.

We chatted for a while, sharing news of New York, and agreed to have a coffee at the Sanctuary the following day. His parting words left an impression on me. He said he might be able to trace something that might interest me, in which case he would send it to me. I could not understand what he meant, but I caught sight of my cousin determinedly striding toward us, so hastened our goodbye.

It did not take me long to fathom my relative's sudden interest in talking to me. My cousin informed me that a small plot of land on the island now belonged to both of us. She felt it was best to make use of this visit to settle all the paperwork and divide our inheritance. I understood full well that she just wanted me to let her have the whole plot.

She was so pushy that I told her I would give her my answer after the funeral. I wanted to discuss the matter with Vasilis first. Not that I was interested in owning property on the island. She ignored my request and kept pushing her case, forcing me to tell her abruptly that it was inappropriate to discuss such matters before Zoe had even been laid to rest.

I remained on the deck, mulling things over, then returned to the lounge. I sat beside Vasilis, who had seen my cousin follow me outside. He said, "Now that you understand why your cousins have suddenly remembered Zoe, make up your own mind. I know you will ask for my advice, so here it is. Give them everything. That place is cursed."

I did not ask him why. Instead, I turned to look at my relations, who smiled at me across the table, waiting to see whether they had gotten what they were after.

My grandmother's funeral had been scheduled for early afternoon. As soon as we arrived on Samothrace, we stopped at Vasilis's house to drop off Destine, then drove to Paleopolis. The cemetery was situated on a beautiful spot overlooking the sea, and I immediately understood why Zoe wanted to be buried here.

I did not know most of the funeral guests, but saw that most were familiar faces from Maronia, along with a handful of locals. The American archaeologist and Alkistis were among them. I appreciated her coming, and thanked her profusely.

It was a brief service. I lingered on as everyone made their way to the coffee shop, where refreshments awaited. Vasilis walked up to me and said, "All your ancestors on your grandfather's side are buried here. All except one."

"My grandfather."

Vasilis bit his trembling lip, then changed the subject by pointing further up the hill, to a spot sheltered by two cypress trees. "That one is booked."

I looked at him questioningly, and he laughed. "I kept a nice little plot for myself."

Vasilis turned to go, but something made him freeze to the spot. He stood, gaping, at the top of a hill across the cemetery, where a man stood looking down on us. It was too far away to see who it was. I could just make out a silhouette in dark clothes. "Who is it?" I asked.

He did not immediately reply. "I can't see; it's too far away. I'm going to the car."

His evasiveness surprised me. The man at the top of the hill did not move, and we both stood rooted to the spot, staring at each other as if in a standoff. Then the man abruptly turned and disappeared down the hill.

How odd, I thought to myself, as I turned to look at the mound of fresh soil that covered Zoe's grave. I had already buried three people I desperately loved; I was almost becoming used to it. I've always believed that those we love only die when they are forgotten, when the last person who knew them passes away, taking any last memories with them.

I kneeled down, leaving a yellow rose beside the grave, and placed my palm on the moist soil. Then I stood up, impatient for the formalities to be over and to find myself on my own at last.

Even though I had an eerie feeling, I felt I would like this island. Vasilis had been a treasure trove of information on what to visit, and I intended to make the most of the water pools and woods the following day. I would be visiting the museum and the Sanctuary later in the afternoon. First, I had to deal with my cousins and their demands …

Dominion of the Moon

When all the post-funeral formalities were over, I dropped Vasilis off at his house to rest, and we agreed to meet the following day. With no outstanding matters to attend to, I could not wait to finally be left alone. I followed his advice and, without even going to see the plot of land I had inherited, I told my cousin I waived all my claims and I would sign everything needed for the land to pass to her in its entirety. As politely as possible, I asked her not to bother me with this matter again.

In the meantime, Vasilis had managed to both surprise and move me. He asked me if I wanted to stay at the house Elizabeth had lived in during her time on Samothrace. It had been renovated, and was now rented out to tourists. It had a large, secure garden, which meant I could safely leave Destine alone, and it was immediately available. We went to the house with the owner and, after a brief tour, he handed me the keys and left me there.

Yellow roses covered one of the garden walls in its entirety, and the garden was cool and shady, dotted with fruit trees. A hammock hung between two tree trunks, the perfect picture of a relaxing holiday. By the staircase, a large pomegranate tree stood, laden with fruit round and bright like the decorations on a Christmas tree. The courtyard was filled with all kinds of potted plants, mostly geraniums and herbs. I ran my hand over a basil plant and brought my palm to my nostrils, a movement I had learned from my grandmother, inhaling its delicious aroma.

So many memories woken by a simple scent! At afternoon Greek classes in New York, my teacher's name was Basiliki, and I'd always thought she was named after the plant.

I set my memories aside and admired the beautiful house. Made of old stone, its two floors were exceedingly well maintained. I would stay on the first floor. The basement had not been used in years. Even the door keys were those giant iron keys you rarely found these days.

Destine could not get enough of the place, sniffing everything. As soon as I stepped inside, I was met with the sweet smell of jasmine. I looked around, but there were no flowers in the house. Walking further in, I was overjoyed at the sight of an antique four-poster bed standing in the middle of the high-ceilinged bedroom.

The house was old, but so warm and welcoming it immediately felt familiar. Its walls were covered with old black and white photos, possibly left behind by Elizabeth. They showed the group of archaeologists who had been there in the forties at work. I stood before a photo I had seen thousands of times at our home in New York. It was one of the rare photos we had of my grandfather. He stood beside Zoe and the rest of the team, around the headless statue of the Winged Victory they had just discovered. Only the date was written beneath. I did not know whether any of the people in that photo were still alive. My grandmother was probably the last of the group, and now she was reunited with them.

As soon as I unpacked, I left Destine in the courtyard and headed out in search of lunch. I would then visit the archaeological site. I pulled the carved iron gates shut behind me, and my beautiful German Shepherd stuck her nose between the bars and watched me until I turned the corner. The people I passed on the way to the car seemed friendly and polite; welcoming.

A few minutes later, I drove to the Chora, situated on one of the most beautiful locations on the island. Here, too, people seemed kind and warm. Only once I was at the square did I notice a woman pointing me out to a group of elderly men, who then turned to stare at me with odd expressions. I paid no attention, and sat at a small taverna Vasilis had recommended. The weather was splendid, and the shade beneath the enormous plane tree soothing. A few tourists milled about, taking photos of the old houses covered in red bougainvilleas.

I asked the waitress to pick my lunch for me. I'd never forgotten the wonderful taste of Greek fish dishes, and looked forward to tasting them once again. The elderly men who had been giving me odd looks were now marching in my direction like a firing squad. A few others had joined their ranks. They walked past me, and looked at me as if they had just seen a ghost. I did not want to add water to the rumor mill, so I ignored them, picking up my phone to check my mail.

I saw an email from Jill asking for photos of the island. I lifted my phone and turned the camera in the direction of the elderly men. They looked great against the scattered coffee tables in the square and the old buildings. They were startled to find themselves photographed, and quickly dispersed. I smiled and raised my wine glass at them. Obviously, that was not the response they had been expecting. A few minutes later, they had all left the square.

Jill emailed me back quickly, enthusing over the cute, little, old men, and bringing a sarcastic smile to my face. I settled down to a hearty lunch of fresh fish and local vegetables and then returned to my car, to head down to the famous Sanctuary of the Great Gods.

I was finally inside the museum at the base of the hill. Although I had expected it to be bigger, it was still imposing. I had just spoken to the American Head of Excavations, and Alkistis was kindly giving me a tour of the museum, which was being renovated.

Her voice echoing against the walls, she filled me in on the museum's history. "Building began in 1939, but was only completed after the war in 1955 by the American School of Classical Studies in Athens. It was designed by Stuart Shaw of the Metropolitan Museum of Art in New York. The building was expanded in 1960, with the addition of the northern wing. As I told you in Athens, it mostly houses the finds discovered at the Sanctuary of the Great Gods. Most of them are at the Acropolis Museum for the exhibition right now. They are returning tomorrow.

"Your grandfather came here at the end of the war, and his contribution during his brief time with the team was significant. The work of those people continues today, and is the basis of many of our present discoveries, teaching us how the past is reflected in the present. Inspiring us to continue their work ..."

Alkistis walked further ahead and paused before a wall. "Normally, the inscription that was found then would hang here. It forbade entrance to the uninitiated. I think you saw it in Athens, though. Let's go to the storeroom, where you can see the plaster replica of the Winged Victory. The original is in the Louvre, as you know."

I nodded and followed her. Covered in a large white sheet, the famous statue stood at the center of the room. Alkistis tugged at its corner, and it fell away, revealing the headless statue. "Your grandfather was fascinated by this goddess. I read the entries in the Americans' logs, and I could tell how desperately he hoped that the head of one of the Winged Victories would someday be found."

"All the statues have been found headless?" I asked, surprised.

Alkistis nodded despondently.

"Isn't that strange?" I insisted.

"Strange as it sounds, many statues are found with missing parts, either damaged in earthquakes or vandalized. We could well find a head at some point in the future. It could be anywhere. It could be buried somewhere on the island, at the bottom of the sea, or even decorating the home of a wealthy collector anywhere in the world."

Filled with zeal, and eager to impart knowledge, she spoke animatedly. "The island of Samothrace was one of the most important religious centers of the ancient world. The cult of the Great Gods revolved around the figure of the Great Mother. There is an impressive lack of detail as to what the Cabirian Mysteries actually entailed. There is a theory that Phillip of Macedon met Olympias here, and that Alexander the Great was conceived after their union at the site. Homer refers to Samothrace as *Zathay*, meaning venerable, holy. He also calls it the Sacred Land. '*Venerable Samothrace, where ceremonies strike fear, performed for the sake of the gods and remaining hidden to mortals ...*'"

Despite the warm day, I felt a shiver at those words. Alkistis pointed to a photo on the wall, showing a ring evidently discovered many years ago. "The power of the Mother of the Rocks was expressed in the stones and magnetite they used to make these rings. Every prospective initiate received such a ring while preparing for initiation into the Holy House. They believed that wearing the ring brought mortals in direct contact with the divine."

She led me outside the room, speaking in a low voice. "We know very little about the past and the present. In any case, shortly after your grandfather's disappearance, the Lehmanns formed the theory that the temple was, and may still be, the most important site of the secret religious rites of ancient Greece. During excavations in 1949, the bones of sheep and pigs were discovered at the *Hieron* Temple. The altar where the votive sacrifices took place was constructed so that the blood of the sacrificial animals would descend straight to Hades. Animals played an important part in those rites. Homer adds that witches would turn the marrow of the slaughtered animals into love potions."

We stepped out into the sunshine, and my attention was caught by a curious sight. I felt Alkistis tense beside me. A group of visitors, all dressed in white, was making its way along the narrow path and would soon be passing before us. In their midst, I noticed a woman wearing a scarlet belt. The long scarf draped over her head hid her features. Like a flock of swans, they drifted in front of us. For a moment, the woman with the headscarf raised her eyes in our direction, casting me a glance. It was so fast that all I could see was the spark in her eyes.

As soon as they were out of sight, Alkistis explained with a smile, "Many ceremonies take place on the island on the night of the full moon. People come here and celebrate their own religion, interpreting whatever information we have on cult rites whichever way they like."

"And how is this group of people related to ..."

She looked around to make sure no one was listening, and pulled me away from the building. "Some of the people you just saw are locals. The rest are delegates, if you like, from other sacred sites of Ancient Greece: Eleusis, Delphi, Athens, cities in Lower Italy, and other areas that were cult sites of the Ancient gods. I have been told that these ones claim to be the heirs of the cult of the Cabeiri. Of course, none of them will confirm that."

"What are they doing here, then?" I asked, trying to understand.

"As I told you, I am doing research on cult rites and ancient initiation ceremonies. For some reason, this year and this month's full moon is very important to them. The fact is, I don't know exactly what they will do, because the whole thing is shrouded in complete secrecy. Remember what I told you? Those participating would take a vow of silence. Punishment for breaking that vow was death."

What she said was intriguing, but I was preoccupied by something else. "Who was the woman with the red belt?" I asked with forced nonchalance.

"I didn't see her face, but I imagine she is a high-ranking member of that group. I feel I've seen her before, but I can't put my finger on it," Alkistis replied, frowning in their direction.

I was impressed by what she had said. My travels and my work had shown me that there were many who still believed and practiced various ancient religions. In many Latin American and African countries, black magic rituals had spread like wildfire, and they were beginning to show up in the West, too. Based on the cases that were coming to light, it was easy to see that most times people were just satisfying their sexual perversions under the cloak of a cult or an invented, misleading religion.

A man stepped outside the museum and called Alkistis. "How long will you be staying, in the end?" she asked, looking at me intently.

"Still undecided, if you can believe it," I said evasively.

"I believe it. It is best not to decide. The island itself will show you whether it wishes you to stay, and for how long ..."

I raised my eyebrows quizzically. She did not reply, just said she would love to talk again. I smiled awkwardly, thanking her for the tour, and we parted ways.

As I walked toward the exit, I tried to picture the temple complex as it must have looked thousands of years ago.

Seeing the site filled me with pride for my grandfather. For some inexplicable reason, I could not get the image of the headless statue out of my mind ...

Dominion of the Moon

In the company of the archaeologists and Vasilis, the evening went by quickly and pleasantly. We were on the outskirts of Paleopolis, dining at the aptly named taverna *Ta Kymata*: The Waves. Our chairs were on the sand, a hairsbreadth away from the waves. We lifted our legs whenever the wind rose and washed the waves under the tables. Everything we ate was so fresh you could almost taste the saltwater, as if it had just been fished beside us right there and then.

If I ever returned to Samothrace, I would like to stay at the guestrooms atop the taverna and enjoy the sea views; the open, uninterrupted horizon. I had travelled far and wide, but nowhere had I encountered the beauty of Greece.

We drank wine and chatted about old folk stories and island lore. Whenever I turned the conversation to my grandfather, though, Vasilis would change the subject, looking at me pointedly, as if not wishing to talk of him in front of the others.

I was still unaccustomed to the late hours the Greeks kept, and after a few glasses of wine, I felt it was time for me to return to the lonely Destine. Despite my tiredness, I wanted to take her for a long evening walk along the path that led from the back of the house to the woods. First, though, I would be giving Vasilis a lift to his own house.

The American head of the team somehow got hold of the bill and paid for everyone. I felt bad. I should have been the one paying tonight. He would be returning to France the following day, to resume his mission at the Louvre. Alkistis had joined us, and we agreed to meet up sometime in the next couple of days. I could sense she might like me, and I did not want to lead her on. She was a pretty, likeable woman, but I did not feel ready even for a harmless flirtation at this time.

Driving back to his house, Vasilis was unusually quiet. "The house is filled with photos from that time," I said, trying to break the melancholy silence.

Vasilis did not reply, so I decided to unburden myself and voice what I had been dying to ask all evening. "Vasilis, what happened to my grandfather that night? I feel like you might know more than the rumors that spread after his disappearance."

"I wish I knew, son. The agony of not knowing has not left me in all these years."

I could tell he was tearing up, and I touched his shoulder, trying to communicate my sympathy. Luckily, I kept my eyes on the road, and I stepped on the brakes just in time to avoid the dark shadow that sprung out from the nearby bushes.

The fox, hypnotized, froze and stared at the headlights. Luckily, Vasilis was wearing his seatbelt, or he would have landed on the dashboard. He stared back at the fox in surprise. I honked, and the fox snapped out of its trance and sprinted off to the side of the road. With a sigh of relief, I drove on.

"I find a dead fox every few days; it's as if they are committing suicide," Vasilis said, leaning back against the headrest.

"You were about to tell me something, just then," I gently reminded him. "About my grandfather."

Vasilis took a deep breath, lost in thought for a few seconds. "So many years have passed since then. If your grandfather had been alive, he would have turned up somewhere. If you are asking me what I think happened, all I can say with any certainty is ..." Another long pause followed, as he tried to keep his composure. "He never left the island ..."

I could feel my curiosity flare up inside me. "Who accused him of stealing, back then?"

Vasilis sighed once again, and turned toward me. "It's good to let sleeping dogs lie. If it's any help, none of them are alive today. My advice is: don't dig up the past. Enjoy your present, your time here, and do not burden yourself with anything else."

I realized that was all I would get from him. I pulled up beside his front door and asked one last question. "Do you know anything about the ceremonies that are going to take place on the night of the full moon?"

He seemed surprised. "Who told you about this?"

I smiled; Vasilis spoke to me as if I were a young boy. "Come on, Vasilis. It's no secret these things happen here! I knew about them even before I came to Samothrace. I'm not talking about tourists, though. I'm asking about the people who live on the island."

He picked up his walking stick and opened the door. Hobbling around the car, he came over to my side and leaned with his elbow on the roof of the car. "Have fun on your excursion tomorrow. Swim in the water pools; feel the soul of the island. They say that if you duck underwater, you can hear a beating heart. Don't drink the water, though! Another legend has it that if you drink water from the springs of Samothrace, you will marry shortly, so if you don't intend to ..."

Vasilis laughed heartily at his own joke, then suddenly sobered up. "Remember what I told you. Don't go stirring up the past. Let sleeping dogs lie. You have been through a lot, and need to rest. Enjoy the rest of your stay. Goodnight, Andreas." He nodded to me, and then hobbled away.

I watched him in the dim light as he opened his garden gate and disappeared down the short path that led to his house. Maybe I should heed his advice, I thought. Have a real holiday, without any worries. Take Destine for a walk, then spend a quiet night going through the sketchbook my grandmother had left me. Although I feared that doing so would only make my curiosity about what had happened to my grandparents on Samothrace even greater.

Dominion of the Moon

As soon as Vasilis opened his front door, a voice rang out in the dark. "Don't lock the door, Vasilis. I won't spend all night here."

Seated in an armchair, Alexandros Varvis lit a candle and motioned to Vasilis to close the door and come near him …

Destine was already waiting impatiently by the garden gates when I reached the house. I attached her leash and set off for the footpath behind the building. The moon was waxing and would be a bright, round disk in a few days. We walked uphill through the woods and came out at a clearing near the top of the hill. I removed the leash and let Destine run ahead.

To the right, the imposing shadow of Mt. Saos stretched up toward the sky, as if trying to reach the moon. Although the full moon was near, the stars sparkled in the clear skies, trying to steal some of its glowing glory.

Destine's low, menacing growl pulled my gaze away from the star-studded dome above, and in the direction of another hilltop in the distance. Someone had lit a large bonfire, its glowing tongues flickering against the dark skyline. I tried to see if it was a campfire, but it seemed to be unattended. I bent down and patted Destine's head, trying to calm her down, feeling the vibrations of her continued growls against my palm.

That's when I noticed a second fire, further to the right, lighting up the stony landscape. I stood up and turned around. Another, larger, bonfire, to my left this time.

Finding my bearings, it suddenly dawned on me that the three fires marked north, east, and west. I turned to the south and, sure enough, saw the orange and red flickering flames up another small hill. Strangely enough, they all seemed unattended, burning ever brighter as if of their own volition. Whoever had lit them was taking care to go unseen.

Destine's eyes remained fixed on the fire she had spotted to the north. Ears pricked, back legs angled out behind her, she turned her head to the side, a sign she was picking up sounds I could not hear.

I realized that I was standing at the center of the four flaming points of a cross. Destine suddenly began to walk off in the direction of the fire. The hill we had climbed up dropped abruptly on the other side, and I ordered her to come back. She barked aggressively at the fire that had angered her so, but turned back nonetheless. There was no point in staying here any longer. The fires were too far away to make any sense of their purpose. No matter how desperately I wanted to relax, the bizarreness of what was happening was making me tense.

Back in the house, I finally began to unwind. Lying down on the couch, Destine at my feet, I put down my wine glass and picked up Zoe's sketchbook. I began to leaf through it, carefully this time, picking out every detail. The figure of the Winged Victory of Samothrace dominated most of the drawings. Among them, portraits of my grandfather. I had only ever seen a couple of photos.

Her sketches vividly depicted the man she had loved more than anyone in the world. Looking at the details, taking in the love and passion every stroke of her pencil exuded, I wondered whether the only love to stand the test of time was unfulfilled love. Were lifetime lovers only those whose love affair was cut short, before it became altered by day-to-day life, by continuous contact? I felt the same way about Eva. I lost her just when our love was at its most vibrant, its most beautiful.

In the history of humanity, strong love stories that stood the test of time were those that went unfulfilled. Lovers separated, often violently, their myth gaining eternal life through the centuries. My grandmother always believed that one day her lover would return. She kept staring out at the sea, hoping to see a boat bring him to her. Just like in the sketch that I now held before me. I had never seen her drawings before, had not realized she had an artist's talent.

I felt my eyelids grow heavy, and rose with difficulty to make my way to my bed. Destine lifted her head off the carpet, alert, following my every move. When I turned the light off, my guard dog rose and came to lie in front of my bedroom door. Feeling safe, we abandoned ourselves in the arms of sweet Morpheus …

Destine's eyes glowed in the dark, as if the fires she had seen earlier had left their flames burning inside them. She kept her eyes wide open until she heard the breath of her master grow deep and steady. Only then did her eyelids slowly close, and the faithful dog fell into deep, yet anxious, slumber.

In the silver light of the full moon, Andreas slowly walks through a clearing in the woods. He pauses; looks up at the sky. The howl of a wolf raises the hairs at the back of his neck. Afraid, he looks around, trying to spot the origin of the nightmarish cry.

Small flames spring up in a circle all around him, trapping him there. He spins around anxiously, trying to find a way out. As soon as he finds a small gap in the ring of fire, he hurriedly moves toward it, but suddenly stops when the wolf appears.

The wolf is hunched low, white fangs bared, ready to attack. Having no other option, Andreas retreats back into the ring of fire. He can now feel the flames burning hot, scorching his back.

Another wolf steps out of the woods. Growling, the two animals menacingly move toward him. He has no other option but to fight for his life. He steps out the ring of fire, waving his arms.

With a sudden leap, one of the wolves lands on his chest, knocking him back. Pinned to the ground, he feels piercing pain in his arm. The other wolf, fangs locked into his flesh, begins to drag him back into the burning circle. More sharp pangs, all over his body. His cries mingle with the crackling of the flames and waft up to the sky.

The shadow of a man stands above him. A man holding a sword, pointed to the ground. Andreas struggles, trying desperately to free himself from the wolves' grip. They keep him on the ground, arms stretched as if he has been nailed to a cross.

The man kneels beside him and raises his hand, ready to plunge the sword into the prostrate man's heart. Just then, a shadow falls on him, tearing off the arm holding the sword ...

Destine kicked her legs and whimpered. The noise woke me suddenly, and I feared someone had broken in. I had heard her dream before, but never so intensely. I called out her name, but she did not seem to hear me, trapped in the world of her nightmare.

I turned on the light and walked to her, stretched out my hand to calm her down. Before I could even touch her fur, she lashed out like a cobra, and my wrist was caught in her mouth. I felt her teeth press my skin, but she immediately stopped, opened her eyes, and gave me a frightened look. She licked my hand as if nothing had happened, and her enormous yawn reassured me that the bite had been intended for someone else.

Beside my wrist tattoo, I saw the imprint of her teeth. I patted her and she lowered her head, looking ashamed. I remembered the words of the Muslim woman in Komotini, about how Destine had a human soul. Maybe that explained her bond with Eva. Eva asked for Destine even in her final moments, and they both glowed with happiness when they met.

I stroked her for a few moments and, having made certain she was calm, returned to bed. That was a close call, I thought to myself, as I caught sight of my wrist while stretching my hand to switch off the bedside lamp.

Vasilis and Alexandros sat across from each other in the living room in the dim light of the candle. On the coffee table between them stood a half empty glass jug and two wine glasses. Alexandros refilled his glass before he spoke. "So, the archaeologist's grandson is a policeman?"

"Not exactly," Vasilis said. "I think he works for an agency that goes after war criminals."

Alexandros seemed startled, but recovered quickly. "When did you say he leaves?" he asked suspiciously.

"He'll stay for a couple of days, and then go back. He wants to spend his holiday in Maronia, to rest. If she hadn't died, he might never have set foot on the island. He even gave away the plot of land, where the house that burned down was. I don't think he likes it here."

"That's good. He is lucky there was a funeral; otherwise, I would have had them chase him away. He's even got the same name as his thieving grandfather."

Vasilis stared at him pointedly, but held his tongue. Undeterred, Varvis continued. "Has anyone told him that his grandfather stole our ancient artifacts and then disappeared?"

Vasilis swallowed hard before speaking. "He doesn't care about all of that, boss. He knows very little, and I still don't think he cares much. He didn't seem interested in the past. Like I told you, he is leaving in a couple of days."

"How come you took him to the house where the American had been staying?"

Vasilis downed the dregs of his glass, trying to think of how to phrase his answer. "I needed to find him a place to stay where the dog would be welcome. It wasn't easy. The house has a garden ..."

Varvis gave him a look of disbelieving suspicion and leaned forward, returning his empty glass to the table. "I hope that is the case, Vasilis. Don't forget you have been making a living all these years thanks to us. If it hadn't been for my father, you would have lost this house when everyone abandoned you. Do you remember how the Americans turned their backs on you after Stais disappeared? You'd be living under a bridge if it weren't for my parents."

Vasilis nodded in silent agreement. Alexandros lowered his voice menacingly. "Make sure he is nowhere to be seen the day after tomorrow, then."

The old man tried to reassure him. "Don't worry. It will all happen as I told you."

Varvis picked up the jug and poured what remained of the wine into his glass. He handed it over to Vasilis, who stood up, leaning heavily against his stick. Slowly, he walked away to refill it.

Once alone, Varvis raised his glass and threw the wine down his throat. He wiped away the red droplets that trickled down his chin, and swore. Andreas's arrival had stirred up memories long buried. The death of Andreas, and the unexpected early death of his mother, with whom he had enjoyed a special bond. He had spent his teenage years watching his father dishonor her memory, bringing other women into their home. It never occurred to him that he had been doing the same.

His eyes shone in the dark as he remembered the day he had plunged his sword into Andreas's chest. If the grandson decided to start asking questions, he would deal with him, personally. Zoe had come back searching for the dead man, but other than that had never bothered them. He thought it strange that her death and the arrival of the grandson had coincided with the grand ceremony. He twirled the wine glass in his fingers, pondering his next moves.

Vasilis shuffled back into the room with the wine jug. The glass slipped from Alexandros's fingers and smashed onto the floor. As if nothing had happened, he stood up and said, "It's getting late. You make sure he goes, and everything will be fine."

Although surprised at the other's sudden departure, Vasilis said nothing. He had become accustomed to the man's bizarre behavior. He hobbled after him, escorting him to the front door. Just before Alexandros stepped outside, Vasilis asked with feigned indifference, "So, this full moon ..."

As if he had been expecting the question, Varvis grabbed him by the throat with the force of a much younger man, and savagely hissed, "You have no business asking these things. Mind your own business. Understood?"

Gasping for breath, Vasilis croaked that he understood. Varvis released his grip suddenly, sending the old man stumbling backward. He turned and walked off without casting him another glance.

Vasilis's eyes glowed with fierce hatred as he closed the front door. He flung his walking stick to one side and, walking easily, returned to the living room and blew out the candle. Stepping over the smashed glass, he sank down on the sofa, lost in thought.

The early morning light crept through the crack in the curtains and woke me gently. I opened my eyes and immediately saw Destine standing outside the door, waiting for me to call her into the room. I cuddled her on the bed, then walked to the wide windows. I flung the shutters open, and was greeted by a cornucopia of sensuous delight: the lush greenery of the garden, the fresh air carrying with it the salty scent of the sea, the smell of flowers and thyme, the chirping sound of birdsong.

For the first time in days, I felt light, as if I had left all my burdens on the mattress behind me. I looked down at the hammock and wondered why I had not tried it yet. First thing I would do, after a quick coffee.

The moment I stepped into the garden, coffee cup in hand, Destine ran to the garden gates, barking a greeting. I saw Vasilis standing outside, beckoning me with his walking stick.

"I'm afraid she'll take me for a thief and attack me," he said as I let him in.

I laughed. "I don't think she's ever attacked anyone, and I don't think you'll be the first. Good morning."

He handed me a grocery bag containing bread and freshly baked pies from the village bakery. I was surprised he had managed to walk all the way here, as his house was some distance away. He looked at the murky mess in my cup, took it from me, and emptied the coffee into a flowerpot. "At least it's good fertilizer," he said, and shook his head as he walked inside the house.

I sat down and hungrily ate a vegetable pie. It tasted good. Real food; I had missed that. Vasilis reappeared with two steaming cups of Greek coffee and sat across the table. I noticed that his walking stick seemed to be more of an option than a need. He moved rather well with both his hands full. I did not comment as I took my first sip of coffee and leaned back contentedly.

Vasilis seemed serious. "When are you thinking of going back to Maronia?" he asked.

Surprised, I pointed at the beautiful garden around us and said, "I'm in no hurry. I'm starting to like this place." I saw his face darken. "What's the matter? Do they need the house?"

"No, the house is available. I just thought you were planning to leave tomorrow."

"You thought right, but if it's okay with the owners, I'd like to stay until the full moon. I heard it's beautiful here."

Vasilis put down his cup and stood up. "I think it would be best if you returned tomorrow, son," he said, avoiding my eyes.

I was taken aback, but I suspected I knew the reason behind those words. "If this has anything to do with my grandfather, I really don't care. I've noticed the strange looks, but it's water off a duck's back. Anyway, I have mostly heard nice things about him. I'll believe them rather than those who enjoy a good gossip behind people's backs. It's all in the past, anyway."

"If you only knew how often the past finds a way into the present and changes everything ..." Vasilis took my hand and looked me in the eye. "Enjoy your stay today, and then may God show you the right thing to do. I just want you to be careful. Very careful." His eyes were moist, tense.

I wondered whether I should press him for more details, or ignore all the small-town gossip. "I'll be careful, Vasilis ... Don't forget I have a shepherd to look over me." I pointed to Destine, who had come to stand beside me.

Vasilis did not return my smile. He shook my hand and made to go.

"I can drop you off, if you want," I offered. "I'm going to go out, too."

He raised his stick as he walked away. "I can still use my legs. Have fun, Andreas. If you are back early, come have a glass of wine. Be careful by the water pools. Don't let a fairy enchant you!"

I did not understand what he was talking about, so I just smiled and waved. I was puzzled by his urging me to leave, but as I settled into the hammock and turned up to look at the clear blue sky, I decided to let Samothrace show me the way.

Iro exited the stables, leading a black horse by the reins. She had just saddled the stallion; its dark coat glistened in the morning sunlight, the heart-shaped white spot between its eyes glowing brightly. She checked the saddle straps and tenderly stroked the horse's neck, before jumping onto its back in one swift motion.

She was wearing a long white shirt and tight black trousers tucked into her riding boots. A black scarf was wrapped around her neck. She pulled her hair back into an elaborate knot, then tugged at the reins.

Miltos's voice halted her just before she rode out through the gap in the tall fence. She turned the horse around to face him as he hastened toward her.

"Good morning," he said. "I didn't know you were going for a ride. Will you wait for me to saddle up?"

Iro hesitated, trying to find a way to decline without offending her fiancé. "I'm riding out to the water pools. I won't be long, so don't bother getting a horse ready."

Smiling, he asked, "Do you want me to accompany you, or not?"

"Yes, of course," she replied with a smile. "I just don't want to be late."

"Good. Then you start, and I'll come find you. We can ride back together. We'll meet at *Fonias*." He turned his face up to kiss her.

Iro bent down and barely brushed her lips against his. She softly dug her heels into the horse's belly, then galloped away toward the woods.

With a frown, Miltos watched her leave the estate. Then he turned back inside the stables. His horse neighed in recognition, anticipating a pleasant ride through the woods.

Dominion of the Moon

I drove along the coast for a while, then parked in the shade of a large plane tree and followed the stream up the mountain slope. I had stopped at a taverna to get a bottle of water, and its owner had suggested I hike out to *Vathres tou Fonia*: the Murderer's Water Pools. She explained how, after a half-hour climb, I would find myself at one of the most beautiful spots on the island. The streams reshaped the ground every year, so there was always something new to see. If my legs could stand the climb, a further two hours away was the island's largest waterfall, falling from a height of a hundred and fifteen feet.

Destine walked ahead, never straying too far as we entered the dense woods. The sun's rays snuck in through the lush green canopy, highlighting the rocks and making the river's surface sparkle. I knew that walking against the course of the stream would lead me to the first water pool. Destine's reactions up ahead gave me a heads up whenever someone was making their way down. We crossed paths with many smiling tourists returning from their hikes.

A few minutes later, we came across the first large water pool. A group of naked swimmers splashed around inside it, squealing that the water was cold. They invited us in, but I shook my head. They were brave to go swimming in the icy September waters. Even Destine cast them a look of surprise.

As soon as the pool was behind us, silence reigned in the forest. I began to enjoy the sound of trickling water, the birdsong, the gentle rustle of the tree branches swaying in the breeze. I stopped to take a picture of a small waterfall, and tried to send it to Jill. There was no signal up here. I took a few more photos of Destine posing by the waterfall and then sat on the ground. A quick break, and then I would walk until I got tired again. It seemed unlikely that I would make it all the way up to the large waterfall.

I was playing tug of war with Destine when she suddenly stopped and pricked her ears, turning to look upstream. She growled at something behind the waterfall. Imagining that some kind of wood creature had spooked her, I asked her to sit beside me, but she ignored me.

I leaned back against the tree trunk and gazed at the blue sky and the small white clouds chasing each other as they sprinted over the island. I hadn't felt like this in a long time. I did not know whether it was the energy of the island, which many visitors claimed to sense, but I felt at one with everything that was calm and peaceful on this land. Life had been tense, and moments such as this rare. Moments where you feel nothing, and that nothingness means everything.

I suddenly heard Destine bark. She was standing beside the rocky ledge over which the water cascaded. I had not even noticed her slip away. I shouted at her to come back, to no avail. On the contrary, she sprinted away, her barking getting fiercer by the minute.

I jumped up and hastily began to climb over the rocks to the top. I saw Destine in the distance among the large tree trunks, manically barking at a horse. Its rider desperately tried to calm down her nervous steed.

Just then, the horse reared on its hind legs, ready to bring its hooves down on Destine. My heart pounded in my chest as everything seemed to move in slow motion. The rider desperately tugged hard at the reins. The horse missed Destine, but landed hard on its front legs, causing the woman to lose her balance. I watched in horror as she fell to the ground.

I ran up to them, grabbed the now-terrified Destine by the collar, and forced her to sit. The horsed galloped off into the woods, leaving its rider behind. Making sure Destine stayed rooted to the spot, I approached the woman, apologizing at the same time.

She was kneeling, holding her hand. Her long hair fell across her forehead, masking her face. I kept asking if she was okay, but she did not speak. Only when I touched her shoulder did she make an effort to stand. I took her by her uninjured arm and helped her up. She brushed the hair away from her face and looked me straight in the eyes, still not speaking a word. I returned the look, trying to interpret her expressionless gaze. She seemed vaguely familiar, but I was too shaken to think straight.

"I'm okay," she said, breaking the awkward silence. She gripped her wrist and winced in pain.

"I think you've hurt yourself," I said, unthinkingly touching her arm.

She pulled away. "It's just fine, thank you. It's nothing serious."

She stepped forward to look behind me, where Destine kept her nose to the ground, ashamed. Then the woman looked at her horse, which had stopped its gallop and was now grazing a few feet away. She knelt down and thumped the soil with her hand, calling Destine to her. Destine half-walked, half-crawled in her direction. To my great surprise, she put her muzzle on the woman's lap, as if she knew her.

"Many dogs are really afraid of horses," she said, running her fingers through Destine's coat.

I was impressed by the reaction of both. They behaved as if they were old friends, not as if Destine had just attacked her horse. I felt a twinge of jealousy as woman and dog bonded. As I hovered awkwardly, I noticed a tattoo just below her shoulder. Her long hair fell over it, and it was impossible to read. Her response to the whole incident made me feel even worse about what had just happened. Without any thought for herself or her injury, her first concern had been to soothe the unfamiliar dog.

Finally, she stood up, pulling her hair over one shoulder. Her black eyes scanned me from head to toe before speaking. "I had a German Shepherd a few years ago. She never managed to like horses either. Is she yours?"

For a few seconds I was lost as to what to reply. "Yes, she is with me now. Seeing how she's acting with you, though, I wouldn't be surprised if she walks out on me one day."

Dominion of the Moon

"Don't be fooled by what you just saw. She might be playing with me now, but she only has one true master she really cares for. He is the one she looks after; he is the one whose emotions she picks up on. Dogs are capable of breaking even the sturdiest chain when they sense we may be in danger. My experience has shown me there is something deeply human about them." Her voice was filled with passion as she spoke, but then she winced again.

"Please accept my apologies, and ... Are you sure your hand is okay?"

"It's nothing," she said, stroking her wrist. She looked at my arm. "You seem to have hurt yourself, too."

I looked down. Only then did I notice the blood trickling down my arm. I must have cut myself climbing up the rocks.

She took my arm and pulled me toward the stream. "It's not terrible, but it's still a deep gash. Come, we need to clean it." I felt her fingers tighten their grip.

We knelt by the small stream, and I abandoned myself to her care. With gentle, knowing motions, she began to clean the dust that had settled on the wound. She rinsed my arm carefully, pausing to look at the tattoo on the inside of my wrist. "On the island, we say that when a person's blood mixes with our water, a part of their soul stays on the island forever," she said.

I was impressed by what she said, the dreaminess in her voice. She changed tones, however, suddenly becoming very practical. "We need to dress your wound. Wait here," she said. She pushed herself up and scanned the ground around her.

Destine watched us carefully from a distance. I was concerned by the abrupt changes in her behavior ever since we had arrived on the island.

The woman knelt back down beside me, holding a plant. She pulled the leaves off the stem in one swift motion and crushed them between her palms. She then placed them on my wound, and tightly wrapped the scarf she had been wearing around my arm.

"This should keep it disinfected until someone can see it," she said, and gave me another one of her intense looks.

"Thank you. Forgive me, but ... I'm sure I've seen you somewhere before." I immediately regretted blurting out such a commonplace phrase.

She didn't reply, but examined me more closely. She shook her head "no" and gripped her injured wrist again.

"Are you sure it's not badly hurt?" I pressed.

I touched her wrist tenderly. She did not pull her hand away this time. A small bruise was beginning to show against her white skin.

"We both had a lucky escape," she said.

Something glinted on the ground beside me. I bent down and picked up a black ring, which hung from a thin leather string that had snapped in two. I noticed the phases of the moon carved all around it. A small black stone decorated the disk of the full moon. "This must be yours," I said, offering it to her.

Her raised her hand to her neck, checking for the necklace, then reverently took the ring. "Yes, it's mine. It must have snapped when I fell."

She hurriedly tied the two ends of the string into a knot and pulled it over her head, bringing the ring around so it rested at the hollow of her neck.

"I apologize for my rudeness," I awkwardly said. "My name is Andreas."

"Iro," she said, and gently pulled her hand away.

"And this is Destine."

"Destine," she repeated, absent-mindedly toying with the ring.

The sound of horse hooves approaching made her turn serious and take a step back. Destine was already on her feet, growling.

A man appeared astride a white horse. Iro raised her hand in greeting, casting a quick look in my direction. I was startled by the shadow that seemed to flit across her face. I cried out for Destine to stay as I walked to her and attached the leash to her collar.

The man on the horse crossed the stream, muddying the waters in his wake. Once he was over on our side, he dismounted, his eyes flitting between the two of us. He kept his eyes on me while Iro explained what had happened.

"Miltos ... Andreas," she introduced us.

"Pleased to meet you," I said. "I apologize once again; it's my dog's fault." I offered him my hand.

Miltos hesitated, and then reluctantly shook my hand. "You need to be very careful with animals. Accidents do not take long to happen. My fiancée might have been seriously injured," he declared solemnly, proprietarily informing me of his relationship to Iro at the same time.

"It was nothing," she said, trying to break the tension. "I am not blameless. I should have immediately dismounted."

"No, it's my fault," I added, in as friendly a tone as I could muster. "I did not have time to stop her; it all happened so fast."

"You are not from these parts?" Miltos asked, staring at his fiancée's scarf wrapped around my arm.

"Yes and no." I kept my tone as light as I could. "My father's family is from Samothrace. I was born and raised in New York."

"First time on the island, then." Somehow, he managed to make the statement sound like an accusation.

"I came for my grandmother's funeral."

Just when I thought the atmosphere was cold enough, it plummeted to new depths of iciness.

"What did you say your name was?" he asked, almost aggressively.

I was beginning to get annoyed. "Look, I already apologized. Now I feel like I'm being interrogated, so if you'll excuse me, I need to be on my way."

I tried to catch Iro's eye, but she kept her gaze fixed to the ground. I pulled Destine back up to her feet and we began to walk away.

"Is your last name Stais, by any chance?" Miltos shouted after me.

I froze to the spot. Sensing the anger rising inside me, Destine growled. Turning to face him, I said, "Yes. Stais is my last name."

"So you are the thief's grandson."

His words hit me like a punch. It's different knowing people are saying things behind your back, and having those words thrown in your face. Iro looked at him, confused. I touched Destine's head, fearing she might become aggressive.

"I am the archaeologist's grandson. You can keep your lies to yourself, where they belong."

Iro bit her lip, giving me a look of apology. It took all my self-control to turn away. Miltos, on the other hand, still had a bone to pick. "You are not welcome here. Go pack your bags! You have no place on this island."

Iro shouted at him to stop, but he ignored her.

"Unless you've come back to return the stolen goods," he taunted me.

This time, I could not control myself. I walked back toward him, holding Destine by the collar, and only stopped at a distance that would keep him safe from my dog's fangs.

"There is a limit to my patience. You can thank the presence of the lady standing behind you ..."

"Or what?" he interrupted. "You'd tell your dog to bite me?"

Iro stepped in front of him, holding her arms wide. Her open arms seemed like wings, spread between us to keep us both safe.

I realized that if I lingered any longer, things could get ugly. I glared at Miltos for a moment, looked at Iro, then turned and walked away, this time determined not to turn back no matter what I heard.

I could hear their voices arguing behind me, especially hers. I kept walking, and only when I was a safe distance away did I remove Destine's leash. It was one of the few moments in my life when I'd felt myself lose my cool, and it had always happened under the pressure of work, never in my personal life. I took a deep breath and exhaled deeply, trying to blow the tension I felt away from my body.

Maybe the place helped; I recovered my sense of peace very quickly as I walked among the trees beside the streaming water. When I returned to the first water pool, the swimmers were gone. I removed my clothes and Iro's scarf without too much thought, and slowly entered the water.

Like a wave, the coldness spread over my body. Without hesitating, Destine jumped in after me, and we both found ourselves swimming in the *Vathra tou Fonia*. I plunged my head underwater and heard a sound like a beating heart, rising up from the bottom of the pool. Vasilis's words came to my mind, and I rose to the surface ...

Iro had brought her horse close to Miltos. "I don't like your manner. You were rude, and you almost got into a fight with a man who did nothing to you."

Miltos looked at her in disbelief. "How I behave is up to me, Iro. Didn't your father tell you what that guy's grandfather did?"

"What's his grandfather got to do with any of this? Since when do the sins of the father fall on the son?"

"You obviously don't know enough, then. I'm surprised you're standing up for him, like you know him."

"I'm not standing up for him. I don't care what he does. I don't know the guy. That doesn't stop me from being fair."

"Your scarf was tied around his arm. I'd say you care," he said sarcastically, shifting in his saddle.

Iro gave him an angry look and mounted her horse. "You really don't know me," she said coldly.

He seemed unrepentant. "Shall we return? There are final preparations to be made. Tomorrow is your big day, remember?"

Disappointed, Iro shook her head. "You go back; I'll head the other way. I'll see you back home."

Leaving him no time to react, she spurred her horse uphill. She only covered a few yards, and then abruptly turned around, as if suddenly remembering something. She trotted back to the astounded Miltos.

"And if you must know," she said pointedly, "my family never proved that the archaeologist actually took anything."

She touched the horse's flank, and it galloped away at great speed. Her fiancé stood still, staring at her until she disappeared from view. He pursed his lips and turned in the opposite direction.

Miltos returned to the tower and looked around anxiously for Alexandros. He asked a servant where he was, and she pointed in the direction of the back garden. He found Alexandros kneeling on the ground, planting seeds in the holes he poked with the flat end of a crowbar. He sensed Miltos's presence and stood up.

"Why are you back already?" He took in Miltos's expression, and a look of worry came across his face. "What happened? Did anything happen to Iro?"

"No, but it could have." Miltos bowed his head.

"Where is she? Why are you not together? What happened, son?"

Miltos asked him to sit down, and then recounted everything that had happened by the waterfall. Troubled, Varvis spoke through gritted teeth: "No matter how many years pass, we'll never be rid of them. They always turn up at the worst possible moment. I had a bad feeling about this, from the moment I saw him at the cemetery."

Alexandros pushed himself up and leaned hard against the table. "You should have buried them there on the spot, him and his dog."

Miltos's eyes bulged at what he was hearing, trying to understand if the old man meant what he had just said.

"You never should have left her there," Alexandros continued. "You should have brought her back with you."

"What could I do? She galloped off. But I don't think she'll be long. She knows she needs to come back to prepare."

"Look," Varvis said, regaining his composure, "if he bothers us again, we'll have to take steps."

"What could he do? He just came for his grandmother's funeral. I don't think there will be anything else. He'll have his holiday, and we'll never see him again."

"Don't you know he is a policeman? Not here in Greece; with Interpol."

Miltos looked confused. "So? Do we have anything to fear from an American policeman?"

"Maybe nothing, but who knows what trouble he could cause if he starts digging around. His family comes from the island." Alexandros huffed, and kicked at one of the holes in the soil. "Look how everything is being stirred up again." He turned back to the puzzled Miltos. "Call Iro and tell her I need her here. Talk to her nicely, calm her down. When the preparations are over, it may be time for you to learn the rest."

"About the American?"

"About the grandfather. You need to know; it seems like you are the only one I can count on."

Miltos dialed Iro's number. "She's either switched it off, or there's no signal where she is."

"Keep trying to reach her until you get hold of her." Alexandros returned to his gardening, plunging the crowbar into the soil.

I felt better after the swim. I sat on a rock standing in a gap between the trees where the sun shone through to dry. Thankfully, no one turned up as I lay naked on the rock.

I did not take any of Miltos's threats seriously, but I nonetheless wondered whether it wouldn't be best to return to Maronia. Have a holiday away from tensions and worry, at my grandmother's sanctuary of a home. Even though Samothrace was friendly, some of its residents were less welcoming. But the eyes of that woman ...

I kept trying to remember, but I could not determine whether I had actually seen her before, or if she just reminded me of someone. I picked up her scarf and brought it to my face, inhaling her distinctive perfume, before placing it inside my pocket. My arm had stopped bleeding, but it needed to be tended to. I would have to get to a pharmacy soon. Luckily, my tattoo had escaped unscathed. Poor Destine tried to lick my arm, wanting to care for me too.

We resumed our return trip to the car. I had to scold Destine for shaking her fur and covering me in water droplets.

We passed a couple of Greek tourists making their way up the slope. In the quiet of the woods, I could hear them talking about *Pyrgos tou Fonia*, the Murderer's Tower, close to the torrent's estuary. I greeted them once they were in sight, and asked them about the famous tower with the unusual name. They laughed and explained that it was named after the torrent, *Fonias*. The peaceful stream I had been following would turn into a dangerous, sweeping torrent in the winter, which carved up the land as it gushed down to the sea, reshaping the landscape every year. The tower was a medieval building, worth the visit.

Having parked near the foothills, I had not seen the tower. As it wasn't too far, I decided to keep walking downstream all the way to the sea. A few minutes later, following the course of the river, I spotted the stone tower, standing proudly on the edge of a small peninsula, surrounded by admiring tourists.

Just then, I spotted the familiar shape of a black horse walking in the sea, the water reaching the line of its belly. I recognized Iro on its back. A dark silhouette, framed against the bright blue expanse behind her. She was too far away to call out to her or wave. I did want to see her again, but made no move in her direction, realizing how inappropriate that might be, for the both of us. It was the first time I'd felt attracted to someone after the death of Eva.

A wave of guilt washed over me. I felt as if the mere act of admiring someone from afar was a betrayal of everything Eva and I had shared.

Destine followed my gaze, and together we watched Iro as she rode away. As always, Destine let a low growl at the sight of the horse, and suddenly I felt it was time to leave, forgetting all about the tower.

We reached the car, and all I wanted was to eat something and find myself back in the garden, stretched out on the hammock. I was fit, but the hike and the intensity of the altercation by the waterfall were taking their toll.

I did not even bother trying to get Destine to sit in the back seat. Driving side by side, I turned the radio on. A cover version of *Summertime* I had never heard before blared out. I loved that song! I turned the volume up and started to sing along in my tone-deaf voice. Destine lowered her snout and covered her ears with her paws. I laughed, heartily, for the first time in days.

The sea breeze wafting in through the open car windows carried all my worries away, leaving me only with the memory of a pair of dark, captivating eyes. All of a sudden, Destine pushed herself up and began to bark in the direction of the sea. I turned to see what had caught her attention.

Iro, close to the shore, had heard Destine's barks and stopped in the water, looking in our direction. I pulled over and hushed Destine, turning the radio off. Without even realizing it, I stepped out of the car and slowly walked around to the other side.

We looked at each other, neither moving, under the bright sunlight. The horse, as if of its own volition, stepped out onto the beach and moved in our direction. Our gazes still locked, Iro passed in front of me and, without stopping, crossed the street and disappeared into the woods.

I looked down at my hand, which was gripping her scarf. I had taken it out of my pocket, intending to return it, and then changed my mind. I just fell silent and watched her ride by. I could not explain what was happening. I could only feel myself helplessly being pulled into her magnetic field, the moon to her sun.

Destine nudged me with her snout as I stared at the forest in a trance, hoping Iro would reappear. I snapped back to the present and patted her head, reassuring her we would be on our way. I drove on, in a daze, and somehow found myself before our front door.

I was woken up by my ringtone, the phone vibrating in my pocket. I flung off the thin blanket and sat up in the hammock with great difficulty. I realized the sun was setting. I had slept through the entire afternoon; an unusual occurrence for me.

The caller was Vasilis. He asked me to dinner, and I suggested we meet at the nice taverna I had visited on my own. We hung up, and I leaned back in the hammock. The song of the crickets, right above me, began to lull me back to sleep. Reluctantly, I got up and went to sit at the long table. Luckily, the house had a well-stocked first aid kit, and I had been able to tend to my wound. I stretched, Destine at my feet, trying to blow away a web cobwebs hanging from the table's underside.

I scrolled through my email and noticed that the German Nazi saga was still playing out in the news, but the tide was turning in my favor. Jill was fielding interview requests, something that the agency did not permit in any case. Nor did I wish to be the face of a crusade against war criminals.

I then searched information on Samothrace: local news, or other events happening on the island. The first item on the search results was a video of a large symposium that had taken place a few days ago. I could not believe my eyes when I saw a familiar woman walk up to the podium and give a speech. I thought it might be someone who looked like her, but no. It was definitely Iro.

I turned up the volume and understood that she was, in fact, the host. I saw her take her seat between her fiancé and an elderly man. Based on what she had said, it seemed to be her father. I was burning with curiosity. I entered her name in the search box, and was flooded with a long list of results. President of the Axieros Foundation … aiming to promote Samothrace … most significant sacred site of the cult of Cabeiri … ancient rites… rituals …

Alkistis's number flashed up on the screen, interrupting my search. She asked me how my day was, and if I wanted to join her for a drink at a nice bar near the port. I explained I was having dinner with Vasilis, and I'd give her a call to meet later. She asked me if I enjoyed *praousti*. I had no idea what she meant, but before I could reply, I heard her voice outside the garden gates. I turned and saw her enthusiastically wave a shopping bag. I liked her, but was not exactly thrilled by the unannounced visit.

Destine ran down the garden path, and a few minutes later we were back at the table, a box filled with local sweets called *praousti* spread out between us.

Alkistis looked at my hand and asked me what happened.

"It's nothing serious," I said. "Just a small scratch, down by the sea." I took a bite. "It's very kind of you, although I'm not really a sweets person. It's very tasty. I hope you don't mind that I won't be eating much."

"Never mind," she said, smiling. "It's the local specialty. I thought you knew. You can't find it anywhere else in the world." Suddenly, she became serious. "Please don't force yourself; I did not mean to impose."

"You don't have to tell me if you don't want to, but is something bothering you?"

"I'm sorry. Something is bothering me, but ... I don't want to burden you with my own worries."

"Please tell me."

"I just found out they are not renewing my contract. I'm very upset about it."

"I'm sorry, but I don't understand what this means," I said, puzzled.

"It means I have to leave at the end of the month. I won't even get to see the full moon. I have to be in Alexandroupolis tomorrow afternoon for an event, and return the following day. I was going to ask you if you wanted to join me at an open air concert on the night of the full moon, but that won't happen now."

"Why did they not renew it? Did you want to leave?" I asked, ignoring the part about going to a concert.

"No, Andreas. I would stay here forever if I could, but unfortunately ..."

"So what happened, all of a sudden? Why are they firing you?"

She picked up a sweet and put it in her mouth, then licked the sticky syrup on her index finger. "I guess it's because I asked too many questions."

"Questions? I'm not following."

"Remember how I told you that I am doing some research on ancient cults and secret religious rites ...?"

"That rings a bell," I said uncertainly.

"It seems some people did not like my looking into this. But I don't want to talk about it. What matters is I'm leaving."

"I don't want to push you if you don't want to go into the details. It's strange all the same."

"If you knew the Varvis family, you wouldn't find it strange at all."

I felt as if I had been jolted by a live wire. Varvis—the same last name as Iro.

"Who?" I asked, with feigned nonchalance.

"I'll tell you, but I don't want to get into any more trouble. I made the mistake of speaking to them, and you saw what happened."

"You can trust me. If you are not comfortable discussing this, though ..."

"Varvis. Alexandros Varvis and his daughter, Iro. And you, indirectly," she whispered, looking around her suspiciously, as if anyone could overhear us in this secluded garden.

I was dying to find out more without revealing that I had become acquainted with one member of that family. "What do you mean, me? How?"

She looked me in the eyes. "I discovered that Alexandros Varvis's father had accused your grandfather of stealing, of antiquities smuggling. There is nothing in the police files, but you grandfather disappeared at the exact same time."

"I don't understand what you are implying, but it all happened a long time ago anyway. They are both dead; it doesn't matter now," I said, knowing that was the way to get her to open up.

"Not quite. Alexandros Varvis was alive back then. According to my information, he must have been around nine years old. I don't know if Vasilis told you anything, but he must know most of what happened back then. I guess he won't." She grimaced, showing her dislike. She turned to look at the house. "What a beautiful house. The American archaeologists used to stay here ..."

"You can visit; it's open," I said, picking up my phone.

She did not need to be told twice. She disappeared inside the house and came out ten minutes later. "What an amazing house! Fantastic bedroom! What a shame I didn't know it was being rented out to tourists; I would have liked to have spent a couple of nights here." She picked up another sweet and looked at me closely. "You seem like you have a lot on your mind too, Andreas. I could tell from the first time I met you, in Athens. I don't mean to pry ..."

I took a deep breath, and decided to return the confidence. "No, I appreciate your concern. I lost my partner a few months ago, and I am still not over it. Then my grandmother died, and ... it was all too much." I wondered as I spoke to her whether I was really telling the truth. At present, I had been thinking about everything other than what I had just told her.

"I'm sorry for your loss," she whispered. "Had I known, I wouldn't have brought it up. I appreciate your honesty. These days, dishonesty is all I seem to encounter."

As if my confiding in her had opened up the floodgates, she confessed how hard it was for her to meet someone open to a long-term relationship. I listened attentively, giving her what advice I could. I laughed as she comically shared her stories, mimicking the voices of men and her disastrous dates. I noticed with a start it had gotten dark, and I had to get ready to go meet Vasilis. I escorted her to the garden gate.

"We'll talk again when I'm back … if you are still here," she said. "About what I told you before, well, maybe you are right. Maybe it is best to let go of the past and move on. It's what I should do too, right? Forget all the men that hurt my feelings."

We laughed at her brief synopsis of all the advice I had given her. She kissed my cheek and thanked me for everything. "You are a good person, Andreas."

I smiled as I watched her disappear down the narrow alley. I had wanted to find out more about the past, but had chosen not to press her any further. In any case, I was about to see the man who, according to Alkistis, knew much more than he had so far revealed.

A large group of people had gathered on the tower ramparts facing northeast, where the moon would soon be rising. This time, no torches broke the thick darkness that had descended over the tower. Patiently, everyone waited for the moon to cast its silver light. Only the shadow of their silhouettes occasionally stood out against the twinkling lights of the distant houses.

A monumental fight between Iro and Alexandros had preceded the arrival of the guests. They had argued violently over the incident with Andreas. Miltos had tried to mediate between father and daughter, calming one and cajoling the other, until a tense peace had descended over the preparations. It could all wait. It could all be dealt with later.

Holding a small drum, Erato climbed the stone steps leading to the ramparts. She walked to a fragment of a marble column and sat on it. Placing the drum firmly between her knees, she beat out a slow rhythm.

In the distance, the first dim light appeared, foretelling the arrival of the heavenly body that affected everyone's presence on Earth, one way or the other. This evening's small ceremony was the final rite before the all-important full moon of the following day.

A few minutes later, the rounded edge of the moon peeked timidly over the horizon. Alexandros gave the signal, and the chanting began: hymns accompanied by the beating of Erato's drum. As more of the moon's silver disk appeared, the chanting and the drum beat got louder and louder.

At the sight of the full round disk, everyone fell silent. A small flame flickered in a large clay bowl, and everyone moved to the far edge of the rampart. The flame filled the bowl, casting an orange glow on the face of Iro, who stood behind it, blindfolded with a black scarf. The reflection of the red flames on her dark vestments matched them to the color of the moon as it made its journey toward the center of the sky.

When the fire began to die down, the guests walked up one by one, emptying the scarlet liquid in their cups over the flames. Each cup weakened the flames and released thick plumes of smoke, which were then carried away by the breeze.

Miltos was last; he emptied an entire jug on the embers, putting out the fire. The flames extinguished, Erato stepped behind Iro and loosened the blindfold. The first thing Iro saw was the bright yellow disc of the moon. Her eyes softened at the sight.

Like a caress, Erato ran her hands all over Iro's body, whispering sacred words. When every inch of Iro's body had been touched, Erato began to unfasten the cords that held her dress up. She pulled down the fabric, revealing Iro's shoulders, then breasts, then letting it drop to her feet.

Iro, naked, stepped out of the dark circle of cloth and stood still on the ramparts, facing the moon. Everyone else walked back down to the courtyard. There, they gathered in neat rows, looking up at Iro's naked silhouette, framed by the moon.

Between the thick leaves of a tree, I saw the enormous moon that had already risen. If I did not know better, I would think the full moon was tonight. I moved to a bench at the corner of the garden, away from the trees, and felt the light of the moon wash over me.

I had just received a call from the American archaeologist on his way to France. He reminded me of our conversation on the ferry, about how he might have something for me. It turned out he had asked the archives department to send him Elizabeth's notes from the time of my grandfather's disappearance. He stressed this was an informal request, and that the mission's notes and diaries had only recently been digitalized.

I looked at my phone, impatiently waiting for the scanned documents to arrive. I remembered Elizabeth telling me in New York that I had my grandfather's eyes. Other than that, she avoided reminiscing about that time, and I never asked. I absentmindedly stroked the head of a yellow rose beside the bench as I waited.

As soon as I heard the phone ping, I downloaded all the documents and began to scroll through them. Unfortunately, there were parts where Elizabeth's handwriting was indecipherable. Perhaps I would have better luck on a proper computer screen, but for now, I had to make do. I sat there reading, absorbed. Some things I knew, but most information I was discovering for the very first time.

When I finished reading, I realized what an incredible coincidence meeting Iro was. Our family histories seemed inextricably linked. Why had my father or my grandmother never spoken of the events Elizabeth mentioned in her notes?

The only man alive who could possibly answer the questions burning inside me was Vasilis.

It was getting late by the time I met him at the local taverna. The moon hung high in the sky like a spotlight, casting its silver light on the table and Vasilis's white hair. He gave me his seat and, as soon as I sat down, I realized why. The castle up at the Chora glowed high up on the hill, stealing some of the limelight.

"Greece is full of castles," I said, enjoying the sight.

"It's true," he replied. "I still haven't decided whether they are built to keep the people outside from getting in, or the other way around." He smiled and raised his hand to beckon the waiter.

Few of the tables were full, and everyone was enjoying the evening. We made casual conversation about my life in the States, and my work. When we finished eating, I decided to tell Vasilis about my encounter with Iro and her fiancé. He gripped my injured arm as if he could not believe what he was hearing. He turned pale and urged me to give him even the tiniest details. I could sense I had a man of many secrets before me, though I could not understand why.

When I finished telling the story to his satisfaction, he took a long sip of wine and spoke anxiously. "Take the first boat back tomorrow morning, son, and leave it all behind."

This time, I was in no mood to content myself with vague allusions. I cut straight to the chase. "Vasilis, how are you linked to the Varvis family?"

He shifted uncomfortably in his chair and tugged his hair over his missing ear. "I don't know what you mean. No more than anyone else on the island. We all know each other here. I even worked for them as a farmhand at some point, but that's all."

"I don't mean to interrogate you, because I know my grandmother loved you very much."

"I loved her, too," he said hoarsely.

"I will be honest with you. I want you to be honest with me, too. Most likely, I will leave soon and not be back in a very long time. We may never meet again. I would like to know everything you are keeping locked up inside you; everything you aren't telling me."

Vasilis's eyes welled up. He took another long sip, trying to fortify himself. I knew this was my only chance.

"What happened in the days before my grandfather's disappearance, Vasilis?"

He wiped a tear that escaped down his cheek, and spoke in a shaky voice. "You are right, Andreas. I don't know how much time I've got left. I never came to Maronia when you were there; I didn't want to be a burden. We might never meet again, so now is probably the best time to unburden my soul. I did not want to tell you because I did not want to drag you into the past. I thought it would all pass, be forgotten. I'll start at the beginning, with how they met ..."

I already knew some of the things he was recounting, but I did not want to interrupt his flow. I let him talk, at his own pace, watched his eyes as he was transported into the past. We laughed when he described how my grandfather fell in the water pool when he startled him. Then he became serious once again.

"The island brought them together in such a way that nothing could tear them apart. Even if their time with each other was so brief ... Alexandros's father, Nicholas, did not want Andreas excavating his land. He is hiding something there, mark my words." Vasilis tapped the table emphatically. "They tried to blame Andreas and Zoe for the theft of some artifacts from the Varvis house, but they failed. Ha! I stopped them. I took away the things they had planted. Nobody ever knew. Not even Zoe ..."

Vasilis chuckled proudly, before turning serious once again. "After your great-grandmother's house burned down, they stayed in Elizabeth's house—the same place you're staying in now. In the space of two days, Andreas Stais met Zoe again, as if by a miracle, and she was present when they found the statue. In that same time he lost his mother, and then disappeared forever."

Elizabeth had written about the fire that had claimed my great-grandmother's life. I kept my face expressionless, so as not to interrupt his train of thought. "How did the house burn down?"

He gave me a bitter smile. "No one ever knew. At first, I thought it was Varvis, trying to frighten your grandfather. Then, when I worked on their land, I changed my mind.

They had a steward working for them, a real snake. Maybe he was responsible for the fire, but ..."

Vasilis glanced around, making sure no one could overhear. "If you want to know what I think, Alexandros is not Nicholas's son. He is the son of Simon, the steward. His mother used to sleep with him. He can brag all he wants about he and his daughter being descendants of the Cabeiri, but they are just two ordinary bastards. He keeps that man, Miltos, close at hand, has him at his beck and call. He even calls him his son, now that Miltos is about to marry the daughter. They've been betrothed since they were children, to keep the bloodline pure. Ha! I hope Nicholas found out he was raising his servant's son, not his own."

I could not believe my ears. Such tangled webs, casting their shadows over my grandfather's disappearance. I kept silent, letting Vasilis finish his wine before he continued.

"Alexandros would not be happy to find out whose son he is. When I heard Simon had died of a strange illness, I thought Nicholas might have been behind it. Maybe he had found out what Simon was up to, and got rid of him for good. I don't think Iro is like them. I spoke to her a little; she's a different type. But she can't escape her destiny. Be careful. She is bound to her heritage."

"Who else knows all this?" I asked. I looked around suspiciously too, caught up in the conspiratorial mood.

Vasilis pointed to his heart. I wanted to know more, and urged him to tell me everything.

"The storm split the island in two that night," Vasilis said. "So many people died in the flashfloods. Some were found by the sea, carried there by the torrent. In the morning I went to the port and told your grandmother to leave."

"I remember that. But why did she leave, if she hadn't found him?"

Vasilis seemed annoyed by the interruption. "I thought Andreas was just trapped on the other side of the island; many people were caught there in the aftermath of the storm. I was worried the police might change their minds and arrest her. Maybe Varvis would accuse them of something else. I was afraid for her, did not want her to be in any danger. She was going to travel to Maronia anyway, so I told her to leave. I would tell Andreas where she had gone, so he could contact her."

He paused and looked at the moon, which was disappearing behind the rooftops.

"What happened next? Before my grandmother returned?" I asked, refilling his wine glass.

"We realized the scale of the storm the following morning. Many people lost their lives, as I said, but we never found your grandfather. Everyone said the torrent must have carried him to the sea. Only Nicholas insisted that Andreas had tried to break into their house again that evening, and then ran away to Imbros when detected, before crossing the border to Turkey. He accused your grandfather until the day he died, saying he was selling antiquities to foreigners. Even when the police, pressured by the Americans, stated no evidence had ever been found. His slurs stuck to this day, as you can tell for yourself."

I nodded, but kept my eyes on Vasilis, indirectly pressing him to keep talking. "What do you think happened to my grandfather, Vasilis?" I asked, touching his hand.

He pulled it away, as if he felt guilty. "All I can say with any certainty is that he never left the island."

The waiter interrupted us, asking if we wanted any dessert. I politely declined, and Vasilis continued, taking a deep breath. "Elizabeth returned the following day. As soon as she heard what had happened, she came with us, up the mountain, down the gorges, looking for him. She got very angry with Varvis, and demanded that they return all antiquities in their possession. They returned much, but I'm sure they are keeping the best pieces well hidden. They must be getting money from somewhere, all these years. I've worked on their land; no way is it making that kind of money ..."

"What do you mean?" I asked, guessing the answer but wanting him to confirm my suspicions.

Vasilis picked up his knife and stabbed a last piece of meat, placing it on his plate. He kept poking it with the point of his knife as if it were an animal he wanted to finish off. "I'm sure they are smuggling antiquities. They accused others to divert attention from themselves."

"How do you know that?"

He smiled as if he had heard something funny. "I know a lot, Andreas. Unfortunately, the Americans did not keep me on. I had to find work where I could get it. Even with Varvis." He gave me a questioning look, waiting for me to react. I kept silent. "For years, foreigners would arrive at the tower in the middle of the night, leaving as secretively as they'd arrived, with their hands full. I overheard many conversations. They never mentioned Andreas."

"Do you remember what happened when my grandmother returned?"

"She came back two days later, not knowing what had happened. She had heard rumors: that Andreas had drowned, or had been arrested, or was imprisoned. I'll never forget her sitting on the ground at the Sanctuary, weeping in Elizabeth's arms when she found out he was still missing. She could not believe it. Then her own plight began. She blamed herself for what happened to him. She walked over the entire island looking for him. I would set out every day looking for her, trying to get some food to her."

"She kept looking on her own? What about my grandfather's sister and brother-in-law?" I asked, stunned.

"Calliope and her husband left the island the following day and never came back. Only the Americans helped Zoe. She stayed with Elizabeth, and only stopped looking for him when she realized …" Vasilis hesitated.

"Realized what?"

"That she was pregnant with your father. Only then did she seem to find some peace, took it as a sign. The Americans helped her, used their influence to get your grandfather's name on the birth certificate as the child's father, even though they were not married." He stopped, looking exhausted.

I let him catch his breath, advising him not to drink any more. He ignored me, filling his glass and downing the wine in a single gulp.

He reached for his walking stick to get up. "But you don't need it," I said.

A sardonic smile spread on Vasilis's lips. He let go of the stick, put his palms on the table, and pushed himself up with great ease, as if he no longer cared about maintaining the charade. "I have my secrets, too," he whispered, and walked steadily toward the bathroom.

I don't know why, but the words of one of my teachers during a psychology class came to my mind. It was during a lecture about truth, secrets, and lies, and about how people handled them. He had scribbled the following sentence on the blackboard, and asked us to write down our answers:

If the truth sets you free, why does no one choose it?

He then read our replies and smiled, telling us we were all correct because none of us had replied truthfully ...

At the beginning of this journey, I never expected it would all come to this. In all these years, I had never shown any interest in this part of my family's past. My father had subtly guided me in this direction too, changing the subject whenever I asked questions, as if he did not wish to reveal anything. Thinking about it now, I realized that maybe he didn't know much of what I was now hearing.

Kostas Krommydas

I wasted no time when Vasilis returned to the table, and asked, "Did you know my father well?"

"No, son. Theodore did not visit Maronia often, and I don't think he ever set foot on the island. If he did, it must have been secretly, without even telling his mother. I only saw him twice, and we did not say much. He was a reserved man, your father. Theodore ... God's gift. That's why she named him that. The doctors had told her she could never have children after everything she had been through, but they did not know the powers of Samothrace."

"What happened next?" I asked, like a child eager to hear the rest of my bedtime story.

"It was a heavy winter. Just before Christmas, Zoe fell ill. Elizabeth managed to convince her to go to the States with her, to have the baby there. No one knows what I am about to tell you. Everyone thinks she never set foot on the island again. However, whenever she was in Maronia, she would cross over in secret and look for your grandfather. She used to hide at my house. It went on for years. Sometimes she would spend the night in the woods, and I would worry something happened to her. Luckily, the Varvis family never found out. One day, she decided never to return. I never knew why. She would sit at her balcony to the sky in Maronia, waiting for him. Until the very end ..."

It was the first I'd ever heard of my grandmother's secret visits. I felt like Vasilis was handing me missing pieces of a puzzle that had been inside me all these years, but of whose existence I had never been fully aware.

"What's the story with the Varvis family?" I asked.

"As I told you, they think they are the heirs of the Cabeiri. They might be; who am I to judge? Maybe Simon was a descendant of the gods." Vasilis broke into loud laughter, causing a few heads to turn in our direction. He stifled his laughter and looked at me hazily; I could tell he was beginning to feel the effects of the wine. "I wish you had not met Alexandros's daughter today; no good will come of it. I think I am tired. I'm not used to drinking." He rubbed his forehead.

It was true. He was having difficulty focusing, and it was time to get him home. I asked the waiter to bring the bill, and left the money on the table. Then I helped Vasilis up, and we made our way to the car, the walking stick back in action as a theatrical prop.

"Why do you use it if you don't need it?" I asked, unable to contain my curiosity.

"That is the only secret I will never reveal," he slurred, and walked away from the car.

"Don't you want a lift?" I asked him anxiously.

He waved his stick in the air and walked unaided, showing he was just fine.

"Vasilis, wait up!" I walked up to him and lowered my voice. "I have one last question. What's going to happen tomorrow night, on the full moon? Do you know where they are gathering?"

His smile vanished, and I could tell he was going to try to avoid the question. So I quickly added, "You told me the only secret you would never reveal is the walking stick, remember?"

Vasilis looked at the moon, clearly visible from where we stood, and recited his reply. "On the night of the full moon, tread the path where two shadows follow you. One is yours. The other is the shadow of the one you will never meet. The shadow that warms you will lead the way. But first, tread the path."

He slung his walking stick over his shoulder like a bayonet and marched off. I watched him until he turned the corner, walking steadily for the most part. Whenever he stumbled, he would halt and find his footing again.

I looked up at the moon, and suddenly wished to watch it set on the other side of the island.

Dominion of the Moon

I drove along the coast, settling in for a long drive. Unlike Vasilis, I felt alert despite the wine. It was probably due to all the thoughts still swirling through my head, replaying everything I had heard that evening. Iro's scarf, stained by my blood, lay on the seat behind me. I had left it there, undecided about what to do with it.

There were few cars on the road at this hour. I wanted to drive to the Murderer's Tower and then drive back. If I still felt alert, I would stop by the sea near my house and watch the moonset. I did not want to be too late. Poor Destine was all alone back at the house.

I saw a car parked by the side of the road, facing the water. The surface of the water reflected the beams of the headlights, a long, shimmering replica of the line traced by the moon. As I neared, the lights in the car came on and a woman stepped out of the car. She looked in my direction, blinded by the headlights, then turned and walked to the rocks. To my surprise, I saw it was Iro. The man in the car was probably her fiancé.

I slowed down as I drove past, wondering what they were doing out here at this late hour. A voice inside me kept telling me to turn around. Turn around, and do what? Pull up beside them and say, "Good evening, how are you?" After everything that had happened?

Kostas Krommydas

I was sure her fiancé would try to punch me the next time he saw me. I thought it was none of my business, and stepped on the gas, but not for long. A few seconds later, I turned the wheel to face the sea and pulled over. Half of me wanted to turn back, the other half to drive off, ignoring this random meeting. I thumped my temples, trying to knock some sense into myself.

I reversed, and stopped in the middle of the road. I was still undecided. A car coming behind me decided for me. I reversed and retraced my steps. I let the car take over, and slowly drove back to where I had seen them.

I could not see their car. I imagined they had switched off the headlights to enjoy the full moon. When I reached the exact spot where they'd been parked, I saw that the car was gone. I felt like a creep, coming back to spy on a couple. Angry with myself, I reversed once again, determined to stick my original plan and drive to the Murderer's Tower.

As I maneuvered, the headlights shone on the rocks and I saw Iro, sitting by the water. She turned in my direction, shielding her eyes. I froze, and carefully scanned the area for her fiancé. She seemed to be all alone, and annoyed by this sudden intrusion.

I parked the car and stepped outside. My eyes took their time adjusting to the sudden darkness. She must have been having difficulty seeing who it was, too. I heard her call out, "Miltos? Is that you?"

I wondered what to say as I saw her stand up. Silhouetted against the bright moon, she looked like a painting. Worried, she cried out once again, "Who is it?"

"It's me, Andreas. We met in the woods today," I called back, and stepped over the sharp rocks toward her.

"What are you doing here?" she asked, puzzled.

"I was making a turn, and I saw you in the headlights."

"Making a turn to go where?" she asked suspiciously.

I was impressed by her speed, her alertness. I blurted out the first thing that came to mind. "I got a bit lost. I thought the Murderer's Tower was nearby."

I could not see her eyes, but could feel her penetrating gaze. "The Tower is much further down the road. Strange you got lost; you took the exact same route this morning, if I'm not mistaken." She clearly didn't believe a word I had just said.

I felt like a child caught with his hand in the cookie jar. "Fine," I said, shrugging. "I was driving to the Tower and I saw you in the car, by the side of the road. A little further down the road—and believe me, I don't know why—I decided to turn back. When I saw the car was gone, I assumed you had left, and I tried to reverse and head off in my original direction."

She fell silent as she took in everything I had just said. "You saw who we were?"

"Yes, your headlights were on and you opened the car door."

"So why did you come back? To confront Miltos over what happened at the waterfall?"

"No! No, I swear!" I cried out, unable to explain even to myself why I had turned back.

"Then why?" she asked as she sat back down, still facing me.

I regretted the words the moment they came out of my mouth. "I thought I should return your scarf."

She burst out laughing.

"No, it's true. It's in my car. I'll go get it if you don't believe me."

"I believe you," she cried out when she saw I meant it. "Are you going to stay, or will you head back to the Tower?"

I laughed too, and sat beside her. She turned toward me, and her face was suddenly visible in the moonlight. Black streaks on her cheeks indicated that she had been crying before I arrived. I was surprised, but didn't ask.

"Do you want to tell me why you really came back, or shall we just drop it?" she asked, turning to gaze at the silver streak of moonlight on the water's surface.

"Let's leave it for now. I just want to reassure you that I'm not following you," I said earnestly. I genuinely could not explain why I had turned back.

"Three times in a row; I don't know if I can take that as a coincidence," she said, throwing a pebble into the water.

Three? I had only ever seen her twice. "We've only met twice: once at the waterfall, and now. When was the third time? Am I missing something?" I said, scanning my memory for any other encounters.

Iro was silent for a moment. "That's right, twice. I got confused."

I was not convinced. I turned to look at the road and asked, as casually as I could, "Is your fiancé coming back?"

"I don't think so," she replied curtly. Clearly, it was a touchy subject.

"It's pretty here," I said, trying to stop us from sinking into awkward silence.

"Yes, very." She sighed. "I don't know what it is you are after. I just want you to know, our families may have had their differences in the past, but I've got nothing against you. I hope you feel the same way, because I can sense you are after something."

"It's a complicated matter. I don't think we have enough time to get into it right now."

"Let's approach it, at least," she replied, waiting for me to begin.

"Look, Iro. I think it is best not to dwell too long on the past. We should enjoy what the present has to give."

"What does the present have to give?" she asked.

"I think it gives us moments we can enjoy," I said, pointing to the moon making its way down the horizon.

The breeze was turning cool. "Maybe you are right," she replied, looking at the moon.

We both gazed at the sky, listening to the sound of the waves gently splashing against the rocks. She broke the silence first. "When are you leaving?"

"I don't know. Maybe I'll go tomorrow, maybe the day after. I'll see."

"You should stay tomorrow evening, since you are here. Tomorrow's full moon will be unique, and you are in the best place in the world to see it."

"What's so different about it?"

"It's a complicated matter," she said, and smiled. "I need to be getting back; otherwise they'll start looking for me, and I don't think Miltos will be pleased to see you again. Especially here."

"I can drive you back," I offered.

She was adamant. "No, I'll walk back. We shouldn't be seen together." She tried to get up.

I rose and helped her to her feet. "We are not doing anything wrong," I said, still holding her hand.

Iro did not attempt to pull it away. I felt her stroke my palm gently. I returned the caress, entwining my fingers in hers. She looked down at our hands. Slowly, tantalizingly, our fingers met in a dance, stroking fleetingly, pressing down strongly, meeting and withdrawing, sending waves of delight from my fingertips all the way down my body.

The lights of a passing car fell upon us like a sudden spotlight, and our hands parted abruptly, leaving a cold void between us. Iro walked past me to the road, leaving the scent that had infused the scarf behind her. I followed her. When we reached the car, she turned around and looked at me.

"I really do have it. Would you like it back?" I asked, and she smiled.

"No, you can give it back to me when we accidentally meet again for a fourth—sorry, third—time."

I was surprised she repeated the same mistake. I looked at the dark woods up the hill. "Isn't it dangerous to go back that way?"

"Don't worry, it won't be the first time. I like what your tattoo says, by the way. I wanted to tell you this morning, too. I wish I could feel what it says. I wish I could get a tattoo that said something similar." She spoke lightly, but her words were infused with undertones of bitterness.

"I hope you do. Do you speak Spanish?"

"Just enough to understand that *esterase siempre en mi Corazon* means you will always be in my heart," she said with a smile.

I felt a mountain of guilt crush me. Without another word, she raised her hand in a silent farewell and turned to go.

"Can I ask you something?" I called out. "I heard about a path: if you walk it on the night of the full moon, two shadows follow you. Any idea what that might mean?"

In the dim starlight, I saw her face turn to stone. "There is no such path, Andreas," she said coldly. "You can't believe any old wives' tale you hear on the island."

I was surprised at her strictness, as if I had overstepped some mark.

"Goodnight," she said. "I hope you return to the island someday. Take care." She hurried off before I could even utter "You too".

I stayed by the car until the darkness of the forest swallowed her up, and then drove back. I wondered whether it was time to return to Maronia, to leave all the strange things happening on the island behind me. I felt terrible, letting my feelings show like that, without any restraint. It was too soon. I felt I was betraying Eva's memory, seeking something from Iro that even I could not understand. Ever since I had met her that morning, I felt swept away by her, as if I was under a spell. Iro had not done anything to provoke this. Was I causing it, and trying to blame it on her to assuage my guilty feelings?

By the time I reached the house, I had made up my mind, not without difficulty. I would be returning to Maronia on the first boat the following morning.

I was surprised not to find Destine waiting for me by the garden gate. I called out her name, but received no reply. There was no sign of Destine anywhere. I ran inside and turned every single light on looking for her. Once I was certain she was not in the house, a terrible fear gripped me...

I don't think I slept for more than an hour that night, I was so busy looking for Destine. I walked all around the house, without finding a single trace of my dog. I then drove around until dawn, but she was nowhere to be found. I jumped in the car and drove to a print shop, to print photos of Destine along with my phone number, hoping to track her down.

I had spoken to Vasilis, who assured me that he would spread the news. He told me not to worry, that she would be back soon. He mentioned dogs often got lost on the island, but most of them returned a few days later; something to do with the island's magnetic fields. I found that hard to believe.

My guess was that Destine had somehow managed to get outside while looking for me, and her curiosity had led her astray. I did not even want to contemplate that she might have met with an accident, or worse ... I was going nowhere until I found her.

Having printed out the flyers with Destine's photo, I went to the island's small police station. As soon as I walked in, the young policeman behind the front desk stood up and greeted me with a warm handshake. I was puzzled, unsure whether I had met him before.

"It's a pleasure to meet you, sir. Please accept my condolences."

I wondered how he knew who I was. His next sentence solved the puzzle. "We heard you are on the island. We are happy a Greek colleague is doing so well abroad. I saw the video ..."

I had forgotten all about that. I quickly explained what had happened, and he eagerly assured me he would do everything he could; he even made photocopies of my flyers. He then asked if he could take a photo with me, and whether I would allow him to post the photo on social media and the police station's website.

I thanked him and let him take a picture. All I wanted was to find my faithful dog as soon as possible. "Anything you need, we're right here for you!" he called out as I left.

I resumed my search, first on foot, then by car. I stuck flyers all over Paleopolis and the port, hoping someone who had seen Destine would call me. My guilt had now doubled. I beat myself up, wishing I had returned to the house earlier, or taken her with me. I drove all the way to the Murderer's Tower, stopping at every seaside taverna and store to ask if anyone had seen her, and to put up flyers.

Vasilis called to let me know none of his acquaintances had any idea where she might be, either. He asked me again when I would be leaving, so he could come and say goodbye. I replied that I would not be leaving without Destine. I was angry, angry with myself. If she turned up and we could still catch a boat, I would gladly leave that very day.

Exhausted, I stopped in the early afternoon at a small seaside taverna to grab a bite. I picked at my food, trying to eat something to keep up my strength, but my appetite was gone. I grabbed the phone as soon as it rang, hoping it would be good news. My heart sank when I saw it was Jill.

I ignored her call, then felt bad and answered. Straight off the bat, she asked me what I was doing in a restaurant stuck in the middle of nowhere. I smiled, realizing she had been tracking me again. She sensed something was wrong, and seemed genuinely upset to hear Destine had gone missing. Then, as if struck by a sudden thought, she hastily hung up, telling me she'd call me back. A few minutes later, the phone rang again, and Jill told me that with a bit of luck she might be able to help me.

A tiny spark of hope flared inside me as she explained she was trying to find out whether Destine's GPS tracking chip was still functioning. It wasn't a well-known fact that our dogs were fitted with tracking chips, and she asked me to keep the information to myself and wait for her to report back to me. She made sure not to get my hopes up, telling me that it was unlikely her chip was functioning after all this time, if it was still there. In any case, she'd keep me posted.

As I paid, the waiter asked me where I would be watching the full moon that evening. The last thing on my mind was moonlight and romance. I drove back, praying that I would find Destine.

By the dock, just before the turn that led up to the house, I saw a large fishing boat enter the port. Instead of fishermen and their nets, it was filled with people dressed in white, just like the group I had seen at the Sanctuary. Even more members of whatever cult they worshipped waited on the shore, also dressed in white.

I slowed down and watched as one of the passengers stepped down from the boat, holding a lit torch. He knelt down and handed it to one of the waiting men. I'd never had a problem with whatever people wanted to believe in, but these extravagant displays from this ancient cult were beginning to annoy me. I wondered whether they had taken leave of their senses, and averted my gaze.

I pulled up outside the open garden gates, hoping to see Destine waiting for me. I had left everything wide open, just in case she returned. The house was still empty ...

I was so tired that it took me a while to realize my phone was ringing again. Seeing the US country code on the screen, I almost dropped it in my haste to answer. An old colleague of Eva's was on the line. He explained our stroke of good luck. Destine's tracking chip had been deactivated when she had retired, but not removed. They would be able to locate her in a short while.

I jumped up and down in joy. We agreed to talk again when they had a location, and he would talk me through finding the coordinates of her location on my phone.

It was already dark outside, and the last boat was leaving soon. I would be spending another night on Samothrace. I promised myself that if I found Destine, if she was unharmed, I would return to Maronia first thing in the morning. I hurriedly jumped in the shower, wanting to be ready to go as soon as I received the next call. Only then, when I finally felt slightly more relaxed, did my thoughts turn to Iro.

Phone in hand, I approached the spot indicated by the flashing red dot on the screen. Vasilis was accompanying me, but was struggling to keep the pace. I realized that, although he was not limping, the terrain was difficult for him. We each held a flashlight in our hands, and tried to follow Destine's signal, which kept moving. Whenever we seemed to get near it, it would move further away. I shouted her name, but received no response. She always seemed to be about a mile ahead, if the tracker could be trusted.

Vasilis pointed out that the signal now seemed to be down a small gorge with no easy access. "I don't want to hold you up, Andreas. I think I'll wait for you in the car. It's a difficult trek for me. You go ahead, but please be careful. Give me a call when you find her. If she is in the gorge, don't go down by yourself. There is no safe way in or out. Come back, and we'll go get some help."

"I'll do that. You take care on the way back."

He turned his flashlight toward me. "Be careful, my boy. The moon will be out soon, and it will be easier to see where you are going. Find her, and then immediately return to the car. Be careful."

Vasilis slowly lowered his flashlight and started to walk back down to the car. A half hour later, the moon was my ally, rising in full glory behind the mountain. I would be seeing this special full moon in the end, at the place to be, according to everybody, although under less than ideal circumstances. I paused to catch my breath, watching the majestic moonrise. I had to admit, it was the most impressive full moon I had ever seen.

Following the signal, I found myself off tangent in relation to the point from where we had set off. It would be difficult to find the car again. In the distance, the Chora and its castle were the only visible signs of civilization. All around me, all I could see was the gully and a silver expanse of water.

Finally, after an hour, the red dot seemed to stop moving. I headed in that direction, stumbling in my haste. I forced myself to slow down and carefully pick my way. It was hard to keep my eyes on the screen and the ground at the same time.

I cupped my hands around my mouth and bellowed out Destine's name. I thought I heard a distant bark, but it could have been another dog. Ten minutes later, the location on the map finally showed that Destine was some distance above me. The steep climb that separated us seemed near impossible to surmount. Again and again, I called out her name as I scrambled up on all fours.

Finally, on the edge of a rock, I saw her bright eyes glowing in the dark. She was growling, and nervously pacing up and down. I kept calling her name, but she did not seem to want to come near me. It would have been easier for her to climb down than for me to struggle up the nearly vertical slope.

I did not stop calling her. Just as the distance between us seemed to be getting smaller, she gave a small bark and disappeared as suddenly as she had appeared.

I finally reached the spot where I had seen her. I took out my flashlight and scanned the landscape around me. Large rocks rose before me, barring my way like castle walls. I was surprised at Destine's reaction. It was the first time she had ignored my calling her to me. I shone my light all around the tiny plateau, trying to understand where she could be. There was no way but down from here.

Suddenly, I noticed a small opening in the rocks, like a tiny cave. It was the only possible hiding place. I crouched down and shone the flashlight through the opening. Her eyes reflected the beam of light. I kept calling her, but she kept ignoring me. I crawled through the opening on all fours, gripping the light in my mouth. Once inside, I saw that this was not a cave, but a long corridor. Another opening, as if someone had carved out the base of the tall rock, stood at the other end. Destine stepped through it before I could get to her.

A strange light glowed beyond the second opening. I realized it was the light cast by a fire. Puzzled, I saw a narrow path wind down from the opening, a large bonfire burning further down the path. The sound of crackling wood echoed against the rocks.

I stood upright and took out my phone. The red dot was moving wildly, appearing next to my location, and then miles away a few seconds later. I checked to see whether there was no signal, but it was strong and steady.

The path split in two. No one seemed to be attending the fire. In fact, there was no sign of life anywhere. I called out to Destine once more, and waited to see if she would appear. I walked to where the path split and hesitated, trying to decide which way to follow.

I turned back, and my heart jumped in my throat. Two shadows seemed to follow my movement. I thought one must have been the shadow of someone nearby, and I turned around, alert to danger. I felt the flames warm my face. My pulse settled down when I realized both shadows were mine—one cast by the flames, the other by the full moon.

As the sound of the roaring fire filled the air around me, Vasilis's words rang in my ears. *On the night of the full moon, tread the path where two shadows follow you. One is yours. The other is the shadow of the one you will never meet. The shadow that warms you will lead the way. But first, tread the path.*

I thought I must be dreaming. Two shadows before me, the burning flames against my face showing me which path to follow. I looked around suspiciously, trying to understand whether I was the victim of an elaborate prank. No one was around. Slowly, I moved forward, following the path that led to the fire. I stood next to the roaring flames and looked at my phone once again. Same as before. At this point, I had no option but to walk ahead.

The path widened into a small opening, tall rocks rising on either side. The sound of people's voices made me stop in my tracks. I thought I spotted someone walking in my direction. I hastily climbed up the rocks, hiding behind a boulder. A man walked right beneath me, holding a flaming torch. He walked up to the fire, planting his torch in the ground. He picked up a bundle of wood lying beside it and threw it on the flames. The red and orange tongues rose toward the sky, lighting up the tiny gorge.

I crouched even lower, trying to remain completely hidden. Although none of this made any sense, I assumed it had something to do with the ceremonies taking place all over the island this evening. I heard chanting in the distance, and realized many people were gathered further down the path. I could not follow the path there without giving myself away. My hands were already scratched, and the wound on my arm had bled during my climb.

I slowly stood and climbed further up the rock, where the light of the flames could not reach. I stared, open-mouthed, at the sight that met my eyes.

A large number of people dressed in white tunics stood in a circle around an enormous pit. A large clay bowl lay at its bottom. A woman in a crimson tunic knelt at the edge of the pit. A white mask covered her face. The people forming the circle held small lanterns. Torches had been mounted on the faces of the rock all around, lighting up the space. The soft sound of a drum came from a woman sitting apart from the group, enhancing the air of mystery. She seemed to be the only one sitting outside the circle, on a slightly raised rocky mound across from where I stood.

Absorbed as I was by the imposing sight, I forgot the reason I was up here for a second. I looked around to see if

Destine was anywhere to be seen, but I could not spot her. Carefully, I rose to my feet. That was when I noticed the man sitting on a large rock right beneath me.

The group continued to chant, in a whisper as irregular as the fluttering of the breeze, rising then falling. I had never seen anything like it before, and I confess I was entranced. I could not understand what they were doing, but every movement seemed practiced, familiar. I was convinced they would react badly to my presence, so I kept as still as I could.

The drumbeat died down along with the chants, and nobody moved. I guessed the ceremony was nearing its end. I decided to return to the narrow passage and get as far away as I could, then try to retrace Destine's steps, whose signal had now disappeared. Fun show while it lasted, I thought, but it was time to go.

Just before I turned my back on the gathering, I detected a slight movement. The woman who had been kneeling down stood up. Her tunic seemed to become a more vibrant red, as if a secret spotlight had been trained on her. The drum began its hollow beat. Some put down their lanterns and began to sprinkle liquid on the ground from small clay jars. When they stopped, one of the women walked up to the woman in the mask and loosened her hair.

Someone else brought a torch and flung it into the large clay bowl inside the pit. Large flames sprang up, lighting up the faces in the circle. More women approached and began to undress her, touching the naked body that was slowly unveiled in the moonlight. Glowing amber in the light of the moon and the fire, she looked like a statue.

Unable to tear my eyes away from the spectacle unfolding before me, I crouched on my heels and watched the strange rites being performed.

The naked woman, wearing only her mask, stepped down into the pit. The man sitting below me stood up and walked forward, passing fearlessly close to the flames. When he was in the pit beside her, she bowed her head as if she was kissing his hand. The beat of the drum got louder, the rhythm faster.

The man, who must have been elderly, climbed out of the pit with aide from the others, and stood across from the woman. She kept her masked face turned to him, and I could only see her back. Her long, black hair reached her waist, emphasizing the milky whiteness of her skin. I felt goose bumps watching the ceremony unfolding before me.

Another man approached behind the elderly man, carrying something on his shoulders. A cry like laughter rang out, and I realized he was carrying an animal: a large, black ram.

The naked woman knelt once again, her back glowing red under the torches and the fire burning in the large bowl. The drumbeat reached a crescendo, and I could feel the rock vibrate under my feet. The man placed the ram at the feet of the old man, pinning its legs to the ground.

The chanting picked up again, and the people in the circle stepped forward, raising their voices, until they formed a tight circle around the pit, vibrating with intensity. The old man took a dagger from his belt and raised it to the sky. He then bent down and pressed it against the neck of the ram, which began to cry like a terrified baby. In one swift movement, he slit its throat as if its skin was made of paper. The man who had been carrying the ram picked it up and placed it in the slaughterer's arms.

Blood was splattered on the old man's face and white hair, but he did not seem bothered. On the contrary, he appeared to welcome it. He held the ram over the head of the woman and let the steaming blood wash over her. It trickled down her hair and over her naked body, dying her skin red, drop by drop. The figures, the voices, the blood, and the beating of the drum all merged, building up to a dense, hypnotic climax.

Every now and then, I thought I could make out a word that seemed slightly familiar. *Axieros.*

The man put down the carcass of the ram and brought the knife close to the woman's neck. She instinctively pulled back, as if she had not been expecting it. In another swift movement, he cut something that was hanging around her neck, and held it up. She slowly raised her right arm, offering him her hand.

The voices grew louder, and everyone raised their arms to the skies, swaying as if held in a trance by some unseen power. The white-haired man took her hand and, speaking loudly in what sounded like ancient Greek, put a ring on her finger.

She turned to face the fire. Her body looked smudged, clumsy, like a child's drawing. She brought her hands behind her head and removed her mask. I felt time stop. The hairs on my arms rose as if someone had just walked over my grave. Iro!

I struggled to breathe. My mind refused to accept what my eyes were telling me. I thought I was hallucinating. Covered in blood, Iro stood naked before the flickering flames. She seemed frightened, but I could not be sure whether that wasn't just the play of the flames, casting shadows on her face and distorting her expression. I ducked as she turned around, thinking she had seen me. I was wrong; she had turned to face the fire again. It all seemed to be part of the ritual.

The image of the woman wearing the scarlet belt at the Sanctuary flashed before my eyes in sudden realization. That's what she'd meant when she'd said we had met three times in all.

A naked man stepped into the tight circle of worshippers, wearing a mask like hers. He walked down to Iro, without touching her, and stood facing her, hiding her face from my view.

Forgetting all about hiding, I moved along the rocks until once again she came into view. She seemed surprised. Her body was shaking, and I could tell she was afraid, as if she was there against her will. The old man and some of the worshippers, no doubt the inner circle, came and sat on the edge of the pit. Even the woman holding the drum came and sat beside the high priest who had slaughtered the ram. My gut told me that he must be Iro's father.

I remembered everything Vasilis had said about Alexandros and his ancestry. The couple stood in the circle, beside the fire, which now burned low. In the absolute silence that reigned, all that could be heard was the crackling wood and the low whistle of the breeze as it skimmed over the rocks.

The naked man touched Iro's shoulders, pressing her to sit down. She turned to look at her father, as if she did not want to obey. The naked man grabbed her wrists and pushed her roughly to the ground. She tried to stand up. Two men who had been sitting beside the pit jumped down and pinned her to the ground. I could not tell whether what I was watching was part of the ritual, or happening against her will. Everyone's calm demeanor seemed to indicate the former, but her struggle to free herself told another story.

Impassive, her father spoke loudly: "We have gathered here today, bearing sacred soil from the four corners of the Earth, to celebrate the full moon and honor our new Great Mother in the moonlight. Tomorrow, a new era begins for all of us who have carried the legacy of our ancestors for thousands of years. For this reason, we all bear witness and participate in the union that will bring us the next generation, blessed by the gods who stand beside us this evening. Let us drink to that before the ceremony begins."

A woman handed cups of wine to everyone. It was plain to see that the old man was an expert manipulator, a demagogue who could sway everyone attending in his favor. My eyes returned to Iro. I saw her open her mouth to speak, but one of the men holding her to the ground slapped his palm over her mouth. I wondered whether I should intervene. Again, I was not sure whether what I was witnessing was real danger, or part of this incomprehensible ritual. Poised to run, I waited to see how far this madness would go.

I felt my phone vibrate, and saw Vasilis's name on the screen. He was obviously getting worried. I switched it off and returned it to my pocket, keeping my eyes fixed on the strange proceedings unraveling by the pit.

Alexandros was standing up. He took a sip of wine, and emptied his cup beside him. Scarlet as the blood of the sacrificial animal, it splashed on the ground. The others followed suit.

He signaled to the man in the pit, who stepped closer to Iro and removed his mask. To my great surprise, I recognized her fiancé, Miltos. He knelt between her legs. Iro struggled to keep her knees joined, to repel him; he struggled to push them open. Her cries occasionally escaped through the palm of the man keeping her muffled. Miltos overcame her resistance, violently prying her thighs open and trying to enter her.

She suddenly freed her mouth and let out a desperate scream, like an injured animal caught in a clever trap. I stood up to shout at them to stop. Before I could open my mouth, I saw something move like a flash across the clearing, jumping over the seated men and falling on Miltos.

Destine!

She grabbed Miltos's arm in her jaws and violently dragged him away from Iro. Commotion followed the stunned silence, as everyone tried to understand what had just happened.

Iro escaped her startled captors and stood up, trying to cover her nakedness with her arms. A battle waged between dog and man, and I began to climb down toward them.

That's when I saw Alexandros approach Destine, holding a sword. Before I could even cry out a warning, he plunged the steel blade into the dog's flesh. I doubled over as if the blow had gone through me. Destine let out a terrifying howl. She let go of Miltos's arm and fell to the ground, panting heavily, still bearing her fangs at anyone who tried to approach her.

A deafening roar escaped my throat as Alexandros raised the sword once again. It echoed against the rocks, amplified as it rippled to the top of the mountain. Everyone turned in my direction. Destine leapt out of the pit and vanished into the darkness.

I climbed down the sharp rocks as quickly as I could, and jumped onto the ground. Iro, smeared with blood and soil, was hastily pulling her tunic on. Miltos, blood streaming down his arm, was doing the same. Alexandros walked up to me holding the small sword. Destine's blood glistened on the blade.

"What are you doing here?" he screamed.

I had no doubt he would not hesitate to use the sword against a human. For the first time, I regretted leaving my gun in the States, but it was too late. The others came to stand behind him, even Miltos, whose eyes were blazing with hatred.

"What are you doing here?" Alexandros shouted again, coming even closer.

"I was looking for my dog, and I heard her howl. I only wanted to help," I said, trying to inject a touch of reality, of reason, in the insanity that seemed to have gripped everyone.

"You have no right to be here. You are trespassing, understand?" He raised his sword once again.

Miltos grabbed Alexandros's hand and pulled it down. "This is the second time you've dared show your face to me," he shouted at me. "You interrupted something very important. Who told you to come here?"

I looked at all of them, and wondered whether I would get out of this alive. Iro remained by the pit, looking terrified.

"No one told me to come here. That doesn't mean I'm here on my own."

Most of them turned to look at the rocks. I took out my phone. "They already know where I am, and who else is here with me. So, if anything happens to me, they'll know where to start."

Miltos grabbed the phone from my hand.

I lunged at him, but felt the point of the sword press against my chest. I pushed the sword away and lowered my voice to a growl. "Give me my phone," I hissed.

Miltos examined it for a second, and then threw it to me. "I suggest you get going. Now. "

Varvis protested, but Miltos nodded that he knew what he was doing. "You have five minutes to get out of here."

"I'm not going anywhere until I make sure she is okay," I said, pointing to Iro.

"She is fine. You can go," Miltos said, pointing to the path behind me and pushing me with his injured hand.

"I want to hear it from her. Don't you dare touch me!" I planted my feet firmly on the ground.

Varvis and Miltos looked at each other. The old man turned toward me. "Listen, stranger. You invaded our land, interrupting something you can't even begin to understand. If they weren't such cowards, you'd already be in the ground like a black ram. Leave, and don't try my patience any further."

"I know you slaughter animals without a thought," I sneered. "I'm not going anywhere until she says she is okay."

The small crowd parted, and I saw Iro approach. "I'm fine. Go," she said, and turned away.

It was the last thing I'd expected to hear. Anger swelled up inside me at her coldness. Miltos sneered, and pointed to the path once again. I looked at them all in disgust, and turned to go. Varvis's voice followed me. "I won't think twice before gutting your animal, either, if I find her."

Luckily, I kept my cool and walked away. A few minutes later, I was crawling through the tunnel to the small plateau where I first saw Destine that evening. I felt crushed with disappointment, and annoyed with myself for feeling that way. What did I expect from a woman I barely knew? Obviously, it was all part of their sick ritual. A wave of nausea swept through me at the thought they would now pick up from where I had interrupted them.

I took out the phone. No red dot. I called Jill, who told me they had lost Destine's signal too, suddenly. I could not bear it, knowing she was injured and alone.

I called Vasilis and simply told him I hadn't found her, and was on my way back. He said he had gotten so worried he was about to call the police. An hour later, I reached the car and found him snoozing in the passenger seat.

Vasilis woke with a start when I turned on the engine, and asked me what had happened. He stared at me open-mouthed for the rest of the journey back, as I recounted the evening's events. Occasionally, he would put his head in his hands, but made no comment. I told him the story dispassionately, briefing him coldly, still seething inside.

He only spoke when we pulled up outside his house. "I'll come stay with you tonight."

Despite my fatigue, I laughed at the way he said it, as if he wanted to stand guard. "Thank you, Vasilis, I'll be fine. I don't think I'll be getting much sleep. I will keep looking for

Destine. She is injured and needs help. Go get some rest. We'll speak in the morning."

He sighed. "I don't know what to say. Be on your guard until sunrise, and then leave. Please. Leave, and never come back. They ..."

"I'm not going anywhere until I find Destine," I interrupted.

His eyes welled up. "That's what Zoe said when she was looking for Andreas."

I reassured him I would be careful, and watched him as he walked inside his house. I was sure he would be spending the night awake, too.

The moon was about to dip down below the horizon, taking the secrets of the night with it. Both the good and the bad ...

Miltos and Alexandros entered the tower's courtyard, closely followed by Iro. Near the staircase leading to the upper floor, Alexandros, still holding the sword, turned to Iro and spoke in a harsh voice, "Go wash. Tomorrow morning, we need to talk."

"We need to talk. Right now," Iro replied.

Alexandros's face turned crimson. "I said go," he hollered.

She did not seem startled or afraid. Even though she was determined to confront her father, she chose to wait. Not out of fear, but out of the need to think seriously about her next move. She knew that her life would never be the same again. She looked at Miltos with contempt, and walked under the passageway, her bloodstained dress sweeping the flagstones.

The sound of the door closing echoed through the courtyard. Alexandros pulled Miltos by the hand and, looking at the bite, said, "He must not go unpunished. He offended us and everything we represent."

Miltos spoke in a lower voice. "Father, we must be careful now. He knows a lot about us. I fear someone has been feeding him information."

"Then we should find the traitor and bury them both. Bury what they know for good," Varvis hissed.

Low on the wall behind them, a small basement window soundlessly opened, just a crack. Two eyes shone in the dark behind them, going unnoticed. Whoever was standing there could hear every word clearly.

Miltos tried to calm his future father-in-law down. "I think it's best to leave him alone and just keep an eye on him, see what he does in the following days. He will most likely leave and we will never see him again. Don't forget, he is a policeman. If anything happens to him ..."

Varvis grabbed his shoulders and shook him. "He insulted us, don't you understand? He defiled our rites. Everything you see around you is drenched in the blood of our ancestors and those who stood in their way. We must obliterate him, like the archaeologist and his mother."

Miltos seemed perplexed, looking at Alexandros as if he had suddenly lost his mind. "When you say obliterate, what do you mean? What has this got to do with his grandfather running away?"

"You young people think that everything will be taken care of as if by magic, without you getting your hands dirty." Alexandros puffed his chest out proudly as he lowered his voice. "I'm the only one alive who knows what I'm about to tell you. When the archaeologist threatened to search our land, my father ordered Simon to burn down their house to scare him off. His mother did not make it out in time, and burned like a rat."

Miltos could not believe his ears. He was not so immoral as to accept murder.

"That scum still did not give up," Alexandros continued. "He was spying on us. A few nights later, he showed up in a field where my father and Simon were digging up gold artifacts to sell. He threatened to turn us in." Alexandros chuckled at the memory.

"What happened next?" Miltos asked, now reeling from the discovery that the family of his future wife were not only arsonists, but antiquities smugglers as well.

"He is still lying in the pit," he replied with evident glee. "I still remember his smile when I stabbed him with the twin of this sword. As if he enjoyed getting knifed …" Alexandros turned the handle of his sword and pointed to the carving. "See what it says here? *Axieros*. Worthy. What my daughter should have become tonight. That's why I'm telling you this. That man must die. If you are too scared, I'll do it with my own hands …"

The window behind them closed softly at these last words. Whoever had been standing there did not want to hear the rest.

Miltos stepped back in horror. He was silent for a while, as he tried to come to terms with what he had just heard. "Alexandros, this is the first time I've heard any of this. I don't think anyone in my family knew about this. I followed you because that's what was preordained. That's what I was brought up to believe. You led us all these years. However, there is a world of difference between standing up for your beliefs, and murdering people. And you just said you sold antiquities, too ..."

Varvis's breathing became heavier while Miltos spoke. Paying no heed, the younger man continued. "I am leaving as of this moment. I will not reveal your guilty secrets, but I will not collude to any crimes. I need to speak to Iro and see what will happen between us, although I don't think there is any reason to continue with this engagement. She seems to be doing everything out of a sense of duty, not because she loves me."

Varvis's breathing became increasingly labored, as he tried to control his mounting rage. Miltos was undeterred. "Allow me to give you a word of advice," Miltos added, "because you seem so blinded by hatred. Forget what happened tonight, and do nothing that might embarrass you or Iro. No one knows about what happened in the past; you are safe from it. If anything happens to the archaeologist's grandson, however, all will be revealed. Did Iro know any of this?"

Varvis gave him a look of pure hatred. "She is not worthy of knowing any of this. Nor are you! I was going to accept you as a son, but you are not worthy of even standing in the same room as me. Get out of my house!"

Miltos looked cautiously at the sword the old man was gripping hard, and carefully stepped away. He walked to the passageway when Varvis called out again, "That's not the way out. You are no longer worthy of passing under those arches!"

That was when Miltos realized he was being kicked out of the house permanently. He did not want to push the old man any further, so he quickly walked away. He would talk to Iro the following morning, get his things then.

Once the wooden door closed behind him, Alexandros let out a scream of white-hot rage. He flung everything to the ground, slashed at the potted flowers and the bushes with his sword, kicking and flailing about like a madman.

The servant appeared at the top of the landing in her bathrobe and ran down the stairs. "What's the matter? What's happened to you?" she asked, trying to calm him down.

Alexandros leaned against the table, panting with exertion. "Nothing happened. Go back to bed and, no matter what you hear, do not leave your room," he said, weighing the sword in his hand.

Frightened, she scurried upstairs as Varvis disappeared under the passageway. He entered the house and stopped outside the door of Iro's bedroom. He opened the door softly, slowly, trying not to make any noise. He could not see clearly in the dark. Keeping the point of his sword turned to the ground, he fumbled for the light switch.

His eyes bulged when he realized the room was empty. Only the crimson garment lay in a pile on the bed. He called out his daughter's name, but received no reply. Enraged, he flung the door open, smashing it against the wall. The curtains fluttered in the sudden current. The bedroom window was wide open ...

I spent a couple of hours driving around, looking for any sign of Destine, but my search proved fruitless. I spotted one dog in the distance, and for a moment hope surged inside me, only to be extinguished as quickly as it had appeared.

I wondered how Destine had ended up on the mountain where the ceremony was taking place. The only link was Iro. She was the one Destine had tried to save when she sensed she was in danger.

I decided to return to the house before dawn, just in case Destine did the same, following a scent trail back home. I would catch a couple of hours' sleep, and then keep looking. I now feared that the others might get to her first, and finding her became all the more urgent.

I parked, and immediately noticed the garden gates were closed. I had left them open in case Destine came back. I exited the car cautiously, on the alert for anything unusual. Quiet as a cat, I walked into the garden. A shadow fell on one of the garden chairs, and I felt the hair on the back of my neck stand up. I took out my flashlight and shone it in that direction.

Iro stood in the garden, staring into the light, unblinking. There was no end to the evening's surprises. I switched it off and hesitatingly approached. After everything that had happened, I expected the worst.

"I'm alone," she said.

"Why are you here?" I asked coldly, keeping a tight rein on my emotions. I would not allow my feelings to rule my head this time.

"I don't know. All I can tell you is that I'm alone." She sat on a chair and pushed her hair back.

I sat down on the chair furthest from her, trying to understand what was going on.

"I'm worried about Destine. Did you find her?" she asked anxiously.

"No, she is still out there." I sighed, and turned to look at the gates.

"She is injured. Surely she'll be back soon so you can take care of her. Those dogs are very smart. Poor thing tried to protect me."

"I might have found her if your father hadn't stabbed her. Tell me, why are you here?" I asked again, hoping to understand the real reason for her visit.

She looked down at her hands, struggling to reply.

"The things that happened during the ceremony ... Did they happen with your consent?" I asked, trying to make some sense of the evening.

"I don't know when you started watching, but up to a certain point, yes. I knew what would happen. It was all arranged."

"Which part did you not know?"

I did not expect her to answer, and I was surprised to see her reply so openly. "I knew everything up to the point where he put the ring on my finger. The ritual was supposed to end there."

"So why did you refuse my help?" I asked angrily.

"If I took your side right then, we might not have gotten out alive. I did it to protect you ..."

I was touched by her sincerity, but I tried not to show it. "So, after I left, did you carry on?"

"No, Andreas. Everything stopped. No ceremony had ever been interrupted before. Nobody knew how to proceed. It caused upheaval, turmoil."

Our eyes locked across the table. The light was dim, just enough to see each other. It wasn't a simple glance between people. Like the first time we met, I felt hypnotized by her eyes, unable to resist.

"I'd still like to hear why you are here," I insisted.

"Would you believe me if I said I had nowhere else to go?"

"I don't know what to believe anymore so just go ahead and talk. I will listen. That doesn't mean I'll believe you."

She seemed hurt by my words, but nonetheless continued. "As I told you, everything stopped after you appeared. Thank you for trying to help me, both you and Destine. I don't even want to contemplate what would have happened if you hadn't been there."

"Do you want to tell me what you were doing up there?"

She sighed. "It's a long story."

I leaned back in my chair and stretched out my legs. "Do I look like I'm in a hurry?"

"Very well. At this point, there is no need to keep any secrets. My family is supposed to be one of the oldest families on the island, its roots stretching all the way back to ancient times, when the Cabirian Mysteries were the main religion on Samothrace." She paused for a moment, and then asked, "Do you know anything about them?"

"I know a little," I said, nodding attentively.

"Last night's full moon had been set as one of the most important of all time. It is said that a new era of great change for the planet and the lives of men begins today."

"What was your part in all this?"

"If I had been born a boy, I would have become the next leader when my father passed away. Today, I was anointed Great Mother. The *Axieros*, she who is worthy … If I ever give birth to a son, he will become the next leader." She turned around and pulled her shirt down over her shoulder, showing me her tattoo.

I remembered trying to read it by the waterfall. I now read it clearly: *Axieros*. She turned back to look at me. I could sense she wanted to say more, but hesitated. "Andreas, so much has happened these past couple of days, and especially tonight. I would like to know how you ended up there. Someone told you, didn't they?"

"No. Like I told everyone else, I was looking for Destine. She led me to you. Nobody said a thing."

"You knew something, though, when you asked me about the path of two shadows …"

I had forgotten all about Vasilis's riddle. It was obviously linked to the site where the rituals took place. I did not want to give it away, so I changed the subject. "I still don't think you've told me the real reason why you're here. I would appreciate you telling me; otherwise, I will have to ask you to leave. If anyone finds out you're here, it will stir up a world of trouble for us both."

She seemed taken aback that I might ask her to leave. "I told you the truth. I have nowhere else to go …"

"That's not the only reason, though." I looked at her intently.

All the night sounds became amplified in the silence that followed, as if someone had turned up the volume. She shifted uncomfortably in her chair, and there was a catch in her voice when she spoke next. "No, that's not the only reason. Please don't press me for an answer. I don't want to have to lie. Go to bed, if you want, and ignore me. I will sit here in the garden if you let me, and leave at dawn. I just want this night to be over. Please, it's the only thing I ask of you."

Conflicting emotions rising inside me prevented me from thinking clearly. I could not believe she had nowhere else to go, but I still could not fathom why she would be here. I got up without a word and walked inside. I needed the physical distance to decide what to do.

I walked to the bathroom and splashed cold water on my face, trying to clear my head and buy myself some time. I turned the bathroom light off and walked to the window as I dried my face. Iro had not moved.

I returned to the bedroom and picked up a blanket, then stepped back into the garden. She turned her head to look at me as I draped the blanket over her shoulders. She reached back to grip the edges of the blanket, and our fingers accidently touched.

I did not pull my hand away; nor did she. We gently stroked each other, my body giving in to the same sensations that had rippled through me as we sat by the water, fingers merged in a sensual dance.

Wordlessly, eyes locked in silent understanding, I found myself standing in front of her, unable to tell whether my own footsteps or Iro's magnetic pull had brought me there. She rose slowly, letting the blanket fall from her shoulders, and leaned into me. She tilted her face as I lowered my head, our lips a breath apart.

In an enchanted trance, we stood there, as if we drew life from a shared breath. Our fingers entwined, caressing, pressing, preparing us for what we now both anticipated. All sense of reason was lost. I silenced a tiny voice of caution inside me. All I wanted was to abandon myself to the spell this woman had cast on me from the moment we first met.

Pulling one hand away, she fleetingly turned her eyes to the front door, issuing a seductive invitation. I felt her lead me there, and I followed unsteadily, drunk with delight at the way her touch made me feel. As soon as we were inside, we both hesitated, caught in a confused, intense awkwardness as the evening hung in the balance. One wrong move and the passion would be extinguished. One right move and the simmering fire that burned inside us would consume us.

I stroked her hair and let my hands follow their course, over her shoulders, down her sides to her waist. I felt her tremble at my touch. Putting a hand around her waist, I pulled her roughly toward me. She leaned her head back, exposing her long, white neck to me. A small vein throbbed wildly as her heart raced, and I felt her crazed pulse against my lips as they hungrily explored her neck.

I gripped her shirt and started to undo the buttons one by one, kissing her all the while, feeling her hot breath in my hair as she gasped with pleasure. The little voice of caution tried one last time to knock some sense in to me, telling me I should stop. As if she could sense the presence of doubt, she suddenly gripped my hair and pulled me in for a hungry, lingering kiss while I roughly tore away at the rest of our clothes.

Her moist lips brushed against my neck and my chest as her hands tried to feel every line in my body. I did not even realize how we ended up in the bedroom. She pulled back and looked deep into my eyes, her fingers tracing the outline of my face and my lips. She brought her lips close to my ear, and her hoarse voice sent shivers of delight through my body.

"I want you," she whispered. "I have wanted you from the first time I saw you. That day at the Sanctuary, when I looked at you, even though I had never seen you before, even though I did not know who you were ... I dreamt of you that night."

Gasping with desire, I gripped her by the shoulders, turned her around, and pushed her on the bed, falling beside her. My hands explored the curves of a body whose naked form I had admired a few hours ago, and which was now burning with desire. In the dimness of the light shining down the corridor, I stroked the few speckles of blood that still stained her skin after the sacrifice of the ram in her honor. There was no fear in her eyes now, only a thirsty flame lit by our touch.

I felt my heart was about to explode when she turned over and, in one swift movement, hovered above me. She teasingly brushed her lips against mine, before sliding all the way down my torso. She straddled me, just high enough to avoid touching me, close enough that I could feel the tantalizing heat of her body.

I grabbed her hands and pulled her down to me, wildly kissing her lips, unable to bear it any longer. She sat on my stomach, tortuously delaying what we both yearned for. I raised my body, forcing her to slide further down, until our two worlds finally met.

She raised her hips and allowed me to enter her slowly. In the darkness behind my eyelids, I felt her vocalizing everything I felt. Her groans came from deep inside her, like the sounds of a wild animal struggling to be free, but unable or unwilling to do so.

My breath came fast, ragged, swept away as I was by the intense currents of pleasure jolting through my body with her every move. I gripped her waist and we both swayed in a sensuous dance, guided by the rhythm of our moans of pleasure.

I sat up on the bed, and we faced each other. She stopped moving for a few seconds, touching my face as if trying to lock it inside her memory forever. I pressed the small of her back with one hand, and mirrored her movements with the other. She still wore her ceremonial ring, which scratched a thin line on my skin as she moved her hand from my lips, to my neck, to my chest.

I pushed against her, harder and harder. The ring dug into my back as she trembled, her moans getting louder, her lips locked on mine ... I felt her quake in my arms as waves of ecstasy shook my body.

With not an inch between us, we became one body, one breath, as the flames of desire became a raging fire that consumed us. The light of early dawn crept through the window, projecting the shadow of the branches swaying in the same rhythm. Lost in endless pleasure, whenever I opened my eyes, the shadows took on the shape of terrifying, mythical creatures for a second, before turning back into leafy shadows.

I was woken up by the sound of birdsong as the early morning sun poured in through the open window. I turned toward Iro and, to my surprise, I saw her lying on her side, looking at me.

"You are already awake," I said, shuffling closer to her.

"I opened my eyes a few minutes ago. You were talking in your sleep."

I smiled. The only dream I could remember was the one I had shared with her a couple of hours ago. "What was I saying?"

"Just random words ..."

I don't know why, but I didn't believe her. Once again, I got the feeling she was hiding something. I pushed myself up and walked to the window, hoping to find my beloved dog waiting outside.

"I'll come looking for her with you," Iro said. She sprang up and started looking for her clothes.

I walked up to her and touched her shoulder as gently as I could. "Iro, I don't think we should keep seeing each other. Maybe it is best our roads part right here. You are getting married soon. This was too good to be true ..."

Her face darkened, and she turned away. "I don't know what I'm going to do next, but I understand if you want to carry on with your life and return to the woman you love."

"I don't understand."

She pointed to my tattoo, and everything clicked. I had not told her anything about Eva. I pulled the bandage away, revealing all the words. "Six month ago, the woman I loved died. Just before she passed away, knowing the end was near, we both got the same tattoo on our right hand, so we would never forget what we had shared."

Her eyes filled with tears. "I'm sorry, I did not know."

I touched her cheek. "It's not your fault."

We both stood awkwardly facing one another, and I hoped she would not make a move. I knew I would be unable to resist her. Thankfully, she turned around and began to get dressed.

"I won't join you since you don't want me to, but I will go looking for Destine anyway."

Unable to control myself, I walked up to her and hugged her from behind. "Don't you understand we can't be together?"

She gave me a long look over her shoulder. I pressed my palm on her lips, hoping to keep her away. She gently pulled my hand down and turned to face me. "Andreas, my life changed last night. I will not stay on the island. I am leaving tomorrow at the latest. I don't think I will ever come back."

I was dumbstruck. "What about your engagement? Your father?"

"All I know with any certainty is that I want to get away from everyone and everything."

"Then why did you come to me?"

She froze, as if she did not know how to reply. She turned to the bed and began to pull the sheets off. I noticed they were muddy, and some of the blood on her skin had rubbed off on them. "We should change the sheets. And then, if you don't mind, I'd like to take a shower. I'm sorry; I washed in a hurry before I came here …"

I grabbed the sheets from her hands and flung them on the bed. "Why did you come here? Will you finally tell me the truth?"

"To protect you," she shouted.

Her strength suddenly abandoning her, she sagged on the mattress. I sat beside her and took her hand. "Protect me from whom? Your family?"

"We should be able to leave it all behind; carry on with our lives free from the past," she mused.

"What's stopping us?" I whispered.

"The past itself …" She sighed. "I don't know how much you know about what happened in the past. Last night, I found out some things I think you should know. It won't change what happened, but you should be careful."

Ever since I set foot on Samothrace and started to hear various stories, a sense of foreboding had been growing inside me. As it did now.

A loud knock on the front door made us both jump. We exchanged a scared look, as if we had been expecting this. I made to move toward the door, but Iro grabbed my arm. She soundlessly formed the words, "Be careful," then let me go.

"Hide," I whispered, but she shook her head and walked to the door with me.

The knocks grew louder as I gripped the door handle. I heard Vasilis's voice call out my name, and felt my shoulders relax. I opened the door, and almost laughed at the shock on his face when he saw Iro.

"What's the matter, Vasilis?" I asked.

Like a fish, he opened and closed his mouth without a sound. I waved my hand in front of his eyes, and only then did he snap out of it, exhaling deeply.

"They found Destine. Someone called me and said he saw her on the Varvis estate, close to the Sanctuary. She was limping ..."

I almost kissed him with delight. I ran inside and grabbed my phone. I saw the red signal had come back on. Iro watched as I threw on some clothes and explained the tracking device to her.

I grabbed my car keys and hurried out the door. Vasilis could not stop staring at Iro, as if she were a ghost. Before we got in the car, he turned to her and solemnly said, "She is on your land."

Iro did not reply, but climbed into the back seat, letting him ride shotgun.

I almost flew down the road, following Vasilis's directions and the GPS signal. The sun had just risen but, in the distance, toward Alexandroupolis, dark clouds raced over the sea, sailing toward us. The signal showed Destine at a fixed location, quite a distance away from the Temple of the Great Gods.

We entered the Sanctuary and drove on, pulling up further down where Vasilis assured me there was a hole in the fence separating the site from the Varvis lands. Indeed, behind a thick bush, a small gap in the fence allowed us to enter the estate, which stretched to the foothills. The ground here was smoother, and we walked easily, heading in the direction indicated by the tracking signal.

Vasilis was silent. He leaned heavily on his stick as he walked, casting sideways glances at Iro. Farther up the hill, the tower's ramparts were visible above the orchard that stretched around it. The distant sound of rumbling thunder told of the approaching storm.

We finally reached the small hill behind which Destine appeared to be lying. The dot had not moved at all in all this time. Fear gripped my heart that we might not get to her in time. I would know soon enough.

Vasilis fell behind as I half-walked, half-ran to the peak of the small hill. No longer caring about pretenses, he walked once again without the aid of his walking stick. Iro caught up with me and held my hand as we climbed.

The first thing I saw over the hill was Destine, lying on the ground among a group of large stones that rose like a temple around her. Cold fear gripped my heart. Iro squeezed my hand. A bolt of lightning tore through the sky and touched the peak of Mt. Saos.

I ran to Destine. She was lying on her side in a hole she appeared to have dug. I knelt beside her and felt for a heartbeat. Her hind leg was caked with blood. Iro crouched low on the ground and placed her ear against Destine's belly. Her face lit up, and she pried Destine's mouth open with her hands. Vasilis knelt beside us anxiously.

"She is alive," Iro said, "but her pulse is weak." She seemed to be thinking of what to do next. "Help me get her out of here," she said decisively, pushing her hands under Destine's body. I did the same, and we lifted the injured dog out of the hole.

I tried to place Destine on her side to prevent her injury touching the soil, and turned to see what was keeping Iro. Still as a statue, she stared wide-eyed at the hole, and at what Destine's body had kept hidden.

I kept looking at Iro, trying to understand what had happened. In the end, I got up and walked toward her. She was staring at the ground, at what looked like a short, thick stick.

"What's the matter, Iro?"

She bent down and tugged at the stick. It wasn't a stick at all, but rather, a rusty steel sword. She wiped the soil off with the hem of her shirt. She looked closely at the handle, and then dropped it to the ground as if she had been stung.

Iro knelt beside the hole and began to dig, scooping up the soil with her hands. Vasilis picked up the sword and squinted closely at its handle. "*Axieros,*" he whispered.

I could not understand what had come over them. I walked back to Destine and picked her up in my arms, ready to go find a vet. I had only taken a couple of steps when I heard Iro's cry. She sat back from the hole, one hand covering her mouth in shock. Vasilis looked ashen as he stared at the hole.

The first heavy drops of rain fell on my head, and the rumble of thunder shook the ground. Staggering under Destine's weight, I walked to the edge of the hole. I stared at the top of the human skull, dumbfounded. Iro hugged herself, rocking back and forth.

"What is going on? Who is this?" I asked, feeling Destine's heart beat weakly against my fingertips.

"I'm not sure … but … but …" Iro stifled a sob.

"Take the dog to the vet and call the police," Vasilis said, with an authoritative tone I had never heard before. "Don't stand there looking at me," he barked when he saw us hesitate. "Save the dog! I'll stay here and wait for you to come back."

Iro stood up and looked at the tower in the distance, as if expecting someone to appear. "Let's go," she said, tugging at my sleeve.

"Don't touch anything else," I told Vasilis. "There could be evidence. Leave everything as it is until the police get here."

Vasilis nodded and waved us off.

We reached the car drenched to the bone. My arms burned with the effort of carrying Destine. Iro sat beside the dog in the back seat, and I set off for the port, where the vet was.

"Whose skeleton is it? You know, don't you?" I whispered, looking at her through the rearview mirror.

Iro stroked Destine, whispering something that sounded like a prayer. Tears rolled down her cheeks.

It was raining hard, but Vasilis had not moved an inch from where they had left him. He eschewed the shelter of nearby trees and knelt on the ground, his palms resting in the mud, water dripping from his hair and clothes, part-mourner, part-sentry beside the shallow grave. Indifferent to the flashes of lightning that split the sky, to the loud crack of thunder.

Vasilis only heard the horse neighing behind him when it was but a couple of feet way. When he saw who the rider was, he shifted slightly, covering the small sword with his legs.

Astride his tall horse, Varvis stared down at Vasilis, his eyes filled with hatred. Spooked by the storm, the horse was jittery. Alexandros dismounted with difficulty, landing hard on the soft earth. He held the sword that had pierced Destine in one hand. He walked up to the pit and cast a casual glance at the bones. As if nothing was amiss, he sat down beside Vasilis, rain streaming down his face. He poked the ground with the point of his sword. Vasilis looked straight ahead, waiting for the newcomer to make the first move.

"It's a terrible feeling to be betrayed by your own child," Alexandros said. "You will not drink that bitter cup as you never had children, right?"

Vasilis did not rise to the bait.

"Do you know who is buried here?" Alexandros asked, wiping his mouth with the back of his hand.

"If it is who I think it is, I even know who dumped him here," Vasilis replied, looking Alexandros straight in the eye.

A clap of thunder startled the horse. It reared on its hind legs and galloped away. Vasilis turned to look at it, but Alexandros calmly said, "Don't worry about him, he'll find his way home." He touched Vasilis's hand with the point of his sword. Vasilis did not pull away.

"Who do you think dumped him here, then?" Vasilis asked.

"Your father and that scum, Simon," Varvis replied, pulling the sword away sharply. Then he laughed, and waved the blade under Vasilis's nose. "Yes. What you don't know is who finished him off. Who plunged a sword just like this one into his heart and sent him to Hades."

Vasilis froze. He had always assumed something terrible had happened to Andreas, but he'd never imagined a small child killing a man.

Sensing his discomfort, Varvis goaded him on. "I still remember the smile on my face as I plunged my blade into his chest. Happiest moment of my life ..."

"Why are you telling me this?" Vasilis demanded.

"So you understand that our breed always clears away the rubbish life throws in its path. My father did the same; got rid of anyone who stood in his way. It's in our blood." He laughed.

"I don't know what was in Nicholas's blood, but it's certainly not in yours," Vasilis said with a smirk.

Alexandros looked like he had just been slapped. His knuckles turned white as he gripped the hilt of his sword. "What do you mean?" he hissed.

"All these years you thought you were the chosen one who would carry on the family name. Ha! Ancient ancestors; what a joke."

Varvis gripped him by the collar and violently shook him. "What are you saying? Speak up, if you don't want to join your friend in the pit ..."

Vasilis pushed away his hands, and pulled out the sword hiding under his legs in one swift movement. Before Varvis could react, he thrust it forward with all his strength. Varvis's eyes bulged, and his face twisted with pain. He tried to return the blow, but his sword slipped from his grasp. All he could do was grasp the handle of the sword embedded in his flesh, staining his shirt red around his heart.

"You were Simon's spawn, you pitiful man ... A bastard," Vasilis said, propping him up by the shoulders. "Say hello to Andreas and Zoe for me until I come meet you all ..."

Varvis opened his mouth to say something, but blood poured down his jaw, gurgling in his throat. With a last spasm, he stopped moving, his body leaning against Vasilis's palms. Vasilis pulled his hands away, and Varvis's body toppled into the shallow grave. The old man burst into tears, burying his face in his bloodstained hands.

Dominion of the Moon

We had just dropped Destine off at the vet. The nurse did not seem too optimistic about her chances. She called the vet, who was attending a donkey in a nearby village. He would be back within the hour and, if Destine held on, he would tend to her. It was hard to leave Destine. At the same time, after everything Iro had just told me, I knew we had to return to Vasilis. There was nothing I could do here. My stomach was in knots.

Iro had called the police while I completed the paperwork at the vet's. We barely spoke on the drive back, lost in our own thoughts. For years, my grandmother had waited for my grandfather to return, unable to believe that he was dead. The reality was that he had been murdered. At least, that's what it looked like. Work had trained me to remain cautious until I had hard evidence and facts. I would have those once DNA evidence identified the skeleton buried there.

We pulled up by the gap in the fence and stepped out of the car. Iro took my hand. "Whatever happens from now on, I just want you to know ..." She struggled to find the right words.

"I think we feel the same way. Maybe it's best to let things take their course ..."

The rain had stopped, and the sun's rays shone weakly through the patches in the clouds. I saw the police car pull up and park behind my car. The young policeman waved from afar, and we walked ahead without waiting for them to catch up. I could not understand, as I neared the grave, why a man was lying inside it, Vasilis sitting beside him, head bowed as if in silent lament.

Iro's cry as we neared frightened me. She ran ahead and flung herself on the body, turning it to face her. I ran up after her and saw the man she was holding in her arms was her father, stabbed through the heart. Vasilis's hands, and the tears streaming down his face, bore witness to his act.

"Who did this?" Iro screamed, stroking her father's frozen face.

Vasilis silently raised his bloodstained hand. Before I could restrain her, she let out a choked cry and lunged at him, her hands tightening around his throat. I tried to prise her hands away, speaking gently to calm her down and save Vasilis from her wrath. Tightening her grip, she shouted at me to leave them alone, cursing Vasilis for what he had done. It was impossible to loosen her fingers without breaking her arms. Luckily, the two police officers came and helped me pull her off him.

Vasilis's face had turned red, and a bruise was already forming around his neck as he gasped for breath. Iro flailed her arms and legs, hitting me clumsily in the face. I was stunned by the blow, and felt warm blood trickle down my nose. I went and angrily stood before her. When she saw my bloodied face, she seemed to calm down. I helped Vasilis to his feet and looked around, trying to understand what had happened in our absence.

Kostas Krommydas

The two police officers listened in stunned silence as I explained what had happened. Vasilis filled in the missing pieces without holding anything back. The young policeman walked back to the grave where Iro sobbed quietly, cradling her father's head. The sword was still in Varvis's chest, but the policeman asked us not to touch anything. I saw his partner take out a pair of handcuffs, then change his mind. He asked Vasilis to remain seated.

He brought out his phone and, in a dramatic voice, informed headquarters what had happened. My nose had stopped bleeding, but my face still smarted from the strong punch. I approached the grave alongside the young policeman, who was busily jotting things down in a notebook. He bent down and started to scrape away the soil around the skull with the back of his pen.

With an exclamation, he lifted his pen up. A chain hung from it, something covered by a clump of soil dangling at the end. He took it in his hands and rubbed the soil away. The red clay particles fell to the ground, gradually revealing something that looked like a large coin. He looked at both sides and then raised his eyebrows sharply. "Your name is written on it," he said.

It was nearly dark, and a crowd had gathered outside the police station. News spread fast on the island. Vasilis was spending the night in a cell, having confessed to killing Varvis. The young policeman told me that because of his age, and the problems with his leg, he might get away with house confinement. It was just a theory; murder was a serious charge. When they asked Vasilis if he had acted in self-defense, he was adamant. "No, he did not threaten me. I just did the right thing ..."

He seemed unrepentant when I saw him. He spoke little, and only of the debt he owed to his beloved friend, of all the years spent not knowing what had happened to him. He asked me to leave the island soon, to stay away from Iro. Even now, he still feared the Varvis family.

The coroner would be arriving the following day to take a DNA sample from the remains, which appeared to be my grandfather. The truth is, I remained unconvinced that it was he. Anyone could have stolen his medal and carried it with them to their grave. Perhaps I was in denial.

Varvis's funeral was scheduled for the following day, and I wondered whether I would go. I was initially taken aback by the depth of Iro's grief. Then I realized that no matter what kind of man Alexandros had been, he still was her father. All these years, he had kept her under his control, filling her head with her ancestry and her own destiny.

She had not spoken a single word to me since his death. She left when they came to take Alexandros's body away. She only looked at me, in shock. It was hard to tell what else she may or may not be feeling. The police took photos and samples, but only Vasilis, Iro, and I knew the story behind my grandfather's murder and Varvis's confession. The crime scene had been sealed off, and a police officer stood guard there. Given their meager means, the police had been exemplary.

A number of missed calls flashed up on my phone screen. Alkistis and Jill had repeatedly tried to reach me. I was in no mood to talk about what had happened. I got inside my car and, a few minutes later, I was at the vet's. More bad news awaited me there. The doctor informed me I would have to make a decision, so Destine did not needlessly suffer. I was not ready to decide anything, and I asked him if I could wait until the following day. Would taking her to Alexandroupolis increase her chances of making it? He shook his head sympathetically. He, too, had heard the news, and reassured me he had done everything that could be done for Destine.

I went to the back room to see her. All she could do was raise her tail limply for a moment. Nothing more. That was her first response in hours, according to the vet. I sat next to her, petting her and urging her to hold on, until the vet announced it was time to go.

I walked by the port, along the side of the road that was lined with souvenir shops, coffee shops, and picturesque tavernas. People greeted me politely, as if not wishing to intrude. I could feel more stares than ever before. I was trying to decide if I should seek out Iro tonight. I wanted to see her, but wondered whether she might wish to mourn her father in solitude.

Tired and sleep deprived, I sat down at the first taverna I came across. People sat at tables all around me, or strolled past me on the street, and yet I felt utterly alone. I would wait and see how things developed the following day, and then I would finally leave this island. I still could not understand whether Samothrace was trying to keep me or send me away. Maybe it would be best to leave Greece and return to work. Maybe holidays were not the thing for me.

Someone sent over a jug of wine, and the kind gesture cheered me up a little. Soon enough, though, I succumbed to my oppressive loneliness and decided to return home. Unable to resist, I did not turn to Paleopolis, but drove to the Varvis tower. I did not intend to see her. I just needed to be nearer to her, even in this manner.

I could spot the large torches blazing on the castle walls from some distance away, as if they were trying to raise the building to the sky. I imagined it was part of some funeral ritual. I drove as close as I could. People milled on the ramparts. I looked for Iro, but she did not appear. Afraid someone would spot me, and my eyes growing heavy with fatigue, I decided to return home. A difficult day awaited me tomorrow.

The bed was just as we had left it that morning—stripped bare. Her scent lingered in the room. I hurriedly made the bed and stretched out my exhausted limbs. Then I picked up my grandmother's sketchbook. Instead of a drawing, the last page contained a single sentence, like an epilogue.

No one will ever know the secrets of the moon ...

I gazed at the cover with the large full moon, and the word *Ouranoessa* written in her cursive handwriting. I turned off the bedside lamp and released myself to the sweet obscurity of sleep.

The hours passed with tortuous slowness. I spent the whole day attending to procedural matters: meeting with the police and the coroner, who took a sample of my DNA to see if it matched the murdered man's remains. He told me it would take a while to take the corresponding sample. He had to carefully remove the soil first. After all these years, the tiniest evidence could prove significant.

The police had kept the medal bearing my grandfather's name, as well as the old sword that had become Vasilis's murder weapon. The other side of the medal bore an image of the statue of the Winged Victory, and an inscription I could not make out. I do not know why, but all these years I'd always thought that my grandfather was alive somewhere. Maybe I had absorbed my grandmother's wish to see him return to us some day. In a few days, I would be certain.

I was met with hostile looks as soon as I entered the cemetery. I recognized the faces of some of the people who had been at the moonlit ceremony, but paid no attention. I stood some distance away from them, and waited.

A procession of cars pulled up, and I saw Iro slowly walk in our direction. Her eyes were hidden behind a pair of large sunglasses, and her hair was pulled back. She was appropriately dressed in black. Behind her, a group of pallbearers dressed in white removed the coffin from the car. Iro hesitated by the entrance, and her face froze when she noticed me. Miltos came up to her and put his arm around her shoulders, and she fell in line behind the coffin.

I don't know why, but I did not expect to see him beside her after everything she had told me, after what he had tried to do to her during the ceremony. I wondered whether I should leave, but remained undecided. Being at the funeral of one of the men responsible for my grandfather's death was strange. I suddenly realized that the funeral was not the reason for my presence.

A melody like a flute floated through the cemetery. I looked around, but could not determine its provenance. I walked behind the crowd, unable to decide whether I should stay or slip away. Large cypress trees sprouted among the tombs and swayed gently in the breeze, creating the illusion that the earth swayed with them.

A woman's voice accompanied the music until we reached a spot far away from the tombs. Here, the graves bore no crosses or other religious markings. They stopped before a large, stone building with lists of names in ancient Greek carved on its walls. Nicholas, Marika, and other ancestors of the Varvis family must be buried there. An inscription on one of the walls read:

"Death will come then, when the Fates command it."

I tried to spot Iro, but she was hidden by the assembled crowd. A small ceremony was followed by wine libations over the body. Then the coffin was sealed and placed inside the mausoleum, accompanied by whispered verses in ancient Greek.

People began to disperse, and Iro came into view, in Miltos's arms. I don't know why I did not leave. Perhaps because I knew this was the last time I would ever see her. Perhaps because I felt I was to blame.

All that could be heard was the rustle of the wind blowing over the tombs, whipping up a feeling of abandonment inside me. The service had been simple, unadorned, but I imagined the bulk of the rituals had taken place at the tower before they arrived.

I did not even notice Iro and Miltos walk up to me until they were standing quite close. Miltos evidently hadn't realized who I was, because as soon as I turned to face them and he recognized me, his expression turned sour. Iro asked him to give us a minute. Reluctantly, he walked away.

I took Iro's hand and told her how sorry I was. The feel of her skin against mine woke up all the feelings of the first time we'd touched. This time we both pulled back abruptly, feeling the same discomfort.

"Destine?" she asked, and removed her sunglasses, revealing eyes swollen from crying.

I shook my head. "I don't think her chances are good. I'm leaving tomorrow and taking her with me, in case anything more can be done. The doctor is not hopeful."

"She has a lot of strength. Help her fight," Iro said. "So ... you are leaving."

"Yes. I need to go to Alexandroupolis and testify, with Vasilis."

She grimaced at the sound of his name, and turned away. I changed the subject. "If the DNA results prove it is my grandfather, I'll be back to bury him beside Zoe."

"It is your grandfather, I'm certain. Thank you for not revealing anything about my father. I appreciate it. I don't know if he was telling the truth; if he really killed your grandfather. I guess we'll never know. He bragged about many things he never did. Of course, you are free to do as you like ..."

"There comes a time when the past must be left behind," I said.

She turned to look up at the sky. "At least your grandparents can be together now. Their story reminds me of the words of a Greek poet. Tasos Livaditis. Do you know him?"

I shook my head, and she spoke softly, in a whisper. "And when we die, bury us close to one another that we may not need to get up in the night to embrace ..." Her voice broke. "Goodbye," she said, and walked away.

In the afternoon, I went by the police station to visit Vasilis. He seemed in good spirits. I was impressed by the number of people coming to pay him a visit. The following day he would be transported to Alexandroupolis, to testify before the prosecutor. He ran the risk of not being granted bail, and having to wait for his trial in prison. I made sure to hire one of the best lawyers in the area to represent him, hoping they would grant bail and he could return to his home.

Vasilis sat on the bunk bed in the small cell, looking at the dim light that crept into the room through the bars on the window. He felt free at last. He'd always felt that his beloved friend had never left the island. He may have already suspected that Varvis had something to do with his disappearance, but violent murder in cold blood had never crossed his mind. He kept Alexandros's confession to himself, and planned to take the secret to his grave.

Everything had fallen into place, and the only thing that troubled him now was Andreas's relationship with Iro. He could sense their feelings were strong. He feared Varvis's daughter, though. He feared all the Varvis women; they hid inside them aspects that made them even fiercer than the men. Her secret name, *Axieros*, did not just refer to the Great Mother … it was the name of a demon, too.

He intended to tell the archaeologists where he had hidden the artifacts that Nicholas had planted in Elizabeth's house to frame Andreas for their theft. He wanted to clear his friend's name once and for all.

He slowly removed a crumpled photo from his pocket. He brought it close to his face and tilted it toward the light. It showed Zoe sitting in her chair by the sea, looking out to Samothrace and smiling.

She was the only woman he had ever loved, even though he knew it wasn't right. She had never guessed anything. He had hidden his feelings well. Besides, Zoe had never gotten over Andreas. She'd waited for him until the very end, leaving Vasilis no room to express his feelings.

He returned the crumpled photo to his pocket and wiped a tear from his cheek. Then he stretched out on the narrow bed, closed his eyes, and drifted off to the land of memories ...

Time seemed to have slowed down all of a sudden. Minutes dragged on like hours, hours like years. I was restless. I kept driving around the island, trying to order my thoughts. My phone had been ringing nonstop, word of what had happened spreading like wildfire. Even my director had called from the States, asking if I needed anything. I wished someone could just tell me what to do. I kept making up my mind, only to change it five minutes later.

With nightfall, I found myself pacing around the garden, trying to unwind. I stopped in front of the basement door. Vasilis once told me my grandfather had slept there, many decades ago. I pushed the door, but it was locked. The edge of a key glinted under a pot of basil. That was probably my way in. I looked toward the street, checking no one was passing by, and I unlocked the door. It creaked and jammed as I opened it. I fumbled for a light switch, but found nothing. Using the light from my phone screen, I entered the basement.

The stale air inside and the massive cobwebs confirmed that no one had entered the basement in years. It looked like a small, abandoned antiques store filled with old furniture, oil lamps, and frames. Objects that were once considered precious now lay abandoned to mold and mice.

How many memories had these forgotten things been part of?

The horn of an old gramophone was turned upside down on a table. I lifted it up, and discovered the body of the gramophone beneath it, an old, dust-covered record on the turntable. The crank had come unscrewed, and lay beside it.

I picked it all up and carefully carried it to the garden, laying everything out on the table. Using a soft cloth, I meticulously cleaned every part and screwed on the crank. I slowly replaced the horn on the gramophone and leaned back to admire my work. Time to see if it worked.

Before winding the crank, I poured myself a glass of wine, turned the lights off, and lit a couple of candles. It must have been years since the old gramophone had produced a single sound, and I felt the need to celebrate something. I took a long sip, then placed the needle on the record, winding up the crank. The sound of static was quickly followed by the sound of a violin, trying to liberate its music through all the scratching.

I leaned back and looked at the sky, enjoying the atmosphere of nostalgia released by the music. I whistled along, trying to follow the rhythm of the waltz. That was when I sensed a presence in the garden, and bolted upright.

Iro stood before me, gazing at me without moving. "I could watch you for hours," she said.

I pushed down the happiness that had spontaneously surged inside me. I knew she should not be here. "Hello, Iro."

She stood there, silently. She wore jeans and a white t-shirt. It was the first time I had seen her so casually dressed.

"I'm sorry ... This was a mistake," she said, while I gawked at her like a love-struck teenager.

I sprung toward her, knocking my chair back in my haste. "Wait ..." I said, and gently turned her to face me. Her eyes were moist, and I could not stop looking into them. "Would you like some wine?"

She nodded as if she really needed a drink, and I guided her to the table. I returned with a glass, filled it, and sat across from her.

"It's very pretty at this hour," she said. "The music makes me feel like I've travelled back in time."

"That's probably when this gramophone was last used. Back in time, so now it wants to carry us there."

I raised my glass. She mirrored the gesture. "I want to ask you something else. It is the last thing I will ever ask of you," she said. "As of tomorrow, my life will take a different path. I would like to spend tonight with you."

It was the last thing I'd expected her to say. Before I could reply, she lowered her voice and hurriedly explained, "I want to stay here ... Nothing more. To spend the evening in each other's company. Drink wine, and talk about anything—except our families, and what happened between them. Talk as if we've only just met, talk until dawn. Then I will leave ..."

I hesitated. "You do realize that if someone comes looking for you here ..."

"No one will come looking for me," she said with certainty.

As much as I knew that her presence here was a mistake, I could not resist the urge to be with her. What else could happen to us, anyway? I raised my glass and covered her hand with my palm. The clinking of the wine glasses coincided with the end of the record. "Where do we start?" I asked, following her rules.

"Talk to me about this woman who will always be in your heart."

I felt a knot in my throat. I pulled away the bandage and looked at the tattoo. My first dramatic meeting with Eva flashed before my eyes. I raised my gaze to Iro, and smiled as the words tumbled from my lips.

I opened my eyes with difficulty the next morning, a fierce headache hammering my temples. The bedroom spun as I tried to get up. Despite the copious amounts drunk the previous evening, I recalled every detail. We had talked for hours in the garden, sipping wine and losing track of time and place as we connected.

A sudden cloudburst had forced us to run inside and seek shelter. The awkwardness had returned then, as we silently looked at each other, as if rethinking all of the reasons that were keeping us apart.

It had been impossible not to feel a quaver of excited anticipation at the memory of what we had shared the previous evening on this same spot. Iro had looked at me intensely, and I could read my own thoughts in her eyes.

A raindrop had dripped from my hair down my face, waking me from my reverie and interrupting the flow of images flashing through my mind. Rather abruptly, I had offered her a seat on an armchair in the corner, and I sat down on the bed across from her. Not without difficulty, we'd managed to overcome the uncomfortable moment, and continued sharing stories from our lives, mostly beautiful moments, keeping our eyes from lingering on each other.

I cannot tell how many hours passed until we finally fell asleep, after a prolonged silence. The last thing I remembered feeling was the weight of her body pressing down on the mattress beside me. She'd leaned her head on my chest and stroked my face. My mind, my senses, had been awake, but I'd preferred not to show it. I'd kept my eyes shut, knowing that if I opened them, I would be unable to resist the sensation of Iro leaning against my body.

I got up and walked to the window. She wasn't in the garden. I found her note on the kitchen table, on top of my grandmother's sketchbook. I unfolded the piece of paper, and a ring fell out. I picked it up and immediately recognized it. It was the ring her father had put on her finger during the ceremony, the ring that had left its marks on my body that same night. I placed it in my pocket and read her farewell.

"If our paths ever cross again, you can return it. Thank you for the clear skies. Take care. I."

I handed the owner the house keys, and asked if I could take a pomegranate with me. He told me I could take as many as I wanted, just mind the thorns. I carefully picked a ripe pomegranate, the red seeds peeking through a crack in its skin, and left the beautiful house. I put my luggage in the car, intending to visit Vasilis first, and then the spot where we had discovered the shallow grave. Destine and I would then travel to Alexandroupolis, hoping her life could be saved. I could not put her down, as the vet suggested.

I had only driven a few feet when the phone rang. Alkistis spoke rapidly, unable to contain her excitement, so fast I could not understand most of what she was saying. Something about the coroner asking for the help of the Archaeological Service, about some old artifacts found beside the remains.

Alkistis begged me to go there immediately. I wasted no time turning around and driving to the Sanctuary, parking at the now familiar spot and walking up the hill. I was impressed by the number of cars parked on the hill, and the crowd of people gathered around the grave like bees around a honey pot.

I looked up to where the Varvis tower stood. On the ramparts was a woman who could have been Iro. The wind tore at her hair and long, white dress as if trying to sweep her away.

Alkistis called out my name, forcing me to turn to her. She walked up to me, put an arm around my waist, and asked me to follow her. Everyone fell silent and parted to let us through. The coroner stood at the edge of the trench, as well as an elderly man in a straw hat. He was holding a small brush, gently sweeping the soil away. Almost the entire skeleton had been uncovered.

Around the human remains, pieces of marble were scattered. I mentally joined the dots, and thought I could make out something resembling a wing. Alkistis informed me the man in the pit was an archaeologist who worked at the Sanctuary of the Great Gods. He stopped what he was doing when he saw me. With a smile, he gave me his hand to help me down into the pit. I could feel everyone's excitement pulsating through the air.

"Look," he said, pointing to where the hand bones ended.

"What's going on? What is this statue?" I asked, looking around. No one spoke. Everyone had turned to look at the archaeologist, hanging on to his every word.

He put his hand on my shoulder. "We can safely assume that the broken wings and the head of the statue behind you ..."

I closed my eyes, feeling time stand still.

"... belong to the Statue of the Winged Victory, which is housed in the Louvre. The Nike of Samothrace."

I opened my eyes and looked again at the statue that emerged from the ground. My grandfather's fingers spread across the cheeks of the sculpted head, as if trying to bring it even closer to him. The face of the goddess was turned toward him, as if she had been talking to him all these years ...

The title of the article took up most of my mobile screen. *A Historic Discovery. Winged Victory at last complete.*

In a strange twist of fate, the remains of a murdered archaeologist who went missing in 1949 lead to the discovery of the head of the statue …

I could not even remember how many articles I'd read, in Greek and in English. The news, the unusual circumstances, had gripped everyone's attention.

I switched off my phone and placed it on the table. A month had gone by, but the story was still doing the rounds. Across the bay, besieged by thick clouds, Samothrace was somehow still visible. I always loved gazing at the shades of reddish soil, fainter by the coast, sharper when it reached the edge of the small cliff hanging over the shore and stretching as far as the eye could see. The autumnal melancholy brought on by October was sweeping summer memories away, along with everything that had happened on Samothrace.

I did not know if and when I would return. My grandparents' graves were my only link to the otherwise beautiful island. DNA results had proved that the remains, including the hand that held the statue's head, belonged to my grandfather. His reputation rehabilitated at last, he was now celebrated as a hero.

He had always wanted to excavate that piece of land, as if he could sense something important was buried there. He'd led everyone to the statue he had been hunting all his life in the end, thanks to Destine. I asked many dog experts, but no one could explain how she could have smelled the buried remains.

Alkistis claimed that the island gods had led my dog to the grave, and had given her the strength to do so. The truth was that even I could sense the strange energy of the island, even now, gazing at it from afar.

The discovery of the Winged Victory's head had started a conversation about where the statue belonged, and what should happen next. Some insisted that the statue should stay at the Louvre once its missing parts were reattached. Others argued that it was time for it to return home and go on permanent display in the Sanctuary of the Great Gods, as it had thousands of years ago. Others still offered a compromise: complete the statue at the Louvre, and share the statue between Paris and Samothrace.

Overwhelmed by the dramatic developments, I grieved at never knowing my grandfather, although now I felt as if he had been watching over me all these years. I felt great sadness that Zoe and Andreas, two people who loved one another so wholeheartedly, had only shared a few days together. Everyone but Vasilis was now gone. Because of his age and his health problems, he was placed under house arrest while he awaited trial. His limp had swayed the prosecutor.

Before Vasilis returned to the island, I asked him once again why he pretended to have a limp all these years. "Always keep a secret for yourself," he replied, pointing to his stick. "One you will never reveal. This is my secret."

He cried as he told me how much he had loved my grandmother, how he had never confessed his love for her. I was taken aback when I heard that, but I could feel his love, his attachment to her. Another selfless love, a love unfulfilled that never saw the light of day. I promised to go visit him whenever I came back to Maronia, but something inside me told me that was to be our last meeting.

Sitting in Zoe's favorite spot, I felt guilty I had not spent more time with her, especially during the last years of her life when she wanted to spend all her time here. I'd often asked her to visit me, but she refused to travel to the States. "You are always away at work, Andreas," she'd say. "What am I going to do all alone for so many hours? The sky keeps me company in Maronia, talks to me ..."

Much had happened in the last month. My life had changed irrevocably in ways I would have never expected when I set off on this journey. I would be returning to work in a few days, but I did not feel ready to continue with my old life. I knew that back in New York I would have to make some brave decisions about my life, about how I wished to spend it from now on.

The moist tip of Destine's nose against my hand startled me, and I pulled it away, turning to pat her as soon as I realized who it was. Her right hind leg was now gone, and she was trying to learn how to walk again. The vet in

Alexandroupolis had gone way beyond the call of duty to keep her alive. Although Destine was still recovering, she was ready for the flight back. A medal from the Archaeological Service joined her collection of medals for bravery earned during the time she had worked with Eva.

I felt arms slide over my shoulders and stretch down to pat Destine. Iro walked around the chair and sat on my lap, gazing into my eyes.

"Is it time?" I asked.

A long, lingering kiss was her reply. Destine gave a low, complaining whine, and we broke into a fit of laughter. "Someone is jealous," Iro said.

"Where were we?" I asked, seeking her lips.

She pretended not to understand. "You asked me if it was time ..."

"And?"

"It is time, Andreas. Before you go, I want to ..."

I reached out and placed two fingers gently against her lips. There was no need for words. It was as if we knew each other's thoughts before they were even spoken.

I broke the silence that followed, trying to lighten the mood. "We'll talk every day ..."

Iro nodded, and her eyes brimmed with tears.

"I guess I should get going ..."

"Yes, if you want to make the evening flight. Unless ..."

I pulled her against me and kissed her deeply, at the same time avoiding giving an answer. Once again, I was transported by her touch, her lips. Softly, our lips parted and we turned to look at Samothrace. Who knew how long it would be before I saw it again.

Destine whimpered and cried as we all three gazed at the island. Reluctantly, I got up. "I have to bring in the things from the garden ..."

"Sophia and I will take care of it after you go. Can we stay here a little longer?"

Every second that passed carried me further away from the place that had led us to each other's arms. With her head against my shoulder, Iro's gaze led mine over the sea, the island, up to the sky, until our eyes filled with blue.

We got up with a start, as if we had fallen asleep. Arm in arm, we walked to the car that would take me away from her. Mechanically, I opened the passenger door and pointed it out to Destine. It was impossible for her to hop inside the car. I bent down and picked her up. She whimpered softly when she noticed Iro staying behind. Even when Destine was in the seat and I had closed the door, she rose with great difficulty and snuck her snout though the window's opening, her cries getting louder. Iro approached her and stroked her, brushing her cheek against Destine's.

It was clear Destine wanted Iro in the car, and for a second I wondered whether I should ask her to join me. Luckily, my head overruled my heart. "You can stay at the house for as long as you want, until you sort things out," I said.

I was trying to hide my real feelings. I knew that at present, after everything that had happened, the distance would be good for us. Everything had happened so suddenly, we both needed time to gain perspective.

"Thank you for everything," she said, and fell into my arms. She hugged me tightly, then kissed my cheek and hurriedly turned back toward the house. I saw her raise her hand to her cheeks to wipe away tears as she quickly walked away. She did not turn back to look at me, even once I was in the car and driving through the large gates.

Through the rear view mirror, I saw her walk to the chair under the gazebo and sit, facing Samothrace. I stopped the car, trying to sear the picture of her sitting there in my memory. Then I released the brake, and the car gently rolled down the hill, the leaves of the plane tries blotting out Iro and the *balcony to the sky* piece by piece.

The sun was setting, and Iro remained seated. In the distance, Samothrace glowed gold in the sunlight. The clouds had dispersed, and in the sharp crispness of the evening the island seemed so close that she could almost reach out her hand to touch it.

Gazing at the land that had marked and shaped her whole existence, tears glistened like diamonds on Iro's cheeks as she surrendered to her feelings and wept; as dusk gave way to night and the full moon rose once again in the sky.

The End

Kostas Krommydas

About the author

When Kostas Krommydas decided to write his first novel, he took the publishing world of his native Greece by storm. A few years later, he is an award-winning author of five bestselling novels, acclaimed actor, teacher and passionate storyteller. His novels have been among the top 10 at the prestigious Public Book Awards (Greece) and his novel "Ouranoessa" has won first place (2017). He has also received the coveted WISH writer's award in 2013. When not working on his next novel at the family beach house in Athens, you will find him acting on the acclaimed ITV series, The Durrels and on various theatre, film, and TV productions. Kostas also enjoys teaching public speaking, interacting with his numerous fans, and writing guest articles for popular Greek newspapers, magazines, and websites. If you want to find out more about Costas, visit his website, http://kostaskrommydas.gr/ or check out his books on Amazon: Author.to/KostasKrommydas

More Books

Lake of Memories

Based on a true story

In Paris, a dying woman is searching for the child that was snatched from her at birth over twenty years ago. In Athens, a brilliant dancer is swirling in ecstasy before an enraptured audience. In the first row, a young photographer is watching her for the first time, mesmerized. He knows she is stealing his heart with every swirl and turn, yet is unable to break the spell. And on the Greek island of the Apocalypse, Patmos, a man is about to receive a priceless manuscript from a mysterious benefactor. Destiny has thrown these people together, spinning their stories into a brilliant tapestry of romance, crime, and timeless love. How many memories can the past hold? Is a mother's love strong enough to find the way? Based on a true story, Krommydas' award-winning book firmly established him as one of the top Greek authors of his generation.

More Books

Cave of Silence

A Love So Strong, It Ripples Through The Ages.

Dimitri, a young actor, is enjoying the lucky break of his life—a part in an international production shot on an idyllic Greek island and a romance with Anita, his beautiful co-star. When his uncle dies, he has one last wish: that Dimitri scatters his ashes on the island of his birthplace. At first, Dimitri welcomes this opportunity to shed some light on his family's history—a history clouded in secrecy. But why does his mother beg him to hide his identity once there?

Dimitri discovers that the past casts long shadows onto the present when his visit sparks a chain of events that gradually reveal the island's dark secrets; secrets kept hidden for far too long. Based on true events, the *Cave Of Silence* moves seamlessly between past and present to spin a tale of love, passion, betrayal, and cruelty. Dimitris and Anita may be done with the past. But is the past done with them?

More Books

Athora

A Mystery Romance set on the Greek Islands.

A tourist is found dead in Istanbul, the victim of what appears to be a ritual killing. An elderly man is murdered in the same manner, in his house by Lake Como. The third murder is the most perplexing of all: the priest of a small, isolated Greek island lies dead in the sanctuary, his body ritualistically mutilated. Fotini Meliou is visiting her family on the island of Athora for a few days, before starting a new life in the US. She is looking forward to a brief respite and, perhaps, becoming better acquainted with the seductive Gabriel, whom she has just met. It is not the summer vacation she expects it to be. A massive weather bomb is gathering over the Aegean, threatening to unleash the most violent weather the area has ever seen. When the storm breaks out, the struggle begins. A race against the elements and a race against time: the killer is still on the island, claiming yet another victim. Locals, a boatload of newly arrived refugees, foreign residents, and stranded tourists are now trapped on an island that has lost contact with the outside world. As the storm wreaks havoc on the island, how will they manage to survive?

Kostas Krommydas

Very soon, more novels from Kostas Krommydas will be available on Kindle. Sign up to receive our newsletter or follow Kostas on facebook, and we will let you know as soon as they are uploaded!

Want to contact Kostas? Eager for updates?

Want an e-book autograph?

Follow him on

https://www.linkedin.com/in/kostas-krommydas

https://www.instagram.com/krommydaskostas/

https://www.facebook.com/Krommydascostas/

https://twitter.com/KostasKrommydas

Amazon author page:

Author.to/KostasKrommydas

If you wish to report a typo or have reviewed this book on Amazon please email onioncostas@gmail.com with the word "review" on the subject line, to receive a free 1680x1050 desktop background.

Thank you for taking the time to read *Dominion of the Moon.* If you enjoyed it, please tell your friends or post a short review. Word of mouth is an author's best friend and much appreciated!

Printed in Great Britain
by Amazon